Dead of Winter

ELIZABETH CORLEY

Allison & Busby Limited
12 Fitzroy Mews
London W1T 6DW
www.allisonandbusby.com

First published in Great Britain by Allison & Busby in 2013.
This paperback edition published by Allison & Busby in 2014.

A CIP catalogue record for this book is available from
the British Library.

10 9 8 7 6 5 4 3 2 1

ISBN 978-0-7490-1632-6

Typeset in 10/14.75 pt Sabon by
Allison & Busby Ltd.

The paper used for this Allison & Busby publication
has been produced from trees that have been legally sourced
from well-managed and credibly certified forests.

Printed and bound by
CPI Group (UK) Ltd, Croydon, CR0 4YY

To Ben, with love

PROLOGUE

The young girl ran through the woods as if the devil himself were behind her. The afternoon sun was obscured behind black clouds, bringing with them the weight of rain in air already heavy with the smell of decay. It seemed a lifetime ago that she had slipped away from her friends into a private game that was exciting at first, then became a lonely adventure and had now deteriorated into threatening isolation. In the crawling fear between her shoulder blades the girl knew she was no longer alone; he was coming.

A crashing to her left forced a yelp of panic that she tried to swallow into silence. She veered right and ran even faster, her backpack slapping heavily onto her spine. The stitch in her side made her wince and she held a hand tight against her ribs, trying to ignore its sharp pain. She was a good runner, the fastest sprinter in her school, but he was even faster.

The girl whimpered as she darted through a narrow gap in some brambles, raising an arm to protect her eyes from whipping tendrils that snatched at her as she pushed deeper into the thicket. She was soon scratched and bleeding; a lurking stinging nettle lashed her bare elbow unnoticed. Her trousers weren't thick enough to stop thorns stabbing deep into her thighs as she forced through vicious old stems that protested her intrusion. The stitch was agony and she had to stop and bend over to ease it. This was no good.

Behind her the heavy footsteps came nearer. She limped

forward looking for somewhere to hide. The brambles cleared into a patch of bracken surrounded by trees. A country girl, she knew without being aware that they were ancient oaks and beeches, mixed with hazel and rowans wherever light penetrated to the woodland floor. She stopped and looked around; where to go? There was a storm-blasted tree ahead of her, its roots standing skeletal in the dimming light. She would be small enough to slip into the hollow beneath, now overgrown with bracken and the seed-spikes of wild foxgloves. She ran forward but stopped almost at once; it was too obvious, the first place he would look, but it had given her an idea.

For long minutes there was silence except for the wind in the trees. The sounds of pursuit ceased; the birds were dumb, alarmed by her intrusion into their world. The girl muffled her rapid breaths in the crook of her arm and squeezed her eyes shut. Had he given up? A flicker of hope stuttered in her chest as her breathing eased from panicked hyperventilation to the panting of exertion. She waited unmoving in her improvised shelter. Her hiding place was in the raised root system of a giant beech. At most there was a foot and a half of space between the roots and the earth, too tiny for anybody but a slim, determined eleven-year-old tomboy who didn't care about insects and rodents as she had pushed her pack far inside and then wriggled in after it.

Her calf muscles were cramping but there wasn't enough room to straighten her legs. She held still, her face screened by leaves of a broken branch with which she had hurriedly swept the forest floor of her tracks, before dragging it in above her head.

Her stillness encouraged tiny creatures to stir in the soil beneath her. Something wriggled past her cheek and she stopped breathing as it explored the outer folds of her ear before moving into her hair. She started to count out the time: *one-crocodile, two-crocodile, three* . . .

Where was he? It would be dark soon but would he simply

give up? He might still be out there waiting. To escape him she would have to hide overnight and hope that she could find her way home in the morning, by when he would surely have abandoned the hunt. In her small backpack she had food, water, a torch and other essential supplies for the adventure she had planned so carefully the day before.

Her parents would not start to worry until morning. They knew she was on her big adventure, the last trip before the start of the school year. They had approved her outing, knowing she would be with responsible company and that their tomboy daughter had too much unresolved thirst for adventure to go easily into her first year of senior boarding school without one last flash of freedom.

She had overheard them rationalising their decision to allow her to camp overnight with friends; her mother nervous but realistic, her father laughingly proud. As they had reassured themselves, sipping red wine and listening to a new blues CD, she had crept upstairs to her bedroom and pulled out her survival kit. It was in two parts: the larger one she would show her parents in the morning, to comfort them that she was well prepared. The smaller kit, packed into a square, waterproof survival pouch, was her secret.

On the floor by the bed furthest from the door she had laid out the contents to check them one last time, aligning each item with rehearsed precision that suggested an obsession with planning and control, young as she was. She opened the treasure box that not even her mother would look inside and extracted a battered book that she had 'borrowed' from her grandfather, meaning to return it but never quite managing to do so. Pappy had been in the army and his dog-eared copy of an SAS survival handbook was her most valued possession.

She emptied first a reused two-ounce tin of pipe tobacco, again borrowed from Pappy; the contents were all in order so she started to repack them, double-checking against the book as she did so: ten safety matches, their heads dipped in melted candle wax to make them waterproof; a small square of candle, as much for lighting fires as for light; a magnifying glass that she had bought second-hand from a stamp collector's shop, to the delight of her mum who had hoped that maybe her wild child was starting to calm down; needles, thread, fish hooks and line (thank you, Pappy – he has so many he wouldn't notice they were missing); a compass; and a sewing kit from a hotel her dad had stayed in once and brought back as a memento. Then there was her most prized possession: a proper fire flint from a specialist camping supply store on Buckingham Palace Road.

There had been a bubble of excitement in her stomach because this time she wouldn't just be using them in a game but in a real adventure. There were some recommended kit items that she didn't have of course, like snare wire (she had a pet rabbit and couldn't imagine killing one of Snuffle's cousins). The flexible saw had been impossible to find, though there was a small hand hacksaw in her 'official' pack. Her medical kit wasn't really good enough; it comprised a few plasters, antiseptic wipes, a small tube of Savlon and a strip of painkillers.

She did have a condom though, still in its mysterious foil wrapper, stolen from her father's bedside drawer. Even looking at it had made her cheeks burn and she didn't really like to touch it but the book had insisted that it would make a good water bag, enough to carry almost two pints. She pushed it quickly beneath the plasters and snapped the lid closed, making sure that the seal was tight. The tin went into the zipped pocket of her combat trousers so that she would never be without it.

The sharp edge of the tin dug into her thigh as she lay still, listening and waiting; nothing. Maybe when she had slipped through the brambles she had lost him? Thinking of her survival tin made her feel better. She was a good planner, even her exasperated mother admitted so, and she was clever – everyone said that from the head teacher at her old school to her new form mistress. Not that the girl cared about being clever; if anything she considered it a curse because so much more was expected of her when all she wanted to do was go with her father on his next trip to Africa or, failing that, paint alongside her mother until the daylight faded and they would sit together by the fire, reading and telling ghost stories to each other. She would miss that at boarding school, a lot.

Beyond her refuge the sound of evening birdsong returned and the girl closed her eyes, exhausted but no longer terrified. She reached down and patted her rucksack in comfort. It contained her 'official' survival kit, the one she had shared with her parents before leaving home that morning. They had tried not to laugh, knowing it would infuriate her, but she had seen the amusement in their faces as she displayed the contents on the kitchen table.

'Firelighters?' her dad had asked, the corners of his mouth twisting in an effort not to smile.

'Well where was I supposed to find hexamine fuel tablets in their own stove container, for heaven's sake? You wouldn't buy them for my birthday and no shop will sell them to me because I'm too young.'

'Right,' her mother was biting her lip and avoiding her husband's eyes, 'but we did get you a nice compass and the electrolyte sachets you asked for.'

'Yes, they're good.' The girl didn't mention that the compass had been a silly girl's thing that she had exchanged for a waterproof, shockproof one three times the price, spending most of her pocket money on it.

'And what's in here, Issie-pop?' Her dad was using his special name for her because he could see she was becoming annoyed.

'My map, emergency rations: instant soup sachets' – Pappy's book said *a good brew raised spirits* but she hated tea and coffee –

11

'apple juice, chocolate, Kendal mint cake. And that's my spare socks and a jumper in a waterproof bag.'

'And your penknife?' Mum asked.

'Here.' It wasn't an impressive knife, not like a Parang – the Malay knife that was supposed to be invaluable for forest survival – which is why she also had a Stanley knife in her jacket pocket, borrowed from her dad's toolbox that morning.

'And this, Issie – it looks like a couple of black plastic bags, or are they a special survival secret?' Her dad was grinning in that really irritating way that he did when he thought he'd made a joke, usually at her expense. He was the best dad in the world, but really!

'No, Dad, they're bin liners from the roll in the drawer but that doesn't make them any less useful to keep me or my equipment dry.'

'I see.'

Thinking of her parents and the home she had left only that morning relaxed Issie. She wondered if it would be possible to reach the last squares of chocolate in her rucksack, but even as her fingers moved towards the clasp of her pack there was a noise in the wood outside and she froze.

Was it the wind or maybe an animal coming out to feed at twilight? Silence. Nothing. A slow sad sighing of the wind through the branches and then stillness. The girl released her breath slowly.

'WHERE ARE YOU?'

The voice was a bellow immediately above her head, making her jump and bringing her face into sharp contact with a jutting piece of root, just missing an eye.

'I KNOW YOU'RE HERE SOMEWHERE! SHOW YOURSELF.'

He sounded furious, angry enough to do anything, and he was so close. If he stepped back he could almost kick her.

'Come out, come out wherever you are.' The knowing sing-song was worse than his shouting. 'You know I'm going to find you . . . come on, little Issie. Let's get this over with. Come out . . . NOW!'

Issie shivered. His use of her name made it worse. No way was she going to show herself – even though it was somehow tempting to give in and get it over with. Perhaps he wouldn't be so bad. Maybe her terror was teenage hysteria that her mum warned her about. Had she imagined his hand lingering on her thigh every time he thought no one was looking; and that leering smile so inappropriate for a responsible adult? She shivered and fought back tears.

Something trickled across her forehead and onto her eyelids, warm and sticky, but she didn't dare move to wipe it away. He was kicking at the leaves now. Her eyelids glowed red as he turned the beam of a torch at the tree. Issie froze. Was her face visible? She'd smeared it with mud at the start of her adventure. Was the camouflage still intact or had sweat and her tears wiped it away? She held her breath, frozen still.

'For heaven's sake, this is stupid. You know I'm going to find you. Come out now and make it easy on yourself.'

Issie drew her head in tight against her shoulders as if she could disappear. He was right there above her. All he had to do was bend down and kick the branch away and he would be sure to see her. She heard him sniffing, like the Nazgûl in *The Lord of the Rings*. Issie's imagination furnished him with red burning eyes and cruel fingers. She bit her tongue to stop herself sobbing out loud. She heard him swear, using a word that was never allowed at home, and the silent tears came harder.

Go away, go away, go away. Please God, make him go away. If you do I promise to go to church every Sunday and join the school choir like Mum wants me to. Please. She screwed her eyes tighter shut.

Long minutes later her prayer was answered. She heard him walking away, hesitantly at first, then more purposefully, breaking into a jog that retreated until his footsteps were indistinguishable from the noises of the stirring wood. Issie stopped crying and opened her eyes but otherwise remained immobile. She didn't trust him, not one bit, never had from the moment he had joined their party that morning, inviting himself along as an additional helper. He could still be waiting somewhere, maybe he was hiding behind a tree close by. She decided to stay where she was for at least an hour, counting to eight thousand slowly. *One-crocodile, two-crocodile, three . . .*

Her head ached and the stickiness in her eyes was blood; she had tasted it to be sure. Her stomach rumbled and her legs cramped. She became aware of the scratches on her arms and face and the deep thorn pricks on her thighs that hurt most. They might already be infected but that didn't matter. As soon as she reached eight thousand she would move, set up a night shelter and clean herself up. She'd love to light a fire but that would be stupid, so it would be cold grub, like it said in her Pappy's book. *One thousand, one hundred and three crocodiles, one thousand one hundred and four . . .*

Her mouth twisted into a smile, and then she snorted softly like a little animal as a chuckle escaped. A laugh tried to break free and she suppressed it in the crook of her arm, burrowing down, her face squished up against her chest. Soon she was giggling helplessly, almost hysterical in relief. It lasted a dangerously long minute but he didn't come back. Night animals began to forage, dismissing her as a harmless creature, as hunted as they were.

Issie eased her body away from the ground, ignoring the agony of pins and needles, and rolled uncomfortably onto her back. Staring up into the pitch dark of the root system inches from her face, she smiled.

'I won,' she murmured. At that moment it was all that mattered.

By the following morning she was cold, wet, starving hungry

and in quite a lot of discomfort from her various injuries, the cut on her eyebrow being the worst, but the memory of victory over her own fear and compulsion to give in was strong. She realised now, of course, that she would have been missed. Her parents would be worried sick. The thought made her guilty but not enough to outweigh the enormous sense of achievement for having survived the chase and the night alone. As Issie stowed everything neatly in her backpack, she knew that she was a different person from the girl who had turned a simple game of hide-and-seek into a life-threatening chase. She hoped her parents would have the sense to realise this; she was not returning as a child.

PART ONE

'The feeling of being misunderstood and not understanding the World does not accompany the first passion, but is the only Cause of this that is not random. And it is itself an escape, Where being with another person means only solitude doubled.'

Robert Musil,
The Confusions of Young Törless

CHAPTER ONE

Late November

Nightingale stretched her toes towards the flames of the wood-burning stove in her top-floor flat, an Edwardian conversion that she had bought for a knock-down price with a mortgage at such a low rate she still couldn't believe it. Her brother thought she was mad to trade in her previous flat, modern and efficient, for something where she had already had to replace half the sash windows and fix leaky bathroom plumbing.

His aversion to 'old with character' was understandable since he had inherited their parents' house, which she knew he secretly wanted to sell but didn't dare because it had been in the family since 1879. It had never been maintained properly and now consumed so much money in upkeep that her brother said he might as well dedicate his whole salary to it. Hence his warning: buy new, avoid a money pit, enjoy life without the unnecessary delights of poisonous lead pipes, quaint imperial measures and the impossibility of ever keeping the place clean or warm. Every time she tried in vain to stop the draughts Nightingale recalled his warnings, but with a smile.

The warmth of real fire on the soles of her feet, the moulding of vine leaves and clusters of improbable grapes in the light rose above her and the original parquet floor all argued against his logic. Nightingale grinned again and took a sip of good Bordeaux, another indulgence when she should be sensible, but ahead of her were the first days off she had enjoyed in weeks. Outside the weather was miserable, with sleet driven by gale-force winds. She sighed deeply with contentment.

The night deserved a good bottle of wine and going out for a meal did not appeal. So she had decided to slice a fresh, crusty granary loaf, defrost some of her home-made chicken soup and open one of the wines she kept for special occasions, rationalising that it would still cost less than dinner in her local restaurant. The soup was simmering gently as wind gusted around the chimneys, rattling slates that she knew were loose but tonight she didn't care; she was in her own world. Nightingale picked up her book and found the page where she had paused to enjoy the moment.

When the phone rang she let it go through to the machine.

'Ma'am, Inspector Nightingale, if you're home could you pick up, please? This is Sergeant Wicklow in Operations. We need you here urgently. There's been an incident that requires your attention.' The tone of voice changed and became personal. Wicklow had looked out for her since she had joined the force as a graduate trainee. 'Sorry, Louise, I know it's the first day you've had off in a month but this one needs you. If you're not here soon they'll call in Blite and I don't think . . .' There was a pause as he remembered all calls were taped. 'If you could come in, ma'am?'

'I'm here, George, what is it?'

'Another rape; a nasty one – I know they're all nasty,' he rushed on, perhaps remembering Nightingale's suspicion that half the blokes on the force considered rape a minor crime, that it was only sex after all.

Wicklow was right; it was better she dealt with this than that Neanderthal Blite. Since the cutbacks, more and more sex crimes were being passed to regular CID instead of to the overwhelmed specialist Sexual Assault Investigation Unit. At least she had been trained, whereas he . . . Nightingale suppressed a shudder and turned the heat off under her soup.

'OK, George, but can you send a car? I don't want to risk

driving in this.' She didn't mention the wine; if anything she did tonight led them to catch a rapist the fact that she had had a drink would inevitably be used by the defence, however irrelevant. Sussex Constabulary was trying to put a line under drinking while working, an uphill struggle in her opinion – which she kept to herself – but while the effort lasted she needed to treat it with respect.

'It'll be about fifteen minutes, given the weather.'

'No problem.'

In fact quite the opposite; just enough time to enjoy her supper and finish her glass of wine.

Nightingale knew that she had not been asked for by name. The new superintendent, Alison Whitby, had replaced Quinlan four months previously. She was in her early forties, ran marathons and had won the Sussex women's pistol competition four years in a row. What's more she was married with eight-year-old twins. To say that Nightingale found her intimidating would be to miss the point. Her frame of reference now included a more senior woman who combined professional and family life with demanding sports that she mastered to county level. And now approaching thirty, Nightingale was no longer the wunderkind.

Whitby wouldn't expect her to interrupt her time off. It was George Wicklow who was looking out for her. His dislike of Blite was unshakeable, not just because the man was an arrogant bigot who would climb on anybody's back on his way to the top, but because he had virtually forced one of their colleagues into retirement on shaky medical grounds. Wicklow missed Bob Cooper almost as much as Nightingale did. Harlden CID wasn't the same without his rotund, dependable presence.

Nightingale stopped off at the station to pick up the incident report and find out who was on the team. The CID room was full despite the hour. Monday night was sometimes busy, particularly in the run-up to Christmas as people relaxed their inhibitions and softened the slow drag of work or unemployment in the manner of their choosing. As December neared, an increasing number of otherwise upright citizens would indulge in serious drinking and opportune sex. The human cost of inebriated abandon kept police forces across the country busier than any other single cause.

Nightingale had a small cubicle in the corner of the CID room that she could call her own. When she had first become an inspector she had moved into a tiny office, but Whitby didn't believe in offices. She liked open-plan, glass walls and free-flowing communication. So most offices had been replaced by cubicles. The careful use of computer screens, files and reference books meant some privacy despite the attempt at transparency. Nightingale suspected that Whitby saw how the old ways lingered but so far had chosen to ignore the problem. A step at a time appeared to be her motto.

Nightingale wasn't the worst offender. One side panel was clear of visual impediments, though two others were conveniently covered. She hated the idea of people being able to stare at her back and look over her shoulder.

'Nightingale! What you doing here?' Jimmy MacDonald, inevitably Big Mac to his mates because of his American football physique, waved a lazy greeting from his desk.

'Called in for this rape, Mac.'

'But you've worked a straight twenty; you won't impress Miss Whiplash by collapsing from exhaustion.'

'Well I don't have your pin-up looks to help me, do I?' Nightingale smiled the sharpness out of her words. 'You know anything about this one; where the assault happened and who was attending officer?'

'It's your lucky day! The Milky Bar Kid was first on scene. I think he even managed to avoid puking this time, though the poor girl's a bit of a mess.'

Constable Roy Rogers (yes, really; some parents can be cruel) had only just made it through the recruitment medical and had lost weight since. He was a pale, acne-cursed scarecrow of a lad who had wanted to be a policeman since childhood, which he appeared not long to have left behind. There was a running bet that he didn't yet shave. To the old hands in the station house he was a gift. Nightingale had come across him before when he had attended an attempted murder. She found him a decent, thorough boy with a lot of compassion for the victim – probably more than would be good for him.

'Good,' she said, ignoring Big Mac's raised eyebrows, 'he'll have preserved the scene until SOCO arrived and will have been gentle with the victim. Where is she?'

'West Sussex General, still in A&E last we heard. Milky's with her. You going over yourself or would you like me to do it?'

Nightingale looked at his two hundred and ten pound, six foot three frame, walnut skin and permanent sarcastic smile and decided he might not be the best officer, even though he was technically as qualified as she was.

'I'll do this one.'

'Can I come along?' He saw her look of surprise. 'I might learn something.'

What was he up to?

'You're on call.'

'I've got my mobile and anyway, you need a good driver.'

Nightingale opened her mouth to protest but he pre-empted her, adding in a whisper, 'Mouthwash is a dead giveaway.'

Thirty minutes later Nightingale tried to control her anger as she waited in the corridor for the forensic technician to finish. The girl in the room behind her was little more than a child and knowledge of how she must have suffered filled her with hatred towards the attacker, mixing with the dread that this might be the latest in a series of increasingly vicious attacks.

The incidents had started in May, always taking place between

Guildford and Harlden. The first crimes had been sufficiently different for the police not to connect them: an aggressive flasher; someone trying to molest teenage girls in a shopping centre; an assault outside a nightclub; so it went on. Then an enterprising trainee detective had gathered and compared descriptions of the attackers and remarked to their mentor, who happened to be Nightingale, on the physical similarity of the perpetrators.

When a heavily built, thirty-ish, dark-haired, blue-eyed man between five-ten and six foot had leapt out on a girl walking through Harlden Park from a youth club to her home, alarm bells had rung. CID nicknamed the attacker Flash Harry after his first attack. Nightingale avoided the term.

As the incidents escalated she had taken a personal interest and was given the lead to investigate. The assaults continued, one roughly every month, with the perpetrator evading capture. Her small team had been through every file, re-interviewed victims and witnesses and organised reconstructions but they had learnt little. It appeared that the attacker wasn't so much clever as lucky. He wore gloves and a baseball cap that concealed most of his face.

Nightingale had feared the escalation meant that they would soon be dealing with something very serious. To her bitter regret, she had just been proved right.

The unnamed girl had been found at the bottom of a short flight of steps behind Bedford Row to the east side of Harlden at seven-thirty. She was unconscious and had been raped. In A&E she had been X-rayed, the registrar refusing to let the police forensic specialist near her until they could be sure there was no brain injury.

'All yours, ma'am.' The forensic technician grimaced.

'Thanks, Sally. How seriously did he hurt her?'

'It was non-consensual for sure; there's bruising and tearing to the vaginal wall and scratches and bruises on her thighs. The doctor said the concussion is due to a blow to the back of her head consistent with her having fallen. She was lying at the bottom of a flight of steps when she was discovered and I found cement fragments in her hair so perhaps he didn't hit her.'

Nightingale looked at the unconscious girl and tried to guess her age; fifteen, sixteen at most. She looked underfed and her hair and fingernails were filthy. Maybe she was a runaway. There weren't many street children in Harlden, partly because since Superintendent Whitby's arrival, police patrols had teamed up with social services and some local charities to deal with every minor they found living rough in order to find them temporary accommodation and, when necessary, counselling. Unfortunately Harlden's position halfway between London and Brighton where homelessness was endemic meant that they were dealing with the spill-over from a chronic problem.

She knew what running away from home felt like; she had slept rough many times before a WPC had talked sense into her on a night that had changed her life. Would she be able to do the same for this girl? She doubted it. Counselling wasn't her strong point. The only remotely personal side she allowed herself to show at work these days was a protective sarcasm that was starting to persuade her male colleagues to drop the teasing and give her some room. It had earned her the reputation of being tough but remote; an ice queen. She told herself she didn't care.

'When do you expect her to regain consciousness?' Nightingale asked a nurse who came to check on the girl, and then dropped her voice in response to the critical finger he raised to his lips. 'It's important.'

'She's badly concussed. It could take up to twenty-four hours.'

'She didn't say anything when she was brought in?'

'She was out cold.'

She said goodnight to Milky, who was stationed by the girl's bed, before heading into the freezing night, collecting Big Mac on the way. He had done little but chat up one of the nurses since arriving. At least that explained his interest. Outside the air misted with a thick, chilling drizzle that seemed to freeze the stale fumes in the air. Jimmy drove her home before heading back to the station. He didn't mention the nurse so neither did she.

Nightingale ran a bath, added lavender oil and soaked while enjoying another glass of the Saint-Estèphe. It was midnight when she slipped into bed, hearing the wind attack the slates around the chimney with increasing fury as the weather deteriorated. She expected the sound of it would keep her awake but was asleep within minutes.

CHAPTER TWO

The pealing of church bells woke Nightingale. She lay in bed disorientated before remembering that her flat was close to the centre of old Harlden, on a street at the end of which was St Mark's parish church. The bell-ringers must be practising. She had intended to spend the day doing some Christmas shopping but the memory of the girl lying unconscious in hospital was too much. As soon as she was dressed she drove to the hospital. The roads were white with a treacherous frost and she drove slowly, easing into corners.

At the hospital she realised it would have been wiser to call ahead. The girl was still out cold, though a second scan again showed no brain injury. The doctor on duty wasn't concerned; the girl's vital signs were stable and she was being hydrated and nourished intravenously. He advised patience and Nightingale tried her best to follow doctor's orders.

She decided to drop into work and review her report from the previous night. That way she could make sure forensic evidence from the rape was being analysed quickly and uploaded to the national DNA database, just in case the rapist was not Flash Harry and already on file. She was at her desk just after nine, with a double-shot coffee and low-fat bran muffin for company. The CID room was quiet; the few detectives there showed no inclination to chat, which suited Nightingale.

At twenty to ten her phone rang and she answered quickly, hoping it might be the hospital.

'Nightingale?' The familiar voice made her catch her breath.

'Andrew.' She hadn't heard from him in months. The hand holding the receiver went clammy.

'Of course, how are you?'

'Fine. You?'

'Great, never better.'

He sounded buoyant and Nightingale felt a stab of rejection that was as illogical as it was painful. Andrew Fenwick had never tried to develop a relationship with her while they had served together at Harlden despite an open invitation from her to do so. Since he had taken on his new role heading Major Crimes they had barely spoken. It hadn't been a deliberate break but he had gone away on holiday and when he returned she had been away. Without realising it three months passed.

Meanwhile, her relationship with Clive, her then boyfriend, fell apart. He was increasingly needy and demanding, resorting to emotional blackmail in an attempt to strengthen his hold over her. Nightingale had witnessed a similar game up close and far too personal with her parents. With sickening clarity she realised that she had chosen in Clive a shadow of her father. She had declined his panicky offer of marriage and they separated. She could have called Fenwick then but she didn't and waited instead for a call that never came.

She had sent him a card the previous Christmas but hadn't received one in return. The oversight hurt disproportionately and for a year she had assumed he was finally out of her life. Why would he ring her now?

'What can I do for you?' She made herself sound relaxed.

'A fingerprint from a recent assault you're investigating matches one we have from an inquiry I'm about to open. The investigating officer is' – there was a rustle of paper – 'DS Jimmy

MacDonald; do you know him? Only I thought it would be easier to start with a call to you rather than someone I'd never met.'

'Naturally.' He missed her sarcasm. 'Big Mac is a colleague. Are you referring to the series of sexual assaults?'

'That's right; all linked to a suspect you're calling Flash Harry.'

'I see.' Her grip on the phone tightened; it was her case and she didn't want to pass it to MCS. 'May I ask why you are becoming involved?'

MCS didn't just take on the odd case here and there. The Major Crimes Squad had been established to tackle serious and complicated investigations. Nasty as Flash Harry might be he did not warrant their attention.

'What do you mean?'

Belatedly she remembered she was addressing a senior officer. Did he even remember they had once been friends?

'Doesn't sound like one for you, Andrew, that's all.'

'There are reasons we're involved.' A brush-off.

'I see. Can I help at all?'

'No need, but I'd appreciate it if one of my team could speak to this chap MacDonald.'

'No problem; whom should he call?'

She jotted down the name while her mouth went into overdrive.

'I might be able to help myself, Andrew. I know the case well, you see . . .'

'That's not necessary. I expect you're busy. I don't want to take your time.'

'If it's important enough for you to call personally I'm sure I can find the time to pop over to MCS and—'

'The roads are terrible and I only called because I thought it would speed things up.'

She sensed defensiveness but ploughed on.

'I'm still confused as to why such routine cases are consuming the head of Sussex Major Crime Squad's time.' She laughed unconvincingly in an attempt to mask her insistence. He didn't join in.

'Not that it's of particular relevance to you, but I'm worried there might be an escalating pattern of violence.'

'There definitely is, that's why I've taken the lead on the latest incident; it was a rape this time. Perhaps we could discuss why we both feel there's a growing risk here?' He sighed loudly and without knowing she did so Nightingale winced. 'Look, I was only offering to help, but if you don't think it's necessary . . .'

'I don't, at least not at this stage. Just have MacDonald call, all right?'

'Sure, no problem; as soon as he gets in.'

'Fine.'

There was an awkward pause. At one time the conversation would have been easy.

'Ah, right, well we're both busy . . .'

'Quite.'

'So, yes, well . . . oh, how's Clive by the way? I saw his promotion to DI came through.'

'Did it? I wouldn't know.'

'Oh, I thought you were . . . that is, I hadn't realised. Well . . . back to the grind then. Good to talk to you, Nightingale. My number's the same if anything new comes up. Bye.'

'Bye.'

She replaced the receiver with extreme care.

'Someone died, Nightingale? You look like you're about to go to a funeral.' Inspector Blite had chosen that moment to put in an appearance.

'The only funeral I plan to go to is yours but you keep me waiting.' Nightingale smiled, lemon-sweet.

'Ooh, bitchy, bitchy. I always seem to catch you at the wrong time,' he paused and added sotto voce, '*of the month.*'

Her hackles rose but she told herself she had asked for it.

Better to ignore him. She busied herself writing a note for Big Mac but as she did so she was replaying the conversation with Fenwick over and again.

You idiot, she told herself. *You practically begged to go over there . . . And you were cocky. He's a superintendent now; he's not your pal any more. You're lucky he didn't put you firmly in your place!*

She shook her head and rubbed her eyes. How could he still make her behave like a girl half her age? She took a drink of coffee but it was as bitter as her mood so she decided to go out for a fresh one. It was raining hard, a chill downpour that was almost sleet and penetrated to her bones as she ran the short distance to a Caffè Nero on the corner. She was served quickly, her loyalty card stamped twice by a Polish graduate she barely noticed. Despite the rain she walked through town afterwards, restless and resentful but at what she wouldn't have been able to say. She wasn't in the mood for shopping. Should she go home and enjoy the rest of her day off or trudge back to work? Without actually making a decision her feet found their way.

By the time she arrived back, the CID room was buzzing with the arrival of the second shift. Big Mac was booting up his PC and grunted a hello in her general direction.

'Message for you, Mac; could be important.' She passed him a yellow Post-it note.

'Andrew Fenwick, the chief inspector who got that commendation a year or so back?' His voice held a trace of admiration that really irritated her.

'He's a superintendent now, but yes, otherwise the same.'

'Wow. You worked with him didn't you?'

'Uh-huh.'

'Why would he bother to call himself? There must be more to it than he said.'

'I don't know but it looks like MCS is sniffing around Flash Harry and that's not good news.'

'Probably because we haven't caught him yet.'

'No, but we will . . . would have, anyway.' She did not see why the investigation that had started because of her insistence should simply be handed over as it became interesting.

MacDonald shrugged and dialled the MCS number. Nightingale tried not to listen.

His casual remark that there had to be a reason for Fenwick's call stayed with her as the afternoon passed. Just after four the hospital called to say that the victim of the assault had come round briefly, enough to say that her name was Jenni – with an 'I' she had insisted – before drifting into a sleep her doctor wanted to continue naturally.

Fenwick had a propensity to become over-involved. Of course that was why he had called. What other reason could there be? He wasn't looking for an excuse to see her; that much was obvious. Maybe MCS wanted to check out Big Mac? That could be it. He was bright, hard-working and developing a bit of a reputation as a sorter-out of problem cases.

But he came through to me. He could as easily have had someone else leave a message for Mac.

Despite telling herself that she was behaving like an adolescent Nightingale found it hard to concentrate so decided to attempt an hour's Christmas shopping after all. She was in her car when the hospital called to say that Jenni was awake and the doctor would allow a short interview. Easy to change direction. Minutes later Big Mac rang her mobile.

'I thought this case was going to MCS, and why didn't you tell me you were going to the hospital?'

'They haven't taken it yet and I couldn't wait, Mac. She's awake; you weren't around.'

'I'll meet you there.'

He broke the connection before Nightingale could argue or ask why he was so interested. Maybe he had promised MCS to keep an eye on it . . . or perhaps it was that nurse.

Jenni was half sitting, propped up by pillows, with a female officer at her bedside. A look of fear crossed the girl's face as Big Mac walked in behind Nightingale.

'I'm not talking to him! No way.' The girl's voice was high-pitched, its toughness forced.

MacDonald backed out of the room. He was surprisingly gentle when interviewing victims of sexual attacks but he was too wise to try and persuade the girl to trust him so soon.

'Who are you?' Jenni demanded and then turned to the officer beside her. 'Why's she here?'

'My name's Louise Nightingale.' Despite her best intentions Nightingale was touched by the girl's bristling vulnerability. 'I'm a detective inspector.'

'When can I go?'

'As soon as the doctors say that you're fit enough. Have you asked them?'

'They won't talk to me.'

'I'll ask them, if you like, Jenni.' Nightingale smiled, surprised at how unpractised the muscles felt.

'I'm not a child, y'know.' Her voice was hoarse and she sipped from a plastic cup.

'I know. Can I sit down?'

Nightingale took the shrug of indifference as agreement.

'I'd like to talk to you about last night. Can you tell me what happened?'

The girl's cheeks reddened but she said nothing.

'Will you do that for me?'

'Nothing happened. Fell over and hit my head, that's all.'

'Is that so?' Nightingale tried to look her in the eye but the girl turned away. 'Can you remember how it happened?'

31

'No.'

'Or what you were doing immediately beforehand?'

'Hangin' out, like. Look, can I go now?'

'As I said, that's up to the doctors but I suspect they'll want to keep an eye on you for a little while longer.'

'Well maybe you can go and ask them for us.'

'I will, as soon as we've had a proper conversation.'

'Nothing happened. Got it?'

Jenni tugged the blanket up towards her chin.

'I ran away from home when I was your age.'

Jenni looked at Nightingale in surprise but recovered quickly. 'Rubbish!'

'It's true. I got as far as France once. Only problem was I didn't speak French and I only had English money on me. Not the best idea I ever had.'

'Stupid, if you ask me.'

'You're right, I was but it didn't stop me. I ran away four times in all.' Out of the corner of her eye she could see Jenni trying to look disinterested. 'First time I was ten; didn't have a clue. Only had my pocket money on me, which I spent on a bus ticket to a town six miles away where I promptly drew attention to myself by stealing fruit very inexpertly from a market stall.'

'Pathetic.'

'Agreed. The next time was a bit better but my real *pièce de resistance* . . .'

'Thought you didn't speak French,' Jenni grinned, pleased with herself, and Nightingale encouraged the fleeting thaw with a laugh.

'Good point.' She paused.

'Well go on, then,' Jenni said, trying to sound bored.

'Well, my best attempt was my last. I managed to get to Glasgow. My parents had succeeded in finding me in England, and even in France where I was arrested and deported.' It sounded big and Nightingale could sense some grudging respect.

'So Scotland was, like, neutral territory,' Jenni ventured.

'Exactly, I knew you'd get it. Anyway, I travelled there no problem, found somewhere to hang out. It was good – particularly while the weather was warm.'

'So what went wrong?'

'I did. Took some stuff that affected me really badly. It was typical, the first time I'd tried something and I had this allergic reaction. I ended up in hospital, a bit like you, really. I was lucky, though; there were no permanent side effects and I was well enough to leave after two weeks.'

Jenni was looking at her with real interest.

'So . . . like I said, what went wrong?'

'It was what went right, actually,' Nightingale said softly. 'I'd given a false name—'

''Course.'

'—so nobody knew who I was. I was planning go back to my mates as soon as I could. Except,' she paused, finding the next part of the story surprisingly hard, 'except there was this do-gooding policewoman who insisted on visiting me. It started with her wanting to know where I'd got the stuff.'

'Like you were going to tell her . . . not.'

'Precisely. I never told her – you don't shop your mates – but, the thing is, even though I wouldn't tell her anything, she insisted on describing to me what had happened to another girl the night before. She'd been experimenting, went off her head and ended up thinking she could fly. She couldn't.'

Jenni was looking away, her cheeks bright red, eyes too bright.

'That's when it sunk in; I wasn't indestructible. That could've been me. It was just luck that I was lying there eating rubbish chips and Angel Delight when this other girl was in intensive care on the floor above. It could so easily have been me.'

Nightingale had to stop. The power of memory constricted her throat. There was silence in the room broken only by the sounds of activity in the ward outside. The girl waited patiently while Nightingale poured herself some water.

'What happened to her?' Jenni asked eventually.

Nightingale coughed.

'She was still in hospital when I left but afterwards . . . I don't know. I meant to go back and see her but the whole thing shook me up. I ended up telling this policewoman my real name, why I kept running away, stuff like that. My parents came but before they saw me she spoke to them. I don't know what she said but I'd never seen my dad so put in his place. He apologised to me, can you believe it? I thought I'd get the usual lecture but this time it was different. I never ran away again.'

'And that's why you're a policewoman?'

'Yes.'

'I'm not hurt. Not like that other girl. I'm going to be fine.'

'I hope you are, Jenni.' Nightingale reached out and touched the girl's fingers where they clutched the blanket. 'You seem smart, strong, there's no reason why you shouldn't make a full recovery, but you were also incredibly lucky. No other girl was assaulted last night, I won't pretend that for the sake of the story, but there are other girls in similar situations to you who are not OK. Don't push your luck.

'What I'm trying to say is that life on the streets comes with so many additional risks. If you're lucky you can go on avoiding them but . . . well, I don't want to scare you, but you put yourself in the way of so much potential harm out there.'

'I don't do drugs, not like you.' Jenni was scornful.

'Good; but I didn't either. I only tried them once, when I was feeling low and everybody else was having fun. I felt on the outside and I wanted in. Don't tell me you haven't already experienced that.'

A shrug.

'How long have you been living rough, anyway?'

'A week.' The words were out before Jenni realised they'd been spoken.

'Do you want to tell me why?'

'No.'

'Fair enough, it's none of my business.' Jenni looked at her, surprised. 'It's not. I want you to be safe and well but that doesn't entitle me to pry.'

'Right. So you're not going to insist I go home?'

'I can't tell you what to do but I can give you some advice if you're interested.'

'You might as well.'

Fourteen, Nightingale thought, watching a few of the defences peel away.

'If you choose not to go home the hospital will have no option but to call social services because you're under sixteen.'

'I am not!'

'You are unless you can prove it. Sorry, I don't make the rules. Just let me tell you the rest. They'll put you in a council-run facility – and yes, you'll probably run away from that within twenty-four hours, though my advice is to take advantage of the bathroom while you're there as it's tough to keep clean on the streets.

'Anyway, you run away; you stay clean of drugs – for a while; you keep clear of men – possibly for even longer. Then at some stage your luck will run out. Now the alternative, if you don't want to go home . . .'

'I can't, I really can't.' Tears were suddenly dropping onto the blanket.

'I understand that feeling, Jenni,' Nightingale's fingers tightened on her hand. 'The alternative is for me to try and get you into one of the shelters. There are a couple right here in Harlden. They always have more demand than they can cope with but I know one of the organisers and I can try—'

'Would you?' It was a plea.

'If you want me to. They're strict, sometimes more than at home, but they're fair. All they want is to give you time to sort yourself out.'

'That's all I need, a bit of time. I didn't think I'd be sleeping rough, not in weather like this. My cousin said I could stay but, well, he wanted me to, like, well . . . it didn't work out, that's all, and I couldn't go back.'

'I'll see if I can find you a place.'

Jenni's expression started to relax for the first time. Nightingale looked at her seriously.

'I need your help though, Jenni, not in return, or anything like that. The offer stands whatever you say next but I'm asking you, please, to help me. You didn't just bang your head. You and I both know that; and the man who hurt you – yes he did, Jenni – that man is going to do it again to other girls unless you help me find him.'

'But I didn't see anything!' Jenni wailed. 'It was dark; he hit me he just . . . hit me. I couldn't see him.' She started to cry loudly and a nurse bustled in.

'Really, Detective, I think that's enough.'

Nightingale ignored her but Jenni's crying became hysterical.

'Jenni, listen to me. I know this is really hard but you have to be honest with yourself. You're too strong a person to want to kid yourself about what happened for the rest of your life and the sooner you can bring yourself to talk the quicker you'll start to recover.'

'Detective! I must insist.' Nightingale ignored her. 'I'm going to call the doctor.'

'Jenni, here's my card. It's got my personal number on it. Call me when you're ready to talk or speak to the officer we'll leave here; that will be just as good. Just do it, love, please, for the sake of the next girl.'

Big Mac was waiting outside, holding the registrar back with difficulty. He didn't speak until they were alone in the lift.

'That,' he said finally, 'was good. Even if you haven't had the advanced training you avoided most of the mistakes and got her to identify with you; she definitely started to open up. The tears will help and as long as the hospital doesn't sedate her there's a good chance she'll be ready to talk tomorrow. Well done.'

'Thanks.' Nightingale didn't know what else to say.

'That story, though. It was amazing. You almost had me believing you!'

'But you saw through me, right?'

MacDonald nodded and Nightingale managed to keep a straight face.

CHAPTER THREE

Issie reached out an arm and fumbled for her alarm clock. She grasped it and managed a hard throw against the far wall. Its incessant beeping stopped as it hit but she knew it was only on snooze and that she had ten minutes to persuade her body to get out of bed. Monday morning; a whole week of college ahead and she felt like death. No, worse than death, she reasoned, because when you were dead you must lose all sense of feeling whereas her body was on fire with pains she couldn't even describe.

It was self-inflicted, as her patient but exasperated friend Puff had told her yesterday. Old news to Issie but she hadn't had the strength to argue. She didn't need Puff to tell her she was drinking too much, of course she was; that was the whole point. And as for the drugs; well Puff had never actually confronted her outright, probably because she didn't want to know as she would then be faced with the hard choice of informing the school counsellor or not. St Anne's had zero tolerance for drugs and would not only expel any pupil who took them but also suspend those who covered up.

Poor Puff; she was so nice, so *decent*, it was better she didn't know. Last night her friend had almost been in tears as she had confronted her. '*Do you want to kill yourself?*' she had asked in exasperation before leaving her room. Well, the simple answer was yes; she just didn't have the guts to do it.

Her life was a living hell, one that she knew she was making worse, but so what? Who really cared what happened to her? Her mother was too wrapped up with her lousy second husband, a man old enough to be Issie's grandfather. He was so different from her beloved dad. God, how she missed him.

Fat tears of misery rolled down Issie's cheek and soaked into her pillow. When the alarm started again she struggled out of bed, swallowed a dose of Resolve and scrubbed her face and hair clean under the shower. It was how she started every day.

The morning passed in a blur. She was given two signatures for late coursework; another and it would mean a detention. The threat meant nothing to her but a detention would lose house points and that she did want to avoid. After her last class she went to one of the computer labs to catch up, which was where her other close friend Octavia found her.

'Hi. Fancy stopping by my room later? I've got some chocolates.'

Issie's stomach heaved.

'Got to finish. I'll be here 'til lights out.'

'Boring.' In one word Octavia managed to infer that study meant nothing to her.

Issie wasn't fooled. Whatever she said, Octavia Henry cared like heck. Beneath the too-pretty, rebellious veneer, Issie recognised deep conventionalism and a burning desire to please her parents. Issie didn't resent or despise these feelings; she envied them, which is why it had been interesting to see her own behaviour push Octavia out of her comfort zone as she had tried to keep up with her self-destruction. Unfortunately it had done nothing to dampen Issie's misery and she no longer wanted to be the cause of Octavia's problems. Let her find her own.

'Look,' she said, running fingers through spiky auburn hair that was growing back from the buzz cut she had given herself at the beginning of term, 'let's be honest; you want to get strong grades this term, don't you?'

The alpha females stared at each other. Throughout their time at the college they had been rivals as well as close friends. Issie excelled in maths, English, sport and science; Octavia in Classics, languages and history. Only in art was it difficult to determine who might be better. Issie's raw creative talent was truly unique but Octavia had a better mastery of technique that Issie had yet to match.

Octavia looked down at the essay Issie was working on.

'You're trying to be top of the year again?'

'No,' Issie sighed, 'I'm not interested in winning.'

'Yeah, right! Like I believe you.'

'It's not important any more. I don't really care how I do.'

Octavia shook her head in disbelief.

'If I didn't know you hated men I'd say you were in love.'

Issie flushed.

'You aren't, are you?' Octavia laughed as her friend looked away. 'Who is he?'

'Leave it, Octavia.' Issie stared at the screen, ignoring her. 'Just leave me alone.'

After a few minutes Octavia did just that but Issie's concentration had gone. Her friend was so wrong. For reasons she would never reveal, Issie was terrified of sex but in her current frame of mind that made the idea of it all the more compelling. If she could force herself to give her body to a man it would be the ultimate act of self-destruction. She would finally prove to herself that she was worth nothing and maybe then killing herself would be easy.

'All the more reason for you to accept that date next week,' she muttered to herself. 'He'll be willing to do the honours.'

The idea was repellent. Issie tried to concentrate on Shakespeare's poetry. The words pulsing on her computer screen seemed somehow appropriate: '*Come away, come away Death, / And in sad cypress let me be laid.*' She rested her burning forehead against the cool of the screen and tried to think. Having sex wasn't clever but it would be satisfyingly destructive. Thinking of him, a man almost old enough to be her father, stupid enough to think she could fancy him and arrogant enough to believe she would give herself to him out of desire, made her shiver. All she needed to do was call him.

The first flakes of winter's snow swirled in the wind beyond the window as she typed the quote she had finally selected to complete her essay: 'Not a friend, not a friend greet / My poor corpse, where my bones shall be thrown.' As she wrote she imagined a stand of Scots pine, their shade cool on even the hottest day, and her bones glowing white in green twilight. She smiled.

CHAPTER FOUR

Steve was worried about Dan. The past few months he had been behaving weird, like he was only half there. Not that Dan had ever been fully 'there' but certain things used to interest him, like darts, drinking and sex. Now his interest in everything but sex had vanished.

Dan was only really focused when they went to visit Mum. While he was with her he was almost normal; talking to her, switching channels on the telly every time she asked, which was constantly. Dan never tired of jumping up to do as she wanted; adjusting the brightness, the volume, the channel again; opening the curtains, closing them, pulling them half-to so that the sun wasn't on the screen.

Their visits made Steve's skin crawl. When Mum was still at home they hadn't noticed that she was crazy. She always had outbursts, more towards Dan than him it had to be said, but that had been their mum. In the care home he heard the assistants call her Batty Betty behind her back. Here they restrained her when she grew violent.

Steve had learnt early to keep a low profile, something Dan never did. No matter how angry or dangerous their mum became Dan would try and reason with her, sometimes holding her arms tight to her body until the rage stopped; even putting her on top of the wardrobe once until she had calmed down. It was good for Steve because it meant that she couldn't get to him but Dan always copped it later.

She would pretend to be normal, nice even, and persuade Dan to let her go – or lift her down, unlock the cupboard door – depending on what he had done to control her. Then she would turn on him. Not straight away, where was the fun in that? Sometimes it would be an hour, once it was a whole day, before she had her revenge but it was certain and he couldn't understand why Dan never saw it coming. She used whatever was to hand: saucepan, rolling pin, ornament. She even put toilet cleaner in his tea but Dan had been so sick, and there were so many questions at the hospital, that she never did it again.

Social services had come round after his dad left because one of the neighbours tipped them off as to the goings-on at number 42. But she was smart, made sure Dan was hidden out of sight – away with friends she had said – and paraded Steve in front of them. Of course he never had a mark on him. His mother's torture of him took the form of psychological intimidation until he grew old enough to work out what reactions satisfied her and learnt to produce them on cue.

But he was worried about Dan. At first when Mum became poorly Dan had started staying over at her house; he had virtually moved in by the time Steve persuaded him that they needed professional help. It was the hygiene that had finally got to Dan. Changing her incontinence pads, clearing up when she couldn't – or wouldn't – make it to the toilet in time. Steve was disgusted by her but he hid it well and limited his visits. He was a married man, after all.

When she went into care he thought Dan would move into number 42 and leave the caravan he called home but he said he couldn't live in the house without his mum there. Dan's caravan was cold and damp, even in summer, but it was where he had always taken his women, those he paid for as well as those he didn't. Not once had he had a woman under his mother's roof and that didn't look like changing now that she wasn't there, even though the council had agreed they could keep the house until it was decided one way or another whether his mum would be sent home again.

Steve could have coped with Dan avoiding the house. What really worried him was that his brother had become secretive. He always used to boast about sex and he was a man of constant needs. If he couldn't find a woman drunk enough to have him at the end of a night in the pub he would buy it on his way home and brag next day. That had stopped. Steve had tried talking but Dan shrugged him off, telling him he was worried about Mum and to give over for a while. Dan still had that after-sex look on his face sometimes in the mornings and Steve was certain that his sex life was continuing; the question was how and where?

Looking at him now without seeming to as his brother stood up to reopen the curtains he noticed scratches on Dan's neck that hadn't been there the day before. He had that telltale lazy look on his face. He hadn't been in the pub, hadn't persuaded Gloria or Ruby to give him one. Steve doubted he had been with a prossie because Dan hadn't asked for a borrow and it was Monday; he was always skint after the weekend. As he sat down Dan caught him staring.

'What?'

'What what?'

'What you staring at?'

'Nothing.'

'You are too . . .'

'You what?' their mother shouted, stirred from her half-sleep by the start of their quarrel.

Both boys froze.

'What you two on about?'

'Nothing, Mum,' Dan said, moving to the side of her bed.

'Don't lie to me!'

She caught Dan a slap on his cheek that left an immediate red mark. Very weak, the nurses called her but what did they know?

'He was staring at me,' Dan protested, not bothering to rub his cheek.

'Pathetic!' Spittle flew from her mouth onto her bedjacket. 'Pathetic, that's what you are; a miserable specimen of a man. My God, when I think of the pain you gave me when you was born. Wasn't worth it, the neither of you were.'

She lay back on the pillows, exhausted by her outburst.

'Have some tea, Mum. They brought it in a while back and it'll be going cold.'

Dan lifted the cup to her lips and she took a long drink that brought a smile to his face. It vanished in the spray of brown, viscous liquid she spat at him, covering his shirt. Steve shut his eyes and shook his head. Dan should've known. He went to the paper towel dispenser by the side of the sink and pulled out a handful, half throwing them at his mother.

'You've dripped some on your sheets. Better mop it up if you want to be clean; they won't be changed today.'

His mother glared at him but did as she was told, her gestures so uncoordinated that Dan took the towels from her and finished the job, pausing to wipe his face before bundling the soggy mess up and throwing it away. He hadn't offered one word of complaint.

'More tea!' she demanded and Dan made to lift the cup.

'No.' Steve quickly moved the cup away.

'You what?'

'Hey!'

Dan and his mother stared at him, one confused the other angry.

'You don't deserve it,' he said calmly and enjoyed the flush of colour that ran into his mother's face.

'But, Steve, she's thirsty, aren't you, Mum?'

Dan looked upset but Steve carried the cup outside, laughing silently as he heard his mother's screech of fury at being disobeyed by one of her sons. A carer came up to him.

'Having another of her turns?' she asked, her face showing her disapproval of their most ungrateful resident.

'A fit of temper, that's all.' He didn't want them chucking her out; that would be a nightmare.

There was another great cry and the carer frowned.

'Maybe I should page a nurse to come and sedate her.'

'Just give me a minute; it may not be necessary.'

Steve stepped back into his mother's room and closed the door. On seeing him again she opened her mouth to scream but he forestalled her.

'Wait. Before you decide to do that, think. They'll come and sedate you, put you out. Is that what you want?'

She swore at him, a flow of expletives that bounced off a skin thickened to armour.

'Your choice,' he said, 'but if they have to drug you too often they'll decide you're too much bother and lock you up in the loony bin. You'd hate that; with all those crazies around you.'

The shouting stopped and his mother looked confused.

'Want to go home.' She picked up Dan's paw of a hand. 'Take your poor old mum home, son,' she said to him, tears in her eyes. 'Let me die there in peace. Please?'

Dan lowered his head onto her hand where it gripped his.

'Don't talk about dying, Mum, not you. You can't die. Course we'll take you home, won't we, Steve?'

Above Dan's bowed head his mother beamed a smile of pure malice at Steve. His bowels churned but he managed to smile back as he said.

''Fraid not, Bruv. I signed the papers to admit her, if you remember, 'cos you were too upset. So it'll take my signature to have her released and I'm not doing it.'

Dan let out a growl and was on him before he had a chance to defend himself. One hand grabbed his sweatshirt, twisting the fabric so that it choked him. The other slammed into the wall

46

beside his head, close enough for Steve to think the punch was for real.

'Sign the fucking papers, little brother, or I'll kill you.'

'No,' Steve managed to gasp, too aware that if Mum ever left the home his life would be a constant hell.

'I'll beat you to a pulp,' Dan said and raised his fist. Behind Dan's back his mum chuckled.

'Hear that? She's loving this.' Steve tried to swallow air. 'You can't look after her any more, mate, the council won't let you.' The pressure on his throat lessened and Steve took a painful breath. 'Even if I asked them to send her back they wouldn't agree. She's too sick; you know she is.'

Dan dropped his fist and turned away. Steve had won the battle – for now. Behind them his mum realised she had lost and started her screaming. Steve picked up his coat and dragged his brother outside where a qualified nurse was talking to the carer.

'She's all yours,' Steve said, pulling Dan away with difficulty.

It was dark outside with frost glinting on windscreens even though it was barely five o'clock. They walked in silence to their vehicles. Steve lit up and offered a fag to Dan who was always out of smokes on Monday. Dan shook his head.

'Go on, take one. It'll do you good.'

'You cheeked our mum,' Dan said by way of reply.

'Put her in her place that's all. She needed it.'

The pain in his jaw was nothing to that in his head as his skull hit the concrete. He blacked out briefly and saw stars when he opened his eyes. His face was on fire, his brain scrambled by the punch. He lay there, the cold penetrating his back as he tried to clear his head.

Dan carried on walking without a backward glance and reached his van. Steve rolled on his side and pulled his knees up to his chest but the movement set his head thumping. He barely noticed the van's engine stutter to life, too preoccupied with his

47

own pain, but when the headlights flashed onto main beam and Dan gunned the vehicle towards him Steve's head came up sharply. The rusty grey van was bearing down on him fast, wheels sliding on the icy tarmac, the back slewing as Dan brought it back under control and put his foot down.

Steve managed to roll to one side into a space between two parked cars, headache forgotten. The van sped by him less than a yard away and he had a brief glimpse of Dan's white face and staring eyes.

'You could've fucking killed me!' he shouted into the exhaust fumes. 'Bloody idiot!'

'Are you all right?'

A lady in her seventies, in a thick tweed coat and woollen hat, was standing over him.

'I have his registration number, you know, and I saw him drive at you after you'd fallen over. I would happily be a witness should you wish to call the police.'

That was the last thing Steve needed. After years of avoiding the attention of the law he didn't want it to start now.

'No, thanks, love, I'm OK.'

'He really was driving most dangerously. I feel we should alert the police in case he does some damage. Maybe he had been drinking.'

'He hadn't. I know him, see, and he's not a drinker. He was upset; been visiting his mum, like, and she's not well. I don't think he even saw me.'

'Well, if you're sure . . .' the lady said, perhaps softened by the idea of a distraught son.

'Really,' Steve smiled at her. 'No harm done.'

He walked back to his car slowly, deep in thought. He really was very worried about Dan.

CHAPTER FIVE

Fenwick's regular meeting with Acting Chief Constable Alastair Harper-Brown was on the first Wednesday of the month at nine o'clock. He wasn't looking forward to it. Today's discussion would be dominated by Harlden's lack of progress in tracking down the sex pest turned rapist, Flash Harry, and the need for MCS to assume responsibility for the investigation. Fenwick should have called Alison Whitby a week ago but he had been reluctant to trample on Nightingale's patch. Her prickly response to his phone call made him uncomfortable whenever he thought about it.

Harper-Brown would argue that it was beyond Harlden's ability, which might be true but if the case was going to be moved Fenwick would rather it were transferred to the specialist sex crimes unit. Harper-Brown was nothing if not a logical man and Fenwick was rehearsing his arguments as he packed his briefcase and left home, running to the car because it was starting to snow.

Fenwick had allowed time for a coffee and stopped at his favourite provider, a supposedly Italian café in Harlden. Run by two Polish brothers, one of whom had done time, it served the best espresso in town and he indulged in two each morning. Fenwick declined 'Luigi's' offer of complimentary biscotti, pulling his coat collar up as he left.

It would take him an hour to reach HQ on roads made dangerous by fresh snow over ice. If he had wanted, Fenwick could have asked for a driver, but on Wednesdays he preferred to look after himself. It gave him complete privacy to think. How much room to negotiate would Harper-Brown give him? Not a lot but more than when he had first become head of MCS. Since taking over two years ago he and Harper-Brown had come to respect each other, despite their very different approaches to detective work.

Fenwick still believed in the hard graft of policing, with science and profiling as aids to, not substitutes for, brains, legwork and proper-sized teams. Harper-Brown was a modernist, eager to embrace each new management technique thrust onto the force by consultants, encouraged by civil servants who sought improved efficiency and reduced costs without their ministry appearing weak on crime. Their different philosophies led to conflicts and the men would never like each other but Fenwick's detection rate was one of the highest in the south of England and the statistics he had to submit at tedious intervals helped Harper-Brown's averages.

Fenwick was stuck in a traffic jam when his mobile rang. It was Dawn, Harper-Brown's secretary.

'Can you hold for the chief constable, please?' she asked with a snap of authority that indicated she didn't require a reply.

Acting, he thought.

'Fenwick?'

'Good morning, sir.'

Fenwick just fitted his earpiece in time as the traffic in front of him eased forward.

'Where abouts are you?'

'On my way to see you for our nine o'clock.'

'Turn around.'

'I beg your pardon?'

'I need you in Guildford, at St Anne's, as soon as you can get there. A girl's missing and you're assigned as senior advisor.'

'That's not our patch and what's a senior advisor, for heaven's sake . . . sir?'

'Just that. This is a very sensitive case and I'm seconding you for as long as they want.'

'Who'll run MCS? We have a huge caseload and five vacancies . . .'

'Richard Quinlan will step into your shoes while you're gone.'

'Quinlan; and he's said yes?'

'He will do when I tell him.'

Fenwick's old boss was counting the months to retirement since being moved aside to make room for Alison Whitby at Harlden. Although he was a decent leader he wasn't a detective.

'Why are we involved?'

'The missing girl is Isabelle Mattias.'

'I still don't understand, sir.'

There was a pause, and then Harper-Brown said in his most dismissive tone.

'Do you live in another world, Andrew? Jane Mattias, née Simpson, is the daughter of Robert Simpson, the film director. And Robert Simpson . . .'

'Is one of our best-loved exports to Hollywood. I still don't see the connection.'

'Have you turned around yet?'

'Not quite.' Fenwick had just moved up into fourth gear for the first time in half an hour and was accelerating to forty to take advantage of a stretch of gritted dual carriageway.

'Then do so and call me back. If I have to waste time giving you a tutorial on Britain's leading families I'd like to know that at least you're heading in the right direction.'

Fenwick mouthed obscenities as he negotiated the next roundabout and retraced his route north-west. He was joining the end of the tailback from the roadworks that ran in the opposite direction as he pressed Harper-Brown's preset number.

'It's me,' he said unceremoniously, drumming his fingers as Dawn put him through.

'Where were we?'

'You were about to explain to me why my life's going to be turned upside down because some spoilt teenage brat has gone absent without leave from school.'

'Now, now!' He could hear the amusement in H-B's voice. 'You'd better be in an improved mood before you reach St Anne's. While it might be a matter of truancy the local team don't think so. Isabelle hasn't been seen since Monday night; which means she could have been missing almost thirty-six hours. They are very concerned for her safety.'

'So, tell me again, please; why are we being dragged in?'

'The Home Office have asked for help. They want to be seen to be doing absolutely everything they can to find the girl. Of course Surrey tried to persuade them that external input was inadvisable but they failed. So when I received the call I was in no position to disagree.'

'And you decided to send me why, sir?'

'Good question, Fenwick. Heaven knows there are better police officers than you. However, you have been commended more than once and are therefore "known". And you still live in Harlden, which is conveniently closer to Guildford than Lewes. It makes sense. It's an inconvenience we'll both have to put up with.

'Look, I haven't got all day. This is what you need to know. First, about the school: St Anne's has one of the best reputations in the country.'

'That I am aware of. The daughter of the deputy leader of the opposition goes there, so do countless offspring of diplomats posted abroad.'

'Exactly; it has an excellent academic record plus the best arts department in the south-east. It's an all-girls school. Not only does the aspiring pupil have to have the right aptitude, the family is quietly vetted as well. They give five scholarships a year. Isabelle entered on one but lost it when her grades started to suffer.'

'Any idea why?'

'No, but I'm sure you'll find out. About the Mattiases – well, the Simpsons really. Jane Simpson is the middle daughter of Robert and Mary Simpson. The other sisters are both actresses. Jane wanted nothing to do with acting and became an artist of some sort, before she married Brian Mattias . . .'

'Of course, the Stone Dead lead guitarist. I've got all their albums.'

'Showing your age, Andrew, but yes, you're right. Unlike the rest of the band, Brian took himself off drugs and accumulated a small fortune. By the time he died it's estimated he had over ten million in trust for his wife and daughter.'

'It was a road crash, wasn't it, about five years ago?'

'Yes, in Africa where he was doing a charitable tour. A year ago Jane remarried William Saxby, Isabelle's stepfather.'

'Of Saxby Entertainment?'

'The same. Barrow boy made good. He and his brother Rodney hold over fifty per cent of Saxby Holdings, owners of the *Daily Enquirer*, multiple property interests as well as some sort of import-export company. The *Enquirer* has a readership of millions and currently supports the government on immigration and European policy.'

'So an early success is expected; but Surrey won't want an outsider hanging around such a high-profile case.'

'True, but they weren't given a choice. You can imagine the sort of reception you're going to get in Guildford.'

Again a laugh that suggested his boss was enjoying the prospect of his discomfort. Was it jealousy, he wondered, or simply their mutual dislike? There was a brief pause as Fenwick finally eased his way through single-file traffic control and changed up.

He shook his head in despair as he skirted Harlden on his way north to Guildford.

'I suppose I'll also have Saxby breathing down my neck.' He suppressed a sigh. 'OK – how do you want to be kept involved, sir?'

'Oh, not at all, Andrew; this one is down to you entirely.'

And that was when Fenwick knew that he really was in deep doo-doo.

CHAPTER SIX

'That's simply not good enough! My daughter's disappeared and this excuse for a school still won't tell me anything.'

As he walked into a small office to the left of the entrance hall, a florid man Fenwick took to be Saxby was confronting a skeletal gentleman in his early sixties who towered over him but nevertheless contrived to shrink into subservience. As the school head was a woman, Fenwick surmised that the cringing victim must be either her deputy or the bursar.

'We have given everything we know to the police, sir, and they have instructed us not to share information with anyone during their inquiry. Naturally I very much regret this but—'

'Regret! It's not your bloody daughter who's gone missing, is it, Bursar?'

The bursar's head disappeared between his shoulder blades like a terrified tortoise.

'What further information were you requesting, Mr Saxby? Maybe I can help. I'm Superintendent Fenwick, Sussex Major Crimes.'

'What I want to know is how my daughter was allowed to leave the grounds after lights out and wasn't reported missing for twelve hours!'

'Those are good questions,' Fenwick replied calmly, 'and ones to which my colleagues will be seeking answers. When we have them we will be sure to let you know, but that may be some time.

My first priority is to receive as full a briefing as I can about your daughter and the circumstances surrounding her disappearance.' The office door opened and closed behind him; Fenwick ignored the interruption. 'You can be sure that I will give this case my very thorough attention.'

'It's about time somebody did.'

In the infinitesimal pause before he replied Fenwick debated whether he should defend the local force but then decided he knew nothing about the conduct of the case and would ignore the criticism.

'I suggest you go home, sir. I'll visit you and your wife later today.'

Saxby opened his mouth to argue but closed it again and left in bristling silence, brushing past a woman standing behind Fenwick without acknowledgement.

'Thank you.' The bursar extended his hand. 'I'm Armitage; thought he'd never leave.'

'Superintendent Fenwick. I'll need to interview you later but right now I need to find Superintendent Bernstein.'

'She's behind you.' The voice was thin, dry and decidedly unamused. 'Bursar, if you could give us the use of your office for a minute?' The tortoise retreated.

The woman who had entered the room during Saxby's diatribe walked past Fenwick and sat down behind the bursar's desk. She had a pinched face and the figure of a stick insect. She stared at Fenwick with undisguised hostility.

'Thanks for the words of support there . . . I don't think.'

'There was nothing to be served by entering into an argument with the man.'

'That's not the point; you didn't defend us and made yourself look like his white knight, all in three sentences.'

'I don't think I did, I merely persuaded him to leave.'

'Assuring him of your devoted attention; implying that he wasn't getting it from us.'

'Not at all. Look, I really do think you've misunderstood my remarks. Can we—'

'So I'm thick as well as a crap detective, am I?'

'No.' Fenwick ran his hand through his hair. 'Can we start again? Andrew Fenwick.' He extended his hand, which she ignored. 'I know that I'm on your patch for some spurious reason neither of us fully understands. I don't want to be here any more than you do. I have plenty of work to do in Sussex and frankly putting up with an overinflated, intrusive braggart with connections to the Home Office while advising on a sensitive case is not high up my list of must-do career opportunities.'

He gave her a grin implying mutual interest but she ignored the offer.

'For reasons beyond your control or mine,' he continued, 'I'm here and I hope we can work effectively together. I'm sure you and your team are doing everything you can to find Isabelle already. I don't intend to second-guess you unnecessarily—'

'Good.'

'But I've been asked to advise, so . . .'

'You're going to insist on interfering.'

It was obvious there was no way she was going to be persuaded out of her antagonism.

'I understand you are to remain SIO but that my advice will help set the strategy for the investigation. I'm sure we'll find a way of working together.'

Fenwick watched her raise a mental middle finger before stalking out. He followed. An incident room had been set up in one of the seven IT labs that St Anne's boasted, one for each pupil year. It had cubicles with Wi-Fi Internet access, scanners and PCs with more internal processing power than most police stations. A space had been cleared in the centre and desks crammed together to provide a common working area. The police equipment looked shabby beside the sleek black processors and flat screens in the study units. When Fenwick entered conversation stopped dead.

Bernstein walked to a desk in the far corner without introducing him.

'Superintendent Andrew Fenwick,' he said to the silent faces around him. 'I'm head of Sussex Major Crimes and I've been seconded here as senior advisor on this investigation. I look forward to working with you.'

Most of the officers just stared at him but one stood up to shake his hand as he passed.

'Inspector Basil Holland, Bazza to my mates.'

'Good to meet you, Bazza.'

'I'm leading the team here at the school. If you need anything, just shout.' Bazza grinned and Fenwick saw Bernstein scowl.

Fenwick nodded his thanks and wondered what had motivated the olive branch. He put the question to one side and scanned the room for a coffee machine. As if reading his mind a woman in her late thirties and carrying twenty pounds she didn't need stood up and came over.

'I'm Janice Bolt, sir,' she said in a deep Sussex accent, 'the team administrative assistant. I've sorted out a desk for you over by the window and if you want anything at all, computer, printer, typing – just let me know.'

'Thanks, Janice. Right now I'm dying for a large black coffee, as strong as you like.'

'No problem.'

Bernstein had logged on to her computer and was clicking through messages, her back angled away from the room. Fenwick pulled out the chair opposite her desk and sat down. Aware of every ear in the room straining towards them he affected an easy tone.

'So, you were saying, about the night Isabelle disappeared. Can you take me through it?'

In an equally improbable tone, she said, 'Sure, why don't we go over the crime-board together. It's through here away from prying eyes.'

She led him into a classroom opposite the computer lab, at one end of which the police had set up the whiteboards that were essential in any serious crime investigation. The classy glass version from TV police dramas was too expensive for general use. He pushed the door closed and said quietly.

'Look, I really do want to start this right. Can we at least call a truce until we're surer of each other? I estimate I've got less than three hours before your boss calls me because Saxby's grown impatient. The last thing either of us needs is unnecessary aggro.'

Bernstein considered the suggestion and then nodded slowly.

'OK. I'll ignore how you belittled me in front of Saxby and give you another chance. But that's it,' she said, emphatically, and glared at him.

'So, begin at the beginning and tell me why you don't think Isabelle's a runaway.'

'Three reasons: first, she's taken no money or clothes. Her passport is still in the school safe, along with her cash and credit card – the girls put them there while they're in college. Second, we found blood on a wall beyond the school gates and it matches her type. DNA is being rushed through. There wasn't a lot but enough to make us concerned. Third, she's vanished. We've had more than forty officers searching around the school for almost twenty-four hours and apart from the blood we can't find a trace of her.

'When the school eventually thought to alert us just after midday yesterday, I called out tracker dogs. We were fortunate that it hadn't snowed again. The dogs picked up her trail through the gardens; past a stable block that's now part of the art department and out of one of the staff entrances. We lifted her prints from the security pad by the gate – she must have had to remove her gloves. Once outside the dogs tracked her going south towards the river.

She crossed the bridge and walked a few hundred metres north-east along the B632, where her trail vanished.'

'Picked up by car?'

'We think so. There's no trace of her within a mile of the spot where the dogs lost her.'

'Any chance of witnesses?'

'Not yet but I haven't given up hope. The B632 has only three houses and a farm along a two-mile stretch. Nobody who lives there saw or heard anything and our request for drivers to come forward has produced nothing. Part of the problem is that we don't know exactly when she left the school. She was in her bedroom before lights-out because the housemistress saw her. A friend heard music until midnight but that's not proof she was still there.'

'When exactly was it noticed she was gone?'

Bernstein shrugged.

'Good question. No one realised until she failed to show up for her art class at eleven on Tuesday. Given her prints on the security pad, we're working on the assumption that she left the college voluntarily on Monday night, perhaps shortly after lights-out with the music playing as cover. Why would she risk leaving in daylight with people about? Given that she took nothing with her, we think she expected to be back in time for breakfast.'

'Talking of which, why wasn't she missed before eleven?'

Bernstein walked over to the timeline on the board, annotated in neat black writing.

'Tuesday morning: sixth-formers can have breakfast in their common room if they wish; they only need to go to the main dining room for a full English. The fact that she didn't appear for a fry-up wasn't unusual.'

'But it says here the school curriculum starts at eight; why wasn't she missed earlier?'

She tapped the board.

'The first period was revision. The girls are meant to spend it in the library or in one of the computer labs. In reality they hang out together in their common room. The second period was Classics. She didn't show up but the teacher in charge merely noted the fact in his attendance record to report in due course.'

'Is it normal for girls not to bother to show up for their classes?'

'For girls, no; for Isabelle, yes.'

'So she really could have been missing for over twelve hours before it was reported, as Saxby said.'

'Exactly, and you can imagine what her parents think of that. Our investigation is being hampered by a certain lack of cooperation from the staff.'

'Are they hiding something?'

'More likely they're trying to preserve their reputation and avoid being sued.'

'So what I heard from the bursar, about not telling Isabelle's parents anything on your instructions . . . ?'

'Was a load of bollocks. Of course we've said not to talk to the press or anyone outside the investigation but that doesn't include the girl's parents!'

'Discipline here is meant to be strict, isn't it?'

'I don't know who told you that but it's not true. According to the blurb on their website the teaching style demands a lot from pupils but it's balanced by giving them responsibility for their own conduct. By sixth form, provided the girls maintain their grades, they're trusted to behave as adults. I didn't really believe it – thought it was PR baloney – so I talked to a friend of mine at Oxford University about the girls they admit from St Anne's and she told me they're among the most mature they see.'

'It's a system ripe for exploitation if you're bright, though.'

'Exactly, and I think the headmistress has just woken up to the fact.'

'When can I see her?'

'She isn't here. She was at a conference in Edinburgh and started back yesterday but her flight was cancelled because of snow. Then her train broke down north of Leeds. She spent the night in a village hall and is on her way back now, which is why the bursar was despatched to deal with Saxby. A couple of Isabelle's teachers are interesting, though. After you're briefed you might want to talk to the art mistress. She seems to understand Isabelle better than most. You'll find her in the stable block.'

Fenwick spent the next hour with Bazza Holland and then read the key witness statements. It was clear that Bernstein was running the investigation by the book and what she might lack in personal warmth she more than made up for in efficiency. Fenwick's only suggestion was to check out every railway station around St Anne's in case Isabelle had disappeared to somewhere like London or Brighton and had avoided the local stop. Bernstein saw the logic and added the task to her list.

On his way to find the art teacher Fenwick paused to drink the coffee that had been left on his desk. It was cold and bitter, undrinkable even for him. Despite his body protesting he left without his fix.

The air outside was so cold it hurt to breathe. A chill mist blanketed the school grounds, reducing trees and shrubs to shadows that loomed like a besieging army. His ears started to hurt in the short time it took him to walk from the main entrance towards where he had been told the stable block was located. As he stepped away from the gravel path and onto frozen lawn he looked back.

St Anne's had been established in a Victorian house bequeathed to a trust on the death of its childless owner. She had left the house, grounds and enough money to fund the foundation of a school on condition that, *The facility herein shall be for the sole purpose of the provision of a Proper Education to girls between the ages of ten and eighteen who possess exceptional Intellectual Capacity, Curiosity, a Precocious Talent for the Arts, Manners and Moral rectitude.'*

Since the 1970s the school had grown in reputation and scale, so that the original house was now used only for sixth-form tutorials, common rooms and staff facilities. Further classrooms – a multi-faith centre (alongside the chapel), a new drama building, computer rooms and a science wing – had been added thanks to private fund-raising.

St Anne's was popular with absentee parents who trusted the staff to care for and educate their children, and boarders accounted for most of the pupils. They lived in purpose-built houses named after previous headmistresses, each with its own small garden or courtyard, communal sitting room and accommodation for a housemistress. It had taken Bazza's team more than a day to search the premises thoroughly and they were still working through the grounds. He could hear their fog-muffled voices from points around him.

Fenwick shivered and regretted his lack of scarf and gloves as he pulled his long winter coat tighter around his neck. Behind him the yellow lights from the main house glowed anaemically in the mist. Ahead he could see the outline of a teaching block and he walked towards it, careful of his footing on the slippery lawn, hoping to find someone who could give him directions to the stables. He climbed the steps and pulled open a heavy front door decorated with a holly wreath. Heat engulfed him and his ears said thank you.

A cluster of girls looked up guiltily. They were cradling plastic cups of steaming hot drinks. Fenwick could smell chocolate, sour instant soup . . . and coffee.

'I'm looking for the stables; I'm with the police,' he explained, showing his warrant card, noting that they relaxed.

'Go out of here and turn left, follow the brick path all the way round. Don't go on the gravel and you can't miss it,' one of the girls explained. She was about his daughter Bess's age and as confident. He smiled.

'Thanks. Is there any way I can get coffee from that thing?'

'Have you got a card?'

'A what?'

'One of these.' She held up plastic ID. 'You put cash on it and pay for things at school. We're not allowed to have money in college, only when we go out.'

'I haven't got one. May I give you some money and borrow yours?'

'Only if you don't look at my picture – it's gross.'

Her friends sniggered nervously and then laughed outright when he failed to operate the machine. In the end the girl, Emily he noted surreptitiously from her card, helped him and he took the too-hot plastic cup of coffee with him as he followed their directions to the stables, sipping at it greedily and scalding his tongue.

It was almost lunchtime when he found the art block so he waited in the hall for the classes to finish rather than risk missing the teacher. He drained his coffee and within minutes a bell sounded. Around him doors slammed open, then feet pounded the stairs in a mad rush. He estimated there must have been four classes in progress. As the first teacher passed he asked if she was Miss Bullock and was told she used the main studio behind him.

As he turned, the studio door was opened by a girl who couldn't have been older than eighteen but looked twenty. She was followed by three more, the last of whom glanced at him curiously and held the door for him. He stepped inside. The room had obviously been a barn and was enormous, double height for most of its length, with a mezzanine over the far end under which there appeared to be some sort of storage area. Easels were arranged around an empty central plinth. The north wall had been replaced with glass and there were Velux windows in the roof with electrically controlled blinds, which today were uncovered, showing snow and the close grey sky above.

Fenwick was momentarily distracted by the artwork on the walls and didn't notice at first the two women deep in conversation by the far wall. He dragged his eyes away from the paintings and coughed to attract their attention.

'Can I help you?'

The woman who spoke was older than he had expected, in her fifties perhaps, with long, silver-grey hair pulled back by a tortoiseshell slide. As their eyes met he felt an unmistakeable tug in his chest and a tingle of attraction that immediately put him on his guard.

'I'm Superintendent Fenwick,' he announced, his voice stilted even to his own ears.

'Louise Bullock, how do you do?'

She walked towards him and the light fell onto her face for the first time. It was lined around the eyes and mouth but so finely he couldn't bring himself to think of her as wrinkled. Her eyes were almost violet, angled up at the corners, hinting at laughter. He almost recognised her and wondered if they had met before.

He took her hand, ignoring the slight shock of her touch, and dropped it quickly.

'You can go now, Octavia,' she said to the young woman waiting curiously behind her. 'Don't forget, I need that piece by Friday at the very latest.'

'Yes, Miss Bullock,' the girl said.

Fenwick waited until she had gone before he spoke again.

'I'd like to talk to you about Isabelle Mattias. You were the only person to think her absence worth worrying about and I need to understand why.'

'Of course, but can we do it over lunch? I only have thirty minutes before my next class. It's personal tuition for a gifted student that I'm trying to persuade of her talent. Any excuse such as my being late and she'll scarper. Some days I could murder her supercilious parents. But,' she looked at him again and raised her eyebrows, 'I imagine I'm not meant to use words like that in front of you. Shall we go?'

Fenwick, who had never learnt the art of teasing or of being teased, followed her with growing uncase.

CHAPTER SEVEN

Any expectation Fenwick might have had of Hogwarts-type splendour vanished as he walked into the airy, cream-walled dining room. For sure, there was a raised platform complete with high table but it was empty save for an arrangement of winter greenery. Below it ash wood tables ran in long parallel rows. Most were occupied. At the far end there was a partitioned area for staff and Miss Bullock headed towards it. Six seats remained vacant at the end of one table and she took the two furthest away.

'We have waitress service. That's the menu. I'm sure there won't be a problem feeding you. I'll be back in two ticks.'

She promptly disappeared to talk to a colleague at another table.

Fenwick looked around the room, breathing in the atmosphere. He had been at the school less than two hours but already he could feel the pull of its character: routines and cliques; obscure rules of conduct, even a secret language that linked everybody together to the exclusion of outsiders.

His initial briefing from Bernstein had been thorough if unenthusiastic but she had shared with him her misgivings about Isabelle's favourite teacher, Louise Bullock. Something about the art teacher worried her and despite a second interview she remained uneasy. He had the same gut instinct. There was an air of secrecy about her that he didn't think was deliberate but it was there just the same, and he was beginning to resent the time she was consuming. Still, he had to eat and warm food would be better than sandwiches to keep him going. He ordered beef bourguignon over rice. Louise Bullock returned as their food arrived and talked without prompting.

'Issie is a disturbed young woman but in all the years I've taught her she has never once missed an art class. So I knew something was wrong when she didn't appear yesterday.' She paused to eat some quiche. 'I also have a strong feeling that she isn't coming back. You've hardly touched your food; don't you like it?'

'I'm not that hungry.' He pushed the plate to one side. 'Look, this isn't the right place for us to talk and I really do need you to answer some questions.'

'Let's go to the old staffroom in the main house; it's hardly ever used.'

Five minutes later, Fenwick watched as she coaxed fresh coffee from a machine that looked older than she was.

'Don't worry; this makes the best coffee in the school. Sometimes the older things are, the better they get.'

He avoided her eyes.

The machine emitted embarrassing burping noises as the water heated but he had to admit that the coffee smelt good.

'You're really worried, aren't you?' she said, pre-empting his next question, 'and I mean about Issie, not the coffee.'

'Aren't you? Isn't that why you reported her missing?'

Miss Bullock studied the plate of fresh fruit she had taken for dessert.

'Call me Lulu; everyone does. Yes, I'm concerned; I have been for months. Something's not right about her. Despite Issie's bravado I think she's vulnerable.'

'Go on.'

'Her father's death hit her badly. Before that she'd been confident, mature for her age. It happened just before Christmas in her second year. I was mother for her house.'

'Mother?'

'It's a St Anne's tradition for the first-years, to help them transition from a home environment. Issie didn't really need me in year one; in fact she helped me with other girls, like a big sister. Then her father died and she went to pieces. He was the centre of her world; her best friend. They used to write to each other several times a week – email, or by post when there wasn't a connection. Wherever he was in the world his letters would arrive without fail.

'For a year after his death she couldn't get through a day without crying, but then slowly she started to heal – on the outside, at least – but I didn't think she was right inside. Not that she ever admitted it.'

'Is that when her grades started to suffer?'

'Yes; she lost her scholarship at the end of her second year. Then just before her mother remarried her behaviour completely deteriorated. Issie seems to loathe Saxby. To her he's everything her father wasn't: a bully, opinionated, mean . . . you name a character defect and she thinks he has it. She refused to go to their wedding. The invitation turned up here at school – it was a grotesque, ostentatious thing, I grant you. She sent a "regretfully decline" card as her RSVP.

'It caused uproar at home. Issie weathered the storm for weeks. He cancelled her allowance so she simply stopped spending money; then he forced her mother to withdraw approval for Issie to go on any school trips.'

'Saxby has that much power over the mother?'

'Oh yes, she's weak. Calls herself a "man's woman"; doormat, more like.'

'Did Issie give in and accept eventually?'

'Not for a long time. She was amazingly strong-willed but the last straw came when he threatened to cut her art tuition. She came to see me with the letter, in floods of tears. She asked whether I could go on giving her tutorials even though her mother had withdrawn permission. Of course, I said yes . . .'

The coffee machine emitted a cough like a sixty-a-day veteran. Fenwick looked at it with concern, afraid that it might be a death rattle and with it the passing of his only chance of decent coffee.

'Don't worry, it always does that.' Miss Bullock stood up and turned it off. 'Black no sugar would be my guess?'

'Yes, thank you. Go on – you agreed to continue tuition.'

'Right. *I* said yes but the college refused; said I was undermining parental authority. My arse! Oh, excuse me,' she said and looked at him, genuinely embarrassed. 'I forgot that this was an official police interview.'

He laughed.

'It won't be in my notes. So that broke her resistance and she went to the wedding after all? She must care about her art.'

'It's her passion and yes, you're right, the poor kid gave in.'

'Let's come back to yesterday. What happened when Issie didn't show up?'

'I sent girls to check her room, the library . . . anywhere she might be. They couldn't find her so I went to the deputy head and reported her missing. She checked with the other teachers and had members of staff search the obvious places. By eleven-thirty I was really worried but the deputy said we couldn't be sure she was gone. I'm afraid I had to insist that we report her missing. I threatened to do it myself if the school refused.'

'Not popular.'

'No, but then they need me more than I need them.'

'Why is that?'

Miss Bullock blushed, made a show of eating her fruit and avoided the question.

'I asked why.'

'Oh, this will sound arrogant; but I'm quite . . . known in the contemporary art world.'

He made a note to check up.

'Is there anything else you can tell me about Issie that might help us find her?'

Bullock toyed with a piece of pineapple, pushing the segment around her plate.

'No, that's all.'

Fenwick felt she was holding back and asked again but she shook her head and merely drank her coffee so he rose to go. He had other interviews to complete before he saw Saxby.

'If anything else occurs to you, no matter how trivial, please call me.' He handed her his card. 'I'm really worried about Issie.' He hesitated, watching in vain for the involuntary flinch his words should have evoked. 'There are four possibilities as to what might have happened to her.'

Louise Bullock regarded him for the first time with interest.

'*Four?*'

'Yes.' He ticked each one off on his fingers. 'One, she's run away – though from everything I'm learning I think that's unlikely.'

'Why?' Her question was almost accusatory, as if he were condemning Issie by his assumption.

'Because she's taken nothing with her; her passport, cash, chequebook, credit card, clothes, make-up are all here. What bright girl does that? She didn't leave the school on impulse; she found out the pass code for the staff gate. That took planning.'

'So that's option one,' Bullock said; her voice wavered but her eyes were steady.

'Option two is that she only left for the night but hurt herself and is lying injured somewhere. That's one of the reasons we have such a large search going on, not just here at the school but in the surrounding area as well. With temperatures this low she won't have survived even one night unless she was lucky enough to fall in a sheltered place.'

Miss Bullock cupped her hands around her mug.

'Well go on; what's the third option?'

'There is a chance that she's been abducted – by a stranger or someone she knows – who is now holding her against her will. Of all the options – and remember I don't think she's a runaway – it's the one that gives us hope. It means she could still be alive somewhere out of the weather and that we have time to find her.'

'And the fourth?' Her tone suggested that she had already guessed his answer.

'Is that she's been killed.' He let his words sink in but all she did was study her fingernails. 'So based on all that, Miss Bullock, are you certain you have nothing more to say?'

The teacher dropped her head and stared at her coffee. Seconds ticked away.

'Miss Bullock?'

'Nothing further, Mr Fenwick.'

'Very well,' his voice was clipped, 'then at the least you can tell me which of her friends I should speak to.'

There was a tiny relaxation in her shoulders as she drained her mug.

'That would be Puff and Octavia. Here,' she scribbled on a piece of paper. 'This is Octavia's room number; they hang out there as it's larger than Puff's. You might catch them before their next lesson. Be careful how you handle Octavia. She's the younger daughter of Sir Dominic Henry, a very influential man in the City and generous donor to the College Foundation. Miss Henry more than makes up in self-belief for what she lacks in modesty. Now, to get there, take the back door from the hall and follow the brick path – avoid the lawn and the gravel.'

He followed her instructions, found MacArthur House and climbed the stairs to the second floor. The sound of rock music flowed down the corridor from a room at the end. His knock went unanswered, probably because it couldn't be heard, so he pushed open the door and stuck his head inside.

Two girls the same age, one blonde, the other brunette and extremely pretty, were lying on twin beds, their feet tapping to the beat, cigarettes in their fingers.

'Hello,' he said, realising suddenly that he was breaking all the rules: alone with girls, in their bedroom, no other adult present.

He needn't have been concerned. They were too worried about him reporting their illicit smoking to think of making a complaint.

'Octavia?' The blonde nodded with affected indifference. 'And Puff?' The brunette gulped and whispered *yes*. 'I'm Superintendent Andrew Fenwick. I'd like you to accompany me to the incident room so that I can interview you.'

Fenwick studied Octavia's room. It was large enough for two single beds, an armchair and a desk under a bay window. Across from where he stood was a door to an en suite shower room. The bedroom walls were covered with posters and student works of art. Behind one bed were delicate watercolours interspersed with charcoal sketches of plants and trees. Above the other were violent collages and an oil painting he thought grotesque. Immediately on his left was an abstract study in acrylics, all primary colour insistence. Although he didn't understand the picture he found himself staring, drawn into its passion.

'We've already told somebody everything we know,' Octavia said belligerently, recalling his attention.

'You haven't spoken to me and I want to hear your account first hand.'

'Why?' Octavia wasn't prepared to give an inch. She stubbed out her cigarette and swivelled her legs to the floor, searching with her feet for her boots.

'You're Issie's best friends; she has been missing for more than twenty-four hours and if you had a shred of real feeling for her you'd be willing to help me in any way you could.'

His bluntness shocked her into silence. Puff was already pulling on her outdoor jacket.

In the incident room Fenwick took Octavia to one of the cubicles at the far end and asked Puff to wait.

'I'm meant to be in history.'

'Please feel free to call administration to let them know where you are.'

He gestured to the phone. Octavia ignored it.

'It's a research set, they'll think I'm in the library.'

'You can have a teacher with you.'

The look she gave him could have scorched earth.

'Quite unnecessary.' Octavia glared at him, crossed her arms and sighed as a policewoman came to join them.

Fenwick leant forward, his tone more gentle.

'I want to find Issie, Octavia. I know you think she's run off but we don't, not without money or her credit card.'

'Issie has friends all over; she could be with any one of them.'

'What makes you so sure?'

Octavia took a lock of blonde hair and started to play with it. She affected a bored, suffering look. Fenwick tried to think how he would coax his daughter Bess out of a similar mood, not that she had yet graduated to Octavia's level of indifference, but then she was only twelve. He caught Janice looking at him and nodded for her to come over.

'Janice, could you get me a black coffee please; and what would you like, Octavia?'

'Nothing.'

'Nothing, thank you,' Janice said automatically. Octavia looked affronted.

'She has no right to talk to me like that; who does she think she is? I'll tell my father and then she'll be sorry.'

'Oh, please!' Fenwick raised an eyebrow. 'You're older and more independent than that. You don't need to use your father's name to be taken seriously.

'Look, no matter what you say *I* think Issie's in real trouble. Right now she could be on her own, scared, possibly hurt, freezing cold and hungry, hoping her friends won't abandon her. If you know for certain that she isn't any of those things, then great, I'll be delighted, but if you can't be sure, then you owe it to her to tell me what it is that you do know. If you don't, and God forbid anything bad happens to Issie, it will be on your conscience for the rest of your life.'

He paused expectantly, hoping that somewhere inside the porcelain doll in front of him there was a real girl and that he had reached her. After a long pause Octavia dropped the strand of hair and yawned.

'Can I go now?'

Fenwick swallowed a curse and nodded. She left without a backward glance.

'Failed to crack Little Miss Cool?'

Bernstein was standing less than ten feet away, a self-satisfied grin on her face.

'Not so much as a thaw,' he conceded. 'Did you fare any better?'

'Worse. I tried to tough her out and she complained to her mother. I'm not good at dealing with their sort. So what did you make of the art teacher?'

'I agree with you, she's holding something back.'

'Any idea what?'

'My guess is she has a theory why Issie left college on Monday night.'

'Hmm, possibly. We're looking into her background just in case it's something else. What are you going to do next?'

'Interview Puff, though I have no expectation of coaxing anything from her. Then I want to look at Issie's room before I interview the headmistress, assuming she's arrived by then.'

'Call me when you're done with the girl and I'll take you if you like,' Bernstein offered and Fenwick wondered whether this was a genuine olive branch. 'I hear you got lost last time.'

Obviously not.

He proceeded to waste the next five minutes in an attempt to make Puff talk. As soon as she left he and Bernstein returned to MacArthur House, careful not to lose their sense of direction in the enveloping mist.

CHAPTER EIGHT

Issie's room was smaller than Octavia's. As he walked in Fenwick was struck by a sense of the girl's absence. His breath misted in the air and he noticed that the windows were open above a large desk, in the centre of which was a laptop connected to a printer with a neat pile of text books and essays to one side. Everything was tidy: the edges of the papers perfectly aligned with the corners of the desk; pens and pencils in a pot by the printer, spare paper in a wire basket under a new print cartridge that might never be used. Smudges of fingerprint powder were the only imperfections.

'Was it like this when you searched?'

'Yes; unnatural isn't it?' Bernstein went to close the windows.

'Leave it for a moment; I want to see things exactly as they were left.'

'You reckon the girl lived like this?'

'No, but somebody wants us to think she did. Let's appreciate the scene they've set.'

He pulled his coat tight as he sat down by the desk and opened the top drawer: more paper and pens, a geometry set, scalpel and glue. In the second drawer he found an iPod.

'What teenager do you know who would leave without their music?'

'I don't know any teenagers,' Bernstein replied.

'Lucky you. Why is the computer here? I'd have thought it would be with Tech.'

'It's been there and come back.'

'Within twenty-four hours?' Fenwick couldn't believe it.

'Yes. Apparently this PC is new, hasn't been used. Her mother told us it was a recent birthday present. She doesn't know what happened to the old one and neither does anyone we've spoken to.'

'Computers don't just disappear. It's probably been taken as part of a cover-up and that means whoever did this knew enough to leave the new PC behind.'

'Probably.'

'Hmm.' Fenwick stood up and went over to Issie's bed. The duvet was smooth, the pillows plump.

'Searched,' Bernstein said, 'nothing under the mattress, nothing in the mattress, nothing hidden in the pillows. Trust me, the bed's clean; so is the room. There's *nothing* here.'

'Exactly.'

Bernstein started drumming her fingers on the door frame, an impatient presence willing him to accept that he was wasting his time.'Issie is fanatical about her art. Why is none of her work here?' He pointed to pin holes in the walls.

'No idea.' Bernstein yawned, baring the telltale yellow of nicotine teeth, but she moved a step into the room, hesitated and then took another. 'Do you think it might be relevant?'

'Maybe.'

Fenwick bent and sniffed the pillowcase. Bernstein regarded him in astonishment.

'Do you get off on young girls?'

'Don't be crude. This bedding's clean. What's the rota for changing linen?'

'I don't know.'

'Then if you want to do something useful why don't you find out.'

Bernstein opened her mouth, shut it abruptly and left. Fenwick sat down on the desk chair and lowered his head into his hands.

The feeling of sadness was suddenly overwhelming. *Someone's cleared her away*, he thought, *but she may not even be dead.*

'What are you doing? Get out or I'll call the police.'

Fenwick looked up to see a woman in a tracksuit standing by the door brandishing a hockey stick.

'I am the police,' he was suddenly struggling to maintain a straight face, 'and who might you be?'

'Elaine Horlick,' the woman replied and wiped her lips as if she had a bad taste in her mouth. She could have been in her late fifties, except that the moustache above her pursed mouth was dark, not grey.

'Miss Horlick,' he said, rising with an outstretched hand, 'Superintendent Fe—'

'*Mrs* Horlick.' She ignored him and strode into the room. 'Do you have a warrant?'

'Fenwick,' he continued. 'I don't need one. Isabelle's parents and the bursar have given permission but I have to ask what you are doing here.' He stepped forward.

'How dare you! I'm one of Issie's favourite teachers.'

He noted that she used the present tense.

'Then perhaps you can tell me about her. Please, take a seat.' He gestured towards the easy chair and, reluctantly, she obeyed. Like some other sports people he knew the energy that suffused Mrs Horlick in action seemed to drain from her once she sat down.

'How well do you know Issie?'

'Extremely well. She's a gifted sportswoman. Her tennis is almost county standard.'

'And you are the games mistress?'

'Games, Superintendent? We don't play *games* at St Anne's – we train sportswomen of the future. Our regime is renowned across England.'

'Indeed. And through your . . . ah . . . training regime you and Issie became close?'

Mrs Horlick looked down at her hands where they clasped the hockey stick. With an obvious effort of will she relaxed her fingers and laid it on the carpet.

'I was her mother away from home,' she said.

'Another one.'

She looked up at him, affronted.

'Who else claims to be?' Her frown did little for her looks. 'Oh, of course, that stupid woman Bullock. Just because Issie likes to daub from time to time she thinks there's something special in their relationship.' Mrs Horlick shivered. 'Do you have to keep that window open? It's well below freezing outside.'

'Yet you were playing hockey,' he ventured with a nod towards the stick.

'A true sportswoman plays in all weathers. Unfortunately I had to abandon the match when visibility deteriorated and we could no longer see the goals. Most inconvenient; St Anne's has reached the under-sixteen quarter-finals and I'm not satisfied with our defence.' She sniffed in disgust at the temerity of weather.

'What can you tell me about Issie?'

'Wonderful girl; cursed with a dreadful mother and even worse stepfather.'

'Why do you consider her mother dreadful?'

'She's a spineless wimp of a woman; terrible role model and an emotional parasite. After Issie's father died it was the mother who called her daughter in floods of tears. She never once thought about what Issie might be going through. Then eventually her period of mourning came to an end and she married a man old enough to be Issie's grandfather – and expects the poor girl to be a dutiful daughter to him!'

'So you didn't approve of the marriage to Lord Saxby.'

'That's immaterial. You asked me why I pitied Issie and I told you. Please can we close the windows so that it's warm when Issie comes back?'

Fenwick stood up and obliged. It was only twenty-five to three but outside the day was growing dark as the invisible sun sank into mist that was thickening to fog.

'Is her room always like this?'

'Perishing cold, you mean? No.'

'I was referring to the neatness, nothing left lying around, no posters or artwork.'

Mrs Horlick looked around for the first time and her eyebrows rose in surprise.

'Her paintings and photographs have gone. She kept her best work here. Not the stuff she needed for her A level, of course, but her other studies. I'm certain they're missing.'

Fenwick nodded to himself.

'Her old computer; do you know where we might be able to find it?'

'No. I wasn't even aware she had a new one.' The sports teacher looked distressed, as if she had failed an important test.

'Have you any idea what's happened to her?'

'Run away, of course. This time of year is always hard for her.' Seeing Fenwick's confusion she added, 'It's the anniversary of her father's death on the twenty-first. And if that wasn't enough, there's her official eighteenth birthday party to get through. She was dreading it. Her mother has organised a formal black-tie thing stuffed full of relatives, local dignitaries and girls she mistakenly thinks are close to Issie. Only two of her true friends are invited.'

'Octavia and Puff?'

'Yes. They thought it a real joke; the invitation was gilt-edged, the dress code stupidly old-fashioned. It had all the hallmarks of Saxby's pretension and they teased her mercilessly. I expect she'll be back once that's over.'

'Where do you think she might be staying?'

Elaine Horlick's face collapsed into a worried frown.

'If I knew do you think I'd be sitting here?' She hesitated.

'Go on.'

'Well, recently I think Issie might have made some unsuitable friends. It's only a suspicion but there have been times of late that she's been ill in the morning. I think she was hungover.'

'Did you report this?'

Mrs Horlick flushed and shook her head.

'If it was a hangover bad enough to make her feel ill then she would have smelt of booze. Did she?'

'Once or twice. I warned her about it, said it would wreck her game . . .'

'To say nothing of her studies, which I understand have also suffered. Do you know why she should resort to drink?'

'Resort? No, I assumed it was a teenage fad, not a way of coping with a problem. You think otherwise?'

'Well, I don't claim to be her "father away from home", Mrs Horlick, but I would say that the girl that's been described to me was in desperate need of help, not indulgence.'

Horlick dropped her eyes and he stood up to indicate the interview was over. She just sat there like a side of beef.

'Mrs Horlick, it's time for you to go,' he said gently.

The woman nodded and rose to her feet. He followed her to the door and passed her the hockey stick. When she was in the corridor he said, 'Can you tell me where the laundry room is?'

'What? Oh, there are bins for dirty linen and clothes in the utility room next to the showers. They're emptied twice a week, on Monday and Friday.'

Fenwick watched her leave before closing and locking the door to Issie's room. He found the showers, made sure there were no girls around and went into the utility room adjacent to them.

The laundry hampers were lined up along one wall, helpfully labelled: *towels/bed linen* and *clothing*.

He went over to the hamper for linen and opened it. There was a rumpled duvet cover at the bottom. The container was so large that he was only just able to reach in and flick it carefully aside. Beneath were sheets and a pillowcase, four items in total. He was wheeling the whole bin towards the door when Bernstein walked in.

'You beat me to it,' she said begrudgingly.

'We need large evidence bags. Have you got any?'

'Not big enough. I'll call for some. I'm going to have Bazza's hide for this. He should have checked everything. What else have you found?'

'That Issie's artwork and photographs are missing from her room as well as her old PC.' He glanced at his watch. 'It's quarter to three. I should go to the Saxbys'. You searched the art rooms in the stables?'

'It was part of the initial hunt for Isabelle.'

'You were looking for the girl not her paintings. Tell Bazza to search them again for the missing artwork; it'll be a chance to redeem himself.'

'What good is that going to do?'

'If we find her work we might learn more about Issie and why somebody did such a good job of cleaning up her life before we arrived. This lot needs to go straight to the lab, top priority. Make sure the chain of evidence isn't broken.'

Bernstein looked irritated at being ordered about but nodded as if acknowledging that he had scored a point.

The fog had thickened so Fenwick could see nothing of the grounds of Saxby Hall as he drove up a red tarmacadam drive bordered by white fencing. The 'Hall' turned out to be a modern, ranch-style house with symmetrical wings of two-storeyed red brick and a marble colonnade at the front. It was one of the ugliest buildings he had seen.

He was greeted at the door by a butler who looked as if he wanted an excuse to send him round to the tradesmen's entrance but let him in swiftly when he heard his rank. Apart from a standard lamp by the staircase the entrance hall was in darkness.

Traces of light filtered under double doors to the right from behind which he could hear raised voices. The hall was overheated. As he was removing his coat the doors were flung open and a man stormed out.

'Who the bloody hell are you?' The voice was identical to Lord Saxby's; it had to be the younger brother.

'Mr Rodney Saxby?'

'I asked you a question.'

'Superintendent Andrew Fenwick, Sussex Maj—'

'I don't need your bloody career history. It's about time you got here. My brother's worried sick. This'll be the second day that girl's missing and what have you lot done about it? Sweet fu—'

'Thank you, Rod; we're ready for the superintendent now,' the elder brother interrupted. 'You're welcome to join us.'

'I'm late already. Doubt there's much you're going to tell us anyway, is there?' He dared Fenwick to contradict him with a stare that might have worked on another man. Fenwick merely walked past him and asked, 'Lord Saxby, is this a good time?'

'No time's a good time. Come on; Jane's in here.'

After the darkness of the hall Fenwick had to blink as he walked through the double doors. The room ran the whole width of the house and was furnished with seating at one end and a library at the other. The books looked as if they had been bought by the yard. Lady Saxby was hunched in a dark leather armchair to one side of a log fire. A matching settee dominated the middle of the room, its austere upholstery relieved by a profusion of geometrically patterned cushions. Above the mantelpiece a full-length portrait of the mistress of the house dominated the room. It dwarfed its subject who huddled protectively behind a cushion, legs tucked up beneath her.

She didn't get up when he walked in, nor did she ask, as most mothers would have done immediately, whether he had any news.

He told them quickly what he had discovered at the school,

concluding with the fact that the prevalent belief among her teachers was that Issie had run away.

'Can you think of any reason why she would have done so, Lady Saxby?'

'No.' She pushed a strand of lank brown hair behind her ear; her voice barely a whisper.

Her husband towered over her, contriving to look threatening rather than protective.

'Tell me about your daughter,' Fenwick asked gently, hoping to establish rapport before asking the tough questions he needed to.

'I don't see that this will do any good, Superintendent. The girl's been missing since sometime on Monday night. Your colleagues, inept as they might be, think she's been abducted even if her useless teachers are too short-sighted to see it, and you sit here wanting her biography!'

'Humour me, sir.'

'I don't mind, Bill. In fact I'd like to talk about her; please?'

She looked up at her husband and Fenwick observed a remarkable transformation. Saxby's face softened, affection replacing its customary belligerence.

'If it will help, sweetheart,' he said. 'Would you like anything?'

'Some tea, perhaps – and maybe the superintendent would like some – but will you make it, darling? Only you do it properly; I couldn't bear to drink anything else.'

'Of course.' Saxby kissed the top of her head and left at once.

As soon as he was gone Jane Saxby let out a sigh and leant her head back.

'He means well but his way of coping is to get angry and it's wearing me down,' she explained in a voice far stronger than before.

Despite the repeated remarks he had heard about her weakness, Fenwick had an insight of a clever and possibly manipulative woman, well in control of her environment.

'I married him for Issie's sake,' she said suddenly, as if aware of Fenwick's silent appraisal. 'He loves me, of course, and I'm deeply fond of him. Behind his bluster he's a really sweet man.'

'Why for Issie's sake?'

'Two reasons: money and a father. My husband and I had made wills leaving everything to charity except a small legacy for Issie. We didn't want money to corrupt her you see. When he died – well, I got a job and Issie had her scholarship so we were fine, but then,' she shook her head at the memory, 'with the financial crisis the income from Issie's trust dried up. Then, even worse, we lost nearly all the capital. Our "investment advisor" put a lot of it into questionable investments.'

'Couldn't you sue him?'

'Apparently not; I'd signed all these forms you see – I was half crazed with grief at the time but that's no excuse. We may get something back – we're part of some sort of law suit – and we've had a little compensation. We could still have got by if Issie had kept her scholarship but she went to pieces when her father died.' She looked guilty. 'We both did. Brian was such a wonderful man, you see.' Her eyes filled.

'So I was faced with the prospect of removing Issie from St Anne's. It was her only point of stability. We'd had to leave the family home, and although my parents are wonderful they are very controlling and I didn't want to give up our independence.

'Bill came to one of my exhibitions and bought half of it! He always says he fell in love with my art before he fell in love with me.'

Fenwick's disbelief must have shown because Jane Saxby nodded for emphasis.

'Don't judge him by his public persona, Superintendent. He has to be tough in business but he has a warm, kind heart. When he met Issie he liked her at once. My daughter is a tomboy, Mr Fenwick: very good at games, an excellent rider, with a bright enquiring mind. I'm the opposite. The only thing Issie inherited from me is a love of art, though she is far more talented than me.

'Bill worked hard to develop a relationship with her. He's not a patient man, of course, and his normal style of persuasion is to bully but he's clever and has good instincts. I thought it would work. In the early days it seemed to.'

'What happened?'

'The summer before the wedding – that would be almost eighteen months ago – we went on a cruise around the Greek islands. Bill has a yacht, an Oyster 625, and Issie had never sailed before. She took to it at once, as I'd known she would. The two of them forced the hired crew below decks so they could enjoy themselves. I could see that they started to respect each other, then it grew into liking and trust. Maybe even real affection.' Her eyes drifted away into the past.

'Sounds great,' Fenwick said encouragingly.

Jane blinked and forced herself back.

'It was, until Rod turned up. He was jealous of Issie from the beginning. For a man in his late forties, he behaved appallingly. He soured the rest of the trip. Bill tried to cajole him out of his sulks and of course Issie didn't react well. She doesn't give trust easily and she saw Bill's acceptance of Rod's behaviour as a betrayal. Three days before we were due to come home I think she and Rod must have had a terrible fight – though neither Bill nor I heard anything – because the following morning she ran away. We were anchored off Cephalonia. Issie took one of the tenders and went to the island.'

'Is running away typical of her?'

'Not until then but since, yes. We organised a search and, as bad luck would have it, Rod found her. When they returned to the harbour, she was silent and he was triumphant. She's never spoken to him or Bill again.'

'She blamed Lord Saxby for his brother's behaviour? That seems excessive.'

'She's a strong-willed young woman, Mr Fenwick; once she makes up her mind, it's very hard to change.'

'Hence her attempted boycott of your wedding.'

'You heard about that?' Jane Saxby flushed, unable to meet his eyes. 'I'm afraid we didn't handle that well. Rod was adamant that Bill needed to be firm with her; "no amount of coaxing will do it", he said, and I was overruled. Of course it was a disaster. Breaking Issie's will was the worst thing Bill could have done. I told him so, that he might have won his little battle by having her physically present at our wedding but he'd lost the war. He just couldn't see it.'

'Is Rod Saxby a frequent visitor?'

'A constant one unless I put my foot down but I can only do that so often.'

'Would he have been at Issie's birthday party?'

Something in his tone made her look up. 'Is that relevant?'

'One theory is that she's run away to avoid the party. Apparently she hated the idea.'

Without warning Jane Saxby's eyes filled with tears. She struggled to find a handkerchief in time to stop them falling but failed.

'I'm sorry,' she said, swallowing a sob, 'this is stupid and unhelpful. It's just that the party was my idea, a way of saying sorry to Issie. I'd hoped it would bring us back together as a family, not drive her away.'

'The way the party was described to me, it was very unlikely to find favour with her.'

Jane Saxby looked at him in surprise.

'That can't be right. I told the party planner to do exactly what Issie wanted within budget. It was to be *Issie's* event, a means of her feeling in control of her life again, of us acknowledging that she was a young woman.'

Fenwick repeated Elaine Horlick's description of the event. As he did so Jane Saxby's mouth set in a thin line.

'The bastard!' she exclaimed when he'd finished, 'the bloody-minded, stupid bastard!'

She jumped out of her chair, scattering cushions, a look of fury on her face, and grabbed the phone on the desk. As she punched in a number the door opened and her husband entered with a tray of tea and cake.

'What's going on? Have you been upsetting my wife, Fenwick?'

'Not him, that damned brother of yours!'

'What?' Saxby put the tray down and hurried over.

'Give me the phone, darling,' he said reaching out for it.

'Get off! That bastard has got to the party planner, I know he has.'

Saxby's face flushed and Jane saw it at once.

'What did you do?'

'I only gave him the number. He was going to arrange for her favourite rock band to be there, that's all; he said he wanted to surprise Issie, make up for his teasing.'

'Teasing? He's a sadistic bully and he's wrecked the party. Tell him, Superintendent,' she ordered.

While Lady Saxby tracked down the party planner Fenwick repeated what he knew to her husband. By the time he'd finished Saxby was sitting with his head in his hands and his wife had finished her call.

'It's all true,' she said, defeat in her voice, 'he told them that we'd changed our minds, that we wanted something traditional after all. He said you'd approved it and that I wasn't to be bothered because my health was delicate. How could you, Bill? You should've known better than to trust him where Issie's concerned.'

'That's why she's run away?' Saxby asked Fenwick, the colour in his face changing from white to bright red so quickly that Fenwick worried for his heart.

'*If* she's run away, yes, it could be but . . .' he said.

89

'I'll kill him!' Saxby said, his fists clenching and unclenching as he leapt up and strode about the room. 'This is the last straw. I should have listened to you, Jane. You were right about him all along but he's my brother, I can't believe he'd do something like this just to spite Issie.'

'Not only Issie, Bill. She's the weapon he's using to get at me. He had you to himself for forty-five years until I came along. It's me he wants to damage; poor Issie is a casualty of his hatred.'

Her words shocked Saxby and concerned Fenwick.

'If you're that certain of his feelings, Lady Saxby, I have to ask something, and forgive me if this question is distasteful to you, sir. Could your brother be involved in Issie's disappearance?'

'But you said she'd run away?' Saxby stared at him, confused.

'I said that was the most popular theory at the school. What I haven't yet had a chance to tell you is that I'm not so certain their theory is right. If you recall, my colleague mentioned to you that there were suggestions Issie had been taken against her will.'

'The trace of blood, yes, but she might just have fallen over.' Jane Saxby was staring at him, willing him to agree with her.

'Possibly, but she took no money, no clothes or other belongings with her. Even her iPod is still in her desk.'

'She left her iPod behind?' Jane's hand covered her mouth in shock. 'Issie would never do that! She even went to sleep with it on. It has all her father's music on it, including the working material of the album he was recording when he died. It's her lifeline.' She collapsed back into her chair.

'Oh my God,' she said, fear for the first time audible in her voice. She turned to her husband, anguish ageing her face. 'Bill, my baby's gone!'

CHAPTER NINE

Fenwick hurried across the car park towards the yellow lights that blurred through the fog. There was a security code to enter the block and he had forgotten it, so he called Janice hoping she was still there and would be discreet when letting him in. She was both, laughing at him a little but in a nice way. He followed her rolling hips towards the incident room. Despite the central heating it was cold in the corridor, with snow blanketing the skylights that ran its length. The incident room reeked of the exhalations and odours of too many bodies in close proximity for too long. It was seven o'clock. He had been involved in the case only ten hours but already he felt the pressure for a result.

After seeing the Saxbys and asking Bernstein to track down brother Rod, Fenwick had gone to Surrey police HQ where he had been interrogated by the chief constable, Charles Norman, OBE, who was a close friend of Acting CC Harper-Brown and Fenwick suspected a negative briefing behind his back.

Norman's parting words were echoing in Fenwick's overactive brain as he rejoined the investigating team.

'Keep me informed. This is a highly sensitive case and I've got the Home Office breathing down my neck. I need to know what you're up to and I haven't got ESP.'

Fenwick had nodded, muttering 'But of course.' Norman had looked at him shrewdly.

'We'll see; I'm told you're difficult to work with but good –

this is your chance to prove the latter and quieten the rumours about the former. If Isabelle Mattias is still alive and has been dumped somewhere she won't last long in this weather.'

Fenwick needed no reminding of the urgency of the case and bit off a retort that regular updates would consume valuable time and wouldn't help find Issie.

He had called his children on his mobile on the way back to St Anne's to wish them goodnight. When Bess blew him a kiss he felt his throat constrict without warning, thoughts of another girl rushing in.

His search of Issie's bedroom at Saxby Hall had revealed nothing other than an eclectic taste in music, some astonishing paintings and a wide collection of books. Next to her bed was a battered copy of *The Wind in the Willows* on top of an equally well-thumbed edition of Shakespeare's sonnets. Despite her poor reputation he had started to like her.

He had asked her mother for a picture that would reveal more of her character than a standard school photo and been given a black and white shot of her hanging upside down from a tree branch, T-shirt slipping to reveal a flat stomach with a stud in the navel. It was a great picture, and would come in handy if they decided on publicity, but it wasn't exactly what he needed. So she had found one of Issie after a local point-to-point. She was holding the winner's trophy aloft with a hard grin of satisfaction on her mud-spattered face.

The idea of Issie alone, freezing and frightened, was constantly in his mind but he couldn't let it distract him. Earlier that day he had skimmed reports that painted a picture of a once lovely girl who had 'gone off the rails' and was now considered a bad influence. He felt pity for Issie and he wasn't the only one; she seemed to have the ability to make people love her, a misunderstood child in a young woman's body, desperate for the uncomplicated father's love that had once been the centre of her world. Fenwick had no doubt that Issie was difficult and might have translated her feelings of abandonment into self-destructive behaviour but he couldn't conjure up a picture of her leading someone like Octavia Henry astray.

Bernstein was waiting for him in the incident room, most of the team around her. There was a low buzz that immediately caught his attention.

'Rod Saxby's done a runner,' Bernstein said with satisfaction. 'We went to pick him up for questioning but he was gone.'

'You're sure?' Fenwick felt a spurt of adrenaline.

'Well, his housekeeper said she was expecting him but he never came home from the Hall. He hasn't been seen at any of his clubs.'

Fenwick's hopes sank.

'Hardly conclusive.'

Bernstein looked disappointed but hurried on.

'He doesn't have an alibi for Monday night. He sent his housekeeper out to the pictures and left a dinner party early. There's no trace of where he went, though in his statement he said he was at home. What's more his car's missing from the garage at his house and he takes the train to London when he visits his club, so where is it? We should try for a search warrant.'

'We don't have enough.'

'Jane Saxby as good as accused him of abducting her daughter!'

'As good as isn't good enough, you know that. Anyway, her husband flatly disagrees.'

'So you're backing off because of his connections?'

It was an accusation in public but Fenwick decided to treat it as a joke; there was already too much tension between them and all he cared about was finding Issie and bringing her home. Bernstein's desire to score points at every opportunity struck him as childish.

'Connections? If you've done any homework on me, and I'd be surprised if you lot haven't, you'll know that I believe in connections as much as I do in Father Christmas. And for those of you who still have doubts, I won't be hanging up my stocking by the chimney in three weeks' time. What else did his housekeeper say?'

'Not a lot. She's foreign, Philippine maybe. Hardly speaks any English; can't have been much use.'

There was a rough chuckle from someone at Bernstein's words and she rounded on them.

'What is it, Cobb?'

The man coloured and shrugged.

'Go on, I know that laugh. You were there, what did you make of her?'

'Let's just say I don't think Saxby hired her for her cooking. Wouldn't be at all surprised if most of the serving she did was between his sheets.'

Fenwick turned to Bernstein and raised an eyebrow.

'It's possible,' she agreed reluctantly. 'Kid can't be more than twenty; good-looking, docile. Maybe.'

'Why don't you bring her in for questioning,' he suggested. 'Get an interpreter and hold her in the worst interview room you've got for at least an hour to let her stew. Then start by asking if she's got a valid work permit.'

'Where will I find an interpreter tonight?'

'I don't know,' he said with a smile that had apparently abandoned the idea that it should be humorous, 'use your connections.'

The incident room was quieter after Bernstein and Cobb left. The remaining eight detectives, plus numerous civilian police workers, bent their heads over papers or towards computer screens in spinal curves that would wreck their backs long before they reached retirement. They would work whatever hours it took to find Issie. In the comfort of the tech block they counted themselves lucky not to be in the search parties, still out despite the weather, inching through the surrounding woods and fields.

Bazza Holland came over and hovered by his desk.

'What's on your mind?'

'Do you think she's still alive, sir?'

Fenwick took a deep breath.

'I have to believe so, Bazza, even though the odds are against. It's more than likely she was killed soon after being abducted, or left injured somewhere, in which case she'll be long dead from exposure by now but . . .' He pulled out the photograph Jane Saxby had given him. 'Look at her. She's a great sportswoman so we know she'll be fit . . .'

'Was fit,' Bazza corrected, 'rumour has it she spent most of this term stoned or drunk.'

'Yet there's no trace of booze or drugs in her room – or is there?' he asked, remembering the bedding they sent to the lab.

'No results yet,' Holland coloured, 'I'll let you know soon as.'

'Her friends don't know that we don't know, do they? Why don't you find a friendly teacher and go and interview them again? Take Jake with you.'

He pointed to a heavy-set constable stabbing at a keyboard as if it had done him personal injury. His face betrayed a boxing past and even if it hadn't his ears were a real giveaway. Fenwick had never read fairy stories as a child – a useless waste of paper his mother had called them – but he did so with his children whenever he could. He was reading one now to Chris, and the concept of a troll had been confusing – until he'd seen Constable Jake Somerset that morning. If anybody could terrify these girls into something close to the truth, it would be him.

Holland turned to leave.

'Before you go, what about Issie's artwork?'

'We found loads of her stuff in the loft of the art block. It's still there if you want to see it. Janice's got the keys.'

Fenwick thanked Holland and was about to ask for the keys when his mobile phone rang.

'Fenwick?'

He recognised the voice.

'Lord Saxby, how can I help you?'

'Look, we want to hire a local private detective. My own security people are obviously all over this thing but they don't have local insight.' There was a murmur in the background and Fenwick recognised Jane Saxby's voice. 'Yes, er, that's right, no criticism of you but we have to know that we're doing everything we possibly can.'

'I really advise against that, sir,' Fenwick argued, 'private investigators only complicate matters and in the worst instance they create havoc.'

'I won't be put off, Superintendent.'

Fenwick tried to argue but the man had made up his mind and wouldn't be persuaded. When it became obvious that he was dealing with the inevitable Fenwick did the only thing he could think to limit the damage.

'If you're determined, then at least let me recommend someone I'll be able to trust.'

'I was hoping you'd say that,' Saxby said with obvious satisfaction; a man used to winning. 'Let's have his name, then.'

'Bob Cooper,' Fenwick said, a half-smile of memory on his face for his one-time colleague who had retired that summer after thirty years of service, the last ten of which having been rather more exciting than he'd bargained for thanks to Fenwick. 'Mention my name and he might take you on despite the season. His wife probably has a long list of things for him to do.'

Bob Cooper was up a ladder, paint-roller in hand, old cap on head, when his wife called.

'Not now, Doris!' he shouted back with more acerbity than normal because it was her daft idea that the spare bedroom needed tarting up in time for her sister and brother-in-law's annual Yuletide visit. A dollop of paint landed on the exposed tip of his nose as he returned his attention to the ceiling. 'Bugger.'

'He says it's urgent, Bob. Apparently Andrew Fenwick gave him our number.'

Cursing but curious, Cooper laid the roller carefully in the tray and climbed down the ladder. His back and shoulders thanked him for the break.

'Cooper,' he said abruptly.

He had no intention of taking on any work before mid January and only bothered to pick up the receiver because whoever it was had used Fenwick's name. Doris was watching him intently and he knew what she was thinking. After twenty-eight years of marriage they could read each other's minds.

The sound of the caller's name made Bob's eyes open in surprise.

'*Who is it?*' his wife whispered and when he mouthed the answer the look of curiosity on her face mirrored his own. She sat down on the bottom stair, obviously curious to learn why the infamous Lord Saxby had called her husband.

'I see,' Bob said eventually. 'Unfortunately I—'

There was a long silence in the Cooper hall, punctuated by Bob's increasingly feeble attempts to argue.

'Yes, terrible but . . . no, it's not a question of other work . . . no, it's not about money either . . . priorities . . . well, Gladys is coming with Bernie . . . yes, family are very important . . . Speak to your wife? No; that won't help . . . No! . . . Ah, hello, Lady Saxby. I'm so sorry to hear about . . . yes, it's terrible . . . indeed, very cold . . . impossible, I'm afraid . . . compassion? . . . Of course . . . but . . . well . . . a bit of advice, you say . . . just a chat? . . . Well, if you think? . . . Maybe, but no . . . er . . . yes, but I can't promise . . . all right, then . . . in half an hour. Where exactly? . . . I'll see you th—Oh, she's gone.'

'So you're going,' said without rancour but he searched Doris's face.

97

'Her daughter's missing and in this weather, too.'

'I know; it's all over the evening news.'

'Is it? I've been up the ladder; didn't notice.'

'Well you would've done if you'd have the radio on.'

'I can't concentrate with all that noise.'

'If it was the cricket you'd manage. So, you're going to help them?' she said, reverting to the real the subject.

'Only with some advice. I told them I couldn't take on a new case before Christmas.'

'I didn't hear you say that exactly. Advice, is it? Hmm. . .' She regarded him shrewdly over the top of her glasses. 'I'd best call Robbie, see if I can't persuade him to finish off the latest job his dad's started.'

'I'll be back in no time, Dot!' Cooper protested, taking off his cap and undoing his overalls before making his way upstairs.

'I'll believe that when I see it, Robert Cooper.'

He rushed to their bedroom to change. Ten minutes later he was back in the hall, car keys in hand.

'Wait!' His wife called out as he undid the top bolt.

She ambled up to him waving a wad of kitchen roll.

'I knew you'd miss it,' she said with satisfaction.

The paper was thrust unceremoniously into his face and he smelt white spirit.

'There,' she said, giving a final wipe to the end of his nose as if he were a two-year-old, 'can't have you going off to Saxby Hall splattered with white emulsion.'

And with that she kissed a turps-free portion of his cheek and pushed him out of the door.

CHAPTER TEN

Issie shivered and pulled the grimy eiderdown more tightly around her body. It was cold in the caravan despite the heater in the other room and she was finding it hard to keep warm as dusk fell on her third night of captivity. Her head ached and she felt nauseous, no doubt as a result of whatever drugs had been forced into her. She wasn't hungry but her thirst was becoming unbearable.

As she lay on the stained mattress in the tiny space that passed for a bedroom Issie tried to work out exactly how long she had been there. She had left the school on time for the rendezvous. He had been late but only a few minutes and they had come straight here, driving carefully on icy roads. Every time a car came near them, he had pushed her head down below the dashboard. She had thought it exciting.

At no time in the car had his behaviour made her worried, not even when they pulled up and she realised that their tryst wasn't to be in a country cottage somewhere as he had promised but in a shabby caravan that looked as if it should be condemned.

'Here?' she had asked, shivering in the bitter air as they left the car and walked to the concrete stand on which the caravan leant at a slight angle, one end supported by breeze blocks.

'Why not?' he had insisted, grabbing her around the waist as he pulled her up the makeshift steps. For the first time she noticed that she had cut her wrist somehow and winced as it hit the door frame.

Issie touched the inflamed skin tenderly as her thoughts

tripped back to Monday night, images running in a continuous loop inside her head as she relived the nightmare.

It had been dark inside the caravan but warm in comparison with the bitter cold of the night. Thin curtains were drawn across the windows. She could just make out random shapes of furniture in the gloom.

'This way.' His voice was low, as if he were afraid of being overheard even though they were miles away from anywhere.

He pulled on her arm and she followed blindly, bumping into something that made her yelp with pain.

'Quiet,' he'd hissed. 'Come on, we're using the back room.'

'Where are we?'

'My brother's place; don't worry, he's not here.'

The idea that someone might stumble in on their lovemaking banished the last shred of Issie's romantic dream.

'I don't want to!' she had blurted out in a hushed squeak.

'Don't worry; I'll lock the bedroom door.'

He kissed her again and pushed her through a gap in the panelling that divided the front of the caravan from the back. Issie took an uncontrolled step forward and fell onto a narrow bed, banging her head on the wall on the other side. The room must have been less than six feet across.

'Ow! Gosh, it's cold in here. Can you turn on more heat?'

'I'll soon warm you up, don't worry. Here, have a drink; you'll be toasty in no time.'

He passed a bottle to her and she took a mouthful, spluttering as the alcohol hit the back of her throat. The liquor made her eyes water but it warmed her so she took another swallow, more careful this time, savouring the heat of the oily liquid as it slipped down her throat.

'What is it?'

'Absinth; we get it direct from Marseilles; my brother goes there sometimes.'

'Why?'

'Never you mind.' He kissed her, banishing any further questions. The taste of the absinth on his tongue was comforting but when his fingers groped for her she tensed.

'Relax,' he said, stroking her, 'you'll like it, I promise.'

Issie's self-esteem was so low that she took his interest in her as a compliment. She stroked his neck tentatively, making him shudder. *This is going to be OK*, she told herself, *not like . . .*

'Don't tense up, there's no need to be afraid,' his words were gentle as his fingers moved across her face and down to the hollow of her throat. Issie concentrated on living in the moment and pushed other memories aside.

He pulled the cardigan from her shoulders before she could stop him and started to unbutton her shirt. Issie protested that it was too cold but he carried on anyway. Her skin glowed white in the dimness of the room and he started to devour her with small bites, his cheeks rough, unshaven since the morning. He pulled down her jeans.

'Wait! It's so cold, can we go somewhere else, please?'

'Drink some more of this while I find us a blanket.'

Issie sipped the absinth and felt the beginnings of the familiar fuzziness of intoxication. She had her eyes closed when he returned with an eiderdown and wrapped it around her. It was to be his last gesture of tenderness. What happened next was rough, unsatisfying – at least for Issie – and short. While it lasted she shut her mind and told herself it would get better but it didn't. At least it was soon over.

Afterwards he rolled off her taking most of the eiderdown and his breathing deepened. It was too dark to see her watch but she guessed it was well past one o'clock. She waited for him to suggest that they should be getting back but instead he started to snore. From the other side of the door there was a rustling sound and Issie froze. It came again and she stopped breathing but then there was silence. She risked a nudge to his ribs.

'It's late and I have to be back.'

'Ngh,' he grunted, his back to her.

Issie lay by his side, shivering.

'Please,' she hugged his back for warmth, 'I want to go back.'

'Arnggh.'

'I mean it.' Issie raised her voice.

'Baby,' he whispered in his sleep.

'Come on, wake up.'

'Ooh, darling,' he murmured and reached for her. Her heart jumped; this wasn't what she wanted. Once was enough, she could tell herself it hadn't happened, but twice . . .

'Wake UP!'

He sat up abruptly and shoved his hand across her mouth.

'Ssh!'

'I have to get back.' She mumbled into his palm.

'Keep your voice down, you little idiot.'

Issie had subsided into shocked silence. The room became still. From outside they both heard the unmistakeable shuffle of feet across the floor of the central room.

'Shit,' he muttered.

Issie huddled into his back, her eyes fixed in a dry gaze where she imagined the door to be. For a moment there was silence within the chilly space, then, unmistakeably, came the sound of the door being opened. With an emotion approaching horror Issie realised that he hadn't relocked it after fetching the eiderdown.

'Who's there?'

The coarse bass voice made Issie jump. Worse, she noticed her lover do the same.

'Only me, bro,' he said nervously.

'Whatya doin' here?'

'Needed a place, y'know how it is.'

'You alone?'

'Course.'

Issie stiffened beside him and his left hand stretched out to touch her thigh, almost comforting. Instinctively she held her breath, hoping her silence and the pitch-dark would fool his brother but the hulk in the doorway took a step into the room so that his leg touched the mattress. Issie shrank back even further. There was a sniff.

'I smell a girlie.'

'Nah, I'm on my own. Just needed a place to kip.'

Another sniff.

'Fresh and sweet. You holding out on me, bro? Y' knows the rules. Share 'n' share alike. My place in exchange for a bit of yours.'

Issie's eyes opened wide in alarm. There was silence. She could hear the brothers' breathing, one slow and careful the other rapid and scared; the realisation terrified her.

'Swear to me that you're on your own. On our mother's life and – God willing – our father's grave. Swear.'

She heard a guilty swallow that said it all.

'It was only for an hour, that's all.'

'No,' she had moaned into his ear, so low and desperate that he patted her thigh again.

'Then move over, little man. It's big brother's turn. Is she hot or does she need some warming? There's good shit here if she needs it. You know how I like them.'

'No!'

'Ssh! Don't antagonise him.' He whispered into her ear. 'Just pretend it's me.'

'Noo.' Her voice was a whine, childish and afraid.

'Oh, she's young. Well done, bro, I like them tender.' The lumbering shape took another half step and fell onto the bed.

'NO!'

Issie grabbed her jeans and bolted for the door, ducking low to avoid what she imagined were huge, outstretched arms. She almost made it; in fact she managed to touch the handle before he pulled her back, up and off the floor as if she were no more than a kitten. He laughed and the fumes from his breath made her want to retch.

'No! Badger!' It was her secret nickname for the man who had proven such a useless and dangerous lover.

'Badger! What sort of poxy name is that? I kill badgers, I do; smoke 'em out of their sets, poison their young, crush their skulls like eggs with me spade. There's good money in badger pelts.' His hands were holding her tight about her chest and stomach; his face nuzzled her hair.

'Oh, she smells so clean. Is this your first time, honey? Don't worry about Badger's brother; I'm better than he is. Call me Brock; older, wiser and so much bigger. You're in for a treat.'

'No, please, I need to get back. I'll be missed; I should be in my room, please!'

Issie twisted her head away as his slobbering mouth lunged towards her. His lips connected with her ear and his tongue lunged into it, aggressive, penetrating, disgusting. She reached out a hand towards Badger, begging for help but he was no longer there. Alone in the bedroom she was thrown on to the mattress, the lower half of her body bare, her blouse half-open from the earlier sex. She could smell him; sweaty, musty, hot. As his body loomed over her she had shut her eyes and turned her face away.

At some point during the long night she had been allowed to use their bathroom, a five by five-foot cubicle that stank of unprocessed sewage. On her return she had been given water and absinth and at some stage there were drugs, what and how much she had no idea. By then she was past caring. She had a vague memory of the brothers sharing her and remarking on it as if she were some dumb sex toy. Just before dawn Issie had passed out. They woke her a few hours later with a mug of tea and a bacon sandwich, still warm inside a bag from a local café.

At some point she had been sick. Badger had cleaned her up and made her another mug of tea. He must have put something in it because Issie passed the rest of the day semi-conscious, drifting into an uneasy sleep as Tuesday dragged into Wednesday.

When she had woken up she was on her own. There was mist outside the tiny window of the back room. She had tried the door but it was barred from the outside. Issie started banging on it and then on the window but the noise disappeared into the empty clearing she could see dimly through the thick Perspex windows and claustrophobic fog. She remembered the long track they had driven down, the isolation of the caravan sitting in the middle of woodland.

A bottle of coke and two packets of crisps had been left at the end of the bed. She ate and drank as she tried to work out what time it was. She noticed that her watch was missing. It was the one her father had given her, that showed the date and phases of the moon, as well as the time in two time zones.

Surely the school would be searching for her by now?

She had been desperate to relieve herself and eventually had to give in. She tried to collect her pee in the empty coke bottle but a lot went on the carpet and the smell now filled the room. She was thirsty, hungover, very sore and desperately lonely. Her wrist hurt where she had cut it and she knew she should clean it when she could find fresh water. She kept banging on the door, the effort warming her body against the steadily penetrating cold. As the grey day crawled past she was forced to stop, exhaustion overwhelming her.

Issie longed to see her mother and tried to imagine their reunion, how she would make sure everything was all right again between them. The memories of their arguments, of how she had refused to speak to her mum the last time they had seen each other added to her misery. Scared and feeling very little, Issie tugged the eiderdown more tightly around her shoulders against the cold evening and started to cry.

CHAPTER ELEVEN

Fenwick found his way to the arts block with the aid of a torch and let himself in. He fumbled for the switch and fluorescent light flooded the corridor making him squint. The door to the main studio was locked and it took him several attempts to find the right key, an old cast-iron thing that turned slowly and with great reluctance so that when it opened he felt he was being admitted to a place of secrets.

The calm of natural daylight from bulbs that were used to help the students see true colour was soothing. He walked quickly to the other side of the room and up an iron spiral staircase to a half-loft that was bordered by a waist-high rail.

Issie's artwork was stacked to one side, weighed down by an abstract sculpture that looked as if it captured the memory of a dream from hell. He lifted the moulded clay to one side, suppressing a shudder, and crouched down to examine her work.

On top was a still life; a random assortment of wild plants pushed into a wide-necked earthenware jar of the sort his mother had used to salt runner beans in the days before she gave in and bought a freezer. Despite the innocent subject matter the picture radiated violence. It was sketched in aggressive charcoal strokes, the stems one bold sweep, the leaves dashed off with careless smudges that nevertheless conveyed their form with menace. There was a toadstool at the bottom, bruised where it had been pushed against the rim of the container. He recognised the species from one of Bess's nature books: fly agaric, highly poisonous. When he peered closely he saw a dead spider under the cap.

Above the agaric was a cluster of dark flowers on thin stems that looked almost prehistoric. Foxgloves arched over them, their spotted throats hungry and gasping, next to stinging nettles in bloom. Delicate trailing flowers rimmed the arrangement but he wasn't fooled. He had been warned of their danger as a child and had passed the caution on to his own children: never touch deadly nightshade. Belladonna, lethal to a child. A snail crawled up the stem towards a glistening seed pod; death waiting.

An innocent still life but Issie had loaded the picture with images of death.

'What the hell are you doing?' a voice called out. 'Come down or I'll call the police.'

'I am the police,' he said mildly and looked over the rail to see Miss Bullock bundled into a ludicrously opulent fur coat and brandishing a poker. He could see the hem of a dressing gown even though it was only eight o'clock. Her long hair fell about her shoulders like grey silk.

'Oh, it's you, Mr Fenwick,' she said, lowering the poker. 'Thank goodness, I thought you were an intruder. I saw the lights from my apartment.'

'You should have called the incident room, not come out to investigate on your own.'

He hadn't meant it unkindly but she blushed crimson.

'What are you doing?'

'Studying some of Issie's work. It's deeply disturbing.'

A look of concern flashed across her face, putting him on alert.

'What have you got there? No wait, I'll come up – unless you want to go and see the headmistress, that is. She's just arrived and your colleague is about to see her.'

'One thing at a time, Miss Bullock.'

'Very well.'

She was beside him in a moment, saw the picture he was looking at and her face cleared.

'Oh, that thing. It's far too traditional to show off her creativity.'

'Traditional? Hardly; this is a picture of death dressed up as a summer bouquet.'

She looked at him keenly, a half smile on her face, and bent down to study the drawing. Fenwick caught a waft of sandalwood and something deeper, more exotic.

'Of course you're right; it is an allegory of death. With the agaric, deadly nightshade, digitalis and aconitum . . .'

'The flowers at the front?'

'Yes, monkshood; beautiful and deadly, but not all the plants are poisonous. See, there are nettles, peppermint, vitex berries and raspberry leaves, all well-known tonics; and this is rosemary.'

'So what is the message?' he asked standing up to put more distance between them.

'Well there is one, you're right. It's a sketch she did two summers ago. At first I dismissed it as a practice piece but I too found it disturbing and when I looked again I saw what you realised at once: that it is a very angry picture. There's a possible explanation, though.

'When she was fourteen, Issie decided she wanted to be a white witch. It was a fad that lasted all of two terms and was never harmful; in fact it increased her interest in biology and helped her achieve an A-star grade. I had various books on herbal remedies that I loaned her while the phase lasted. When I saw this picture I used the books to identify the healing ingredients and realised that they were a coded message.'

Her cheeks coloured again.

'Only one remedy I found uses all the herbs in this picture.'

'What is it for?'

She broke eye contact as she stood up.

'Loss of male libido.'

'Libido?'

'Yes; I think her message was very clear: she was wishing death or impotence on some man with a vengeance.'

'Any idea whom?' Her analysis helped to explain his deep unease about the picture, though he was a resolutely unsuperstitious man.

'Her stepfather, possibly. They'd had some sort of falling out while on holiday.'

Now that she was standing he knelt down to go through the other pictures but nothing else shouted a message to him. He sensed there was something missing.

'What have you done with them, Miss Bullock?'

'Pardon?' She turned and started to walk down the stairs, the soft soles of her shoes slapping against the metal rungs.

'You know what I mean; Issie's pictures, the best ones. Where are they?' He bent and rolled up the flower drawing and placed it under his arm.

'I most certainly do not know what you mean,' she said, affecting indignation.

'If you don't answer me, I shall ask you to accompany me to Guildford police station and detain you while I secure a warrant to search your rooms.'

Fenwick looked down on her from his vantage point, unaware that his face was even more threatening than his words. Her cheeks went white. For a moment she looked towards the door, as if about to run, then her shoulders sagged.

'How did you know? Oh, never mind. Come on.' She turned away, defeated and he followed.

Miss Bullock lived in a set of rooms at the top of the original schoolhouse. When he walked into her apartment he smelt spice and saw candles in the sitting room. She hadn't spoken since leaving the studio. When they entered she left him and disappeared into a room to the right. Glancing over he saw the corner of a bed.

The sitting room rose double height into the eaves. One wall was lined with bookshelves floor to ceiling, with a library ladder attached to a rail. Interspersed among the books were small statues, some cast bronze, others intricate carvings in a dark-green stone. Most of them were startlingly lifelike representations of animals and children; a few were abstract. He found them unsettlingly personal, as if he were intruding on someone else's thoughts.

There was a fireplace set into the wall behind a glass door. The fire inside needed tending. The faint smell of woodsmoke mingled with the aroma of sandalwood and spice from the candles, warm and relaxing. Music played softly, a Chopin étude that he recognised. A pile of wood was stacked neatly in a basket next to the hearth.

The rest of the walls were covered with original paintings in oil and acrylic lit from above by angled recessed spotlights. Some of them seemed to be very good. He bent down and selected sticks for the fire. When it was blazing he threw on a split log and watched as the flames licked around it hungrily. He closed the door quickly on sparks that shot from the dry bark. There was still no sign of her.

The herbals she had mentioned were easily identified, including a number of ancient editions that looked to be collectors' items. Next to them were volumes of botanical drawings, mostly nineteenth century, with leather bindings and quaint names. The comfort of the room stole over him, making him drowsy. Despite his intentions he felt himself sucked into a state of semi-intoxication as the heat, fragrance and flickering of the flames cocooned him. After the freezing cold of the night outside he was overwhelmed by the desire to sit down, loosen his tie and relax. Fenwick shook his head and the drowsiness passed.

There was a noise and he turned to see Miss Bullock staggering into the room under the weight of three large canvasses. He helped her set them against the wall.

'This is all I have, other than a few pieces of her sculpture in my garage.'

He turned the first painting around and couldn't stop himself gasping. The picture was painted in an ironic surrealist style – melting trees, an improbable moon and planets in a black sky – but what drew the eye was the scene of a girl being raped by a goat-man in the foreground. The girl's face was blurred but her expression still managed to convey a mixture of hatred and anger that dared the viewer to pity her. He looked at the next picture. It was the goat-man again, the yellow eyes flat and evil, with vertical slits for pupils. Around his neck was a gold chain and medallion with an inscription in Latin.

'It says *"All things evil will be cast into a lake of fire"*,' she said as he bent to read.

'*Revelation*. Who is this goat-man?'

'I have no idea.'

'Why on earth didn't you report this?'

'I didn't see them until after she'd disappeared. Issie had been working on something secret for months, painting them only when on her own. She kept the canvasses covered in the studio and made me promise not to look at them. I respected her wishes . . . until she disappeared.'

'And you didn't think it relevant? You're an intelligent woman; how could you cover up something like this?'

Louise Bullock bridled.

'I did it to preserve Issie's privacy!'

'Privacy? If this is an expression of her own experience, then the girl's been abused!'

'You mean it might be why she's run away?'

'Or been abducted, or killed to stop her talking.' He ran his fingers through his hair in exasperation as Miss Bullock sank onto the sofa and covered her mouth with her hands.

'I never thought of that, I mean . . . Her work had become more violent, really dark and menacing, but ironically it was better than ever. This one, see,' she pulled out the third picture, 'it's absolutely brilliant. I wanted to keep it for her A-level submission but Issie said it wasn't good enough.'

Fenwick studied the painting. It was titled, innocuously, 'Bonfire Night'. An eruption of white light like a supernova dominated the top-right corner, with a smaller yellow starburst away in the distance to the left. The bottom of the canvas was consumed in a swirl of flames from a bonfire, which silhouetted the cluster of people gathered about it. Instead of being a cheerful celebration, to Fenwick it depicted a scene from hell, the fires ready to consume the damned.

'She has real power, doesn't she?' Miss Bullock said with pride.

'Yes, but I'm not here for art appreciation. I need to find Issie. Every minute she's missing in this weather she's closer to death, assuming that she's been kept alive.'

'I was certain that she'd run away. I sympathised with her need for privacy – sometimes one needs that. She has her own right of self-determination and I respect that, even if her parents don't.'

Fenwick looked at the teacher in exasperation as his patience snapped.

'Self-determination? I don't know whether that's naive or just plain stupid! What right do you have to make a judgement like that when a girl's life is at stake? Her rights; her privacy? How about her *life*? You need to get your priorities sorted, Miss Bullock.'

Lulu Bullock hugged herself and looked away. He could see moisture in her eyes and thought *I hope you lose sleep tonight*. It wasn't very Christian but then he didn't feel like forgiving anybody until Issie had been found.

'I'm sorry,' she said, shamefaced, finally daring to look at him. 'How can I help?'

'Tell me everything you know. Start with Issie's drug habit.'

'You know about that?'

He lied and said yes.

'Of course you would. It was pot mainly, though she told me she'd tried a tab of E once and didn't like it.'

'Why didn't you report her?'

'I did better than that; I found her some proper help. There's a clinic I know. Last weekend I took her there for an appointment. She was going back again after Christmas.'

'You have a duty to her parents, to the school. It wasn't up to you to decide how to help her.'

Miss Bullock rounded on him with an anger that almost matched his own.

'Why do you think the poor kid had problems in the first place? It was her parents that drove her to find an easy way out. She was living a nightmare since her mother remarried.'

'But she's only a kid, you just said so yourself.'

'A turn of phrase. Issie is eighteen this term, legally an adult. I knew what she needed; her parents would have had no idea and neither would the school.'

'What made you so certain that you understood her when no one else did?'

She stood up.

'I need a drink; can I get you one?'

He shook his head.

'Answer my question.'

Bullock concentrated on opening a bottle of red wine, leaving him time to speculate.

'We're running background checks on everyone, including a search for previous convictions.' He paused. 'Want to tell me now or wait for us to find out officially?'

She gulped some wine and looked at the ceiling.

'It was a long time ago. I was young, in trouble, everyone did it back then.'

113

'Did what?'

'Drugs.'

'What sort of drugs?'

She rested her head against the wall.

'LSD. I thought it improved my creativity. Instead it nearly killed me. If it hadn't been for Brian it would have done.'

'Brian Mattias; Issie's father?'

'Yes. He helped get me straightened out, then he set me up financially – not that I did a lot with his generosity; I had other problems by then.'

'Such as?'

She shook her head, eyes closed. Fenwick was surprised to see tears on her lower lashes.

'I need to know.'

'I fell pregnant. I didn't know it, and I can't claim that's why I kicked the habit but thank God I did. The baby's father was already married; a real bastard but I loved him.' She blinked a few times and took another sip of wine.

'And the baby; it wasn't Issie, was it?'

His question provoked a bitter bark of laughter followed by an unmistakeable sob that was quickly turned into a cough.

'No, this would have been about eleven, twelve years before Issie was born. No,' another sip, a deep sigh, 'my baby girl died.'

'I am so sorry.'

'Do you have children, Superintendent?'

'Yes; a girl and a boy.'

'You do?' She looked at him in surprise, as if she had expected him to be a lonely bachelor with no experience of parenthood.

Well, one out of two might have been true but that was none of her business.

'So you can understand what it would be like to lose a child.'

'It's my worst nightmare,' he said, meaning it, 'which is why we have to find Issie and you must help me. You may not think

114

much of her mother but she's suffering more than we can possibly imagine.'

She looked ashamed and put down her glass.

'I'll do whatever I can.'

'Did you take Issie's belongings from her room?'

'No!' She sounded genuinely shocked at the idea.

'What was the room like when you last saw it?'

'The typical mess that Issie lived in – stuff everywhere, bed unmade.'

'That's not how we found it.' He described the scene and she frowned.

'Octavia and Puff,' she muttered, 'though heaven knows what got into their heads.'

'Tidying up after their friend. It probably started with removing the bottles and maybe some drugs. Then they realise there's more. Perhaps Issie had a diary and it mentions her habit. Away that goes, her old PC, any clothes that might have traces of booze and drugs on them. Unfortunately they succeeded in removing anything that might have helped us.'

'Little idiots.'

They're not the only ones, he thought but he needed her cooperation.

'If you really want to help, Miss Bullock, you can persuade Octavia and Puff to talk to us. They know something and their silence might be killing Issie.'

'Give me five minutes and I'll be with you.'

He called Bazza's mobile while he waited. He and Jake were back with nothing to show for their visit to the girls except strained patience. It was half past eight.

'Anything from the national database yet?'

'Nothing.'

'Have you prioritised the request?'

'Of course; NPIA are checking the PND against a list we gave

115

them of every single man Issie knew; friends, family, teachers and the rest of the staff.'

'Good. Anything from the search parties?' It was a pointless question; if there had been he would have been told.

'No, sir.' Bazza sounded exasperated. 'And POLSA are back on site as you suggested.'

'Good; we need search expertise for a situation as complex as this. I had a thought. Were there any no-shows for work yesterday or today?'

'Superintendent Bernstein had us check first thing. The only person missing today was the headmistress's secretary who has a heavy cold. She was visited; nothing suspicious. Yesterday several staff had the day off – some work Saturday's in exchange for a weekday.'

'Have them interviewed anyway – you never know. I'll be with you shortly.'

Lulu Bullock came back as he was putting his phone away, dressed in jeans and a thick gilet over a polo neck; coat, hat and gloves ready in her hand. Her hair was back in its ponytail. As she led the way through freezing fog to the girls' dormitory Fenwick could smell her exotic perfume. They spoke to the housemistress who had a lot to say about her charges being disturbed twice in one night. Eventually she let them in because, as she said, 'I trust you, Miss Bullock, to put their interests first.'

'And I trust you to put Issie's first,' Fenwick muttered as they climbed the stairs.

Loud music rolled down the carpeted corridor towards them; Led Zep Four. Lulu caught his eye and they both smiled involuntarily as their knock interrupted 'Stairway to Heaven'.

'Oh god,' Octavia said dramatically when she opened the door and saw Fenwick, 'not you again.' Then her eyes fell on Miss Bullock and widened in surprise. She stepped back.

'Where did you hide Issie's stuff?' Fenwick asked without preamble.

Octavia laughed and bent over to turn up the music.

'Turn it off.' It was a command. Octavia obeyed with a scowl. 'I asked you a question and if you choose not to answer, I shall have no option but to arrest you on suspicion of theft.'

She looked at him with a twisted smile as if she were trying to see the joke.

'This is no laughing matter, Miss Henry. If you choose not to help us with our enquiries you leave me no choice.'

'Oh pur-lease; one phone call to my father and I'll be out of custody in less time than it takes you to write a grovelling letter of apology – which,' she smiled at him, suddenly the coquette, 'I might accept because you're quite cute.'

Fenwick heard Lulu Bullock gasp and it helped him keep his temper. He was struggling with the desire to pick up the spoilt brat and spank her but that would have been a career-finishing move and he suppressed the impulse.

'For heaven's sake, Octavia, this isn't a game.' Lulu Bullock came to his aid. 'If Issie's still alive then we need to find her before the cold kills her. There could be vital clues among her possessions. Octavia, you might be condemning her to death by your silence.'

The smirk left Octavia's face to be replaced by a look of confusion.

'But she's, like, run away, hasn't she? We all know that, you included.'

Lulu sat down on Octavia's bed and patted the duvet for the girl to join her.

'I thought so at first, but now,' she glanced at Fenwick, caught his eye briefly and coloured, 'well, I think I was wrong. The police have evidence that Issie may have been abducted. We have to take that possibility seriously.'

'No way. Not possible.' Octavia stood up and leant over to

select another album. Fenwick pulled the plug from the socket before she reached the iPod dock, earning another glare.

'Very possible,' he said, his voice full of the conviction he felt, 'and maybe by someone she knows: a boyfriend, casual acquaintance.'

'What? Issie hates men. Why would anybody take her; money?'

'Possibly, although we haven't received a ransom demand and normally that would have happened within the first twenty-four hours.'

'So . . .' Octavia screwed up her face in thought. 'If it's not money then . . . not sex?' she said and exploded into an unconvincing laugh.

'Why is that such a ludicrous idea?' He asked, his face a blank.

'But Issie . . . *Issie!* . . . You don't know her, she's just not into sex, I mean . . . no way . . .' But her expression suggested something different.

'She's almost eighteen; very pretty, confident, intelligent. All reasons why men would find her attractive.'

'Please, Octavia,' Lulu Bullock interrupted, 'we have to find her and we need your help. He knows about the drinking and the drugs. Don't look at me like that, I didn't tell him. He *is* a policeman you know.'

'And apparently a good one; I'll have to tell my dad he's despairing over the state of the nation prematurely.' She laughed at her own irony.

'Issie's belongings. Now!' he said, finally losing patience and recognising in his tone the voice he used on his ten-year-old son when he really misbehaved. Octavia turned towards the window. 'It's below freezing out there. What if the cold is killing her right now? Would you be able to live with the fact that you let your friend die?'

Octavia dropped her head. He heard a sniff, saw a tear fall and glanced at Lulu Bullock in frustration. She understood the silent message and put an arm around the girl.

'Come on; it can't be that hard. Superintendent Fenwick won't prosecute, will you?'

'If I receive immediate cooperation there will be no charges.'

'Upstairs,' Octavia murmured and pointed above her head. 'There's a loft space above the landing. Your lot searched it yesterday but didn't find where we'd hidden everything.'

'They were looking for Issie at the time, not her things. Show us.'

There was an extension ladder behind the ceiling hatch. He clambered up into the void, followed by Octavia.

'Over there.'

Against the central timber were a suitcase and a box that had 'Tesco Baked Beans' on the side.

'Go and get them,' he said, not wanting to add his own fingerprints.

She dragged them over to the top of the hatch, struggling with the weight of the suitcase. When it became obvious that she wouldn't manage them down the stepladder he gave in and borrowed Lulu's gloves, squeezing his hands inside the woollen knit, cursing the fact that for once he wasn't carrying latex ones. He hadn't thought he would need them when he left home for a routine meeting with the ACC.

Back in Octavia's room he rang Bazza and asked him to bring evidence bags and warn the lab and tech team that there would be material for immediate processing.

'Was there a diary or something similar?'

Octavia nodded and opened the box. It was lying on top. He picked it up carefully by the edges and turned to Monday 4th December, the night Issie disappeared. There was no entry but on the previous day she'd written *Badger tomorrow night. Right thing???*'

'Who's Badger?'

'No idea; we didn't recognise the name.'

'So you read this?'

"Course.'

'And you still hid it from us, knowing that there was mention of a meeting on Monday night? We've lost a whole day because of your stupidity.'

He expected a sharp retort but for once Octavia Henry was silent and actually looked guilty.

'I won't have you shouting at my girls.'

The reprimand came from the housemistress standing in the doorway, hands on hips. Behind her Fenwick could see the curious faces of other boarders.

'Are you all right, my dear?' she asked, pushing past Fenwick to reach her charge.

Her sympathy had the usual effect and Octavia burst into tears.

'I'll put in a complaint,' the woman threatened, 'you see if I don't.'

'By all means,' Fenwick said as he heard Bazza make his way up the stairs, 'if you wish to make tonight's activities official, then I won't stop you but you might wish to check with Octavia first. Whatever; tomorrow, eight o'clock sharp, miss, I expect to see you and Puff in the interview room to make your statements. Ladies, I bid you goodnight.'

Bazza came into the room followed by Jake, ready to take whatever evidence had been recovered to be processed straight away. Fenwick took an evidence bag off him and put the diary in it, then dated and signed the label.

'If I were you, Miss Henry,' Fenwick muttered under his breath as he passed, 'I'd persuade your housemistress to calm down.'

'Sergeant Holland, they're all yours. If you need me, I'll be with Superintendent Bernstein in the headmistress's study.'

CHAPTER TWELVE

Issie huddled under the eiderdown, squeezed into a tight foetal ball. Her teeth chattered and the only part of her that felt warm was her wrist where the cut was on fire.

It was dark outside. She thought it was still Wednesday but she had been unconscious for an unknown length of time so maybe a further day had passed. She couldn't tell. She hadn't eaten or drunk anything since finishing the crisps and coke. Her thirst was worse than anything she could have imagined. She looked again at the bottle of urine and wondered whether she could force herself to drink, but as she raised the viscous yellow liquid to her mouth the smell made her stomach heave.

In some way the pain in her arms and legs was a welcome distraction. Her muscles were exhausted from repeated physical exercise and her attacks on the window and door. Despite their flimsy appearance, the fittings had resisted every attempt to break them. The door was made from double-thickness MDF with hinges on the other side, impossible to reach; the window comprised two layers of yellowing Perspex that wouldn't break. Even so she had attempted to smash it, again and again, until her knuckles bled and she finally realised that she was wasting precious energy.

When she hadn't been shouting or attempting to break free, she would count to one thousand and then exercise to keep her muscles active and her body warm. Only now that night had fallen did she give in to the exhaustion in her body.

Issie's eyes closed and her head fell back. She slept but within minutes some inner determination forced her out of comfortable unconsciousness and into intense pain.

'No!' she said out loud and pushed herself up, wincing as her wrist brushed against the mattress. 'Sleep is death.'

'Sleep is death,' she repeated and brushed tears from her cheeks. She knew all about hypothermia from reading Pappy's survival books and told herself the pain she felt was a good sign.

Issie started scissor jumps, arms and legs out, closing on the descent. After a count of ten it was hurting too much so she switched to sit ups. Earlier she had managed hundreds at a time but now her stomach muscles spasmed at ten and she had to stop. Still she didn't give up. She hugged her knees into her chest and moved into hip raises until she lost count.

Dehydration meant that exercise no longer raised a sweat but Issie forced herself to continue until she could no longer move. When she finally stopped her body was shaking as she lay on the mouldy carpet. The floor was cold and hard but she was satisfied just to lie there. Her eyes closed.

A noise from outside woke her; voices arguing, two men. She crawled forward and pressed her ear to the door. It was Badger and his brother, the one she thought of as Brock. Issie moaned in relief. She had begun to think they'd abandoned her but of course they wouldn't do that. She squatted down, her ear tight against the door as the brothers continued to argue on the other side.

'—'king can't do that!' she heard Badger shout.

'Your fault if you hadn't . . . deep shit.' Brock's voice slurred drunkenly.

'She won't talk, I . . .'

Issie realised they were arguing about what to do with her and strained to hear. Badger was pacing, his voice ebbing in and out as he moved. There was a mumbled reply from Brock, unintelligible and then Badger again.

'Forget it! How the fuck do you expect to get away with that?'

The hair on the back of Issie's neck stood on end. What had Brock suggested? Her imagination provided a horror show of alternatives as her hands groped in the darkness for a weapon, anything with which to defend herself; but, of course, the room was bare apart from the plastic coke bottle half full of urine. She crawled over and picked it up anyway; there was nothing else. Even the mattress was supported on a cheap plastic frame without metal fittings. She wrapped herself inside the eiderdown and tried not to make a sound.

It went quiet in the room next door. There was the clink of a bottle on glass followed by an unintelligible rumble from Brock. At one point heavy footsteps lurched towards the door but there was a shout, sounds of more drink being poured and whoever it was retreated back into the room.

Were they going to ignore her, pretend she didn't exist? Did they mean to leave her here to die? She felt an urge to cry out despite an inner caution that told her to keep quiet. Issie stuffed the filthy eiderdown in her mouth and started to count in a desperate attempt to stop herself from panicking.

Just after one thousand the door opened without warning. A hand pulled her up sharply by the hair. Another went over her mouth and she dropped the bottle, struggling as she was dragged out.

'Be quiet or you'll wake him!' Badger's voice hissed in her ear.

The light in the main room was dim but her eyes were already adjusted to the dark and she could see everything. Brock was sprawled on the couch in front of a television, an empty bottle of whisky on the floor by his outstretched hand.

Badger looked somehow the same but totally different. His expression was out of focus and he wouldn't look her in the eye as he pulled her towards the door. His brother groaned and they both froze.

'Ssh.' Badger whispered but it was unnecessary. Issie hadn't made a sound since he had grabbed her.

They waited as Brock scratched, half turned on the sofa and emitted a grunt before starting to snore. Issie leant towards the door and escape but Badger didn't move.

'Stay here; doors locked; he's got the key,' he hissed.

She watched, barely breathing, as he edged towards the sleeping figure, his right hand outstretched. When he was by the couch Badger crouched down, inching his fingers forward and into his brother's trouser pocket. He paused, searching, then probed deeper. He started to withdraw his hand as Brock opened one bleary eye. Issie held her breath and shrank into the shadows.

'Wha . . . ?'

'Just looking for a smoke, that's all.'

'Ngh; smoke?'

Brock eased his bulk up, trapping Badger's hand in his pocket by the movement. He looked half asleep but then his arm snaked out and he grabbed his brother's clenched palm.

'Lessavalook.' His voice was an animal growl, the look in his eyes instantly murderous.

Twisting Badger's wrist so that he yelped, Brock yanked the hand into full view. A set of keys dangled from his brother's clenched fingers.

'Smoke! I'll give you fucking smoke!'

Wide awake, Brock brought his free hand up in a swing that connected so hard with Badger's head that it knocked him to the floor. Issie watched as Brock brought up his fist to strike again but Badger rolled aside and the blow missed. As he did so his side brushed the empty whisky bottle and he snatched it up by the neck. Before Brock could hit him again, Badger smashed the bottle against the side of his brother's jaw. The glass shattered on impact and the air was filled suddenly with a bright jet of blood that reached the ceiling.

Issie screamed, so did Badger. He jumped back as his brother clutched at his neck, a look of total surprise on his face. Brock opened his mouth to speak but red froth bubbled out instead, then a hissing sound. Almost in slow motion he collapsed back onto the settee, his mouth opening and closing like a landed fish. Issie shut her eyes and turned her head away. There were gurgling sounds that shut off abruptly and then silence. When she looked again Brock's eyes were set, staring unseeing at his brother in a look of amazement.

Badger hadn't moved. He seemed frozen; the broken neck of the bottle still in his hand, a cut beneath his left eye caused by flying glass oozed a thin trickle of blood, like a shaving nick. It was strange the way it showed up despite the crimson wash that had covered the room in a wide circle with Brock at its point of origin.

'We need to get help,' Issie said, amazed at how normal her voice sounded. 'Badger; I said we need to get him help. Come on.'

She was reluctant to go near the man on the couch but the keys were still in Brock's hand so she forced herself to step forward and open his fingers. The keys slid out, still warm. Badger's eyes were fixed on his brother. Issie backed towards the door and managed to slide the master key into the lock despite the tremor in her arms. At the noise Badger stirred. He moved with startling speed and grabbed the keys from her.

'Where are you going?'

'To get help, like I said.' Issie made her words sound normal but her brain was screaming at her that she was in the room with a killer who might not want a surviving witness.

'He's dead, can't you see?'

'There may be time to resuscitate him if we hurry.'

'No way.' Badger slipped the keys into his pocket and tested the door to make sure it was still locked. 'Wait here.'

He was gone less than a minute.

'Put these on.' It was an instruction.

Issie wrinkled her nose at the musty smell emanating from the shirt, socks and trousers he thrust at her, all far too big for her tiny frame but she put them on, glad of their warmth. The trousers slipped down to her ankles. Badger laughed, a hysterical sound that made her want to cry. She bit the inside of her lip, hard. He took off his belt and passed it to her.

It was far too large but she managed to pull it tight over the waistband of the trousers and held it closed with one hand. Badger watched her, nodded to himself and twisted the belt around so that the buckle and spare length of leather were against her spine. He yanked the loose end and she stumbled back against him, like a dog brought to heel. She was on a leash.

'Time to go.'

'Where?' she asked, and then bit her lip again in case he didn't like the question.

'I'll find somewhere. Come on.'

He unlocked the door and thrust her before him into air so cold that it froze the back of her throat. His car was parked under naked trees fifty feet away. She stumbled to the passenger seat but he dragged her to the back and opened the boot.

'You can't!' she screamed, starting to lose her self-control. 'No, I won't, I'm not going in there. *No!*'

Her protests stopped as he slapped her face, making her bite her tongue. He lifted her off the ground and threw her into the boot on top of oily rags. The lid snapped shut on her muffled screams.

PART TWO

'It is an ancient Mariner,
And he stoppeth one of three,
"By thy long grey beard and glittering eye
Now wherefore stoppeth thou me?"

[. . .]

And now the Storm-Blast came, and he
Was tyrannous and strong:
He struck with his o'er-taking wings,
And chased us south along.'

Samuel Taylor Coleridge,
The Rime of the Ancient Mariner

CHAPTER THIRTEEN

He drove aimlessly for an unreckoned period of time before the shock set in and he started to shake so badly that he pulled into a lay-by. There was no way he could begin to comprehend what had just happened. He was certain that if he just went back to the caravan Dan would be snoring in front of the telly, out of his brain on booze and dope. He would wake him up and they'd go out and buy two chicken tikka masala pizzas and some beers, a bottle of whisk—he stopped himself. Just the beers; then they would return to the van, pop the beers and watch the latest porn movie until unconsciousness or sleep took over.

His eyes misted sentimentally. Despite his refusal to allow the truth into his mind he knew the image was false. He would never see Dan again. They would never pick up women and share them like they used to; never visit their mum together. Mum! He shivered in fear.

Without warning gut-wrenching sobs burst from his mouth. He cried without restraint, collapsed against the harness of the seat belt, his face drenched, hands balled into fists so tight the nails cut his palms. His sorrow was as much for himself and for a future destroyed as it was for his dead brother. Even though he would miss him, theirs had been a relationship forged in the necessities of survival, sustained by shared enjoyment of easy pleasures rather than affection. Superficial, maybe, but it was the only lasting bond he had ever known.

His wife was a selfish cow who grew indifferent to sex within twelve months of trapping him into marriage by pretending to his mum that she was pregnant. Almost as soon as the honeymoon was over she claimed she'd had a miscarriage but he suspected otherwise and what little affection he had felt towards her vanished. Of course, she had called him unfeeling about the baby and what she described as 'the tragedy' but he told her the tears were bollocks and that she should be grateful they wouldn't have the inconvenience of a kid. It had been a bloody argument but one he still felt good about. Dan had thought the whole thing a joke.

Dan. He was the only one who'd ever taken him as he was. The line of self-righteous prats who had looked down on them stretched back a long way, starting with his dad, who'd buggered off when he was ten, leaving Mum right in it with two kids to raise, precious little money apart from benefits and dodgy health. He and Dan had learnt fast and the first lesson had been that life could be better without their dad. With no one to tell them what to do they'd been able to stay out on the streets until too tired to want anything more than their beds. And Dan always had a new game to try.

New tears arrived with the memory of endless versions of hide the neighbour's cat down the drain, moving on to how many plants they could uproot from poxy Mr Sallow's garden after he threatened them with the strap for frightening his little Annie. If he'd only known what his precious daughter liked to do in the park on a Saturday for a bit of extra pocket money he'd have taken his belt to her but he and Dan never told. Why risk spoiling their fun? Annie had grown up sweet and accommodating. Ah, Annie.

The crying stopped as he recalled the girl who had helped him lose his virginity at the age of fourteen, but then started as he remembered she had done it as a favour to Dan.

What had he done? His hands gripped the steering wheel,

trying to hold on to a world that was being shaken apart by the reality of his brother's death. He could feel his muscles spasming as he tried to control the shivering in his arms. From nowhere he realised that he was going to be sick and only just made it out of the car in time. A stream of vomit splattered the frozen ditch at the side of the road, joined quickly by another as his stomach heaved.

The evening was suddenly threatening. Headlights on a distant road became police cars out searching for him because they'd found Dan's body. His fingerprints would be all over the van, even on the broken bottle. He hugged himself, terrified by the thought that he would be arrested and sent to prison.

'Should've burnt the fucking van!' He spoke into the silver stillness, unaware that he had made a noise.

There was banging from inside the boot and he looked at it stupidly. The memory of the girl rushed back like a tidal wave, sweeping him from his feet so that he lost his balance and fell, his hand slipping in the pile of fast-cooling sick. He looked at it with disgust, more concerned about the stink than the returning second slice of reality, erased from his mind by the shock of Dan's death.

'Fuck,' he said getting up and wiping his palm fastidiously on a rag, 'Fuck!'

He went over to the back of the car and kicked it viciously.

'Shut up!'

The banging continued so he found his keys, unlocked the boot and yanked it open, standing over the girl inside with a raised fist, ready to use it. She cowered away, eyes so wide that their whites shone in the moonlight. He frowned; why was she tied up? Oh yes, he'd done it with some nylon ties he had in the boot. He'd made a loop, slipped it over her hands and then down to her legs, his movements quick and smooth, as if directed by a part of his brain unaffected by the traumas shattering his life.

'You either keep quiet or I'll gag you. Understand?'

She nodded and he slammed the lid shut. He waited by the car to see if she dared make another sound. Nothing, so he climbed back into the front seat, suddenly aware that he was freezing cold. The tears had gone but he was physically exhausted, in no state to make the decisions he knew were needed. He had no idea what to do. Life was so unfair!

He was consumed by self-pity, certain he was again Life's victim in a game with rules he'd never been told and which he still didn't understand. The feeling was familiar, one he had lived with since childhood; one that provided excuses whenever things went wrong. It wasn't his fault, he decided. Dan's death had been an accident, the result of an argument that had been the bloody girl's doing. He never should have taken her to the van, wouldn't have done if she hadn't complained about the cold in the car and the smell of exhaust when he had tried keeping the engine running to please her. Picky little madam. Now look at her, hanging around his neck like an albatross, bringing him nothing but bad luck.

Lines from *The Rime of the Ancient Mariner* came back to him from a school lesson long ago. '*God save thee, ancient Mariner! From the fiends, that plague thee thus!*' It was the only piece of literature ever powerful enough to hold his attention for more than the opening line. The coincidence with his name and the sense of doom that filled every verse had somehow echoed his own world order. '*With my crossbow I shot the Albatross.*'

An albatross, yes, that's what she was, but the Ancient Mariner was cursed because he killed the bird and he hadn't done that. So that meant there could still be a way out. He looked at his watch; it read twenty-five past nine. His shock at the time was as difficult to cope with as everything else. How could it be less than two hours since he'd met Dan and they had made their way to the van together? He shook his arm, held the dial to his ear even though it had a quartz mechanism, and then looked at the dashboard. The luminous readout said 21.26. The idea that his world could have changed so completely in so little time destabilised him, bringing fresh tears to his eyes so that he shut them tight, pressing the balls of his palms into them until they hurt.

Red stars burst behind his eyelids, swirling with flashes of white light. In his imagination he saw himself walking along a path with many turnings. Each fork he took brought him closer to the point of Dan's death. Any single choice would have meant things would turn out differently. If he hadn't joined the search party, thinking that it would make him look innocent; if Dan hadn't called, saying they needed to talk at the van; if he hadn't encouraged Dan to stop at the pub first and then smoke more dope than usual in the hope that he would pass out and he could sneak the girl away; if Dan hadn't woken when he did, or had kept his keys on a hook like a normal person. The list went on spooling in his mind; pieces of bad luck, choices made, paths taken.

Slowly it dawned on him that he was still on the path. It lay ahead of him, seemingly endless, with more choices ahead. Perhaps he wasn't yet doomed; his albatross might be trussed up but she wasn't dead.

The idea of escape fell into his mind like a stroke of genius. *Nobody* knew his brother was dead, let alone who'd killed him; no one had any idea that he'd taken the girl or that she was with him. The thought came to him that he could go to the boot of the car, lift her out, dump her on the ground under the trees by the side of the road and drive away. If a car came along and saw her in time she'd live; if not, she'd die. It wouldn't be his fault; it would be Fate. It was tempting and he got as far as stepping out of the car into the bone-numbing chill before common sense took over.

He needed time to get away. If she was found and told her rescuer what had happened, it would all be over. The alternative, of killing her first before dumping the body, never occurred to him. He wasn't a murderer, that much he knew about himself despite his brother's death. If the girl died it would be because of an accident or from natural causes, not because of anything he did to her.

Slowly, his mind started working again and with the thinking came a sense of hope. No matter what Life had thrown at him today he could survive. He'd go away. Somewhere at home he had a passport, a relic of the hopeful honeymoon in Menorca. He'd get on a ferry over to France, hire a car and drive wherever the road took him. Maybe he could work his way to Spain, it would be warmer than here at any rate; he could go even further south: Morocco, Africa, anywhere but here. Mariner slipped the car into gear and executed a neat three-point turn.

As he guided the vehicle carefully on icy roads, always on the speed limit, never drawing attention to himself, he started to imagine his alternative future. By the time he arrived at the familiar semi on Goosegreen Avenue he was already halfway to a new life somewhere warm, where girls would be plentiful and the beer cheap. He steered the car into the garage, locking the door behind him. Leaving the girl where she was he went inside to check his wife was still away at her mother's as he expected; she was. There was a note on the calendar explaining there was shepherd's pie in the fridge for reheating and a casserole in the freezer. That was all; no kisses, not even her name.

The small hall was stuffy and smelt of drying washing. He turned down the thermostat in one of the daily battles in which he and his wife engaged, the futility of his action lost on him. He would stay home tonight – easy to carry the girl in via the back door from the garage. She would have to be gagged of course; no way could he trust her to keep quiet all night. At least they'd be warm. The missus wasn't due back for two days but he'd call her just to make sure. It was a plan.

He went round the house closing all the curtains and made sure that the front door was double-locked. Then he carried the girl inside, stuffed a clean sock from the airing cupboard in her mouth and tied her to the bottom of the stairs while he went and had a long, hot shower.

Dressed in clean clothes he felt a new man as he left his bedroom, only to recoil from the stench on the landing.

'What the . . . ?'

It was the girl. She stank after two days in the van and needed cleaning up. It was easy to lift her, she weighed almost nothing. He dumped her as she was in the shower and turned it on, letting the warm water flow over her huddled body. While it ran he found some clothes that might just fit her. A pair of his wife's jeans she hadn't been able to get into for years and was keeping for some reason he had never fathomed. A T-shirt, jumper and fleece that were all too big for her but were better than the stinking rags from the van. Only the socks were the right size. His wife had little feet.

He turned off the water and undressed her despite her protests.

'Stop wriggling or you'll stay filthy. You can't stay inside smelling the place out. If you won't be cleaned I'll just leave you outside soaked through and you'll be frozen solid in no time.'

That quietened her down. He stripped her and retied her hands and feet immediately. As he soaped her pure, white skin, he felt himself become aroused. *Not yet, not like this,* he told himself, *you're not an animal. She'll be grateful and want you soon enough.* Drying her took all his self-control. Dressing her while she was tied up proved impossible. He undid her feet first and started to put on the clean clothes. The sight of his wife's grey-white grandma knickers over her tight buttocks and slim hips made him laugh. After he dressed the bottom half he re-tied her feet and undid her hands. She started to squirm immediately, like an eel in his grip, grunting against the gag.

He didn't mean to bang her face on the tiles and he had to find tissue for her nose. Then he realised she couldn't breathe and he pulled out the sock quickly.

She took an immediate gulp of air and he clamped his hand

over her mouth, too aware of the thin party wall and his nosy neighbours, who would probably already be commenting on two showers in quick succession.

'Scream, make any noise, and it goes back in. With this nosebleed you'll suffocate.'

He doubted he would be able to do it but she believed him and stayed silent while he cleaned her up and finished dressing her. Her wrist was an angry mess so he rubbed on some antiseptic cream and put big a plaster over it.

'I suppose I'd better feed you. Shepherd's pie and beans all right?'

She nodded and he fireman-carried her downstairs to the kitchen, checking again that the blind was down. He reheated the pie – more than enough for two, the way it always was when his wife cooked – heated the beans and made tea for them both, adding a generous slug of cooking brandy to his. After they had eaten he found an anorak of his wife's and went to put it on her.

'Time to go back in the car.'

'No! Please, not again. I hate it in there.'

'You can always share my bed instead,' he smiled at her.

'Please,' her eyes filled with tears.

'Bed or boot, take your pick. You might just survive the night out there now that you've eaten something, though in this weather . . .'

'Please, Badger,' she flinched, 'I mean Steve. Please, I don't feel well. I hurt all over; all I want to do is sleep.'

'And so you can,' she looked at him hopefully, 'in due course.'

'Please, no,' it was little more than a whisper but then, 'NO!'

'Shut up!' He rammed a tea towel down her throat so hard she fell off the chair and hit her head on the table. 'You should be grateful you little bitch. My brother's dead, fucking dead, and it's your fault. I rescued you! The least you can do is show a little thanks.'

135

He bent down and picked her up with one arm, grabbing the brandy with his free hand. The dishes could wait until morning, breaking another house rule but probably not the most egregious disobedience of the night.

Early the next morning he woke with a cheap brandy hangover and tried to focus on the bedside clock; five-twenty-two.

'Urgh, I feel terrible,' he mumbled and reached out a hand to his wife's side of the bed. There she was, fat lump of lard, snoring away . . . except that she wasn't fat or snoring. 'What the . . . ?'

Mariner sat up in bed so fast the pain behind his eyeballs nearly made him sick. Fumbling for the switch the first thing he saw as the light lanced into his eyes was the bottle to blame for his hangover. He stared at it accusingly, then rolled over to see who he had persuaded back to his marital bed while the wife was away. He screamed and the girl woke up. She started choking almost immediately so he removed the gag, which he noticed was one of his best socks. Why was she was tied up?

'What the . . . ?' he said again.

The girl stared up at him, flinching when he raised his fingers to wipe away dried blood from around her nose.

'Dear God.' He rolled onto his back and shut his eyes.

The headache was terrible but his fear and shame were worse. As he lay there trying to think, fragments of the plan from the previous evening came back to him but everything now seemed impossible. What had he been thinking of? He buried his head in his pillow, breathing deeply, inhaling the scent of sweat and sex.

He had messed up the bed. The wife would go nuts. He rolled the girl off onto the carpet and replaced the gag. Then he went and had a shower. It sobered him up but did nothing for his headache so he took some painkillers with water from the tooth mug.

He let her use the bathroom, insisting that she kept the door open, and then carried her downstairs and tied her up while he changed the bed, threw the linen in the washing machine on hot;

136

put the old clothes she'd been wearing plus his bloody trousers and jacket in a black bin liner to take to the tip; placed the mugs, glasses and dinner things in the dishwasher. He turned on the radio just in case the neighbours were listening in and she tried something, then made fresh mugs of tea and sat down to work out what to do. First things first, he had to stop the damned girl from staring at him. He wrapped her up in the anorak and thrust her unceremoniously into the car boot, ignoring her grunts of protest.

There were two thermos flasks in the kitchen where they always were, one for coffee and the other for soup. His wife was precise in her domestic responsibilities, though not because she cared for him. Oh no; he knew that she looked after him out of duty, not affection, and it showed every time the bread in his sandwiches was a bit dry, or the end of the cake in his lunch box was starting to go stale.

There were plenty of tins in the store cupboard and an opener hanging on the rack. He chose tomato soup and heated it in the microwave while he made more toast. Fifteen minutes later, another can opened and warming for one thermos and coffee on the go for the other, he slipped upstairs and started packing his suitcase.

Now that he was leaving his movements were furtive, like a thief's, but then he reasoned he *was* stealing. He was taking back something that had once belonged to him: his life.

The idea of asking for money came to him as he was looking for the savings tin. Every week his wife put in twenty-five pounds and once a quarter she added three hundred pounds to the building society account in her sole name. He never knew whether the money eventually went on clothes, or presents for her family, or was being saved up against the day she'd leave him, but he suspected the latter. It was the third month of the quarter, so there should be a tidy sum there, enough for a cheap ferry ticket so that there would be no trace of him using his credit card. He was quite pleased with himself for remembering that the police could find you that way and furious with her when he found the tin empty.

The problem was that he had already used up the limit on his cash card. Again his mind slipped gear and he started to panic. He had a vision of living rough in the forest somewhere and spent ten minutes filling the back seat of the car with everything he thought he might need. It was as he was moving the girl's bag from the front passenger seat, thinking it should be hidden, that he had the inspiration to look inside for money.

Sure enough, she had sixty quid in new twenty-pound notes, together with a mobile phone but no cash card. It was typical that she'd have money. She probably had more free cash a month than he did despite his forty hours at the school breaking his back. Thinking of the school with its snooty, over-privileged kids made his blood boil. She was as bad as the rest of them, spoilt rotten by parents with more money than sense.

More money than sense. The phrase lodged in his mind, circling round and around. It drove him back to the kitchen, to another cup of tea with two sugars. As he sipped, the idea came: his albatross was a valuable bird.

He shook his head, too aware of his own limitations. There's no way someone as sophisticated as Lord William Saxby would fall for an attempt to squeeze money out of him for the return of his daughter. But the idea wouldn't go away. As he made patterns in the damp ring left by the mug on the pine table the idea changed from fantasy to reality.

If he didn't at least try to con some money out of Saxby he would never know whether he could have succeeded and the unknown would drive him mad, like having a lottery ticket but not checking the numbers. All he needed to do was make one call. There it was, by the fridge; a beige wall-mounted phone that he had used countless times without thinking. What was to stop him picking up the receiver and dialling? All he had to do was ask. Couldn't be that difficult, could it?

He clenched and unclenched his fists, the blood in the vein of his throat pumping hard, his breathing rapid. One call; one simple phone call, that's all he had to do. That wasn't beyond him, was it? He wasn't such loser that he couldn't manage one call, was he? Anger at himself propelled him back to the garage. He unlocked the boot and roused the girl who seemed to be half asleep.

'Your dad's number,' he shouted at her, then remembered the neighbours might now be awake and repeated quietly, 'Your dad's phone number; what is it?'

Confusion, then hope flared in her eyes.

Issie recited a number. 'That's his personal line, he always answers it.'

The idea that he might have had to talk to someone other than her father hadn't occurred to Mariner but he realised he couldn't remember the number.

'Wait!' he shut the boot and went back inside.

There was a Post-it pad stuck to the wall by the phone. He pulled it off and found a pencil in a drawer beneath. When he opened the boot again she was waiting for him.

She repeated the sequence slowly so that he had time to write it down. 'And please, can I have some more clothes or a blanket? It's so cold.'

He found a sleeping bag he had thrown on the back seat from when he was planning sleeping rough, thrust it at her and watched as she tried to wriggle under it, clumsy within the cords, so he tucked it around her and made to replace the gag.

'Please; it gets so stuffy,' she begged.

'One minute you're cold the next it's too bleeding stuffy.' He slammed the boot shut with unnecessary force.

In the kitchen he picked up the phone but put it back immediately. Maybe Saxby had the technology to trace calls; he was powerful enough. He rummaged in Issie's bag, found her mobile and dialled at once before his nerve failed. The receiver was picked up within two rings and a voice uncannily like his own shouted '*Issie, where are you?*' He had expected patrician cool and was momentarily struck dumb.

'Issie? Who's there? Answer me, damn you.'

'Money,' was all he could say. 'Money; for your daughter.'

The silence that greeted his words made him feel stronger and he took a deep breath.

'I've got her and if you want her it'll cost.'

'How much?'

The question surprised him.

'Fifty thousand pounds, in used notes.' Where had that come from?

'How much?' The voice sounded incredulous; had he asked for too much?

He didn't care, the sum had taken root in his brain and all he could do was repeat it.

'Fifty thou' and don't tell the police.'

'But how do I—?'

'The money; if you want to see her again, get the money. No police or she dies. I'll call back with more instructions.'

He rang off, bathed with sweat; breathless but exhilarated. He had done it! He had actually done it. In the privacy of the kitchen he danced a jig around the table.

The exhilaration of the call took him through packing up his belongings, and when he drove away, locking the back door for the last time, he was whistling.

CHAPTER FOURTEEN

Five fifty-five and the school was pitch-dark apart from lights in the IT block where the police team had assembled ready for the 6 a.m. briefing. Fenwick had been waiting an hour. Unable to sleep he had left home early with an overnight bag well before five. The drive to the school had been slow but once there he made himself some coffee and read the reports he hadn't managed the day before. He had been involved less than a day but the case had already taken control of his life and he knew its outcome would somehow shape his future.

Fenwick couldn't shake a sense of discomfort about this investigation. Normally he was a realistic optimist; confident in the abilities of his team and the scientific and computing support at their disposal. But this time . . . this time his instinct told him something was wrong, that he was being sucked into a dark journey at the end of which there would be a death, maybe more than one. On his own in the chilly classroom he had shivered and drunk coffee, finding it bitter even when fresh, but as the team drifted in none of his misgivings showed.

Fenwick had read a copy of Issie's diary from cover to cover, the original having been sent to the forensic lab already. There was no explanation of who Badger might be nor a hint of his real name. When he saw a cryptic reference to *'losing it'* he had a horrible feeling that he knew what *'it'* was. These girls; these stupid, clever girls, with brains and more money than was good for them but no common sense . . . He stopped the thought. They were young and Issie was a victim, no matter how privileged she was. The inverted snobbery he knew still lurked in him – a lasting influence from his childhood – could hamper his objectivity if he didn't silence it.

The most important fact to hold on to was that Issie had an assignation on the night she disappeared and that meant she might still be alive. Bernstein had had a team working through the night following up with friends, family and school staff, asking about 'Badger', without success. Nevertheless, there was an air of heightened expectation in the conference room as the team assembled.

Bernstein looked angry about something and was deep in conversation with Sergeant Willie Cobb, breaking it to ask Bazza to kick off. He reported that he had sent Issie's bedding straight to the toxicology team at the lab who had run presumptive tests and found traces of alcohol, marijuana and nicotine, nothing stronger.

'Even so,' Bazza reasoned, 'she must have had a supplier. It's a start and I reckon her so-called friends will talk now you've softened them up, sir. That Octavia's a piece of work.'

There were assorted mumbles about the girl and her family that Fenwick didn't think were helpful but Bernstein let the chat run, perhaps glad to feel the atmosphere lightening for the first time. When it died she took the opportunity to round on Cobb.

'Tell them your news, Sergeant.' She didn't bother to disguise her scowl.

'Rod Saxby's still missing. We almost got him but he slipped through our fingers.'

'How did that happen?' Fenwick's voice was mild but Cobb squirmed as Bernstein sent him a killer look.

'He came back to his house and picked up his car, sir.'

'And the officer waiting for him to do just that . . . ?'

'Cobb was taking a leak; has a weak bladder, apparently,' Bernstein interjected.

'Bit of a hazard in our line of work, wouldn't you say?'

Fenwick was too irritated to appreciate his own sarcasm but there was a nervous giggle and someone somewhere muttered 'piss artist' in what was meant to be a whisper but which carried in the silence that followed.

'It's an infection, ma'am,' Cobb protested.

'Then get yourself sorted and keep to desk duties until your bladder's back under control.'

'Presumably RPU are already on the lookout for him?' Fenwick asked.

'Obviously; I called road policing immediately.'

'Then there's nothing more we can do. The question is: is Saxby junior the Badger Issie met on Monday night?'

'We don't know. No one has ever heard of a "Badger",' Bernstein explained. 'Rodney Saxby never had the nickname, which means that it's a priority to find the person Issie arranged to meet.'

She handed out copies of the relevant diary entries.

'So why Badger? What sort of nickname is that?' she asked.

'Someone fat and hairy?' Jake suggested.

'You're in the frame, for starters,' Bazza retaliated but Bernstein went to the whiteboard and wrote up: '*Fat? Hairy?*'

'A girl her age wouldn't go for fat, but hairy, maybe. What else?'

'An older man,' one of the women constables suggested. Fenwick thought her name was something like Anderson. 'It's a comfortable, wise name, like in *Wind in the Willows*. Could be a father figure.'

'Interesting,' Fenwick chipped in, 'there was a copy of the book in her bedroom at home; we should pick it up in case she wrote in it.'

'Agreed,' Bernstein took over. 'We also need to talk to her parents again to see if anything new occurs to them. Bazza, you go and do that as soon as we're done; with sensitivity, please.'

'*Older man. Wise.*' joined '*Fat? Hairy?*' on the board.

'How about some grey hair?' Fenwick suggested, 'That's a badger's colouring.'

'It fits with the other images; anything else?' There was silence. 'OK; unless there are any further ideas, we should keep our minds open that we could be looking for an older man.'

'Or a regular boyfriend with a naff pet name,' Bazza suggested.

'There is that,' Bernstein agreed. 'If that's all on Badger – Andrew, why don't you tell them about Issie's art.'

He stood up.

'We need to investigate the possibility that Issie might have been sexually abused. Cobb, if it doesn't strain the wrong muscles, could you pass those paintings over?'

He showed the goat-man first and there was a 'so what' moment, but when he revealed what he thought of as the rape scene there were murmurs of disgust.

'Issie's work, taken and hidden by Lulu Bullock.'

'Damn woman,' Bernstein spat.

'The paintings were a secret project. Bullock discovered the canvasses after Issie disappeared and I think she was still trying to work out what to do with them. The girl could be a self-portrait, which might suggest Issie was the victim of an assault and this is her way of dealing with it. Does the goat-man remind you of anyone?'

No one volunteered any suggestions.

'Me neither. The medallion is distinctive, though. We need photos of it to check whether any member of school staff, friends or her family has one like it. Add that to your list for the Saxbys, Bazza,' Fenwick suggested, 'and take – er . . . Anderson, isn't it? – with you.'

'Henderson, sir,' the woman corrected and Fenwick was surprised that he had the wrong name as his memory was usually reliable.

144

There were a few smirks around the room but he ignored them until the reason for his mistake flooded his mind, bringing a rush of colour to his cheeks. His subconscious had noted the woman's generous chest and substituted the wrong name. The reason for his slip of the tongue hadn't only occurred to him, and a few of the redder-blooded males in the room were having difficulty keeping their faces straight. He looked down and coughed.

The team dispersed. Bernstein assumed the challenge of locating Rod Saxby. She asked Fenwick if he could meet with the outer search team and brief them. He was happy to oblige, relieved to have something concrete to do.

He drove out to Bryden Hill, half a mile from the school, where the team was using a YMCA hostel as a base. They had worked long into the night until heavy snow towards dawn had made it impossible to see. As visibility promised to return, so too did the searchers, volunteers mixing with police as determination slowly replaced hope.

His feet crunched frozen snow as he made his way to the wooden building, his breath misting around his face and freezing as it settled on his exposed skin. Occasional barks carried through the still air as dogs jumped out of vans, eager to start. Inside the hostel Inspector Steve Watson looked up as Fenwick walked in. A man in his mid forties with sleep-deprived eyes, his face relaxed into a brief smile of welcome when he realised the identity of his visitor.

'Thanks for coming over,' he said simply. 'Coffee? The stuff in that thermos is so strong any leftovers will have to go to Sellafield, but it's all we've got.'

Fenwick poured himself an espresso-sized measure and hid a grimace as the grainy liquid filled his mouth. If Watson and team were living on it he wasn't about to complain.

'Anything?'

'Nada. Her trail disappears at the road. Frankly she could be anywhere and after two nights like this . . .' Watson rubbed his eyes, pulling the skin down at the edges to reveal bright red rims. 'The only thing you might be interested in are these.'

He pointed to a pile of CCTV tapes and photographs.

'The volunteers?' Fenwick asked. It was routine to record them as experience proved time and again that the perpetrator would be compelled to join the hunt for their victim.

'Yes; over sixty yesterday, though there are less going out now, inevitably.'

'Could you have someone go through and pick out all the men and divide them into two piles, under and over thirty; and then sort those with grey or greying hair to the top? There's a chance she might still be alive.' He told him about the reference to a meeting with someone called Badger and their theories as to what the nickname might signify.

The fatigue disappeared from Watson's face as he listened and he excused himself to inform his search coordinators. A hard lead was exactly what they needed to boost flagging spirits. As soon as he had finished he returned to Fenwick.

'We'll go through the surveillance immediately. It will do us good.'

Fenwick was drinking coffee with the civilian clerk providing admin support when his mobile rang. He recognised the caller number and excused himself.

'Bob, how are you? How's Doris?'

'Fine thank you, though I wouldn't visit for a while if I were you, you're not my Dot's favourite person. There's a half-finished ceiling in the spare bedroom needs urgent attention and I haven't even started the walls.'

'Sounds like I rescued you just in time.'

'Well there is that, I grant you, but don't tell her I said so. Look,' his voice dropped to a whisper, 'I'm at the Saxbys' and they're in a right state.'

'What's happened?'

'There's been a ransom demand, five minutes ago; but don't jump to conclusions. It may be a hoax. I was here and saw it happen. Saxby took the call, went white and I knew something was up straight away. Soon as he put the phone down I confronted him. He didn't want to tell me but I pushed him and he admitted that the man who'd called said he had Issie and wanted fifty thousand pounds for her safe return.'

'Fifty thousand – that's nothing from a man like Saxby. Is that why you think it's not real?'

'Partly, but also Saxby said the caller sounded nervous, rushed his words, wasn't coherent. And there's the delay. Why wait?'

'Thing is, Saxby doesn't want you lot to know. The caller said Issie would be killed if the police were involved. Some of your team turned up five minutes ago and that sent the Saxbys crazy. They made me promise not to say anything to them and ushered me away.'

'And you're breaking your promise, Bob?'

'I said I wouldn't tell the officers who'd arrived anything, but that didn't extend to you.'

Fenwick was surprised at Bob's subtlety; if asked he would have said the man was too straight to know how to bend.

'You should come over, sir. I reckon you can make them admit what's happened. The man's going to call again with instructions for a drop-off.'

'I'm on my way.'

Fenwick explained that there had been a development and said a hurried goodbye to Watson who passed him a fat bundle of photographs.

'Here; this lot's copies from when the search first started late on Tuesday and these are Wednesday's volunteers. I'll send over today's later. Let me know if there's anything more I can do.'

Fenwick pushed the pictures and copy tapes into his overcoat pocket and left, turning up his collar against the freezing air. On his way to Saxby Hall he tried to reach Bernstein but went straight through to her message service so he made a snap decision and called CC Norman, insisting he be pulled from whatever meeting he was in.

'We have to treat this as a kidnap, Fenwick. That means by the book.'

Fenwick knew he was referring to the 'official kidnap manual' containing the procedures for abduction. Norman would appoint a Force Gold leader to handle the ransom drop and deployment. Bernstein would be the obvious choice, but did Norman trust her enough? The team would include Silver and Bronzes to back up the Gold commander, handling the outside inquiry, intelligence, media risks and other investigations.

'I'm going to assume control of this critical incident personally,' Norman said. 'I want you to proceed to the Hall and stay with the Saxbys while I mobilise a team here at HQ, separate from the one at the school. I'll have Bernstein as Silver and you and Holland as Bronzes.'

Fenwick acknowledged his understanding, silently frustrated at the bronze role but relieved to be involved.

Holland's car was parked by the faux Georgian pillars when Fenwick arrived at the Hall. There were raised voices from inside.

'—bloody well cannot arrest me, you little turd!' Rod Saxby had returned.

'If you refuse to cooperate, sir, you leave me no alternative.' Bazza's voice was full of anger but under control.

'Take the bastard and lock him up! He drove my baby away. Get him out of here.' Jane Saxby sounded close to murder.

'Your spoilt brat wasn't driven away; she's run off and you're lucky the family silver's not gone with her.'

Lord Saxby's attempt to calm his brother down was lost in a shriek from his wife and the sounds of a scuffle. Constable

Henderson was struggling to stop Jane Saxby from hitting her brother-in-law while her husband attempted to explain something to Bazza Holland. In the confusion Rod Saxby was edging towards the door. Fenwick put his six-foot-plus frame in the way and the man backed into him.

'What the . . . ? Oh, it's you. I'll be lodging a complaint. I might even sue you bastards for defamation of character. Now get out of my way.'

Fenwick held his ground. Around Rod Saxby's neck he had spotted a glint of gold. Bazza saw his glance and nodded; the man wore a chain.

'As I think Inspector Holland will have explained to you, Mr Saxby, you have two choices: you either come with us willingly or we arrest you.'

'On what grounds?'

'Obstructing the police would be a start and your reluctance to help us find your niece is making me wonder whether we could find other charges if we looked more closely.'

'I'm not having this nonsense; I'm calling my lawyer, right now.'

'Please, Rod,' his brother interrupted, sounding so unlike himself that it silenced everyone. 'She could be dying out there. If they need to talk to you, eliminate you from their enquiries or whatever the bloody hell they call it, then just do it. For me, I'm begging you.' He was almost in tears. The effect on his brother was immediate.

'All right, old man; keep your shirt on. I was going to; just didn't like the bastard's tone.'

He walked out of the front door, Henderson close behind carrying Issie's book in an evidence bag. Fenwick told Holland to contact CC Norman without explaining why. When he was sure Rod Saxby wasn't about to bolt he returned his attention to the others.

'We haven't found Issie but I need to update you on a few things, sir.'

'You're staying? There's no need. We—'

'Yes, I'll be staying for a while.'

'Have you eaten, Superintendent?' Jane Saxby asked, her voice on automatic. 'There are bacon sandwiches in the kitchen; Millie made them but we can't eat. Or some tea, perhaps?'

'That's very kind.'

Bob Cooper emerged from the study and followed them into the sitting room. The previous night's fire had burnt to nothing and there was a chill in the corners where cold air fell from the windows despite the curtains. Lady Saxby shivered and her husband lifted a pashmina from the sofa to wrap around her.

'I'll turn up the heat,' he muttered.

'Tea would also be nice, Bill,' Jane prompted and her husband left obediently.

As soon as he was gone she rounded on Cooper, her face furious.

'You told him, didn't you? You Judas; I trusted you. What have you got to say for yourself?' she demanded, turning to Fenwick.

'First, Bob Cooper did the right thing; second, he didn't breach your confidence and tell the other officers, he kept the information for my ears only; third, he trusts my judgement and knows that I'm too experienced to do anything to jeopardise your daughter's safety. He did the right thing – for Issie.'

Fenwick expected another emotional outburst but Lady Saxby seated herself in a corner of the sofa and curled her feet up before closing her eyes in despair.

'There's brandy in the cupboard beside you, Mr Cooper. Could you pour me one?' She opened her eyes to scrutinise him. 'I know it's a strange breakfast but I need it.'

Cooper poured a measure of Rémy and she was sipping it in silence when Saxby returned.

'What's happened?' Saxby asked immediately.

'He knows, Bill, but I trust him. I would guess that a team's already on their way with everything they'll need to trace the next call.'

Saxby slammed the tray down on the coffee table.

'Jane; what have you done? What if the kidnapper's already watching us? What do you think he'll do to Issie when he sees police technicians turn up?'

'We've thought of that,' Fenwick explained, 'they'll be coming in an ambulance. From the outside it will look as if one of you has been taken ill. While we're waiting, why don't you give me details of the call?'

'I can do better than that; all my calls are recorded. You can judge for yourself.'

Fenwick played the call and was inclined to agree with Bob that the man wasn't a professional – but that didn't exclude that he had Issie. There was a noise in the background and he tilted his head on one side as he tried to identify it.

'I reckon it's the news headlines,' Bob said, 'from the radio.'

Fenwick replayed the tape as both Saxbys came closer.

'That's the local station,' Jane said and then glared at her husband. 'Tell him.'

'Tell me what?'

Saxby looked away, seeming close to tears.

'I think he had Issie's phone,' he said hoarsely.

Fenwick rounded on him.

'And you thought to hold that from us?' He shook his head in frustration and forced himself to calm down. 'That means we might be able to trace it. You should have told us at once.'

He rang Norman, to be put through immediately.

'He did use it,' Norman confirmed. 'There's an automatic trace on it and Bernstein just called to say it's been activated. They've narrowed the area down to a triangle to the north-west of Guildford. This changes everything.'

'Possibly, sir, though it might still be someone who found the mobile somewhere and is being opportunistic.'

'I'll be the judge of that.'

'Sir.'

Norman rang off and Fenwick returned to the drawing room. The technical team had arrived, two of them with paramedic vests over their clothes. They set about their work with minimal fuss. Lady Saxby watched every move, a frown line between her eyebrows and a second glass of brandy cradled in her palm. A replacement family liaison officer had turned up as well, a young man with a sympathetic face who introduced himself as Tony. He sat unobtrusively beside Jane Saxby and said nothing. Fenwick approved of his style.

'He called on your private line?' he confirmed.

'Yes, the one in here. That's why I took him seriously.'

'Could you give us your mobile phones, just in case? We can alert the network provider.'

'Of course.'

'While we're waiting, can you tell me more about your brother? He works for you?'

'As a non-executive, yes. He used to be our commercial director but, well, the company moved on and . . . he had other interests; the job became very demanding.'

'What he means,' his wife interrupted, 'is that the other shareholders put so much pressure on the board that Rod was forced to resign. He went out kicking and screaming and it was only after he'd gone that Bill discovered his, ah, unique ideas of client entertainment.'

'That's enough, Jane.'

'And your brother's current earnings are . . . ?'

'That's a bit personal.'

'It will be easier to find out from you rather than obtain a warrant for his financial records.' Fenwick explained and watched

Saxby battle concern versus belligerence before writing a number down on a piece of paper he handed to Fenwick.

'Why are you so interested in my brother? Surely you can't think him guilty of any involvement with Issie's disappearance?'

'At this stage it's routine to find out as much as we can about family and friends.'

'As suspects, you mean? I suppose that includes us. You have to understand we'd none of us hurt her. We love her.'

Saxby looked sincere but Fenwick reserved judgement, too accustomed to stories of grieving parents who were later proven guilty of murder.

'Rod hates her, Bill, and we both know it,' Lady Saxby said, her words slightly slurred as she stood up to pour herself another measure of brandy.

'Easy, old thing. That's probably enough for now.'

She glared at him but replaced the bottle carefully and went back to the sofa empty-handed.

'Tell him about Rod,' she demanded.

'Very well,' Saxby sighed and rubbed his eyes.

Fenwick doubted he had slept since learning of Issie's disappearance.

'Rod is a non-executive with the company. We also pay him a consulting fee for finding new clients . . .'

'Corporate-speak for an open expense account,' his wife interjected but Saxby ignored her.

'Is he comfortably off?'

'He should be but . . . well, Rod has a passion for the finer things in life. It's easy to understand why. He was a director for many years and during that time he naturally benefited from a different level of compensation. Unfortunately, when his circumstances changed his tastes didn't.'

'And how does he finance these "passions" of his?'

Saxby closed his eyes and massaged the bridge of his nose.

'I help him, of course. I give him advances, loans . . .'

'Which are never repaid,' his wife said maliciously.

'Which, I grant you, are rarely repaid but I've made it clear that I don't expect repayment.'

'So, if there was a financial motive behind Issie's disappearance—' Fenwick started but Saxby interrupted him.

'Never! He wouldn't need to; all he has to do is ask and I give him whatever he wants.'

'That must be galling for a grown man, don't you think?'

'I . . . well, no . . . he's my brother; he'd know it was no trouble.' But Saxby didn't sound convinced.

Unexpectedly it was his wife who came to his rescue.

'The idea's absurd, Mr Fenwick,' she said, a look of contempt on her face. 'If Rod were behind the phone call the ransom demand would have been at least ten times bigger.'

The phone rang. One of the technicians held up his hand and when it dropped Bill Saxby picked up the receiver. Fenwick slipped on a headset.

'Saxby.'

'I want more. Five hundred thousand, in cash. You've got twenty-four hours to get it.'

'Can I deliver you the money sooner? We don't need twenty-four hours.'

'No.' The voice was muffled, as if the caller had placed a cloth over the mouthpiece.

'We want her back – today – I'll get you your money, but please can I speak to her?'

Saxby was rushing his words. Fenwick scribbled *slow down, keep him talking* on the pad of paper in front of him. Nodding, Saxby took a deep breath and made a visible effort.

'Look, I want my daughter back. I'll get you the money but I need proof you have her. My wife is very upset, distraught.'

'Is that why you've got an ambulance there?'

The words sent a jolt around the room. Without being told Tony, the FLO, stood up and went to check that the curtains were securely closed. They all were. Fenwick wrote another note, this time for Tony: *Call CC Norman – we need men outside, immediate and discreet.*

'I suppose you're proud of yourself, are you; making my wife ill with worry?'

'You should've kept better control of your daughter. A slut she is; it was only a matter of time before someone took her.'

Saxby controlled himself with effort.

'We just want her home. Please, can I talk to her? Is she all right?'

'When I've got the money you can see her all you like.'

'Wait! Where do I deliver the money to?'

'Twenty-four hours.'

The connection was broken. Lady Saxby burst into tears and her husband hugged her to his chest. Fenwick looked expectantly at the technicians who shook their heads.

'Not quite long enough but he was using her mobile again.'

Fenwick rang and briefed Norman and Bernstein about the call, emphasising the need for absolute discretion. Norman had already despatched a surveillance team to the Hall though they all agreed it was unlikely the kidnapper would hang around. Even so, as he rang off Norman asked Fenwick to stay in place just in case. He looked up to see the Saxbys comforting each other as they huddled on the sofa.

'If you can stand it, we need to hear the call again,' he explained and a tape was slotted into a machine that had been set up on the coffee table.

They listened in silence. At the end Saxby said, 'He's different this time; he sounds more professional, in control. Last time he rambled.'

'Is it the same voice?'

'I think so. Same local accent behind the muffling and the pitch was low. But . . . well he sounds more serious.'

'Better prepared perhaps; he might have been dissatisfied with his performance last time. It still doesn't sound professional. He was on almost long enough for us to trace him; he insulted you and tried to put the blame for taking Issie on her, as if he was excusing himself. A professional wouldn't have bothered. To them, it's just business.'

'So you think he might have her?' Jane Saxby asked.

'It's impossible to say. He offered no proof that . . . of her identity.'

'Say what you mean,' she insisted, wiping her eyes angrily. 'He offered no proof that she was still alive.'

'Right,' he replied carefully, 'and someone who knew what they were doing would have done. It would increase the emotional pressure on you.'

'So what are we going to do?'

'Chief Constable Norman has taken command of the operation; it doesn't go higher.'

'But you'll still be involved, Superintendent?' Jane Saxby looked at him hopefully and he was touched.

'Yes; we're working on the assumption that the kidnapper has her. We will lure him out. Can you find the money in time?'

'One call to my bank will sort it.'

'Good; we'll mark the money – invisibly, don't worry – and put a transmitter in with it that he won't spot. When he picks it up we will follow him and find Issie.'

'Just like that,' Saxby snorted, finding sarcasm from somewhere.

'Just like that,' Fenwick replied, not daring to catch Bob Cooper's eye.

'What can I do?' Jane asked, looking even more drawn and red-eyed than her husband.

'I don't want to be condescending,' Fenwick said, meaning it, 'but the best thing both of you can do is take one of the pills I'm sure your doctor prescribed and try to get some sleep. The more rested you are the better you'll be able to cope with the kidnapper's demands.

'As soon as we can be sure he's no longer watching the Hall, we will leave, but we'll be back tonight and stay here ready for when he makes contact tomorrow morning.'

'Why is he leaving it so long? Surely he'd be keen to take the money and go.'

'I don't know but maybe he needs time to think how to pick up the money.'

With some more persuasion the Saxbys finally went upstairs to try and sleep, leaving Cooper and Fenwick together as Tony went to find the promised bacon sandwiches.

'If he's not a professional and really does have her . . .' Cooper started to say.

'I know, Bob, the chances are Issie is already dead or soon will be. He'll panic at some point, realise he can be identified and kill her. Or botch things so badly she dies. If indeed he has her, but listening to that tape we have to take this seriously. I'm going to head back to the team as soon as the coast is clear.'

'What about your bacon sandwich?'

Fenwick looked at Cooper's impressively dimensioned stomach and smiled.

'Somehow, Bob, I don't think it will go to waste.'

CHAPTER FIFTEEN

Mariner continued to watch Saxby Hall for a few minutes after he broke the call. He was feeling confident again. His thinking had moved beyond escape to the needs of his new life. Saxby had said yes; as meek as anything! What would he have said if he had known his beloved daughter was trussed up in a disused pump station less than ten miles away? Mariner laughed and turned on the radio.

The idea of hiding at the pump house had come to him as he left Goosegreen Avenue that morning before it was light. It had been years since he, Dan and Annie had needed a place but the memory of those hot, sticky afternoons had boosted his unnatural optimism as he drove away from his past without a backward thought. Breaking into the pump house had been easy. The bolt cutters in his toolbox made fast work of the padlock, which he replaced with one of the spares he routinely carried. It fitted through the hasp as if made for the job.

He patted the key in his pocket as he turned on the wipers to clear fresh snow. He should be getting back. The idea of the chill pump station made him shiver. He fingered the sixty pounds in his jacket pocket. Was it enough for an oil heater? Maybe, if it was second-hand; and he knew just where to find one.

Before midday he was locked inside with the girl, his car parked out of sight up the disused road leading to the pump house. There would be car tracks of course but it was snowing so hard they would soon be covered. Everything was going his way. She was where he had left her on a mouldy mattress some squatter had abandoned, trussed up and tied to an iron fitting on the wall. He set up the oil stove just out of her reach.

He fed them both from the store of cans he had taken from home and made them strong mugs of tea with sugar. The girl ate and drank in silence. The only words she spoke were to ask to go outside to relieve herself. The afternoon was growing dark. He had already read his paper and he was bored. There was nothing to do; he hated puzzles and had forgotten to bring a radio. Should he risk going out and finding a pub? He glanced at the girl and shook his head. He didn't want anything to drink. His hangover headache was back and he felt exhausted. Best thing would be to have a nap. He made sure the stove had enough fuel before opening out a camp bed, layering on blankets and zipping himself up tight in his sleeping bag. He shut his eyes and fell asleep almost immediately.

Fenwick returned to spend the night with the Saxbys. Even though the children were expecting him for supper he knew he would never forgive himself if the kidnapper changed his plans and he wasn't on hand. Technically he didn't need to be there; Norman had a team on site, including an abduction expert from the Metropolitan Police, who had arrived dressed as a priest just in case the house was still being watched. Fenwick doubted it was. They had searched the surroundings thoroughly and found nothing but indistinct car tracks.

Bob Cooper had also been asked by Saxby to sleep at the Hall. They would share the guest wing with a police team of seven including the FLO. Tony had volunteered to move in for the duration when the Saxbys asked him to do so.

Fenwick and Bob headed for bed just before eleven.

'Get as much sleep as you can, Andrew. You look tired and this one could run on; you know it's not going to get easier.'

'You have no hopes for tomorrow, Bob?'

'Do you?'

Fenwick shook his head.

'Between us, I have a bad feeling, have had from the moment I arrived at the school but I can't tell you why.'

'My gut's telling me the same.'

Fenwick looked down at the expanded stomach in question.

'Could be the food you consumed today. Their cook was so pleased to find at least one person eating I think you put away the family's rations.'

'I only did it to make her feel better. What about your day. Any progress?'

'Nothing; we've worked through the staff and teacher lists at the school for a second time. The right pre-employment checks were taken; there's no one remotely suspicious employed there. All the alibis for the time of Issie's disappearance have been checked and reconfirmed by the team. I've read their reports, every last page, and nothing leaps out. There are just three people they haven't been able to track down to talk to a second time: a maths teacher, a maintenance man and a music tutor so they are top priority. The teacher went to Cyprus Wednesday evening . . .'

'That's sloppy of Surrey. Surely it's a "don't leave the area" one this.'

'You're right, but he had been off recovering from an operation and had a good alibi so I think they let him go. Even so . . .'

'Exactly. What about the others?'

'The maintenance man is married. He was interviewed Tuesday evening at the school and had a clear alibi; his brother confirmed they were together all Monday night. Still, Bazza's trying to track him down for a second interview, not least because he volunteered for the search party. And the music teacher we can't find.'

'That's not good. I never trust the music teachers, all this one-on-one tuition and they sit so close.'

'He's supposedly gay and uninterested in the girls, which is one of the reasons he was hired. He was at a concert in London on Monday night and stayed up there but now nobody's home when we call. Everything's being double-checked. Anything else happened here today?'

'No. They're going nuts with worry, particularly Lady Saxby. I like her.'

Fenwick noted Bob's soft spot and wondered at it. He typically didn't relate to women – other than his wife, daughter, and Nightingale, of course. Now where had that thought come from?

'They did manage to triangulate the call from Issie's mobile to an area of north-west Guildford.'

'Not precise enough to be much help.'

'No and I'm worried about the press. They're calling Saxby Enterprises non-stop and there's a risk that they'll pick up on the ransom demand.'

Cooper looked sceptical.

'Norman's decided we need a contingency plan just in case. Bernstein's sorting it out.'

Cooper's hand jerked and spilt tea onto the carpet.

'Who?'

'Deidre Bernstein; do you know her?'

'Too well. She's the bi—the one who handled the internal investigation into me last year.'

'The one who found you blameless?'

'Almost, if you remember; she's not someone I'd like to bump into again. So I'll be off tomorrow morning sharpish.'

'What will you do with yourself?'

'Why, do you need a hand?'

'I wouldn't mind benefiting from the Cooper nose.'

'The one my wife accuses of being into everything?'

'That's the one.' He leant over to where his jacket was hanging on the back of a chair and rummaged in the pocket. 'These are copies of stills of the search volunteers. Bazza and his team are going over them but while you're sniffing about, see if you think anything smells.'

'No problem.' Cooper stretched and yawned prodigiously. 'I'll leave you to your beauty sleep. Remember, at least five hours.'

'Five hours, hmm,' Fenwick glanced at his watch. 'Do you want a wake-up call at four-thirty-three precisely?'

'Bugger that!' Cooper stood up, scratching his stomach. 'I'm retired, mate, which means I'm going to enjoy the luxury of a full seven. G'night.'

'Good night, Bob. And don't snore; you're only next door and it'll keep me awake.'

'Do I ever?'

The answer was yes but Fenwick was dead to the world before the first reverberations penetrated the party wall.

His alarm went off at four-fifteen and he pressed the snooze button in his sleep, surfacing ten minutes later when it buzzed again. He was suddenly wide awake, adrenaline directing his movements in a way that left his brain behind. He showered, managed a bad shave with a disposable razor and was dressed before a quarter to five. In his socks, Fenwick padded downstairs and found his way to a kitchen twice as large as the first flat he had owned. He worked the espresso machine by instinct. His first coffee of the day was so good he poured another and then forced himself to eat a mound of toast in order to absorb the caffeine that was mixing with his adrenaline to produce a dangerously strong cocktail that would consume his energy too quickly.

He rang Chief Constable Norman at six o'clock to be briefed on the plans for the day.

'The Home Office called me last night. They want real-time updating on any significant development. You still want to be at the drop itself?'

'Of course, sir.'

'If this goes wrong Fenwick . . . are you sure?'

'The answer is still yes.'

'Is this for real do you think? He hasn't offered any proof of life.' Fenwick grunted. 'I hate these crimes. What must her parents be going through?'

Fenwick thought back to the time Bess had been taken by a suspected murderess. She had been gone less than a day but the anxiety had been crippling.

'A hell neither you nor I can imagine, sir.'

'And Rod Saxby, do you think he's involved?'

'In the kidnap; as the brains behind it?' Fenwick paused, 'I don't think so. Jane Saxby blames him for everything but he couldn't have made the second call and if he was going to hire someone I think he'd have chosen a professional. This is opportunistic or a hoax.'

'You mean someone found Issie, picked her up and kept her?'

'Possibly, or maybe it didn't start out as abduction but ended up that way.'

'Which increases the chance that she's dead, doesn't it?'

'Yes. Amateurs make mistakes, professionals don't. Even if she is still alive, I think the chances of us recovering her unharmed are low. If he's an opportunistic amateur he might have let her see his face. She may even know his identity. At some stage this is going to occur to him and he might force himself to kill her, even if he's kept her alive up to now. The money is his attempt to find a way out. It would explain why the initial ransom was so low.' Fenwick lost his appetite and put down his piece of toast.

'He wasn't thinking straight but by the second demand he's planning his escape.'

'Exactly; he's realised he needs to have something to live on.'

'We had a sniff from the press last night on the ransom demand but the PO fobbed them off. I'm about to spoil Bernstein's beauty sleep so that she can work on a contingency plan with the press officer. Horrible thought.'

'Sir?'

'Bernstein in bed.' Fenwick held his tongue. 'You two getting on all right?'

'Coping with each other; she resents me on her patch and I understand her feelings. It isn't getting in the way.'

'Good. She has a reputation for being prickly – which is politically correct speak for impossible to work with – but I want to keep her as Silver. She's one of my most senior female officers and she'd never let me forget it if I didn't. If you can keep the peace and still make good progress, I'd appreciate it.'

'Of course.'

'I have an excellent officer in charge on location today; Jim Perkins. He's the best. All the team are hand-picked by me.' There was a muttered expletive. 'Is that the time? I've got a briefing planned in thirty-five minutes. I need to go.'

'I could call Bernstein if you like, sir. She'll need to sort out the publicity officer before she starts on Rod Saxby.'

'She's holding him?'

'Flight risk; he avoided us all day and there's a suspicion he might have abused Issie.'

'You wait until his brother finds out that he's in custody. Any points you've scored will disappear faster than a whippet up a hare's arse.'

'I'm hoping that he'll be so focused on finding his stepdaughter that he won't even remember Rod until the operation's over and if he does I'll leave him to Lady Saxby.'

Bernstein was predictably annoyed that Fenwick had spoken to Norman directly. She accused him of keeping her out so that he could take all the glory.

'Or the pain,' he reminded her. 'I'm not confident that this is going to end well.'

'And I suppose you'll blame the crap initial investigation if it doesn't.'

'That remark doesn't even deserve a reply. How you can think about recriminations and covering your own backside when a seventeen-year-old girl is still missing and we've an imminent meeting with her supposed kidnapper is beyond me.'

The words slipped out before he could stop himself, his anger fuelled by worry for Issie, adrenaline and the coffee . . . and he had just been asked by the chief constable to keep her sweet! He heard an intake of breath.

'You're right,' she said at last. 'That was stupid and I'd be grateful if you could forget everything I've said from my grudging good morning until now.'

Fenwick confirmed their previous conversation had never happened.

'Apart from interviewing Rod Saxby and the press side of things, what else does Norman expect me to do?'

His momentary silence said it all.

'So I'm the Silver with bugger all to do beyond PR; great. But I suppose you're allowed to be at the drop-off?'

'Yes.'

'Bloody typical. Well, whether he likes it or not I'm going to join Norman at HQ while he relies on his pal Jim. It'll be better than biting the rest of my nails off in the incident room and wishing I was with you.'

It was honestly said and the call ended almost amicably. Fenwick wondered why she had such a bad rep, then mentally criticised himself for being a fool. She was tough and refused to put up with anything she thought a slur on her character. He realised he had been on the verge of treating her just as programmed: as a difficult woman with too much attitude and not worth getting to know. Did that mean that, deep inside, he was as much a misogynist as the colleagues he looked down on?

With a pang he realised he missed Louise Nightingale. She was the best partner he had ever had. He still regretted that they no longer worked together. With her around it had been second nature to treat women as equals; since he had moved to MCS his world was a duller place.

He shook himself and made fresh coffee. The money was due to arrive at six-thirty and he expected the Saxbys to be awake despite their pills. There was still no sign of their cook so he laid out a tray, added fresh toast, marmalade and butter and made his way through to the sitting room, where Tony the FLO was already awake, waiting for the family and the start of the day in which they might have their daughter returned to them . . . hopefully alive.

CHAPTER SIXTEEN

Mariner woke up starving hungry, stiff and bitterly cold. The stove was out of fuel so he had to go out to the car for more oil. He was shocked at how much snow had fallen. When he returned he realised that it was bitterly cold inside. If he hadn't woken up, he would have died! The realisation scared him. He relit the stove and huddled close but couldn't stop shaking despite the sleeping bag and layers of clothes he had pulled on. The girl lay on the mattress, unmoving. The previous night he had remembered to cover her in a mound of blankets and old newspapers before he went to sleep. She was a constant reminder of a reality his mind had been working hard to deny.

He tried but failed to go back to sleep. At five-thirty he lit a hurricane lamp and the camping gaz to heat water for a brew. All trace of the previous day's euphoria had vanished to be replaced by an unshakeable sense of doom. He looked back at recent events in astonishment, as if they had happened to someone else, unable still to believe that Dan was actually dead; that he was the proud possessor of a teenage girl, tied up against her will; and that Monday night's quest for casual sex had slipped into kidnap and then murder.

NO! Not murder. Dan had died in a stupid accident, which was why he needed the money; to get away.

The idea of Lord Saxby waiting at the end of the phone for a call to summon him to a secret location – one he reminded himself that he had as little idea of as Saxby – made him shake with fear. What had he been thinking of? He dozed as he waited for the water to boil and dreamt briefly of being chased by giant white huskies through a forest of venomous plants. His bladder forced him awake.

He stepped outside to relieve himself. His breath and urine steamed in the freezing air as he tried to write his name, watching the stain on the snow. He gave himself a vigorous shake, zipped up and stuffed his hands in his pockets. The fingers of his right hand brushed her mobile phone and he pulled it out, holding it tight in his palm like a talisman. He knew it was dangerous, which is why it was switched off so it couldn't be traced.

'Never should have used it,' he said to the empty space around him, fringed by the fingers of skeletal trees black against a dark yellow-grey sky but he held onto it, indecisive, hating to throw away a good phone that might come in handy.

A waking rook cawed loudly from the top of a nearby tree making him jump. It was time to get ready. He had things to do, money to collect and places to run to.

It took him five minutes to pack what he needed, a further five to smoke a second morning cigarette but he couldn't pluck up the courage to leave the pump house. He kept staring at the immovable bundle under the newspapers, edging towards it, hand outstretched as if she were a wild creature, before backing away again.

'There's plenty of food here,' he called out, his words bouncing off the brickwork. 'And I've heated up some soup for your breakfast; it's a lentil one.'

He hated lentils but they were meant to be good for you and it made him feel better to think he was leaving her something nourishing.

The bundle didn't stir. Maybe he should check to see if she was all right. Was she even still alive? He had no idea but it would be untrue to say that he didn't care. It was important for him to believe that she was OK. Last night, when he'd forced some of his soup into her, through chattering lips that showed blue in the light of the storm lantern, he had held her tight. She was so little, slumped against him, the top of her head barely reaching his chin. He had chafed her bound arms and legs before bundling her into one of his old tracksuits he had brought with him. At the last minute he had put more blankets and his parka around her on top of the anorak, reasoning that he could easily buy another with the money he was going to collect.

Now she was lying just as he had left her, her face hidden except for a band of forehead that looked white in the gaslight. Maybe he should untie her; he was going to lock the door with one of his padlocks anyway so she wouldn't be able to escape.

He walked over to the wall barely making a sound and pulled the knot apart.

'There, you can move around now.'

There was no answer.

'Do you want to go, er, you know, outside, before I lock up?'

Nothing. He bent down and shook her shoulder.

'I said—'

THWACK! Suddenly he was sprawled on his side, his chin numb from the blow from her fists as they connected with skin and bone. He lay there stunned, blinking to clear his eyes while she hobbled towards the open door!

'You little . . .' He lunged after her, still on his knees.

His hand caught the end of the cord that was dangling from her wrists and he yanked on it, pulling her down onto her back yards from the doorway.

'No!' The girl struggled to rise to her feet.

He scrabbled towards her, keeping tension on the rope until she was within reach.

'Bad girl,' he said, and rapped the back of her head with his

169

knuckles in admonishment, too relieved to have caught her to be really angry.

'Let me go!' She struggled within his grip, lively as a wildcat with nails sharp as claws. Fingers scratched the side of his face and his good humour vanished.

'Enough.' This time the slap was hard enough to shut her up.

He threw her back to the floor, his trust in her docile dependence irreparably damaged.

'There's food over there; I'm going to watch you eat before I retie and gag you.'

He expected her to refuse but to his surprise she sat and ate the soup, then drank hot tea to which she added a ridiculous amount of sugar. She kept asking whether he was going to let her go. He told her yes, of course, later that day, but he could tell from her expression that she didn't believe him and he didn't blame her.

With his suitcase and passport, he could drive the eighty miles to Portsmouth and try and use his credit card to buy a ticket for a ferry. If he left now maybe he could be at sea within five hours. He could have lunch in France, hire a car and be off. Except that he was out of money and his credit limit for the month had already run out.

'Why don't you have a cash card in your bag like a normal person?'

'They have to stay in the safe at school.'

'Someone like you could have more than one.'

Something in the way she looked away made him wonder. He picked up her bag and shook it. It was just a small pack that slipped over her shoulders. She was trying really hard not to look at him but he could tell she was holding her breath.

'Where is it?'

She took a slurp of tea and ignored him so he rapped his knuckles hard on her head. He knew it had to hurt because his mum had done it to him innumerable times; the bruises never showed, you see, so child protection never got to know. She didn't make a sound.

'Next time, I'll break your nose and when I put in the gag you won't be able to breathe. Don't be stupid.'

He watched as she calculated; just like his bloody wife, never straightforward, always weighing up the pros and cons before giving a simple answer.

'Reach inside the zip pocket. There's a hole in the lining. I've got a spare one in there.'

'Smart girl.' He passed her a bourbon biscuit.

He made her tell him the pin number, which she did surprisingly easily.

'If this is false . . .'

'It's not, I promise. And I never break a promise.'

'What's your daily limit?'

'One hundred.'

Not enough to fund an escape, even if the card worked. He had no choice but to go through with the ransom demand.

She asked to be let outside to relieve herself and he let her go behind some bushes, holding on tight to the rope around her wrists, his back turned to give her some privacy. Afterwards he retied her to the ring, inserted the gag and settled her down on the mattress. He left the oil stove on beyond her reach. The remaining fuel wouldn't last more than a few hours but he didn't plan on leaving her that long.

'The door's going to be locked. No point trying to escape,' he called out as he left.

He didn't have an ice scraper so used his useless credit card to clear the windscreen as the heaters blasted on full power.

Where should he tell Saxby to drop off the money? The question fell into the chaos of his thoughts as he sat in the car with the engine running. Although he hadn't planned the day he assumed that he would be returning at some point to do something with the girl; he couldn't just leave her there, could he?

Instead of answering his own question his mind slipped back to the bigger problem: how to collect the money Saxby had promised him the day before. Without realising he had done so he put the car into gear and drove away. As he reached the outskirts of Guildford he noticed that he was almost out of diesel so he pulled up at the next petrol station and put in a tank's worth. He offered the cashier his credit card, holding his breath as it was swiped. A frown crossed the youth's spotty face and he tried the card again, waited, then shook his head.

'Not going through, mate. Got another?'

He offered her card, hoping the lad was too stupid to check the name. He was in luck.

'Pin number?'

It was written down on a piece of paper in his wallet but he hadn't memorised it and to pull it out might look suspicious.

'Bloody forgotten haven't I.' He forced himself to chuckle sheepishly. 'Always do.'

He smiled at the boy, man to man; treating him as equal.

'No worries; I can override it. Just sign here.'

Sign. He had no idea what the signature on the back of her card would look like but he guessed it would be neat so he bent and wrote carefully: *I. Mattias*.

The slip was taken without comment and filed away in the cash register with dozens of others. There was an impatient cough from somewhere behind him.

'I said here you go, mate.' The card was being waved under his nose. 'You all right?'

He blinked and shook his head, aware that he had been staring at the boy's hands, watching the evidence against his fraud instead of taking her card and leaving the shop as quickly as possible.

'Yeah, miles away. Cheers.'

He was still shaking when he pulled into a café two miles

down the road and ordered coffee and a bacon sandwich. The waitress gave him a funny look so he smiled at her. All he got was a raised eyebrow. There was a battered map of the area on the wall by the door. While he waited for his food he took his coffee and studied it. He had instructed Saxby not to tell the police and he thought the man would follow his orders – he had sounded scared on the phone. Even so, he wanted somewhere he could escape from easily.

His eyes roamed the grubby plastic, his finger tracing in wider and wider circles. Nowhere seemed right. If he went for the town centre there was a danger he would be seen as he returned to his car. On the outskirts of town there were plenty of places to drop off a bag but none he could see that offered an easy escape.

'. . . I said your food's going cold.'

'What? Oh thanks, love,' he said smiling again.

'I'm not your love and I want you out of my place as soon as you've finished. I have my standards and I don't care how long you've been on the road – you need a good wash and a shave.'

Embarrassed and angry he slouched back to his table, wrapped the bacon roll in the paper napkin and threw a small note from his precious bundle onto the laminated table cloth.

Stuck up cow. She reminded him of his wife, not a pleasant thought, but her suggestion had given him an idea for what to say to Saxby when he called him.

CHAPTER SEVENTEEN

'The public swimming baths; in twenty minutes,' Saxby repeated steadily. 'It will take me longer than that to drive there, let alone park.'

Fenwick nodded encouragingly. '*Keep him talking; buy us time to stake out the location,*' had been the simple instruction.

'Twenty minutes is all you've got.' The voice was muffled as before but Fenwick, listening on headphones, thought it sounded more aggressive.

'Please, I want to do what you say but twenty minutes really is impossible.'

Saxby had found just the tone of firm supplication that Fenwick could have wished for.

They had had a conference call with a criminal psychologist an hour before to try and assess the mental condition of the supposed kidnapper. Fenwick insisted that Saxby participate, convinced he was strong enough to cope with whatever would be discussed and he had been right. Even when there was frank debate about whether the caller really had Issie, and if he did what the chances were of her still being alive, Saxby had reacted remarkably well. Fenwick's confidence in him was being rewarded as he played his part to perfection.

'Why? You've got a bloody big BMW, shouldn't be a problem for you,' the kidnapper was arguing.

'I don't want to risk a speeding ticket or being pulled over for careless driving in this weather. The last thing we need is for me to draw attention to myself.'

'Hmm.'

'And you know what parking in Guildford's like on a Friday this close to Christmas,' this said man to man as if they were mates sharing a moan about their wives' shopping.

To Fenwick's surprise there was a low chuckle from the caller.

'Too right; took me fifteen minutes to find a place.'

'Is it that bad already?'

'Terrible.'

'I suppose I could always get the bus; never done it before, but if I need to, of course I will. I don't suppose you know the times do you?'

'Look, don't rely on the bus. Tell you what; I'll give you an hour until nine-thirty. OK?'

'Thank you. Where do you want me to leave the bag?'

'In the litter bin in front of the main entrance; the one on the right with green and white stripes. Put the money in a black bin liner and dump it there.'

'Just like that?'

'Just like that.'

'Sounds so simple.' It was said with a hint of admiration.

'Best plans always are.'

'You'd have made a good businessman.'

There was silence at the end of the phone and Saxby hurried on.

'Is Issie all right?'

'Yes.'

'Can I talk to her?'

'I'm hardly likely to have her with me now, am I?'

'So how do I know that you'll hand her over after you've got the money?'

'You'll just have to trust me.'

'Please, we're out of our minds with worry. Is she safe,

somewhere warm? We just want to know that our daughter's going to be OK.' Saxby's voice cracked as the weight of fear threatened to break his self-control.

Fenwick reached out a hand and squeezed the man's shoulder in support. Saxby took a deep breath. In the seconds it took to happen there was no word from the caller.

'Hello? Are you still there?'

'I'm here.'

'If you won't say anything about Issie can you . . . can you at least tell her that we love her? Please?' His voice broke and Saxby closed his eyes.

From the sofa Jane Saxby rose to go over to him. Tony held her back gently.

'One hour. Just turn up with the money and everything will be all right.'

'And after that, we'll have Issie back?'

'I'll call you when I'm safe away and tell you how to find your daughter.'

'Thank you.' The words were forced out through clenched teeth but he managed them, following the psychologist's instructions to the letter. 'One more thing—'

But the line went dead. They all looked expectantly at the lead technician crouched over his computer.

'We've got him,' he said triumphantly. 'A public call box at the swimming pool. He's already there.'

A copy of the conversation was sent to the psychologist. While she analysed it Fenwick called Norman and briefed him.

'If he's already in position you'll need to be very careful,' Norman emphasised. 'Perkins will lead the surveillance operation as Silver.'

'Understood, sir. I've been thinking, maybe we should have air surveillance . . .'

'Hotel 900 is already on standby but I won't send her up until

176

the last minute in case the sound of a helicopter spooks him. Good luck, Fenwick; we'll speak later.'

Fenwick watched Saxby being wired in preparation for the unlikely chance that he would meet the kidnapper. The money was transferred to a bin liner, the transmitter hidden deep inside one of the bundles of notes. Barely a millimetre in thickness it would be unnoticeable to anybody but an expert.

'I'm uncomfortable with the bug,' Lady Saxby paced the room. 'If this man's professional he'll look for something like that and if he finds it . . .'

'He's not a professional, isn't that right, Superintendent?' Saxby looked at Fenwick.

'Correct, and although I'm not the expert, my interpretation of the last call is that he's as keen for this to be over as we are. As soon as he leaves the swimming baths he'll head for Issie,' Fenwick paused, hating what he had to say next, 'if he has her.'

'So you still think this might be a hoax?' Despite her drug-induced sleep the previous night Jane Saxby looked on the point of collapse.

'We have to consider every possibility.'

'Including that she's already dead?' Her eyes begged him to disagree.

'All possibilities,' he said gently, 'but there's no reason to give up hope.'

She took a shuddering breath and weaved slightly before regaining her balance.

'I'd better go and get my coat,' she said simply, to the horror of the men in the room.

'You have to stay here, darling.'

'I'm coming with you.'

'He hasn't asked for you to be there. If he sees another person with me he might think it's the police. We can't risk that.'

'I will not be protected!'

'This isn't about you,' Saxby said with remarkable calm, 'it's about Issie. Her safety is our only priority. Everything we do must be driven by one thought: we want her back safe and sound.'

'Issie might be with him. What if she is? I have to be there!' But there was defeat in her voice and tears filled her eyes.

Instead of answering, Bill Saxby took a long step towards his wife and enveloped her in a hug. The sound of her crying fell against his chest.

'I want my baby back,' she sobbed. 'When she's here again we'll cancel the stupid party and then we'll go away, just the three of us. We'll show her just how much we really, really love her.'

'That's right,' he said, stroking the back of her head, though only an hour before he had listened to the combined opinion of the police and psychologist that, if Issie wasn't dead already, she could be within hours.

'It's time to go,' Fenwick said quietly.

'You'll have to excuse my moment of stupidity,' she said and wiped her eyes.

'It's understandable.'

'Maybe, but it doesn't help Issie, does it?'

On his way to the swimming baths Fenwick was called by Bazza Holland from the incident room at the school.

'Issie's bank has contacted us. We've had a watch put on her account and they told us her second cash card—'

'Second card? Why didn't we know?'

'God knows, anyway it was used at seven thirty-eight this morning at a service station on the A31 just outside Guildford. I've sent someone over to collect the security tape and interview the cashier who accepted payment.'

'Thanks, keep me posted. How did Rod Saxby take his night in the cells?'

'Loudly. He's threatening to sue.'

'Did you and Bernstein learn anything from the interview?'

'Only that he hates his new niece and her mother and doesn't mind admitting the fact; said they were after his brother's money.'

'He's a fine one to talk.'

'Exactly, but one thing is relevant: the chain he wears has a medallion identical to the one Issie painted. Even if he's in the clear for the abduction we might get him for abuse once we find Issie. He's a deluded little shit, s'cuse my French. In his version of reality he's key to the company's success. He claims all the best contracts were down to his deal-making skills.'

'Doesn't ring true to me. Watching Saxby on the phone this morning handling the kidnapper it's obvious he's a born negotiator.' Fenwick sighed. 'So what have you done with him?'

'We've had to let him go as he admitted nothing and we had no basis to charge him. As I left he was yelling at his solicitor to draft a formal complaint.'

'Great. Anything more from the school?'

'It's still early but Bernstein has teams dedicated to following up on the maintenance man and the music teacher. Are we missing anything, d'you think?'

'If you have time you could talk to Issie's teachers again in case they've remembered something; and ask the bursar to tell you what he knows about the non-teaching staff. The kidnapper doesn't sound educated. Don't reveal the ransom demand to anyone but probe to see who at the school might have a money motive. Has the lab found anything more interesting on the bedding from Issie's room?'

'There's no news. I'll chase them.'

'If necessary threaten them with the Home Office; that should sort their priorities out.' With Issie missing since Monday night he was willing to use any tactic.

Fenwick arrived at the rendezvous point a safe distance from the swimming pool to be briefed on the surveillance arrangements by Jim Perkins. They agreed that he would go to the swimming baths and stay in the control van they had there. The car park was full when he arrived and he had to leave his car on the street outside. There were double yellow lines and he couldn't afford to put his official permit in the window in case the kidnapper saw it so he took the risk of being clamped.

Two white vans with commercial lettering on their sides were parked by the car park exits. One proclaimed plumbing services, the other twenty-four-hour van hire. Concealed inside the first were six men in bulletproof vests, with the officer up front wearing dirty white overalls specially trained in high-speed driving. Fenwick entered the other van. The familiar sight of the interior of a mobile surveillance unit greeted him.

Around the car park and by the building itself, six unmarked cars were positioned within a fifteen-yard radius of the rubbish bin. In two of them the drivers were behind the wheel; one, a woman, was drinking coffee and supposedly talking on a mobile phone, the other looked asleep. The rest of the occupants were spread inside and outside the building, posing as maintenance men or mothers waiting for their children to finish their swimming lesson. More were concealed out of sight in the security office behind the reception area. In total Norman had twenty-five officers at the swimming pool in addition to manned unmarked cars waiting outside every exit and on each road that led away in case the surveillance teams couldn't follow immediately because of traffic congestion.

It was twenty-eight minutes past nine. Saxby had arrived five minutes before and was now locking his car under the lens of CCTV security cameras. Images from the cameras had been looped in to the screens in the vans in addition to those from their own surveillance. Fenwick watched the foreshortened grainy black and white pictures; Perkins' voice was a whisper over the radio that linked him to the officers on the team.

'Bear one has arrived and is locking car. Making his way now to porridge.' It was a stupid code system but the random name generated by the computer for the operation was Goldilocks – somehow appropriate for the season.

Saxby didn't hurry; he was a little early and keen to follow the kidnapper's instructions precisely. He kept his eyes straight ahead, ignoring the temptation to look around for the police. At nine-thirty he dropped the bag in the bin, looked at it for a second before walking back to his car. As instructed, he then drove away.

Seconds passed, then minutes. There was an ebb and flow of people entering and leaving the building, mainly toddlers with parents bundled up against the freezing cold but no one wandered over to the bin and lifted the bag. By ten o'clock various crisp packets, empty drinks cans and other rubbish had been discarded on top and someone asked over the radio how much longer they were going to wait. Perkins told them to be patient.

At five minutes past ten, one of the surveillance team radioed in.

'Potential mummy bear has just walked past point bravo. Solitary man, early thirties, approximately five eight, wearing Puma trainers, a grey tracksuit with hood up and brown jacket over the top.'

'We have him on camera; stand by, this could be our man.'

There was silence as the subject walked briskly towards the swimming pool entrance, his shoulders hunched against the cold. When he was almost there he was intercepted by a pool maintenance worker who appeared to have stepped out for a cigarette. The man in the tracksuit stopped abruptly and they punched hands, talking for a couple of minutes while the maintenance man smoked before they headed off in different directions. Neither went near the bag.

'False alarm.'

It started to snow. The drivers waiting in the cars asked if they could turn on the engines. Perkins relented and said yes. The watchers outside started to take it in turns to go into the reception area to keep warm.

181

Perkins ignored the growing moans from the team and waited. Fenwick supported his decision. A halt was called to the operation at one o'clock and the money retrieved.

'He's not coming,' Fenwick muttered to himself, 'no one would be able to leave half a million pounds sitting in that bin being covered by snow for this long. Bugger!' He hit the wall beside him. 'Bugger, BUGGER, BUGGER!'

It was the only sign of emotion he had shown throughout the operation and it released a torrent of frustration in the team around him. Fenwick sat in the middle of their storm of blasphemy with eyes closed until it died down.

'I suppose we had better go and see the Saxbys, tell them the news.' He spoke into the radio. 'Jim, do you want to come?'

Perkins declined.

'I'm going to see Norman. He's bound to want a case conference. See you there.'

'Why didn't he show up, sir?' someone asked.

'Who knows? Maybe it was a hoax; maybe it wasn't. Either way, something happened or he lost his nerve. We need to find out.'

'Did he spot us?'

'I doubt it, but if he calls again he'll be sure to let us know if he did.'

Fenwick called the psychologist as he drove back to Saxby Hall and told her the news.

'It's not entirely unexpected,' she said dispassionately. 'We discussed the possibility this morning, remember, and concluded that if he didn't have the girl or was an amateur his nerve might fail.'

'On the call to confirm arrangements he seemed surer of himself.'

'It was still fantasy then, something he could envisage controlling. When it came to having the guts to walk over to the bin and lift the bag then reality struck.'

'Will he try again?'

'There's a chance, as long as he believes that the police know nothing about the ransom demand and he needs the money. What are you going to tell the parents?'

'That we're doing everything we can to find their daughter; that there's a chance she's still alive . . .'

'Do you really believe that?'

'I have to . . . We have news her spare bank card has been used. That at least is concrete.'

'Good luck.'

They were waiting for him in the sitting room. The fire blazed, incongruously cheerful. He noticed a bare Christmas tree by the front window, which must have been delivered while he was out. Neither of them looked up as he entered. Tony was pouring coffee into mugs. When he had finished he offered a plate of biscuits to Jane Saxby but she stared through them.

Fenwick sat down on the sofa opposite, noting how Bill Saxby was stroking the back of his wife's hand above nails that had been bitten raw to the quick.

'He didn't show up,' he said simply. 'I'm sorry.'

'Not your fault,' Saxby replied, his voice hoarse. 'Looks like a bloody hoax after all. You always said it might be. We just wanted to believe so much that it was real, that we'd get Issie back.' His voice broke.

Jane glanced up at the clock.

'I thought she might be with us by now,' she murmured, 'cold, hungry, frightened, of course, but with us. I've got her favourite pyjamas warming in the airing cupboard and we've bought all the food she likes.'

The men watched her, waiting for the crying to start but she held onto her self-control, even when her husband pulled her into his chest and kissed the top of her head.

'What are your plans now, Superintendent?' he asked, eyes moist, looking away.

'We maintain the trace on your phones in case he calls. Meanwhile, there are other leads and the search continues.'

He told them about the use of Issie's second bank card that morning, cautioning that they shouldn't assume it was their daughter who had used it.

'We'll know more when we've studied the security tape from the garage. I'm going back to HQ now. We still have to behave as if he's watching the Hall so all our comings and goings will be discreet. Even so, we need to agree a cover story.

'In case he rings and asks who I am, I'm Lady Saxby's physician and Tony is a favourite nephew who's come to stay. He won't have seen Jeff,' he pointed to the technician sipping coffee patiently by the equipment and the Saxbys looked at him in surprise, as if the idea of him having a name hadn't occurred to them.

Fenwick stood up, relieved that they could leave two highly skilled officers at the Hall.

'If anything happens, I'll call you straight away. Don't despair, there's still plenty for us to work on.'

They nodded in synchronised pain. Saxby made to stand to see him out but Fenwick waved him back down and shook hands in farewell.

The incident room had been moved to HQ that morning. It was unnaturally quiet when Fenwick entered. So much had happened in the last twenty-four hours but with the failed pickup it felt as if the case had gone cold. Rod Saxby had been released; there was still no sign of Issie and the kidnapper remained a mystery man.

'Have the fingerprints from the payphone been sent off?' Fenwick asked the room and a civilian clerk answered.

'Yes, sir. Inspector Perkins had CST there within fifteen minutes of his call dressed as maintenance so hopefully they'll have some of his.'

'Good; cross-check them immediately against the ones we

lifted from the security pad by the gate that Issie used on Monday night. What about the service station videotape?'

'Already being processed, sir,' Bazza walked in unwinding a thick scarf from his neck. 'Jake's taken it to Tech and will come back with stills ASAP. We'll be able to compare them with photos of St Anne's employees from their records and with the pictures of the volunteers in the search team, plus all the coverage of the swimming pool.'

'Any news from Deidre?'

'She's taken over the search at the YMCA.'

It wasn't a job she should have been doing but Fenwick understood why she had exiled herself to the chilly youth hostel. He knew how she felt. He wasn't sure whether he would be asked to stay on or dismissed after the morning's debacle. Any hope of him being a miracle worker must surely have disappeared.

'Right, well I'd better go and see the CC,' he said without enthusiasm.

Norman was waiting for him with Jim Perkins already in his office. He asked them relevant questions, offered few observations and spent most of the meeting debating theories. Like Perkins, he favoured the hypothesis that the ransom demand had been a hoax. Their discussion did nothing to make Fenwick feel better. It was illogical, and he wouldn't allow himself to dwell on the thought, but he couldn't help feeling responsible for the morning's fiasco. Norman confirmed that he was going to retain personal command of the investigation. Fenwick was welcome to spend the rest of the day and weekend on the case but he had already called the Home Office who had agreed that Fenwick could be reassigned back to MCS from Monday.

Fenwick had expected as much and nodded acceptance. Stepping out of Norman's office he decided he needed a coffee and headed down to the cafeteria. The air outside the stair windows looked as if two giants were having a pillow fight. The sky was full of swirling snow, large soft flakes caught in eddies between the buildings, moving in all directions before settling in drifts on the frozen ground below. Fenwick's heart went out to the police team searching for Issie. There wouldn't be many volunteers today.

He took his mug to a small table at the end of the almost empty room. He was slurping the boiling hot liquid, too impatient to wait for it to cool, when his mobile phone rang. He glanced at the caller id and closed his eyes.

'Hello, sweetheart,' he said in a half whisper, 'I'm so sorry I didn't call you this morning but it's been a very busy day.'

'Daddy, where are you? It's Friday and you promised to take me shopping as soon as school was finished! I need a dress for the school disco and you said we'd get it today, that it would be my special Christmas dress, like every year, and the tree needs decorating and Alice won't let us do it without you here because she says the lights have to go on first and you need to check they're all right and if we don't there might be an electrical fault and then the house will burn down and we'll all die in our beds and how would you like that, and I want to gather ivy from the garden like we did last year to put on the banisters and the fireplace and Chris wants a snowman and he's in one of his moods and won't come out of his bedroom and Alice says she's had enough of us and . . .'

Fenwick lowered his forehead into his hand as her words lanced through him, bringing stinging cuts of guilt. He had forgotten the promise and that it was meant to be his day off. There was no way he could go home. The alternative was for her to go shopping with Alice but his housekeeper complained about the loud music in the stores and disapproved of Bess's increasingly adolescent dress sense.

'I'm going to be working for the rest of the day, love,' he explained as he stood up and started to walk out his tension.

'What about tomorrow instead?'

It was one of his last days on the case.

'I can't make any promises.'

'What's so important that you can't be bothered to spend time with your family this close to Christmas?'

Fenwick missed the little girl who understood why her daddy worked late and was proud of what he did for other people. Twelve-year-old Bess was becoming a handful and too often he was left without the words to manage her. He lowered his voice.

'A girl has gone missing . . .'

'And she's more important than I am, is that it?'

'Bess, how can you say that?' He struggled to keep disappointment from his tone.

'Well it's true, isn't it? Everybody's more important to you than we are. You take us for granted, assuming we'll just be here when you're ready for us. It's not fair!'

'I know it's difficult for you, love—'

'No you don't, you have no idea what it's like for us stuck here with Alice, with you out being self-important, worrying more about your job than your family.'

'That's not true, but there are times when other people's lives are as important. It's my job to—'

'Your job! How many times do we have to hear that? I'm fed up with your job! I want a daddy who loves us, who comes home when he says he will and who wants to spend time with us because we're the most important people in the world! That's the sort of daddy I want.' She burst into tears.

'Bess, please. I love you and Chris more than anything in the world,' he whispered.

Continued sobbing greeted his words.

'Bess . . .'

'I don't want to talk to you.'

The connection went dead.

'Damn,' he whispered to himself, looking around instinctively to see if anyone had overheard but all he saw were hunched backs of indifference.

He drained the rest of his coffee and went to buy another. He was still drinking it when Bazza came running into the room pink-faced and breathless.

'There you are! Some bloke called Bob's on the phone for you. Said he tried your mobile but it was busy and he needs to talk to you urgently.'

Fenwick outpaced him as they returned to the incident room and snatched up the receiver.

'It's Bob. Anything new since the bust this morning?'

'Nothing.'

'Bugger.'

'My thoughts exactly.'

'Well I'm glad I decided to call. Look, I may have something. I've been digging around at the school, where they're being very cooperative soon as I say who I'm working for.

'Anyway, I showed them the pics of the volunteers and they identified one of them as a maintenance man-cum-gardener at the school, one Steven Mariner. Not much in that but the man hasn't shown up for work since Wednesday. I called his missus and she was spitting feathers. She's just come back from her mother's to find that someone has cleared out her store cupboard and stolen most of their camping gear. And there's no sign of her husband either. He's not answering her calls. I'm driving over there now but thought maybe you'd want to make this official.'

'I do! What's the address?'

'Twenty-six Goosegreen Avenue, it's on the outskirts of Guildford, to the north.'

'Hang on; map!' Fenwick demanded and Bazza called up Guildford A to Z on his computer. Fenwick gave him the address. Seconds later he said, 'It's within the triangulated location from the mobile service provider.'

'Bob, we're sending a team over. Hold off until they arrive.'

'No problem.'

'That was Saxby's private detective,' he explained to Bazza, 'he's got a lead.'

'And knew enough to call us rather than bumble in? That's a first.' Bazza watched Fenwick pick up his jacket and followed his example. 'What is it?

'Steven Mariner . . .'

'He's the odd-job bloke I'm still trying to find for a second interview. What about him?'

'I'll tell you on the way. Cobb, can you alert Operations that we might need a crime scene team and then join us at 26 Goosegreen Avenue as soon as you can?'

Cobb's face flushed. Fenwick recognised guilt and glared at the man.

'Out with it.'

'There was a call from Mrs Mariner to the station this morning. She was reporting a possible break-in. When the duty officer there heard her husband worked at St Anne's he sent a copy of the report over. I was going to put it on your desk but it didn't seem that important . . .'

'You tosspot.' Bazza couldn't contain himself.

'Enough.' Fenwick didn't have time to waste on recriminations. 'Cobb, call Operations as I told you. Bazza, get in touch with Superintendent Bernstein and tell her where to meet us.'

His phone rang as he was leaving the building.

'Fenwick.'

'Andrew, it's Deidre Bernstein.'

'Am I glad you've called. We've just—'

'Andrew, whatever you have to say can wait.' Bernstein's tone put him on instant alert.

'What is it?'

'We've found a body.'

CHAPTER EIGHTEEN

Fenwick agreed with Bernstein that DS Holland should proceed to Goosegreen Avenue and told him to allow Bob Cooper to enter. He ignored Bazza's raised eyebrows and took a separate car with driver to meet Bernstein. The deteriorating road conditions made the journey difficult so he was out of patience already before he walked into the miasma of her foul mood.

Bernstein was tapping her foot outside a dilapidated caravan. Scene of crime technicians hadn't finished their work so none of the detectives had been allowed to enter. Fenwick was given extra-large sterile blue coveralls and he put them on over his winter coat, the hood loose on his back. As the short afternoon darkened, the dingy clearing transformed into an arena of combat between murder and modern science. Outside the perimeter Bernstein's team were conducting a fingertip search despite the snow and poor light.

While he waited Fenwick listened to the officer who had found the body of a male, thirty-something, about six feet tall; throat cut, probably at the scene given the amount of blood. The officer had followed procedure. Apart from searching the scene for anyone else he hadn't touched anything. Bernstein could add little. She had contacted the Land Registry for the owner of the site only to be told that it would be shut until Monday. The chief constable had been dragged in to find the mayor and have the office opened urgently.

Fenwick called Bazza and asked him to send to his mobile

a photograph of Steven Mariner. He received two: one from his wedding too small to be helpful and a better one of Mariner drinking with another man. He showed them to the officer who was first on the scene.

'Could the body belong to this man?'

The officer squinted at the pictures and angled the phone into the spotlight. As soon as the beam hit the photo of the two men he nodded.

'The fat one on the right, it's him, I'm sure.'

'On the right, you're sure? Not the other one?'

'Positive.'

Fenwick called Bazza to find out who was in the shot with Mariner.

'It's Dan Mariner, his brother. Apparently they're very close.'

Fenwick motioned for Bernstein to follow him and found a quiet space to talk. He told her about the reported theft from Goosegreen Avenue, Steven Mariner's disappearance, how he worked at St Anne's and had volunteered for the search on day one but had subsequently disappeared.

'So this may be connected. Who killed him; his brother? Issie? Did the brothers have her?' Bernstein chewed gum with aggression.

'Good questions. We need to find out urgently when Dan Mariner died. Are those technician's ever going to finish?'

They continued to wait. Bernstein paced up and down beyond the perimeter, packing the snow into dirty brown ice beneath the spotlights. The mobile scene of crime unit was stuck in snow at the far end of the track leading to the clearing. They were just thinking of going back there to warm up when there was a call from the caravan steps.

'All yours! We'll continue once the body's been removed.'

'At last.' Fenwick put on protective shoe covers and almost fell over.

He slipped his way up the breeze blocks that served the van as steps. Behind him a black Range Rover crawled down the track that led to the site, the driver carefully avoiding the fishtailing that had befallen all other vehicles. Fenwick watched, his brow creasing in concern in case it was a journalist. His expression changed when a large woman, dressed in a puffer jacket that made her look like the Michelin man, climbed out, doctor's bag in hand. She was wearing stout crêpe-soled shoes that carried her firmly across the ice. One of the CSTs took one look at her and put away the blue coverall they had been holding out and passed over instead a man's size, extra-extra-large.

'Doctor Patricia Jamieson,' she said in a falsetto that was out of keeping with her bulk, 'Patty to my friends. It's taken me forever to get here – sorry. There are cars abandoned everywhere and I had to double-back and find another way.'

She held out a hand and Fenwick shook it.

'Superintendent Andrew Fenwick; this is Superintendent Bernstein. You're the new pathologist, Pendlebury's replacement?'

'The same. Now where's the stiff? At least I imagine he will be whatever time he died in this miserable weather.' Her giggle was a little girl's.

Fenwick blinked but didn't laugh.

'He's in there.'

She put on the overall and squeezed through the door with some difficulty, puffing with the effort of climbing the steps. Fenwick and Bernstein exchanged a glance and followed. Dr Jamieson paused a few feet from a man's body sprawled on a decrepit sofa sodden with his blood. Arterial spray coated the ceiling and walls in a crimson umbrella. The corpse's bleached left hand clutched at a gaping hole in the side of his neck. His face was turned away from the door so all Fenwick could see was the side of his head.

Jamieson stepped forward, whistling tunelessly. She crouched down by the body and extended a finger to touch the man's arm in a surprisingly gentle gesture.

'They've taken all the photographs you need?' Her breath misted in the air.

'Yes. Is cause of death as obvious as it looks?'

'If it was, you wouldn't need me except to pronounce, would you?' The whistling resumed, punctuated by small grunts of effort as she moved. She pushed against muscles in the man's jaw, frowned and took a long thermometer from her bag. As she inserted it Fenwick looked away.

'Has that door been open ever since you lot discovered the body?'

Despite the girlish tone she sounded accusing. Fenwick bit back a retort and scanned the preliminary report the CSTs had just given them.

'The door was kept shut while we worked the scene,' Bernstein replied calmly, unprovoked for once. 'The CSTs took the room temperature as soon as they arrived. It was twenty-seven degrees Fahrenheit and the outside temperature twenty-five. There's a Calor heater over there. It was out and cold to the touch when the technicians got here, empty of paraffin. We don't know when it was last filled but they're going to test how long a full tank lasts and take temperature readings of the van while they do it.'

'Good, that will help me to assess ToD. Rigor has already passed.' She tested the man's thigh, then his feet. 'He's wearing two pairs of socks, one . . . two shirts and a sweatshirt, and there's a blanket on the floor. So it was probably cool in here even with the heater going. That,' she gestured to the Calor gas, 'wouldn't be enough to heat a badly insulated room like this very well.'

'Can you give me a time of death?'

'Very hard to say, at least twenty-four hours; rigor is notoriously inexact as a basis for estimation, so don't quote me until your technicians have simulated the temperature curve.' She rolled the body onto its side, his dead weight nothing to her, and pulled down his clothing to reveal bare skin. 'Skin is cold to the touch; liver temp . . . twenty-eight degrees. That would suggest he died much more than twenty-four hours ago.'

Jamieson prodded at purplish patches on pale buttocks.

'Lividity is consistent with the position in which the body was found and is fixed. Forget twenty-four hours; he could have been dead as much as thirty-six, possibly longer.' She scratched her head. 'Decomp isn't nearly as advanced as I would expect because of the probable ambient temperature at time of death followed by the rapid cooling of the environment once the heat ran out. You can move him now.' She struggled to her feet, pulling her weight up against the force of gravity. The whistling started again.

'As for cause, I'd say the obvious is probably right in this case.' She glanced at Fenwick. 'Looks like he went into cardiac arrest as a result of rapid exsanguination; would have been dead almost instantly. Arterial spray is consistent with him being alive when he received the injury that killed him and as far as I can tell it was just one blow that did it.

'Your technicians will be the experts, of course, but there appear to be two major spray areas, suggesting he was moving at the time of the injury – maybe in a fight. The pooling here shows he collapsed onto the sofa and died where you found him. There are no obvious defensive wounds but I'll look for bruising and any signs of a struggle in the PM. Was the weapon a bottle?'

'CST found one, shattered and covered in his blood.'

'An unlucky break,' she gave another giggle. 'I can do the autopsy tonight if it helps.'

'It would, thank you, Doctor.'

'It's Patty, remember.' She smiled at him, a massive, overweight, tone-deaf cherub.

As she walked past him out of the caravan he recognised the tune she was murdering. It was 'Always Look on the Bright Side of Life'. He couldn't tell whether the choice was motivated by irony, lack of taste or indifference; maybe all three.

After she had gone Fenwick went over to the body and stared at the man's face, grotesque with the shock of death.

'Definitely Dan Mariner and it looks as if his brother has left home. Given his wife's report he could have taken not just his regular belongings but food and camping gear as well.'

'Camping gear . . . in this weather?'

Bernstein popped a fresh square of nicotine gum into the side of her mouth, chewed quickly and then slipped it between teeth and cheek while Fenwick pulled out the report Cobb had failed to give him earlier.

'Assuming it's him, he took blankets, camp bed, sleeping bags and cooking equipment as well as food.'

'So he's hiding out somewhere. With or without Issie, that's the question?'

'Exactly; but whichever, his brother's murder is a major complication. It looks like Dan died in a fight: was it over Issie? Was she kept here?'

Fenwick breathed in the icy air of the caravan and shuddered. Despite the cold he could smell mildew, old rubbish . . . and something else.

'It's possible according to SOCO,' Bernstein replied, 'through here.'

They walked in single file into a tiny cupboard of a bedroom. Fenwick wrinkled his nose.

'It stinks.'

'Urine, sweat, sex. The mattress and sheet were covered in traces according to CST; they're on their way to the lab together with short auburn hairs, visually similar to Issie's.'

'So this could be where she was held. Did she see Dan die? Was she killed too and her body taken away?' His voice was heavy.

'What do you think?' Bernstein squinted at him, chewing

195

incessantly while dragging the chill air between her teeth as if inhaling on an imaginary cigarette.

'You tell me.'

The jaws stopped briefly.

'Issie's abducted, right? Maybe it started for the sex. Then they realised . . .'

'They, not he?'

'If it was one man, he's dead and Issie would be here or would have contacted her parents. No, there was more than one.' He nodded. 'Right, well they realise what they've got – sorry, who they've got – and one of them decides to turn kidnapper.'

'Steven Mariner; Dan was dead when the second call came through, if not the first.'

'So, say Steven has her. Before the calls, they keep Issie here, maybe for sex,' she sniffed, 'certainly smells like it. Except something goes wrong – an argument, fight, accident; doesn't matter for now – somehow it concludes with a broken whisky bottle and murder. Fattie ends up dead and the other one – Steven – clears off with Issie.'

'Why so sure?'

'Footprints by the door.' Bernstein looked smug as Fenwick peered over and saw two sets in the dried blood, one much smaller than the other.

'Is there anything to tell us where he might have taken her?'

Fenwick looked at Bernstein hopefully but knew it was a futile question. If there was they would already be heading there. He opened a drawer at random but all it contained was a bottle opener and a desiccated bluebottle.

'We have nothing to go on. The ground outside is too frozen to hold tyre prints. Our best bet is to continue the search and put a marker on Steven Mariner's car. If he's smart, Bazza should already have done so. I'll check.'

'Good; what would you like me to do? Stay here or continue

to Steven Mariner's house?' Fenwick asked. 'And someone has to tell the Saxbys there might be a lead.'

Bernstein's expression darkened.

'Norman will call them personally, I expect. You go to Mariner's. I'd rather stay here in case anything breaks.'

His car was parked beyond the perimeter CST had established, almost at the edge of the wood. As he walked towards it he noticed some of the searchers in the trees nearby, apparently oblivious to the cold, fuelled by a new determination to find the missing girl. They were armed with sticks and powerful torches to penetrate the undergrowth and every other one carried a brush or spade to clear the snow. The search conditions were atrocious but they couldn't, wouldn't stop.

He thought of the latest health and safety guideline to soil his in tray and snorted in disgust. He would like nothing more than to have a few of those Whitehall paper-pushers out here right now. There should be a law against people making regulations who didn't know what they were doing. Make operational experience compulsory for all civil servants, he thought; it might do the force the world of good.

The idea was a distraction; maybe a deliberate attempt by his subconscious to keep him from imagining Issie's body out there somewhere, already frozen as night fell. He pushed the idea away and entered the welcome relative warmth of the car.

Fenwick's driver eased the car forward, feeling the tyres slip then catch their grip. They were almost at the junction when the driver spotted someone trying to catch up. It was Bernstein. The car braked carefully and Fenwick wound down his window.

'What is it?'

'This. We just found it next to the track.'

She held out a sealed plastic evidence bag and he took it from her through the open window. Inside was a small silver stud and loop that he had seen before. In the picture of Issie hanging upside down by her knees from a tree this had been pierced through her navel. She was a clever girl; maybe she had dropped it deliberately as a clue for them to find. If so, it meant she was alive and conscious when she left the caravan. His heart pounded with excitement as he thanked Bernstein.

He decided that he had to speak personally with Mrs Mariner and then he would go and see the Saxbys anyway. The stud was new evidence, an indication that Issie might still be alive, and her mother deserved to hear of it, but first he had to be sure that Mariner was their man.

The lady of the house was waiting for him in the kitchen with a freshly made pot of tea and the central heating turned up high. Bob Cooper was there, pink and sweating, and had removed his tweed jacket, leaving him in just the pullover, shirt and, presumably, his customary vest.

Mrs Mariner was in her early thirties. She oozed respectability and Fenwick apologised for the mess the crime scene technicians were making as they processed her house. The words brought a frown to an otherwise plump, attractive face.

'I think you're wasting your time. Steve's done a runner by the look of things but he's not got the gumption or guts to be a criminal.'

'What makes you so sure?' Fenwick asked, and then listened carefully as Mrs Mariner explained that he was a man dominated by his mother and brother.

Fenwick wanted to understand Mariner in order to try and anticipate what he might do if he really had kidnapped Issie and was now on the run. So far he had found out that he had a decent, hard-working and house-proud wife who probably looked down on him. That wasn't too good for his self-esteem and may be sufficient encouragement for a weak-willed man to chase after young girls. The wedding photograph lying on the table showed him a little shorter than his wife, about five eight or nine, an averagely attractive-looking man but hardly memorable. There was nothing in the picture to suggest why a girl like Issie would go off with him willingly.

Mariner as the perpetrator wouldn't automatically rule out Fenwick's theory of an unintentional abduction but it was hard to create a scenario in which they were romantically involved. His wife was absolutely sure it couldn't be him and laughed when he mentioned the demand for money.

'According to the mobile phone provider a call was made in the vicinity of this house using the missing girl's phone.'

'Near this house? It can't have been; I mean, no . . .' She sat down heavily on a kitchen chair and rubbed her forehead. 'Unless it was his brother, Dan; he's a very strange individual. There have been times when I've had to ask him to leave because of his behaviour, especially when he drinks. He's not quite right – I don't know what it is about him exactly but he gives me the creeps.'

'When did you last see Dan Mariner?' Bazza asked.

'About three weeks ago, perhaps more.'

'And your husband?'

'Monday morning at breakfast and I spoke to him on his mobile Tuesday. He said he'd been out searching for that girl. I told him I'd be back by Friday.'

'How did he sound on the phone, Mrs Mariner?'

The woman frowned and rubbed her lips in agitation.

'A bit odd, but then he is sometimes.'

'Odd?'

'Distracted, not really concentrating on the conversation. The only thing he was interested in was the time I was due back. I understand why now. His passport's gone and he's taken a lot of food, clothes and all our camping equipment apart from the tent, though heaven knows why in this weather.' She sounded angry but confident of the missing items. Fenwick thought she could list exactly what had gone.

When he suggested it might be possible that her husband had started an affair with a seventeen-year-old girl, she laughed.

'In his dreams! That would be his fantasy, his and that idiot brother of his. The Mariners are a sick family and the mother is truly evil. My parents warned me but I was too much in love to see it and married Steve anyway. Trouble is, I'm Catholic and I can't divorce him now, even though I know he's been unfaithful many times. It's usually prostitutes or trollops who trade sex for a night of drinks and a meal at the local but he's never run away before. I'm still a bit shocked that he's had the nerve, quite honestly.'

Her eyes strayed to the wedding picture and she shook her head.

Fenwick went upstairs while Bazza continued searching and Cooper stayed with Mrs Mariner. The place was spotless, as if recently spring-cleaned and a technician he passed said there were virtually no prints. There were two bedrooms and a separate bathroom, all clean and tidy apart from some bedding and clothes drying in the spare room. He noticed that Mrs Mariner wore brushed-cotton pyjamas; hardly a lusty marriage. There was nothing else of interest so he returned downstairs, walking into the kitchen as Mrs Mariner handed something to Cooper.

'Here, my brother-in-law's address. It's the house where he lived with his mother before she was taken into care. What a blessing that was. And this is a photograph of him.'

Cooper passed the snapshot over to Fenwick who studied it. There was no doubt Dan Mariner was the corpse in the caravan.

'We'll need to take this photograph.'

He told Bazza to finish off the search and make sure anything recovered was sent immediately to Cellmark, the forensic laboratory in Abingdon, to be processed at once. A team was sent to the mother's house just in case Issie had been taken there, though that would have been an act of such stupidity he doubted it. He decided to go straight to the Saxbys' and then to Surrey HQ.

They knew who had taken Issie and probably where she had been held immediately afterwards, though they were no closer to learning where she was now. Norman had called a team briefing for eight that evening. It would be a chance to review all the evidence and plan what to do next. Fenwick should have felt more positive, and anyone looking at him would have thought he was, but the sick worm of concern he had felt from the outset twisted and turned in his gut and his inner thoughts were as dark as the winter evening.

CHAPTER NINETEEN

He sat in the front seat of the Ford Mondeo, his eyes fixed blindly on the snow that was steadily covering the windshield. His mind was as empty as his sight, a complete void except for the all-consuming terror that held him rigid.

If asked, even under torture, he wouldn't have been able to say where he was or how he had arrived there. All he knew was that he had a sense of being hunted and that sooner or later the hunters would find him and it would all be over.

The heavy snow had already covered his car in a thick, lethal blanket that would freeze him inside the stillness of its tomb. In some part of his subconscious he knew this, knew that the lethargy he was experiencing was the gentle onset of hypothermia. His eyelids drooped and he couldn't be bothered to blink them open. They would find him soon enough; why worry?

There was a sudden rapping on the window. He ignored it.

'. . . mate, you'll freeze to death in this . . .'

The words and the knocking wouldn't stop, so that he was forced to jerk his head up and struggle to focus. The voice buzzed in his ears like an irritating fly.

'What?' The word stuck in his mouth, kept there by numb lips that wouldn't open.

'Come on, mate! You've bloody fallen asleep. It'll kill you in this weather.'

He heard the words thickly through the frozen glass and his

eyes tracked up to their source. His heart stopped; his jaw dropped open as he stared at the hunched figure in yellow reflective gilet over a blue uniform coat. The policeman bent down further now that he saw the man looking at him.

'I think you should come with me to the hospital,' he shouted, 'get yourself looked at. How long have you been in there?'

A basic survival instinct pushed itself to the surface, stimulating words that he didn't even know he could formulate. He cranked the window down an inch.

'Had a row with the missus,' he said, certain the blatant lie would be disbelieved. 'She kicked me out.'

'On a day like this? That's animal, that is.' The policeman stared at him with renewed concern. 'Your lips are blue. You need to get warm, sharpish. Come on, I've got some coffee in my car.'

He made to open the driver's door but it was locked. Steve fumbled but managed to turn on the car's ignition, shaking his head at the offer.

'S'OK, mate, I've got some of me own. I'll soon warm up now.' He lifted the empty thermos flask from the passenger seat and waved it. The clock on the dash read 13.47; the time since ten-fifteen, when he'd driven away from the pool, had vanished.

'You sure?' The traffic cop stamped his feet and blew on his hands, hesitating.

'Certain, but thanks again. In me own bloody world, I was; miles away. Good that you came by when you did.'

'Right you are, then, but drive safe. The roads are treacherous around here. Council didn't grit this part, did they?'

'Typical.'

'Too right. Well, see you.' The cop thumped the roof and trudged back through snow that was up to the top of his boots.

He watched the patrol car back out of the lay-by and pull away cautiously. He waved and received a short hoot of the horn in response. When he was sure that they really had gone he started to laugh, a chuckle at first, then a proper belly laugh that went on and on, rising into hysterical crying that lost all trace of humour and shook the car with its violence.

'Unbelievable; bloody unbelievable!' He kept repeating the words, laughing and then sobbing in relief. There he'd been, in a snow cave preparing to die and the bloody police had come along and saved him. He wiped his eyes, took a deep breath – and then burst out laughing again. The hunters had saved him.

He was a great believer in Fate, in the reality that Life would happen to you anyway no matter how much you tried to change it. His life, he had long been convinced, would be tough and unfair; no easy chances, no winning lottery tickets or wealthy relatives dying. So there was no point being an optimist or trying too hard. It only opened you up for disappointment. His mum had taught him that from before he could walk.

She had been the same, sticking to what she knew, cautioning him not to get above himself, against trying too hard. '*Know your place, stay there and you won't be disappointed*,' she'd say and he and his brother had been convinced she was right. They watched schoolfriends sweat at their studies, or practise their chosen sport until they were exhausted, and they'd felt superior, knowing they had the right of it. Had all that work changed a single life? Did one of them get to play for Man U, or the Arsenal? 'Course they didn't; and only snotty Philip Baker had made it to university out of the whole class, and that was because his dad beat him if he didn't study.

His mum knew the ways of the world and had taught them well: how to conserve your energy and spend it only on what you enjoyed, how to keep others out and never get tricked into believing that good would happen. It never did, not to the likes of them. It was that conviction that had led him, finally, to drive away from the swimming pool without the ransom money.

On the way there he had repeated his new mantra to maintain

his courage and shifting sense of purpose: *I haven't killed the albatross; I haven't killed the albatross* . . . The sentence resonated reassuringly in his head until he had been certain that, for once maybe, he would be lucky. *She* was his luck and she was still alive.

He had felt good when he made the call to Saxby, pleased that he'd had the foresight to be in place already, to be able to watch the car park to be certain that the police didn't show up. As he had waited though, every arriving car became a potential threat; every van without windows a surveillance trap waiting to snare him. His confidence evaporated faster than the snow melted on his warm windows. He had started muttering to himself, as if hearing the words out loud would boost his confidence.

'I haven't killed the albatross . . . the bird's alive and well . . . the albatross is alive . . . she's alive.' He would pause to swallow some coffee, then, 'If the next car that arrives has a little girl in it my luck's in.'

And when a family estate deposited a mother or father and daughter his spirits rose. If it was a boy it was neutral; no children was negative and his mood would deflate.

'Girl!' He would shout out and punch the steering wheel. Then, 'Blue car!'

Blue was his lucky colour. Anything blue was good, always had been ever since his dad had bought him a Chelsea strip as a present for his sixth birthday, the only birthday the bugger had remembered. It had been a knock-off from the market and last season's design but he hadn't cared. Blue was good, so was white. Yellow was neutral, but red and green – they were bad; real bad luck happened with red and green. His wife had red hair; he should have known better than look at her in the first place. His mum's room in the nursing home had green walls and a red carpet that smelt of sick. With a shock of memory he realised that Dan had been wearing a red shirt the night he'd . . .

A red estate pulled into the car park, followed by a black

station-wagon, a green van and another red car. His hopes spiralled down. He was wearing his lucky blue jumper under the sweatshirt with a hood, which he pulled up over his head as the warmth in the car slowly faded.

'Blue.' A new car came into the car park, but the word was barely a mutter now, almost in vain as if it had no power to balance the weight of negative energy that was piling up around him. But five hundred thousand pounds was a lot of money and the thought of it carried more power than anything Steve had ever believed in before. The idea of owning that much cash worked on his mind, changing his constant calculation of the balance of the fates. Girls versus boys didn't count any more, he concluded. Neither did the tally of cars by colour that were parked around him.

What mattered was his anonymity. Nobody knew him; nothing would have the power to change the good fortune that the girl-albatross was bringing him as long as he remained unknown. It was as if he was in hiding from his fate, camouflaged under the cover of her wings, waiting to snatch a new future before his previous life caught up with him. He decided that if he saw nobody he knew the whole time he was there it was a sign that he was meant to have the money and leave his past life behind.

Inside his hood Steve had smiled, confident that he had found a test that would work. None of his mates had toddlers preschool age to take swimming and they wouldn't be stupid enough to come here themselves on a day like this. By the time he had stepped out of the car his faith in his good fortune was restored.

The confidence lasted while he walked around to the front entrance, blossomed when he saw the bulging bin liner exactly where it was meant to be and was almost beyond containment as he had paced towards it.

'Oi!'

He had ignored the shout, convinced that it couldn't be aimed at him. He didn't know anybody here, right?

'Yo, man! How y'doin'? Haven't seen you in weeks.'

With a dread so deep it was certainty he had turned around to see Jerry Knight, JK to his pals, heading towards him, cigarette cupped in the shelter of his palm. He had stared at his shining face, so out of keeping with the weather, his mind stunned with disbelief.

'Hey man, you OK? You lookin' at me as if I'm a ghost or sommink.' JK grasped his hand sideways and pummelled it vigorously before double-punching his knuckles in his customary salute. He had responded in a trance.

'Wassup? You sick? You want to come inside, get warm?'

He recovered his wits.

'Row with the missus, the usual.'

'You need to dump her, man; she's doin' your head in.'

'Yeah, I know. How're you?' His autopilot was taking over; he even managed a smile.

'Good, good. Managed to find this job, din' I, after three months of lookin'. They laid us all off at the printworks and it's taken me for ever to find somefink else. S'only maintenance, not skilled like before but, y'know, it's a start. I've worked me way up before; I'll do it again.'

He had stared at the overalls and plastic identity pass around his friend's neck and enjoyed a warm feeling of condescension. *Try all you like, you sorry bastard, they'll only grind you down again.*

'Yeah, sure; didn't know you work here.'

'Started last month, in time to save up for the wife and boy for Christmas.'

'I didn't know you worked here,' he repeated. Part of him wanted to punch the self-satisfied smile off JK's face. Stupid bastard had wrecked his chances and all because he'd chosen some poxy menial job rather than queue up for the dole like a regular citizen.

'. . . I said see you at the Bull tonight? Christmas darts special, remember?'

He had forgotten; they'd be expecting him . . . and Dan.

'Yeah, see you then,' he lied.

'Dan coming too? How's the lazy sod doin'?' JK took a drag, holding the smoke deep in his lungs before exhaling a perfect smoke ring.

An image filled his mind of Dan splayed out on the couch, his neck slashed open, blood gushing out and up. He wanted to be sick.

'Lying around as usual,' he said, swallowing hard.

'Typical!' JK laughed, pinched the top off the cigarette and slipped it into his pocket. 'Better get back before they miss me. See you tonight.' He punched farewell and left.

He had squeezed his eyes shut and then opened them again to take in his surroundings. The bag was still there; snow settling steadily on top of it. He had stared at it with longing, even took a pace towards it. Then a lifetime's caution had stopped him and made him dart a look around. Not all the cars were empty. That white one over there had a woman in it reading the paper while waiting for someone; maybe it was him. There was a dark metallic green Volvo to his left with two people in it talking. Its windows were misted up as if they'd been there a while; why?

He had sniffed the air and looked around again. Over there, almost behind him to his right there was a black Ford with a man in it. He was sipping coffee now but he was almost certain he had been staring at him just before. Dangerous; it was too dangerous. He had turned away sick with failure, the heat of the money lying there burning into his back. When he had reached his car he'd driven away at once . . . and somehow ended up here in this godforsaken lay-by.

The taste of defeat was still in his mouth as he sat in the car while the heater blasted away ice and snow from the windows. What was he going to do? Before the traffic cop had arrived he'd been prepared to freeze to death. Stupid thinking, he realised now, but understandable. He had been so close to a fucking fortune. Tears of self-pity filled his eyes but he blinked them away angrily.

It was all JK's fault. If he'd only bothered to tell him that he worked at the swimming baths he'd never have chosen the place. Smug git. JK always acted superior, telling him how he should live his life – try this, do that – and all because he'd managed to scrape together some GCSEs.

JK looked down on him, he was sure, and he had that big-arsed woman of his too, so obliging. He remembered JK's ecstatic description of their honeymoon, what she'd let him do to her, what she had done for him. Everything, that's what; there had been nothing that two people could do to each other in bed that they hadn't tried.

Of course he'd pretended it was normal, that all wives were like that, but it hadn't dampened JK's enthusiasm, or his obvious gratitude that he had somehow ended up with a churchgoing wife who was amazing in bed.

Thinking of JK's exploits made him grow hot. His trousers constricted him and his hand moved to his zipper, a secretive, oft-repeated gesture. Whatever he had boasted to JK and others, his wife was conservative and frigid. He undid the top button of his trousers but then stopped himself. What was he doing? He didn't need self-help, not with that pretty young albatross waiting for him. She would be desperate, wondering whether he had abandoned her; so grateful to see him.

His stomach and groin tightened. JK's missus was nothing compared to Issie. He could barely contain his excitement as he switched on the headlights, slipped the car into gear and eased onto the road, feeling his way over loose snow until he joined a gritted dual carriageway and blended into the traffic.

The track leading up to the pump house was treacherous with fresh snow so he decided to park out of sight in a dip at the bottom of the hill and walk up. He had used some of Issie's cash to buy sandwiches, a bottle of whisky and a razor, as well as more fuel for the oil-fired heater and canisters of camping gaz. His urgent desire for her and a renewed sense of immunity had guided him smoothly through the transactions. Now he was impatient.

The snow in front of the pump house was pristine. She hadn't managed to escape then. The thought made him smile. He walked in a wide semicircle close to the skeletal brambles so that his tracks would be hidden in their shadows, only stepping onto the white covering a yard from the door. One stride and he was at the padlock.

The key took some time to turn in the frozen metal but it opened eventually and he pushed on the door. The gloom inside surprised him until he remembered that the gas lamp was out of her reach. He lit it and saw his breath mist in the stale air. As he shut and bolted the door concern filled him that she might have died and he ran to the bundle on the mattress.

There she was, shapeless in layers of his clothing, zipped up tight in two sleeping bags, her eyes open and staring at him but he could tell she was alive. He remembered her body, the feel of her skin under his hands, how the slenderness of her back and waist swelled into muscle-firm buttocks. She would be so grateful to him for being here that she would do anything for him.

'I came back,' he said proudly, 'I said I would.'

'Can I go now?' she asked at once.

'Maybe,' he smiled, 'depends on whether you're a good girl.'

'He gave you the money, like he said he would?' she demanded. 'You've got the money, right?'

The reminder of his failure made him angry. Snooty little bitch; typical that she would rub his nose in it. Women; they were all the same. She was meant to be pleased that he was here but instead she was nagging him already. His head ached. He cracked open the whisky and swallowed, coughing as the raw spirit hit the back of his throat.

Without looking at her he refuelled the heater and lit it, pushing his palms towards its heat. Then he lit one of the gaz stoves and put a camping kettle of water on it.

She was talking to him, bleating on like his stupid wife, but he ignored her. How could a man think straight with all that noise? He drank some more of the whisky directly from the bottle. Anger at his failure slowly turned on her, his temper simmering like the water, gradually bubbling to the surface mixed with a rush of desire. Ungrateful little bitch.

'. . . please tell me. They paid, right? They're waiting for me; we're going to them? . . . Answer me, damn you!' She screamed at him. 'Answer me, you bloody bastard!'

The flat of his hand caught her mouth, snapping her head to the side as the return stroke knocked her back on the mattress, her head swaying in a satisfying see-saw motion, so he hit her again. It made him laugh through his fury.

'Shut up,' he bayed at her, spittle covering her reddened cheeks. 'Don't you ever shout at me, you little whore. You should be grateful I'm here.'

'I am, I am.' The girl looked at him with wide wet eyes. Her obvious terror made him feel good.

'You are really grateful?'

'Yes, very, very.' She blinked back tears.

He reached down and grabbed a handful of her short hair, pulling her head forward sharply. Some of the tears that had accumulated in her eyes spilt over. The sight of them gave him enormous pleasure.

'How grateful?' He whispered, bending down so that his lips brushed her ear.

She stank of sweat and urine but his desire was stronger than any repulsion and she was trembling, he could feel it through his hands, through his lips as they rested against her salty skin. He started to devour her with little bites.

'I'm very grateful, Badger,' she whispered.

He heard the lie in her words. Her deception was transparent to him now.

'It's Steve,' he said, 'not Badger. Bloody daft name; don't call me by it again.'

'Of course, Steve,' and she reached up to touch his cheek with her bound hands.

He remembered how she had head-butted and scratched him only that morning and jerked his face away. The recollection of her insolence drew his anger back to the surface, bringing with it overwhelming desire. With his free hand he reached down and pulled the sleeping bags away from her. The unwashed smell that wafted out was irrelevant to his lust as he unzipped himself, sighing with pleasure at the release of pressure as he burst free.

'Then it's time you showed me just how grateful you are,' he said, pulling her towards him.

It took a long time for him to finish. He had never experienced such intense pleasure and she had been willing – well sort of – at least by the end.

He hadn't enjoyed hitting her and he'd told her so. It caused him as much pain as it did her, he had explained, but she had to be good. Good girls weren't punished, only bad girls. She learnt her lesson eventually and he was able to tell himself that the sex had been consensual. That mattered. At one point she almost passed out. All he could see were the whites of her eyes and her breath had sounded all raggedy in the back of her throat. He had forced some whisky into her and that choked her back to consciousness.

Satiated, he reached out to touch her. Despite the vigorous

hour of sex her skin felt cold to the touch and her lips were bloodless in the gaslight. He patted the top of her head, not with affection exactly, more with pride of ownership.

She was worth her weight in gold, literally, much more than the five hundred thou' he had asked for. And she was his; there was no doubt about that now, not after what they had just done together. Being with her made him strong. Feeling her body do exactly what he told it to made him the master. It was only when he was away from her he realised that he started to doubt himself. Together they were invincible, like Bonnie and Clyde.

'My little Issie,' he whispered into the darkness. 'What am I going to do with you?'

They couldn't stay here. She needed warmth and decent food inside her. They had to get away, but where? They could hardly waltz into a hotel with her being looked for everywhere.

Steve stood up and stretched. As he moved the girl moaned. She sounded really sick.

'Have something to drink, baby.' He put the bottle to her mouth but she moved her head away feebly.

'Feel sick,' she muttered but he could barely hear her.

Maybe he shouldn't have given her some of his skunk. It was good, really strong and he had thought it would make the sex more fun, but on top of the whisky and with no food inside her maybe it hadn't been such a smart idea.

He rested his hand on her forehead. It was icy and he felt a spurt of fear. The albatross couldn't die.

'Come here.' He bent down and wrapped his arms around her, trying to infuse warmth into her shaking body but the trembling just wouldn't stop.

Steve started to panic. They needed to move now, but where? There was nowhere to go. They were stuck here with virtually no money and the hunt lurking outside. With Dan dead he didn't dare go to his mum's in case the police went there. He hugged Issie tight, rubbing her arms, feeling the chill of her body seep into his skin. She was so cold! How had he not noticed before?

She was going to die; he suddenly became sure of it and moaned. Issie couldn't die; she was his lucky mascot; a sentence of doom would fall on him if he let her die. With no idea where to go other than away from the freezing pump house, Steve began to bundle his belongings into the car, talking to her all the while, running back to her side to hold her between trips to the car.

'Come on, Issie, wake up, baby. Wake up for Badger like a good girl.'

But no matter how hard he tried to revive her, Issie lay dead to the world in his arms.

CHAPTER TWENTY

The car Fenwick was being driven in had to navigate black ice in total darkness as it crawled to Surrey HQ in time for CC Norman's briefing. On the verges abandoned cars were being wrapped in deep blankets of snow as they passed, spraying dirty salt and grit onto pristine whiteness. Including the search teams, Norman had deployed a team of seventy officers dedicated to finding Issie and Steven Mariner but there had been no sight of man, girl or car. The weather didn't help as poor visibility hampered the ability of the Automatic Number Plate Recognition system, despite it being the most extensive in the western world.

The major incident suite was on the fourth floor of Guildford police HQ and a room had already been dedicated to operations Snow White and Goldilocks; the former for Issie's disappearance the latter for the ransom, which would now be combined. The ransom drop had failed and even though CC Norman had taken charge of it personally, Fenwick knew he would be a convenient scapegoat. He was being returned unceremoniously to MCS with attendant damage to his reputation.

That wasn't what was worrying him, though, as he entered the briefing. His only concern was finding Issie and he hated the idea of leaving the investigation to others. The chances of her being alive were remote but he placed his hope in Mariner being a coward at heart, who would find premeditated murder extremely difficult. Another accident though . . . Fenwick pushed the thought away.

Directly next to the door a thoughtful civilian clerk had placed an oversized thermos of coffee and a jug of milk together with a plate of toasted teacakes from the canteen. With the comfort of so many people in the room it could almost have been cosy, except for the wind buffeting the windows and the thought of Issie at the mercy of a killer, out there somewhere.

As soon as Fenwick was seated Norman started the meeting, identifying the case, the time, date and presence of senior officers by name. Rather than run the meeting on his own, he gave Bernstein the lead when it came to Dan Mariner's murder and the scene at the caravan. He nodded for her to speak as Fenwick helped himself to coffee and a teacake, remembering that he had missed lunch.

Bernstein had written down the salient facts about Dan Mariner's murder on a whiteboard and used it to illustrate points as she spoke.

'This afternoon at fifteen-fifty, one of the search teams discovered the body of Daniel Mariner, known as Dan, thirty-seven years old. It was in a caravan on agricultural land outside Haslemere. The nearest farmer claims not to own it and we have an outstanding inquiry with Land Registry. Dan was the elder of two brothers, the younger, Steven, being a person of interest in connection with the disappearance of Issie Mattias. The boys' mother Betty Mariner is a resident at Golden Park Nursing Home. We sent Cobb to notify her of her son's death and to interview her. I'll say more about that shortly.

'Dan Mariner's throat had been slashed with a broken bottle. Whether it was deliberate or accidental we can't yet say – we might know more after the PM. Whatever, he died where we found him almost instantly, according to the pathologist.

'The broken bottle was recovered at the scene.' She directed her next remarks to Fenwick. 'As well as many smudges we have been able to recover prints from the bottle. Two, Dan and Steven Mariner's, we've been able to match to prints recovered from their homes. We don't know who a third set belongs to – they aren't Issie's, nor are they in the system – they might simply be from the person who sold the whisky. The important thing is that we have a perfect set showing that Steve Mariner held the bottle, right-handed, upside down by the neck; a perfect grip for the killing blow. He's our main suspect in the murder of his brother.'

There were no questions. Everyone in the room was listening with absolute concentration, taking whatever notes they needed. At Bernstein's next words there were exclamations of surprise and excitement from everyone but Fenwick and Norman.

'From fingerprints recovered at the scene, we know for certain that Issie was held at the caravan, probably by Steven and/or Dan Mariner. She might have been there from Monday night up to when Dan was killed. If so, that's good news because at least she would have had shelter. The gas heater in the van kept it well above freezing, probably in the low sixties in the back bedroom, which is likely where she was kept as it's lockable from the outside and there was heavy urine staining in one of the corners.

'We're asking for DNA confirmation to match against samples taken from Issie's bedroom; results should come through sometime tomorrow. The lab is working on this as priority over the weekend. We also found this outside the van under a layer of fresh snow.'

She circulated a photograph of the navel ring together with the one of Issie hanging upside down with her tummy revealed.

'We don't know where she was taken after the caravan or even if she was still alive. The search of the vicinity has stopped for now because the weather is so bad it's impossible to continue.' As if sensing Fenwick's disapproval Bernstein rushed on, 'We'll resume at first light and bring the dogs in. Probably hopeless given the snow but we have to give it a go.

'In the meantime, we're trying to establish the previous whereabouts of both Mariner brothers. This is the timeline we have so far.' She gestured to the board.

'Monday fourth December, Steven Mariner was at work at St Anne's College. He knocked off at five exactly – there are reliable witnesses – and went to visit his mother. Dan visited with him the same day. They stayed for just under an hour.

'Tuesday afternoon, Steve Mariner joined the search for Issie for a few hours. This is him here in surveillance pictures taken at two-thirty. That's the last we see of him. We don't know where Dan Mariner was but he definitely wasn't in the search party and so far no one from the school recognises his photo.'

'Was he even alive on Tuesday?' Bazza asked.

'Good question. We don't know. ToD is going to be difficult to establish because of conditions at the scene. CST is going to do their best to simulate the temperature curve in the caravan but we don't know how much fuel there was in the Calor heater or whether there was any other form of heating– there's an electric stove and the van is connected by a Heath Robinson contraption to a nearby power line.

'Back to Steve Mariner: he called in sick on Wednesday. His wife can't vouch for his whereabouts as she says she was visiting her mother in Epsom. We don't think the wife is involved but we're checking her alibis anyway. She gave us a list of places the brothers frequented – it's been photocopied and I want every one checked out. Cobb, that one's for you; take whoever you need.'

Fenwick's heart sank. Why couldn't the idiot-boy have taken a few days off sick? He watched Cobb take the list and picked up a copy himself to slip in his pocket.

'So far as Dan is concerned we have no idea where he was from the time he visited his mum to when he died. But Steven

Mariner is more interesting.' She looked at Bazza who stood up to take over.

'On Wednesday night Steven Mariner returned to his house on Goosegreen Avenue at between twenty-one-forty-five and twenty-two hundred hours. A neighbour recalls Mariner's car pulling into the garage. He's sure of the time because he was waiting for the ten o'clock news to come on. He was keeping an eye out because Mrs Mariner had asked him to – which suggests, by the way, that she might not have been entirely sure that her husband would be sleeping at home.

'Just before 8 a.m. Thursday, a call was made in the vicinity of Goosegreen Avenue using Issie's mobile to Saxby Hall. It was the ransom demand for fifty thousand pounds. Shortly afterwards Mariner left the family home. The wife of that same neighbour looked over on her way to the eight-twenty bus. Snow had fallen heavily overnight and there were fresh tyre tracks outside the garage. We have a marker on with ANPR for Mariner's Mondeo, so far without success. This is a picture of it – note the licence plate everyone, it's customised "ST EV 77".

'And before anyone asks, we don't know where he went or whether Issie was with him. The next we see of Mariner is this morning at seven thirty-eight when he uses Issie's spare cash card at a garage on the A31. The lad on the till has been interviewed twice but is frankly useless. He doesn't even know which day of the week it is. But the surveillance pictures from the petrol station show a man with a resemblance to Mariner.'

One of the civilian support team passed around grainy stills that showed a male of indeterminate age wearing a sweatshirt with hood up.

'The part of the face that's visible is similar to photos we have of Mariner. We've asked Tech to see if they can enhance them as a visual is always helpful at trial but we know it's him from fingerprints on the vendor copy of the sale slip.'

The photos reached Darren Yarrow, a DC who had been with Fenwick at the ransom drop.

'There's something familiar about him, don't you think, sir?' He asked Fenwick. 'We've seen him before.'

Fenwick peered over his shoulder to study the grainy image. 'You're right.'

'Like where?' Bernstein asked, as she popped a piece of nicotine gum into her mouth and started chewing.

'I'm trying to remember. It was recently; maybe at the swimming pool . . .'

'That's where!' Darren almost shouted. 'Sir, do you remember we had a possible pickup – a bloke in a hooded sweatshirt and brown jacket?'

'You're right; we need to check the CCTV from the pool and our own surveillance footage.'

'If it's him it means I didn't spend three hours in the front seat of a green Volvo freezing my balls off for nothing.' The young constable was too excited to remember CC Norman was there.

'Diddums; I'll knit you a ball cosy.' Bernstein chuckled.

Before Norman could intervene, Fenwick continued.

'Darren; we should compare these photographs and the others we took from his house with the surveillance footage from the swimming pool. If he was there, it's very unlikely it's a coincidence and it means he's definitely the kidnapper, not his brother, because Dan was dead by the time of the second phone call. We might be able to pick up CCTV coverage of his car leaving the car park and track him out of Guildford. He could still lead us to her!'

CC Norman ordered Yarrow and two other officers to make an immediate start on checking the recordings. As they left Fenwick watched Bernstein add a possible sighting of Steven Mariner to the timeline during the wait for the ransom drop between nine-thirty and one o'clock. Norman stood up and the room went still.

'What now, sir?' she asked Norman.

'Have a team continue the door-to-door in Mariner's neighbourhood. Cobb should follow up ASAP on Mariner's known haunts; he'll need backup.'

There were some curious glances towards Fenwick as Norman allocated work away from him. Fenwick could feel eyes on his back but ignored them and stood up to study the timeline.

'He used the cash card at the garage at seven thirty-eight: the second call to the Saxbys was at eight-thirty and we know he's at the pool by then. Where's the map?'

A large-scale map of Guildford and the surrounding area was already tacked to a wall.

'So, Saxby Hall is where?'

One of the detective constables put a black pin on the location. Without asking she moved on to mark the swimming pool and, after double-checking her notes, the location of the garage where Mariner used Issie's card. They made an irregular triangle shape with the pool at the east point in Guildford centre, the garage on the A31 four miles west and Saxby Hall to the south-west of Guildford, five miles into the countryside. While Norman, Fenwick and Bernstein watched, the constable added a cluster of pins showing both Mariner houses and the nursing home. She didn't have a map reference for the caravan but Bernstein did and added a red pin almost exactly halfway between Mariner's house and the garage.

'That gives us a clear search area,' Fenwick said, pointing to the triangle. 'With the bad weather yesterday he wouldn't have wanted to drive far. This should be the priority area to cross-check with whatever Cobb finds out about the brothers' hang-outs.'

'Of course,' Cobb sounded almost offended that he had to be told.

'What did we learn from Mariner's mother?' Norman took a step forward and both Bernstein and Fenwick had to sit to give him room. 'Anything that might help?'

Cobb shook his head.

'She's a witch; completely batty and nasty with it. She barely reacted to the news that her elder son had died and when told it looked likely her younger son had done it she burst out laughing like it was the best joke ever. We've had a team searching her house but CST hasn't found a trace of Issie and the dust on the furniture suggests it hasn't been lived in for a while. That's consistent with what the neighbours say.'

Norman looked frustrated.

'So we have no idea where Steven Mariner might have taken Issie after the caravan. Where would he hide her? Bazza, you told me his wife is adamant that neither brother has any property, not even a shed or workshop. He's poorly paid, doesn't have any savings and is very unlikely to risk going to a hotel or B&B. Where will he go?'

There was a flourish of grimaces as the team realised that despite all they had discovered they were no closer to finding Issie.

Fenwick raised his hand.

'We have to find out more about his past. Did he have any favourite haunts, hidey-holes from when he was a kid; anything?'

'His wife mentioned an old girlfriend a couple of times, Annie Sallow. She married a few years ago and left the area,' Bazza threw in but he didn't sound optimistic.

'We should trace her,' Fenwick suggested, 'from everything we've learnt about him, Mariner is the sort to run to ground somewhere familiar. That's where we'll find Issie.'

'Assuming she's alive and he's taken her with him rather than finishing her off and dumping the body somewhere. There's a chance she saw the murder and if so it might have prompted him to kill her.' Bernstein stated bluntly what they were all thinking.

'I know,' Fenwick acknowledged, 'in which case there's a risk we won't find the body until the weather changes and we can use the dogs properly. Meanwhile, we have to work on the assumption that she's alive and that killing his brother wasn't premeditated, which is important. If he thinks of it as accidental then Steve might not consider himself a murderer and Issie has a better chance of staying alive . . . for now.'

Norman allocated the rest of the work, making it clear he expected them to continue through the night. He told Bazza to join Darren in checking the CCTV tapes and gave Bernstein additional resources to look for Annie, including despatching someone to the registrar for details of her wedding. They needed her married name and where she had moved to. There was nothing for Fenwick to do.

Norman then announced that the press office was releasing Steven Mariner's name and car details to the media in time for the ten o'clock news. Fenwick suggested that he add to it a request for Annie to come forward. It might make her life difficult but they were running out of time for Issie.

'I'd like to raise one more thing, sir,' Fenwick asked as the team started to stir. 'Did the Mariners have a local pub where they were regulars?'

'The Bull and Drum on the A281. I've already been there and asked around,' Cobb explained. 'Nobody knew anything.'

'Right,' Fenwick stared at the retreating back of the officer he considered a jinx.

As soon as he was in his temporary office he rang Bob Cooper's mobile number, left a message and then tried his home. Cooper's wife answered sounding breathless.

'Hello, Doris, it's Andrew Fenwick,' he said, forcing bonhomie into his voice in an attempt to defrost the ice he could sense creeping towards him.

'I suppose you'd like to talk to Bob?'

'If you don't mind.'

'Well I do but since when has that made a difference?'

Such rudeness was a rarity from a lady who had been

considered a warm-hearted saint by those who had known her while Bob Cooper had been in the force. Fenwick feared that the favour he was about to ask might not be granted after all. Cooper picked up the phone.

'Hi, Bob, how are you?'

'Fine.' Fenwick heard reserve and caution in his old colleague's voice.

'I was wondering . . .'

'Not tonight, Andrew. The wife's got the neighbours round for drinks.'

'Oh, it's just that—'

'I can't do it, really. I'm not a copper any more and I promised her I'd change my ways.'

'Is your son there?'

'Robbie? Yes, but he's due to go out with his mates.'

'To a pub? Couldn't you join him, just for half an hour? That's all I need.'

'But I'll be missed; it's gone nine!'

'I understand, Bob, but I need the Cooper nose – just for half an hour. Please; half a pint at a pub that's less than fifteen minutes from where you are.'

'I'm begging you, send someone else.'

'I've already tried that and got nothing.'

'So why do you want me to go?'

'You don't look like a detective and you did some of your best work in pubs.'

'I think I resent that.'

'People open up to you over a pint, you know it; and Issie's still missing. Bob, we think we know who's taken her and where they kept her at first but they've moved on and we have to find out where.'

'And half an hour at some pub or other will do the trick, just like magic? You're clutching at straws.'

'Not any old pub, the Bull and Drum.' Fenwick knew it. The public bar was a dive but they served some of the best locally brewed ales in the area and the lounge bar was usually full of real-ale aficionados. 'Robbie would probably appreciate a quick drink with his dad.'

'You reckon I'll only need half an hour?'

'Maybe less. The Saxbys are your clients, after all.'

'I'll have to check with Dot . . .'

'I'm sure she'll understand.'

'I doubt it. You'd better not come round here for a while. She's a sweetie, my wife, but once she loses patience with someone . . .' He left the threat unspecified but Fenwick got the message.

A long minute later Bob Cooper confirmed that he and his son had been granted leave of absence to have a quick half pint together. 'Just a half, mind.' Fenwick asked him to leave at once. While he was on the way he would call his mobile to brief him on everything they knew or surmised.

Afterwards he decided to go and join Darren, Bazza and the CCTV film team to encourage them along. Fenwick ran down the stairs; he had the night and weekend left to find Issie.

The team had requisitioned all the security tape from around the swimming pool as a matter of course after the failed ransom pickup but it had been a lower priority since news about Mariner's identity and the body in the caravan had drawn attention elsewhere. He found them sitting in a room equipped with three TV monitors and a bank of DVD and videotape players.

'Where have you got to?'

'Nine-twenty. I started just before eight-thirty because that's when Mariner called from the swimming pool. I'm looking at the camera footage that covers the main entrance. Darren's taken the east side camera and Pat the west.'

Photographs of Steven Mariner were taped up beside the TV screens, as were stills from the petrol station. Bazza had been watching the tape in real time; tedious stuff. Fenwick glanced at the detective he now knew was called Pat and saw him briefly press fast forward.

'Go back.'

Pat jumped and looked over his shoulder.

'But . . .'

'Go back. While we were waiting it started to snow and the light was bad so the images aren't sharp. Go back to wherever you were tempted to fast forward.'

Pat rewound the tape, his shoulders radiating resentment. On the other side of Bazza Darren continued to watch the images on the screen in real time. It was obvious they weren't good enough to rush through.

'Sorry,' Bazza muttered, 'I should've had my eye on him.'

Fenwick grunted a reply, missing his hand-picked officers from MCS. Minutes ticked past. He had forgotten to blink and his eyes had dried out but he couldn't take his eyes off the screen in front of him. His stomach rumbled loudly.

'The canteen will still be open,' Bazza suggested. 'Do you want something?'

'I didn't have lunch, so yes, anything that can be taken away – preferably something hot.'

'If you're in luck they do a killer Cornish pasty.' Bazza stretched his back, hit pause and looked around. 'I'll go if you like. I could murder a cigarette anyway.'

'That would be great; a pasty or whatever they've got plus a coffee and something sweet. Here,' Fenwick passed him two twenty-pound notes, 'get something for yourself and the others while you're at it. I'll keep watching while you're gone.'

'Cheers.'

Bazza sprinted off, perhaps already savouring the nicotine, and Fenwick took his chair and pressed 'play'. Nothing happened for ten minutes, then Darren called out.

'I think I've got him! Here at ten-oh-four.'

Fenwick and Pat clustered around, peering at the screen where he was pointing.

'There, see, the bloke with his back to us and his hood up? That coat looks similar to the one from the petrol station. He's walking towards the main entrance. He should be coming into your screen next, sir.'

They went back to Fenwick's station and he forwarded to two minutes before in case the clocks were not synchronised exactly. They watched without speaking as seconds crawled past. At ten-oh-five the man they thought might be Mariner walked into shot. His face was clear; in fact he stopped and looked straight at the camera. Fenwick froze the scene.

'Gotcha!' Darren hissed. 'So why didn't he complete the pickup. Did he spot us?'

'I pray to God not.' It was Fenwick's dread: a botched operation that might have cost Issie her life. He pressed play, feeling sick to his stomach as he watched Mariner walk towards the waste-paper bin and five hundred thousand pounds.

When he was less than fifteen feet from the bin he was stopped by a man who fist-punched him in greeting.

'Who the hell is that?' Darren asked not expecting any answer. 'An accomplice; maybe the pool drop wasn't a random choice?'

'I don't know.' Fenwick rewound the tape and put it into frame-by-frame slow motion. 'No, look at his face; Mariner's surprised to see him. In fact he looks almost sick. He didn't expect to meet anyone he knew.' He let out a deep sigh and felt his gut relax. 'That's why he abandoned the pickup. How can he go ahead when someone he knows is watching? The guy's wearing maintenance overalls, so he might even work at the pool. No way could Mariner pretend to him that he had any business rummaging in the bin.'

'Why not wait and go back later?'

'Perhaps he got spooked,' Pat suggested, 'he's not a professional. It must have taken some balls to turn up, and then to bump into a mate like that – well, it could've put him right off.'

'I think you're right,' Fenwick stood up, 'but we need to find this man urgently. We should be able to get his name from the council; if he works at the pool he'll have photo id. Get onto it, Darren, at once. Wake up the mayor if you have to. I want us speaking to that man tonight.'

'They were out of pasties but I've got hot sausage rolls, chips and tomato soup, boss.' Bazza stood proudly in the doorway, smelling of a mix of fried food and cigarette smoke. 'What's up? Oh, don't tell me you found him and I missed it.'

Fenwick laughed for the first time that day as he relieved Bazza of the food.

'That's the problem with smoking, Bazza. You miss out on so much in life!'

He didn't hear Bazza's response as he was already heading to his office to call Bernstein and Norman in that order. After he had made the calls, he remembered with a stab of guilt that it was too late to go home in time to see the children before bed.

With the weather conditions still bad he decided he might as well spend another night in Guildford. While a civilian assistant found him a room in a nearby Travelodge, Fenwick took a deep breath and dialled. Alice answered at once, as if expecting his call.

'Andrew, thank goodness, you picked up my messages.'

Fenwick looked at his mobile and saw he had three missed calls.

'I haven't listened to them yet. What's the problem?'

'It's your mother. She's fallen over and is in hospital.'

Fenwick found he was short of breath and had to sit down. They weren't close but other than the children she was his only living relative.

'Is she all right?'

'Better than they feared at first. The poor dear took a nasty tumble on some ice. They thought she'd broken her hip but it turns out it's only badly twisted. She has a fractured left arm, though, and a mild concussion. Apparently she's quite bruised about and they're keeping her in for observation.'

'Have you got the hospital's number?'

'Of course, I left it on your mobile but here, I've got it to hand anyway.'

She read it out twice and then said, 'I've taken the liberty to send some flowers and the children have made a card already and it's in the post to her home.'

'Thank you, Alice, that's very thoughtful of you. Can I speak with the children? I know it's late but I guess they're still up as there's no school tomorrow.'

There was a slight pause.

'Chris is right here beside me. He's been a real help today, haven't you, love? He cleared the front step and some of the path like a proper little man. Not that we . . . er, ventured out; it's terrible. I won't drive in this.'

'No, of course not. Are you all right for food?'

'Well, I was going to ask if you could bring some fresh bread and milk home with you but don't worry, we can cope, can't we Chrissy? I get the feeling you're not coming home again tonight?'

'*Oh!*'

Fenwick could hear Chris's disappointed cry in the background.

'I'm sorry. We've just had a break in the case and I'm staying here. There's a young girl's life at stake . . .'

'Oh that missing school girl? I guessed that's what's been keeping you. We said so earlier, didn't we, Chrissy? Well, you just make sure you find her so that her poor parents have her home safe and sound for Christmas. Here, have a word with your son, he's desperate to tell you what he's done today.'

Chris chatted for so long that Fenwick thought he was going to have to interrupt so that he could get back to work, but then he stopped without warning and was about to hang up.

'Wait a sec, what about a word with your sister; is she there?'

'She's not talking to you, Daddy, in fact she's not talking to anybody. Thank goodness! She's a real moaning-Minnie at the moment.'

'Chris, that's not very kind.'

'Well, that's what Alice says and she is too.'

'Could you go and tell her I'm on the phone anyway?'

'She knows. She's been sitting at the top of the stairs pretending not to listen but now she's gone and shut herself in the bedroom.'

Fenwick suppressed a sigh and wished Chris goodnight, blowing him a kiss without a trace of self-consciousness. As he replaced the receiver his mobile phone rang.

'Fenwick.'

'It's Bob; I've just left the Bull and Drum and I'm on my way back home.'

Fenwick glanced at his watch; Bob was going to be in the doghouse.

'I found someone at the Drum you must speak to; he's willing to come in and make a statement if you send a car for him – he's had a couple already and doesn't want to risk driving. His name is Jeremy Knight, JK to his friends. He was here for a darts tournament and was expecting to meet up with the Mariner brothers. Knows them both really well from school; and, you'll never guess what . . .'

'Tell me.'

'He saw Steve Mariner today – at the swimming baths! He's just started work there having lost his job as a printer. Says Mariner was really surprised to see him, didn't look too well at all and just went off after a couple of minutes. I reckon that's why he never made the pickup.'

'You're right, we have him on CCTV. Describe Knight to me, Bob.'

'Well, he's, I don't know what I'm allowed to say any more, I get that confused with political correctness. He's of Caribbean extraction – there, is that all right? About five ten, fit – athletic, even – same age as Steven Mariner.'

'That's him. Brilliant, Bob. Thank you! I'll send a car straight away and, Bob, please tell Dot I'm sorry but you might just have helped save a girl's life.'

'I'll explain that to her in my own time. Right now I've got a bunch of flowers and a box of chocs from the garage that'll have to do my talking for me because one thing I know, she won't be in a mood to listen!'

Fenwick organised a car to pick up Knight and then called the hospital where his mother was, to be told that she was asleep. He left a message and tried Bernstein next, found her out with Cobb checking on the list of locations they had been given by Mariner's wife. He was relieved Cobb hadn't been left on his own.

After she listened to his update she told him her own bit of good news.

'We know Annie's married name; it's Jones. Not a great help but we also know where she lives. She's kept in touch with a friend who works at the takeaway pizza place the Mariner brothers went to. She's now in Godalming and I've sent a local round to pick her up, but given this weather she won't be with us for an hour. I was wondering whether I should call her right away. I know it's a risk. If she and Mariner are still thick she might tip him off or even be in on it, but I think that's unlikely. According to her friend she married well and has put her past behind her. What do you think? Any minute now I'm expecting to have her mobile phone number – shall I make the call?'

'Absolutely, yes. We're only twelve hours behind Mariner and we're closing on him. Get everything you can as fast as you can. I'll be here at HQ. If I'm not at my desk I'll be with Operations.'

Fifteen minutes later Bernstein called him. He knew at once from her voice that she had news.

'There's an abandoned pump station two miles south of the caravan. Annie says it was somewhere both brothers used to hang out. It's the only place she can think of that Steve might run to. It explains why he took the camping equipment and food. He could be holed up there. And if Issie is still with him . . .'

'She could still be alive!' Fenwick stood up and grabbed his coat.

'I've informed Norman and he's sending two teams and a negotiator. If I were you I'd leave before he tells you to stay out of it. I'll see you there.'

Fenwick's thumbs were tingling as he broke the call.

CHAPTER TWENTY-ONE

An ambulance, three squad cars and an unmarked minibus carrying eight officers from the local support team converged before the start of the track leading to the abandoned pump station and parked out of sight. Fenwick climbed out of the lead car and walked through snow to Bernstein who was standing in the meagre shelter of a barren oak. She gestured up the unmade, steep icy road, barely a vehicle-width, and the LST deployed silently without torches, the visors of their military style helmets up until the last minute to help visibility. Before them the silhouette of a decaying pre-war brick building rose solid black, apparently deserted. Fenwick paced behind. Norman had allowed him to accompany the operation after all but ordered him not to interfere.

All the way up to the entrance the snow lay virgin fresh, with no signs of a car or footprints. Eight officers deployed around the building; the rest of the team lowered their visors and flexed fingers inside heavy-duty black gloves. They were ready. The rusty chain on the door was already hanging loose.

'POLICE!'

They entered loud and in force, torch beams sweeping the space ahead while Fenwick and Bernstein waited with the officers blocking the track.

'Clear!' The team leader called out and they ran forward, Fenwick slipping and clouting his bad knee with an audible crack.

Cobb offered a hand but he shrugged him away.

From just inside the door Fenwick surveyed the room, lit intermittently by torches until the SOC floodlights could be set up. There was abundant evidence of recent occupation. Beside the entrance a pile of rubbish spread across the dank concrete floor. A cracked camping gas light, just warm to the touch, lay abandoned on its side. In a saucepan were the remains of a can of baked beans. It was 10.42 p.m.

Bernstein made an immediate decision to authorise a search of the building. Fenwick knew she was breaking with procedure and should have waited for the crime scene technicians to process it first, but approved. They didn't have the time to waste on niceties and needed any clue as to where Mariner might have taken Issie. After a frantic fifteen minutes it became clear that there was nothing to indicate where they might have gone – assuming that the recent residents had been Mariner and Issie, of course, but that was an empty question. Fenwick was certain they had been there – barely hours before. The dread in his stomach churned to acid.

He walked over to a stained sleeping bag and old mattress, ignoring the protests from a CST behind him, and knelt to smell them. He didn't need an expert to tell him it was heavy with evidence, and was almost sick – he was a man who could study a decomposing corpse with equanimity; but this he couldn't bear.

'He's still abusing her.' Fenwick failed to mask the disgust he felt.

'And we almost had the bastard!' Bernstein was shaking with anger as she gestured towards the filthy mattress. 'She's just a kid; a year younger than my niece! I thought everyone said he was a normal bloke. It makes you think, doesn't it: what lies beneath.'

Fenwick didn't have time to waste on philosophy.

'We must be close behind them,' he insisted. 'In this weather he won't have travelled far.'

'Norman has ordered roadblocks and released details of the Mondeo. We'll find him, Andrew. Don't forget, the press release was broadcast at ten with Lord Saxby's blessing. We've got the eyes of the public on our side now as well as traffic control and ANPR. But if we could only work out where he's gone . . .'

Fenwick paced the concrete, watching with growing impatience the fruitless search by the technicians for any clue of where Mariner might be heading.

'With a blizzard due overnight he'd have to be suicidal to try and stay outside,' Bernstein offered.

He wished she hadn't said that. Would Mariner snap and kill them both? The CSTs didn't remark on the damage done by the officers who had completed the hasty search. The ambulance that had been standing by went away empty to deal with other tragedies of the night. Reluctantly Fenwick and Bernstein left the scene and returned to Guildford HQ where they could be at the centre of the search operation.

Just before midnight a report came in that a patrol car might have seen Mariner's car that afternoon before the alert was issued. Fenwick read it and his fears that Mariner could be suicidal grew.

'We need to get a profile of him, Deidre. Have you got someone you rate?'

'I have,' Bernstein looked at him curiously, 'but I didn't think you'd have much time for psycho-babble.'

'Not all of it's rubbish; I've been glad of it in the past. Why don't you get them in now? I'm going to read the latest interviews – just in case. There must be some clue as to where he might go. And we need to alert all the homeless shelters within driving distance.'

'You've suggested that already, Andrew,' she smiled at him sympathetically, 'on the drive back here, remember?'

'Have you arranged for posters to go up at all bus and railway stations?'

'Yes, Andrew.' Despite his increasingly brusque manner Bernstein didn't appear to be rankled. Nor did she remind him that his time was running out as advisor. 'I did it when we issued the press release.'

Fenwick ran his hand through his hair and looked around the incident room, as if there might be a clue lurking in a corner that he had missed.

After he had read the most recent interview statements he went up to Operations but they had nothing to tell him. So far the roadblocks and traffic cameras had drawn a blank. After that he paced down to join Bernstein and team who were still going through tapes from around the swimming pool. They had been at it for hours and their eyes were red with exhaustion.

'We haven't been able to find anything else, sir,' Darren said grimly. 'There's no sighting on tape of him leaving the car park or in the roads immediately around there.'

'You should call it a day as soon as you've finished the final tape,' Bernstein said. 'He must still be within thirty or forty miles of Guildford. In this weather it would be impossible for him to drive further.' She sounded positive but with every minute Fenwick knew Mariner was becoming more difficult to find.

At two-thirty Bernstein came back with the profiler's report and complete histories of the Mariner brothers.

'He was a student of average intelligence but a serial underachiever according to his school records; he suffered from mild attention deficit disorder from the age of ten, which made him disruptive and difficult to teach. Until then he'd been a Joe-average kid, but apparently his dad left home never to return and he came under the influence of his older brother. Dan Mariner was a bully who terrorised the neighbourhood. By the time the kids were fourteen and eleven respectively they were known to social services and the police.

'There were numerous reports of vandalism and verbal abuse and they were arrested as juveniles for joyriding.'

'They were never prosecuted?' Fenwick asked but he thought he knew the answer.

'Nope.'

'So Steve Mariner is likely to have contempt for the law.'

'The profiler says that's possible but we shouldn't rule out that he is in awe of authority figures. He wasn't in trouble while his father was at home and seems to have been completely under his brother's influence. Dan was certainly beyond caring. He had a spell in the army but was dishonourably discharged. After that he drifted into a life of casual labour; there is no further record of arrest or conviction. Dan Mariner couldn't hold down a job and was often rough with women. There are two complaints from his late teens, from girls who say he forced them to have sex, but both were drunk at the time and later retracted their statements.'

'Have we matched his DNA to the system yet?'

'In process; Issie's evidence took priority.'

Fenwick was thinking of Flash Harry, the unsolved investigation he had regretted taking from Harlden and Nightingale.

'What about Steven Mariner? How did he manage to end up married and with a job at one of the top girls' colleges in the country?'

'In a minute, I haven't quite finished with Dan yet. There's more from social services. It appears both boys were on their watch list. There were suspicions of abuse though nothing was ever proven. Neighbours reported seeing the boys, particularly Dan, with bruises and once a broken arm but he said he'd got it falling out of a tree and it was left at that. He was a big lad for his age so they took his word for it. Interestingly, Steven was never seen with a scratch on him.'

'Was he assaulting his brother? Surely not?'

'Very unlikely; the profiler suggests it was probably the mother.

She was always screaming at her sons, even now she's bedridden. This week she spat hot tea in Dan's face when he visited, according to one of her carers. It looks as if Steven was smart enough to stay out of harm's way.'

'It sounds like Steve is the cleverer of the two but possibly weak-willed and easily manipulated,' Fenwick suggested.

'Could be; while his brother was in the army he finished school and ended up in a training scheme where he did well as a carpenter. He passed his technical exams and was apprenticed to a coffin-maker, of all things. While there he met the daughter of his supervisor who became Mrs Mariner. She used a contact of her uncle's to get him a job as a handyman at St Anne's when he fell out with her father.'

'He must be used to leading a double life,' Fenwick suggested and was rewarded with raised eyebrows and a small smile from Bernstein.

'That's exactly the profiler's conclusion. She says he's grown up in an abusive home, with a manipulating sadistic mother and an abused bully for a brother. Despite this he hasn't previously appeared to revert to violence or crime in adulthood. Somehow he managed to develop enough independence from his brother at a crucial stage in his life – late teens while his brother was in the army – which saved him from continuing to be totally dominated by him. Then his wife's good influence probably reduced the power the brother had over him. He may even be a bit scared of her, as his only experience of women was previously his mother whom he would have resented and feared.'

'Has he had any straightforward, positive experiences with women?'

'You mean does Issie stand a chance? Well, Annie Jones says he was quite a sweet boy. She had a bit of a thing for Dan rather than him but says he was sometimes with them at the pump house. Annie couldn't believe that he would abduct a girl.'

'Same as his wife. She didn't believe it either.' Fenwick scratched his cheek and yawned. 'That's what makes me think Steve Mariner is two people. Part of him is almost childlike, as if he never finished growing up. It means he might be able to live in a fantasy world, and that's good news for Issie. If somehow she becomes part of an alternative future he can believe in then there's a chance she'll stay alive.

'But the other side of him is the frustrated, dominated, younger brother, hating the world, hating himself but blaming all his failings on others, possibly in particular on women. At some point Issie could become a focus of real rage. She might come to be the reason for all his failures; even the murder of his brother could somehow become her fault. Then he will kill her – perhaps not with a deliberate blow but in a fit of rage, or he'll abandon her and in this weather she'll be dead in no time at all.'

Bernstein's expression had lost its habitual scorn as she stared at Fenwick.

'You didn't need that profiler's report, did you? You've done a better job than she did.'

'I think I'm getting to know him a little, Mariner I mean. We have to find him, Deidre. If we don't there's a real risk that he turns against Issie.'

'Yes, but right now you should try and get some sleep. I'll call you if anything comes up.'

'I'd rather stay; you go home. I won't be here next week. Other than going to see the Saxbys there's nothing else for me to do before I leave . . .' He looked down at a random piece of paper on the desk.

'Well, in case I don't get to see you tomorrow, it's been a privilege,' Bernstein said and stuck out her hand. 'Just so you know, Norman's decision to send you packing had nothing to do with me. In fact, I asked him to change his mind.'

'You did?'

'Yeah; I thought we had the makings of a good team but he's decided otherwise and the Home Office are no longer pushing the idea of a miracle worker from outside.'

'Right, well . . .' Fenwick shook her hand. 'I can do without that sort of label, so I don't regret it but I would have liked to get this job finished. I can't help but feel Issie is partly my responsibility now.'

Bernstein shook her head sympathetically.

'You'd be the same in my position, Deidre. Go get some sleep; that's the least I can do. I'll leave you a note if I think of anything else.'

He walked out of the room, not sure of where he was going and not really caring as long as he could be on his own.

CHAPTER TWENTY-TWO

The view outside Nightingale's window was obscured by sleet. Despite this, the pavement below was full of shoppers struggling through the weather to stock up on food ahead of a forecast blizzard. Christmas was just sixteen days away; the race was on.

Nightingale wasn't looking forward to the festivities and had volunteered to work the unpopular holiday shift, earning her more credit than all her solid hours of detective work. Jimmy's feedback about how she had handled the investigation into Flash Harry, particularly securing Jenni's statement before Sussex Major Crimes had taken it over, had helped to start a subtle thaw of attitudes in the detective room, of which she was as yet unaware.

Quinlan had taken on the Flash Harry case when he arrived to stand in for Fenwick at MCS. Big Mac had been seconded as she had predicted. At least Nightingale was able to keep up to date with progress unofficially. It was bittersweet to her that there had been none.

Jenni still hadn't talked about the rape but DNA results confirmed her case was linked to the other sexual assaults. She was now in a shelter being coaxed towards recovery by a psychologist. Nightingale's heart went out to her; poor kid.

With free time on her hands she had promised to have supper with her brother, sister-in-law and baby nephew. It was three years since the car crash that had killed her parents and the feeling of loss was no longer as raw. She suspected that the softening of grief was due in large part to the arrival of her nephew, Barnabas James, now eighteen months; a bonny June baby who brought constant delight to the cluster of Nightingale survivors.

She remembered with a start that she hadn't bought him a present. Auntie Louise never turned up empty-handed. Her gifts, though not extravagant, were always different and somehow right. She had also promised to drop in on Jenni to see how she was coping but when Nightingale called the shelter she was informed bluntly that Jenni was out.

Nightingale dressed as if for an Arctic expedition for her short visit to town. She was walking down a snow-thick causeway towards the shopping centre when her mobile rang. Assuming it was work she answered with irritation.

'Nightingale.'

'Is that you?' A hushed voice asked.

Nightingale covered her other ear.

'Yes; who is this? Jenni?'

'No,' the whisper insisted, 'it's Bess.'

'Bess?' Nightingale stopped abruptly, earning a curse from the man behind who skidded into her. There was only one Bess that Nightingale knew. 'Bess Fenwick?'

'Yes, who else?' the child insisted.

'Well, hi, Bess.' She moved into the shelter of a wall.

Why on earth would Bess be calling? She hadn't seen her for months.

'Nightingale, I miss you.'

'That's nice, Bess; is that why you're calling?'

'I want to see you.'

'Do you?' Nightingale was flattered, though she struggled to know what to say. Fenwick wouldn't like the idea of his daughter having formed any sort of emotional attachment beyond the family. She asked the obvious question to stall for time. 'Have you discussed the idea with your daddy?'

'He's not here but I know he wouldn't mind.'

'Even so, you should ask. How did you get my number?'

'From his address book. I know your new address too. I could come and see you.' Bess was not to be deflected; Nightingale suspected it was hereditary.

'Whoa! You can't come into Harlden on your own.' She had an image of little Bess at the bus station and her blood chilled.

'I'm twelve now,' Bess said with a touch of belligerence that was new.

'Twelve, mmm, well that does make you more grown up but still, you're not old enough for that sort of travel in this weather.' The Fenwick family home was miles outside Harlden.

'Says who? Nobody'd even notice I was gone.'

Nightingale sighed. At one time Bess and her father had been soulmates, brought closer by the death of Bess's mother after a long illness.

'Look, why don't I come and see you instead?' Nightingale suggested, concerned by the loneliness she heard behind the girl's plea.

'Today?' Bess's voice was brighter already.

'Well . . .'

'Oh please! I could meet you in town.'

'No, the snow is so bad, Bess, but I could come and visit if your daddy says yes.'

'I want to meet you in town. I'm allowed to go on my own now and I've saved up my pocket money so we could go and buy a dress for the school disco.'

Nightingale calculated that she would just be able to buy the dress with Bess and the present for Barnabas and still be in time for dinner with her brother.

'I could come and pick you up if Alice says yes.'

'I'd rather meet you at the bus station.' Bess sounded triumphant.

'No; I don't care if you're allowed out on your own, the weather is terrible and I don't want you to.'

'But . . .' Bess sounded awkward.

'You're already there, aren't you?'

'Yes.'

'Oh, Bess. I'll be there in ten minutes.'

Bess was shivering under a bus shelter when Nightingale found her.

'Bess; this is not good.'

'I was here already when I rang. I told you I could do it!'

'That's not the point; I'm disappointed in you. Behaving as you've done is almost like lying to me. I'm inclined to find a taxi and take you straight back home.'

Bess burst into noisy tears.

'Oh, come on, this is silly. Don't get upset just because you know you're in the wrong.'

The crying continued so Nightingale took her into a nearby café where she ordered two hot chocolates with whipped cream. Bess stopped crying and started to lick the cream.

'Why did you come out on your own? You always used to be such a good girl.'

'I still am,' Bess contended, then looked at Nightingale's sceptical face, 'sort of.'

'Hmm, I'm not impressed. If I can't trust you I won't be able to agree to see you again. You do realise that, don't you.'

'I just wanted to show you I could do it.'

'That's not the point. Will you promise that you'll always tell me the truth in future and that if we agree to something you'll stick to it?'

Bess nodded.

'Say it out loud, please.'

'I promise, always.'

'Good girl, now wipe your face and tell me what you've been up to.'

Bess chattered away, pleased to have an attentive audience. As Nightingale listened she studied the girl, noting a small pimple by the side of her nose, two others on her chin. Beneath a thick pullover Bess was no longer flat-chested. She was leaving her infancy and Nightingale was sadder than she knew was logical. How would Fenwick be coping with the changes in his little girl? She didn't think he'd be doing that well.

'How are Chris, Daddy and Alice?'

'Chris and Alice are always grumpy. And Daddy . . . well, I don't know . . . we don't talk much . . . he doesn't understand me any more.'

'He's a hard man to judge.' Nightingale couldn't suppress a wry grin at her understatement. 'Sometimes he can be surprisingly understanding. I'd talk to him if I were you. Tell him how you feel.'

'I never see him.'

'Is he really not home much, Bess?'

Bess drank her chocolate. Nightingale asked again but received a shrug in reply. Demonstrating yet again that she was her father's daughter, Bess avoided the emotional topic and changed the subject.

'Would you come and help me find a dress for the school Christmas party?'

'Why not go with Alice?'

'She hasn't got any dress sense.'

'That's unkind.'

'Well it's what my friend Lucy and her mum say. Alice is just the housekeeper. They told me I shouldn't start treating her like a relative, it wouldn't be right.'

'I think that's cruel. Alice is a lot more than a hired hand.

She's done a wonderful job of looking after you and Chris – the fancy-dress costumes she makes for you each year; and she's always helping with cakes for the fête – that's not the behaviour of someone who thinks of themselves as an employee, is it?'

'S'pose not. But why does Lucy's mum say so if it's not true?'

'I don't know but it's time you formed your own opinions, don't just copy someone else's. Kind thoughts are a lot nicer to have than cruel ones.'

'Will you come shopping with me?'

Nightingale was saved from answering by the shrill sound of a cat mewing a popular song. It was Bess's phone.

'Answer it, then.' Bess coloured and Nightingale guessed the reason with a detective's intuition. 'Oh no; you didn't go off without telling Alice, did you?' The silence spoke volumes. 'If you don't answer it I will.'

Bess flicked the phone open.

'Yes . . . I'm in town . . . With a friend . . . No, not with Lucy . . . I didn't say I would be with her . . . No I didn't! . . . But . . .' Nightingale glared and Bess subsided into a mutinous silence at the end of which she said, 'Oh, if I *must*,' and hung up, mouthing something unpleasant at the offending handset.

Nightingale ignored her theatrics and picked up their coats.

'Time to go. Come on, I'll find you a taxi.'

'When can I see you again? How about next Saturday; we could look for the dress?'

Nightingale was about to say no, that she wasn't available, but decided that wouldn't be the right answer, given Bess's frustration with her father.

'I think it would be nicer if you asked Alice. Buying a new dress is fun and she deserves to share some of that with you.'

'But she won't know what to buy like you will.'

'Oh, I think Alice could surprise you.'

Nightingale found a female taxi driver on the rank and waited until her car was at the head of the queue. Then she bundled Bess into the cab, gave the driver the address and enough money to cover the fare. As the car was about to pull away Bess gesticulated and the taxi pulled to a halt. Nightingale bent down as the passenger window opened.

'What's the matter?' she asked, huddling under her umbrella from the pattering sleet.

Bess hesitated, her face flushed, eyes uncertain.

'Are you . . . are you, like, that is . . . areyoustillseeingmydad?' The question came out in a rush of embarrassment. Before Nightingale could think of an answer Bess continued, 'Only if you are, well, Chris and me, well, we think that's OK; we'd sort of like that.'

She leant out and kissed Nightingale's cheek, her lips warm against ice-cold skin. Nightingale kissed her back, the gesture badly aimed because her sight was blurred.

Nightingale was at her brother's house by six, having bought Barnabas a bright-green caterpillar that waggled a long cuddly body in ecstatic reaction to being hit between the eyes. Not a politically correct present maybe, but it made her laugh. The door was opened by Simon, looking happy and in need of losing fifteen pounds.

'Sis! Come in. Naomi's just changing Barnabas. Let me get you a drink. You won't believe how he's grown since you last saw him. And he can talk!'

'Was it Mama or Dada first?'

'Mama, of course, but he can do more than that . . . you just wait.'

He poured her a glass of white wine and started chatting about work. He was an orthopaedic specialist and had just been accepted to work with a consultant surgeon. Nightingale was pleased for him and was about to tell him so when there was an excited shriek and Barnabas tumbled into the room on unsteady legs.

'Lou-Lou!' he shrieked, to his parents' obvious delight.

They smiled at their young Einstein and beamed proudly at Nightingale, who was struggling to cope with her reaction.

'What . . . what did he say?'

'Your name, of course,' Naomi laughed delightedly and hugged her sister-in-law with real affection. 'He recognises you from your picture. You were his sixth word, after Mama, Dada, Dog, Nana, Baa, in that order. We thought you'd be pleased.'

Nightingale gathered up her nephew and lifted him high in the air, swinging him around to his delight. Her action diverted his parents from her overbright eyes. It wasn't just the fact that he could say her name that had moved her; it was also what he had called her. How could they know its significance? She hadn't yet told them what she had discovered during her stay at the derelict family farm three summers before. How could she tell the brother she adored that she wasn't his twin sister, just a half-blood cuckoo slipped into the nest at a day old when his real twin sister died?

During that long, hot, terrifying summer at Mill Farm, she had finally unravelled her dead aunt's cryptic clues to reveal a truth that was shocking yet somehow reassuring: she wasn't her mother's daughter, but a bastard ('love child' part of her mind insisted) sired by her father with his long-time lover Lulu. It had all made sense suddenly; her resemblance to the woman increased as she grew up and her mother had pushed her away. She had felt lost, unloved, unconnected in a way that had driven her away from home. The discovery of who she really was had provided a missing piece of the jigsaw that was her life, though she had never revealed it to anyone and still hadn't worked out what to do with the knowledge. She didn't even know whether her real mother was alive; she hadn't even googled her! What sort of denial was that?

Nightingale hugged Barnabas and breathed in the unique clean baby smell of him that made her heart lurch, before placing him on his play rug to unwrap the caterpillar. It was, as anticipated, an immediate hit. When she looked up her eyes were dry.

Supper was typically delicious. Naomi and Simon had gained pounds since they married but at least now they could no longer criticise her for being skinny. She was a healthy weight again thanks to a sensible diet and rigorous exercise regime. Although her appetite still vanished when she was stressed, she now forced herself to eat.

She was sipping claret and nibbling crumbly white Wensleydale while Naomi put the finishing touches to dessert, when Simon started the conversation she had been dreading.

'So who's the lucky man in your life?'

'There isn't one, Simon, as well you know.'

'No I don't. And anyway, I can't believe it; you're just too attractive to be single.'

'I don't need a man to define who I am.'

'That's not what I mean. You won't talk about your future plans because you're so bloomin' private but I know you well enough to recognise that you'd make a wonderful partner for someone . . . you can pretend to be tough all you like but you can't fool me.'

'Whatever happened to that man you were in love with three summers ago?' Naomi asked, staggering in under a tray of desserts that would have fed a rugby team.

'There was no one, Naomi.' Nightingale hated the way her sister-in-law noticed everything. It hadn't been the death of her parents and a terrible period at work that had driven her away to the farm; it had been Fenwick, but that was her secret.

'Rubbish, you had all the symptoms. I thought he was going to be the one.'

'Well, he wasn't,' Nightingale replied sharply, preferring to acknowledge that there had been someone rather than risk the conversation dragging on.

'I'm glad you dumped Clive,' Simon continued. 'Nice enough bloke but selfish.'

'Enough, the two of you. I don't ask embarrassing questions about your love life so leave mine alone!' It was said with a laugh and they both had the grace to blush.

An hour later she was playing with Barnabas, who had been brought down to stop him screaming. He was chasing his new caterpillar, christened Eddie by his father who delighted in hitting its head rather hard in order to see it wriggle and squirm. Simon raised the subject again.

'We're a bit worried about you.'

'What is it this time? My weight's fine – firmly in the target range for my height, thank you – and the security at my flat would foil a safe-cracker.'

'It's the personal stuff. You live for your work. Sure, you're good at it but it won't keep you warm at night when you're flab and fifty.'

'So that's what marriage is all about, is it? A security blanket for middle age.'

'You know what I mean. It's about love, finding a soulmate who makes everything you do worthwhile; maybe even having a family. You shouldn't leave it too long.'

'Simon! I'm not even thirty; do me a favour.'

He raised his hands in capitulation but couldn't resist adding, 'All right, but you do *me* a favour then. Indulge yourself; take time out; have some fun. You don't deserve to end up a dried-out old maid. You're far too good for that.'

Nightingale went to bed shortly afterwards, not so much driven away by their words as by the atmosphere of overwhelming domestic bliss. She didn't envy them she told herself but too much of their contentment made her introspective and broody; because, of course, her brother was right. She ached to find the right partner and have a family; to know that there was someone, somewhere in the world who was worrying about her, waiting for her, caring about what she did, about how she felt, whether she was happy. Someone who would want to be the father of her children.

It was a basic, urgent need and maybe he was right to remind her of it. The only problem was that she would have to feel the same way about that person, to reciprocate absolutely, and so far there had been only one man for whom she had experienced that depth of feeling. Sadly he had made it very clear that he was unavailable, no matter what his daughter might have wished for.

CHAPTER TWENTY-THREE

Thoughts of his final conversation with Bernstein filled Fenwick's head as he waited for the door to Saxby Hall to open on Sunday afternoon. He couldn't just disappear without having seen them. Despite the most extensive search operation he had ever witnessed they had failed to find Issie. Norman was continuing the road checks and had committed more officers. Forces in Sussex, Hampshire and Kent were all on alert for Mariner and his Mondeo but the man had vanished.

At least the weather hadn't deteriorated further. The predicted blizzard had veered south, with Surrey suffering only a flurry. Unfortunately in Sussex, particularly along the coast, three inches of snow had fallen in the last few hours. Alice, bless her, had left him another message that morning telling him not to worry; they were safe and warm and had enough to eat. The news just made him feel guilty.

Fenwick took a deep breath and rang the doorbell. Norman would already have told them that they had been within hours of finding their daughter; what more could he say to them except goodbye?

'Yes? Oh, it's you. Come in.' The door was opened by Saxby himself, looking even older than when Fenwick had seen him two days before.

He went straight to the drawing room where the bare Christmas tree leant forlorn. There was a small fire smoking in the grate and a pile of unopened post on a table by the sofa.

'Jane's still asleep, thank God. The doctor came last night and gave her an injection because she refused to take the pills. She's in a terrible state, Fenwick. It's six days now without any sight of Issie. Even though she – we – still hope, well . . . It's not looking good, is it?' Saxby had tears in his eyes and Fenwick didn't know what to say. 'It's all right; I'm not asking you to lie. It's just . . . I feel so helpless. The one thing that matters most to me is my wife and her daughter and I can't help them. I can't do a bloody thing.'

Saxby folded onto the sofa and pretended to look at the pile of post while blinking rapidly.

'Christmas cards. I've stopped Jane opening them – these need to be cleared away. She breaks down when she sees Issie's name. The letters from other parents at the school are even worse; people that wouldn't acknowledge us before, sending us well-intentioned cards and notes of support . . .

'The birthday cards will start soon. That'll be even worse. A week today she'll be eighteen.'

His voice broke and for a long moment there was just the soft crackling of the struggling fire to break the silence. Saxby shuddered and took a deep breath.

'I just want Issie back and my wife to be happy. Not much to ask is it? So why are you here and not out there looking for her?'

Norman obviously hadn't told them he was off the case. Fenwick thought rapidly and decided it wasn't news for him to break.

'I, er, just wanted to see if you had any questions after the latest development.'

Saxby shook his head but then paused and frowned at Fenwick.

'As you're here you might as well give me your take on the situation.'

Fenwick tried not to wince; he couldn't afford to contradict Norman.

'Well, the evidence is clear that Issie was kept somewhere

253

relatively warm and that she was probably fed since leaving the caravan.'

'Norman told me that much but what he wouldn't tell me was how long she'd been in the pump house or how close you came to catching that bastard Mariner. Will you?'

Fenwick couldn't meet his eye. Would it help to know how close they had come? No, just the reverse but he deserved to know.

'We can't say for sure but if you want my guess—'

'I just asked for it!'

'Then I would say we were hours behind them.'

'So if you'd been a bit more bloody efficient . . .' Saxby couldn't finish the thought and stalked to the far end of the room.

Fenwick watched the tension in his shoulders, regretting that he had made the visit.

'I should be going, sir.'

'Wait! I haven't finished with you yet.' He walked back until he was standing less than five feet from Fenwick, his cheeks deep red, eyes bulging, obviously full of pent-up rage.

'Why was Norman so certain Issie was kept there alive?'

Fenwick could tell by the way he asked the question that Saxby had already guessed.

'At the pump station we found clear evidence that someone had been staying there, two people in fact.'

'How can you be so certain?' Saxby demanded.

Fenwick took a deep breath. He hated what he had to say next.

'It looks as if she was abused by him, sir. I'm so sorry. There is a slight chance it was consensual of course but . . .'

Saxby lunged forward and took a swing at Fenwick, missing by inches as he managed to twist away. He grabbed Saxby's arms and held them tight to his side, standing so close that he could whisper his next words.

'I know; it hurts like hell that the only evidence that Issie is alive is that she's been abused, and I am so, so sorry but if you can bear to, try to see it as the proof of life we so needed.'

'Fuck you, fuck your filthy mouth, you . . .' But Saxby was crying too hard to finish.

'It may even be that the kidnapper has formed some sort of attachment to her. That's the best development we could hope for short of finding her.'

'Jesus help us.' It was said as a prayer, not blasphemy.

Fenwick guided Saxby back to the sofa and eased him down. The man lowered his face into his hands and wept. Realising that he would hate a witness to such a collapse, Fenwick motioned the FLO out and left to find the kitchen. The cook and butler were there red-eyed and white-faced.

'He doesn't like us up there, sir,' the butler explained.

'I understand but we need sustenance. Does he drink coffee or tea?'

'Coffee, sir,' the cook answered and jumped up, keen to be of use.

'Good, make us a big pot, with milk and sugar on the side, please.' He turned to leave.

'If you don't mind my saying so, sir, you could do with something yourself, and more than just coffee. I know the look of a man living on his reserves. Can I make you a nice plate of bacon and eggs?' The cook looked at him hopefully and Fenwick's stomach growled low in answer but he ignored it.

'Welcome as that would be, I don't think it would be acceptable right now, thank you.'

Saxby was stoking the fire when Fenwick returned.

'Can we keep the news of the . . . assault on Issie from Jane?'

'I won't tell her, sir, and I'll mention to Tony that it should be kept quiet but your wife is a smart lady – she will probably work it out for herself.'

'Perhaps, but I'll deal with that when it happens.' Saxby looked at the portrait of his wife on the chimney breast and touched it with his fingertips.

'There's something else that may become public that you need to be aware of.' Fenwick knew he was on thin ice as Norman should tell them, but he judged Saxby to be a man who hated anything being kept from him and had decided during the short visit to the kitchen that he had to know all.

'You are a bird of ill omen, Fenwick; what now?'

'It is very likely that Steven Mariner murdered his brother and possible that Issie saw it.'

'Murdered?' Saxby turned around and stared at Fenwick in horror.

'We found the body of Daniel Mariner at the caravan where Issie was held. The killing might have been accidental; it might even have been to protect Issie. There is a risk that the press will pick up on this even though we have made no announcement. A murder is hard to keep quiet.'

'Murder.' Saxby looked back to his wife's picture. 'If he's killed once . . .'

'As I say, there is a strong possibility that it wasn't intentional and there is nothing in the history of Steven Mariner to suggest a tendency towards violence.'

'There was nothing to suggest he was a kidnapper either, was there?'

'No, but if you recall, we thought the kidnap might be opportunistic. That would fit with what we know about him.'

Saxby glanced at him sceptically but swiftly turned his back when the butler brought in a large tray of coffee and biscuits. He retreated quickly, smiling sympathetically at Fenwick.

'Coffee? I don't need it, take it away.'

Fenwick recognised the tone of the bully taking over from the grieving stepfather.

'But I do and I'm going to have some before I leave, if you don't mind. I can get by on a few hours sleep a night with no problem as long as I have caffeine, but without it I run on empty. Something to eat and drink would do you good too.'

The bluntness of Fenwick's answer surprised Saxby. He opened his mouth to argue but shut it again and went over to the tray and poured himself a coffee with milk and sugar. Saxby added a measure of brandy to his coffee and waved the bottle at Fenwick who shook his head. They drank their coffee in a silence that could not have been described as congenial. Fenwick stood to leave.

'There is something more that I need to tell you, sir. As Chief Constable Norman has assumed control of the investigation he will be keeping you updated personally on developments. There's a team of over one hundred looking for Issie, across the whole of the south-east, with a nationwide alert that is bringing the eyes of the nation's police and general public to our aid. He is determined to find her.'

Saxby nodded in reply, a proud man who would find it hard to apologise for anything and wouldn't forgive a witness to his prior weakness easily. Fenwick picked up his coat, hat and scarf and made to leave. Before he reached the living room door, Saxby stuck his arm out and shook Fenwick's hand, much to his surprise. His second, pleasant surprise was a warm packet thrust at him by the cook as he opened the front door.

'Bacon sandwiches,' she said with a smile, 'for you and your driver. I pray to God every night for our Issie to come home and you're doing his work. It's the least I can do.'

Fenwick closed the door to the Hall softly and paused with his head bowed by her words, but the smell of hot bacon and the chill of the biting wind soon drove him to the shelter of the car.

PART THREE

'Death's a great Disguiser.'

William Shakespeare,
Measure for Measure

CHAPTER TWENTY-FOUR

Nightingale watched Jenni-with-an-I finish her plate of ham, egg and chips and wipe it clean with a slice of bread. The girl looked better, with the polished complexion of someone taking care of themselves. She was still receiving trauma counselling but had so far continued to refuse to give her real name. At least she was out of the cold.

'OK if I see you again next week on my day off?'

The girl stared at her suspiciously.

'Why are you doing this? I'm not going to tell you anything.'

'I'm under no false illusions, Jenni. You're clearly a person who makes up their own mind but someone once helped me rebuild my life. I don't have any expectation that you need me to do the same for you but I do want you to know that you're not alone. That's all. No hidden agenda.'

Jenni shook her head and then shrugged.

'Whatever, I appreciate the meal; it's better than the stuff they serve at the shelter. We all have to muck in with the cooking and none of us is Jamie Oliver, that's for sure.'

'That should be an incentive to learn, then,' Nightingale suggested laughing through Jenni's scowl. 'Can I give you a lift back?'

'Nah, I'll hang about a bit. There's usually a good crowd about on a Saturday.'

'OK.' Nightingale put on her coat, scarf, hat and gloves.

'See you for lunch next week, then? You can call anytime before, if you like.'

'Suit yourself. My diary isn't exactly overfull.'

Nightingale left biting her lip. Jenni wasn't going to change. Outside, the wind funnelled down the open walkway bringing blasts of ice particles and grit that stung her face. It was another gloomy day that the seasonal shop windows failed to lighten, but despite the weather, people were out enjoying enforced camaraderie as they slipped about on crowded pavements.

What should she do next? It was her day off and she really did need to do some Christmas shopping, not that she had that many people to buy for but she was an indulgent aunt and this year she wanted to find something nice for Jenni and for Bess, Chris and Alice.

'Better get on with it,' she muttered and decided to drive closer in to Harlden town centre. She was pulling into the multi-storey car park when her mobile rang. The Harlden number that flashed up on the screen brought an instant knot of tension.

'Hello?'

'Louise? Is that you?'

She recognised the voice at once and her heart rate increased.

'Alice, yes; what's the matter?'

'Thank goodness; it's Bess. I wondered if you might have seen her. Only after last week when she ran off to meet you I thought . . .'

Nightingale could feel incipient panic but she kept her voice calm.

'No, she's not with me. If she'd contacted me I would have let you know.'

'Of course you would, it's just that . . . I hoped – that is, I thought . . . Oh, I'm worried sick. She's not answering her mobile and I don't want to leave the house in case she comes back. And there's Chris to think about . . . what am I going to do?'

'How long has she been missing?'

'I noticed her gone half an hour ago. I've rung round her friends but she's not with any of them. She'd been sulking all morning because she wants a new outfit for the school party on Monday and won't let me take her to buy it.'

'Have you called her father?'

'I've tried but there's no answer. He went in to work this morning even though it's Saturday, but no one there knows where he is. What are we going to do?'

Nightingale noted that she was considered part of the solution and in other circumstances would have been pleased.

'Let me think. You say you've tried Bess's phone?'

'Yes, but there's no answer.'

'If she has caller id and she's in a sulk she may simply be refusing to pick up because the call's coming from home. I'll ring her now and call you back.'

Nightingale broke the connection and rang Bess's number, which still showed on her phone from the previous week. She was answered at once.

'Nightingale!'

'Hello, Bess, how are you?'

'OK, sort of. I'm looking for a dress but I can't find one.'

'Is Alice with you?'

'No.' The tone said *so what?*

'Your friend Lucy and her mum?'

'No,' more defensive now.

'I see. So you'd be on your own?'

'. . .'

'Was that a yes, Bess?'

'Yes,' muttered.

'And whereabouts are you?'

'Guildford.' Nightingale closed her eyes. 'I came on the train; the bus wasn't running.'

'Hmm, that's a long way from home on such a rotten day. When are you planning to come back?'

'As soon as I've found a dress but . . .' There was the faintest hint of a whine.

'. . . you can't find one and the trip hasn't turned out as expected?'

'Maybe.'

'That can happen.'

Nightingale was biting her lip again. Understanding would work better than shouting if Bess's character was anything like her's had been at her age.

'Are you lonely? I know I would be.'

'Yes, a bit,' said very quietly with maybe even a sniff. Nightingale wanted her contrite and cautious not emotional and even more vulnerable.

She kept her voice matter-of-fact even though her stomach was churning.

'Whereabouts in Guildford are you?'

'The Friary shopping centre, in Top Shop.'

'I think there's a café in the Friary isn't there? I want you to go there and wait. When you're at a table ring me back, OK?'

'Yes. You'll come for me?'

'Either me, or Alice, or your daddy but somebody will. Now go and find a table.'

Nightingale plugged her phone into hands-free and rang Alice as she put her car in gear and headed north to Harlden train station. She told her the news and Alice was predictably delighted, furious and worried at the same time.

'How on earth are we going to get the silly little madam back?'

'Can you drive to Guildford with Chris?'

'Not in this weather, dear; I hate driving at the best of times. I only go to and from town. I'd be terrified out on the roads in these conditions.'

'I see. Well keep trying her father. Meanwhile, I'll head for the train station and see if I can catch the fast service to Guildford. It will be much quicker than driving, provided the trains are running.'

Nightingale was stuck at traffic lights when Bess called.

'I'm in the restaurant, Nightingale.'

'Good. Is there a waitress nearby?'

'Yes, why?'

'I need to talk to her. Put her on the phone, please.'

'That means asking her over . . . I can't.'

'If you consider yourself old enough to trot off to Guildford on your own in the middle of the worst winter we've had in years then you are *certainly* capable of speaking to a waitress. Please do it now.'

Nightingale was aware that she was using her 'in charge' voice, the one normally reserved for work. She had to smile as she heard the distant voice of an obviously shocked Bess asking someone to please come to the table for an important message. A wary waitress spoke into the mobile.

'What's your name, please?'

'Angela.'

'Angela, this is Detective Inspector Nightingale of Harlden police. The young lady at your table is lost and on her own and it is of vital importance to an ongoing inquiry that she is safely returned to her family as soon as possible. Please would you serve her a warm drink and maybe some food; but above all, make sure that she doesn't leave the table until someone she knows or bearing police id comes to collect her.'

'Why me? There's a security guard just yards away.'

'Even better; put him on please but make no mistake, Angela, if she isn't there when we come to collect her we will also hold you responsible.'

'But . . .'

'The security guard, please.'

Nightingale repeated her message to the guard, noted down his details and gave him her mobile number just in case.

By this time she was parking at the station. If the trains had been cancelled or were severely delayed, she would have no option but to drive, but if a train was due she could be with Bess in forty minutes. She ran to the entrance. One look at the board told her that the two-thirty-two was leaving from platform four in less than three minutes!

She waved her warrant card in the general direction of the member of staff who had moved to intercept her as she jumped the ticket barrier and sprinted up the stairs. Seven strides along the bridge over the tracks and she was pounding down the stairs to the platform as she heard the beep of the doors about to close.

'Police! Hold that train,' she commanded as her feet hit the concrete. A startled-looking youth in a hoodie obliged by moving his body to block the automatic doors long enough for Nightingale to jump on board.

'Thanks,' she said to him, her sides heaving a bit more than they should have been.

'No problem. Need a hand catchin' someone?'

Nightingale grinned at him.

'Thanks, but I think I can manage this one on my own.'

The doors closed behind her and the train started to move. A guard stalked down the carriage but she flashed her warrant card and he backed off.

'How long to Guildford?'

'Can't say with this weather. The line was cleared earlier and we made it in normal time but the weather's got worse since . . .'

He went away to check and came back to say that the line was still clear and they should be there within forty-five minutes; longer than normal but better than she had feared.

Nightingale found a quiet corner and rang Alice to give her an update. Then she called Bess, who was delighted that her friend was on her way and starting to enjoy her celebrity status far too much in the circumstances. '*What are we going to do with her?*' Nightingale shook her head in frustration and took a deep breath before dialling Fenwick's number. There was no answer and his messaging service was full. Typical.

She had heard from Big Mac that he had returned to MCS the previous Monday and was no longer involved in the hunt for Isabelle Mattias. Speculation was rife about what it meant for his reputation but at least there was someone decent in charge of the Flash Harry investigation again. Much as she liked Quinlan he was a lousy detective. Big Mac was still seconded to MCS and had confided that they had made no progress.

In the two weeks since the case had been passed to MCS she had worked up her own theories and worried over them. Given the escalating pattern there should have been another attack by now and she wondered why there hadn't been. It was something she planned to ask Fenwick when . . . if . . . she saw him. As the train eased forward there was nothing for her to do so she settled back in the seat and wished she had brought her notes with her in case Fenwick showed up.

The train pulled into Guildford station twenty minutes late. She showed her warrant card and bought return tickets from the guard at the barrier before making her way to the Friary. When she left the station it wasn't actually snowing but the wind whipped up loose drifts as she walked through bustling, icy streets.

When she reached the shopping centre it took her a moment to orientate as it had changed since she was last there. A floor plan revealed that there were several restaurants and cafés to choose from and she had tried two of them before taking the escalator down to the third where she could see Bess below her. As she descended, a man approached Bess from behind. Nightingale let out a shout and called Bess's name before running down the last few steps, slipping on the wet floor and into the café – almost stumbling on to Fenwick's back as she did so. How had he made it so quickly from Lewes to Guildford?

'Nightingale.'

'Andrew.'

'What are you doing here?' The abruptness of his words stung.

'Looking after your daughter. We couldn't reach you so I agreed with Alice that I'd come myself to bring her home.'

'Well, that's kind of you but as you can see, there was no need.'

Nightingale stared at him open-mouthed. The man really could be an ungrateful bastard. She was about to tell him so when Bess intervened.

'Daddy, that's not very polite. We didn't know that you'd turn up, did we Nightingale, and Alice was worried sick. If it hadn't been for Nightingale you don't know where I might have been.'

Carried away with her passionate defence of her friend, Bess didn't realise the hole she was digging for herself. Both adults turned to her with identical expressions of disapproval.

'Whoops.'

'Whoops indeed,' they said together. Fenwick smiled at her bleakly.

'Sorry, I was out of line. I should have said thank you for wasting your Saturday afternoon on our behalf.'

'It wasn't wasted. I'm just glad she's OK.' Nightingale turned to Bess. 'You had us all worried sick, you know. This is not the way to behave; I've told you that before.'

'But I didn't lie. I just left the house and came here.'

'Without telling anybody,' Fenwick interjected. 'We'll talk more about this at home.'

He ran a hand through his hair in a gesture Nightingale recognised too well.

'I can take her, Andrew, if you have to be somewhere.'

'Could you?'

'Daddy!'

'Alice said you had to work so . . .'

'It would be a big help.'

'Daddy!'

'Quiet, Bess.'

Given Bess's earlier stroppiness, Nightingale expected an outburst but the child simply lowered her head.

'Do you have time for a cup of tea and something to eat?' Nightingale asked. 'Knowing you, you've probably been living off coffee and scraps.'

'I haven't had any lunch, you're right.'

They ordered three toasted cheese and ham sandwiches, a large pot of tea and a glass of milk. Bess's request for a hot chocolate was denied. As they waited Nightingale wondered how to talk to Fenwick about Flash Harry. When Bess said she needed the loo they let her go on her own as they could see the entrance from the table.

'I really am grateful, Nightingale. Whatever you say, this has screwed up your day.'

'It's no problem, honestly. Look—'

'Earlier you said to Bess "I've told you before". Is this a common occurrence?'

Nightingale told him quickly about Bess's previous excursion into Harlden.

'This is getting out of hand.' He rubbed his forehead and frowned. 'I'm going to have to do something. What would you suggest?'

An olive branch?

'I'll give it some thought, but right now there's something else I need to ask you. How did you manage to reach Guildford so quickly? It said on the news that the A27 and the A23 were blocked and traffic was at a standstill.'

Fenwick flushed and scowled. He opened his mouth but then shut it.

'You were already here, weren't you; following up unofficially?'

He gave a rueful laugh and nodded.

'I should have known you would work it out. Bernstein called me and suggested we meet for a coffee. There's been no trace of Mariner, his car or Issie all week and she's run out of ideas. Despite everyone assuming we wouldn't get on we actually worked well together.'

Nightingale started playing with the crumbs on her plate.

'Not that I'm being any help. Since finding the place where Issie had been kept there's been no decent leads to follow despite the reward the Saxbys are offering.'

'I noticed the case was no longer headline news but I'd hoped that was deliberate.'

'Unfortunately not. Saxby has hired an army of private investigators and deployed a whole investigative journalist team to work on it but even they can't find anything. Issie has simply vanished.'

'I had an idea,' she ventured and winced at the sudden hope on Fenwick's face. 'Not about Issie, I'm afraid, but about Flash Harry.'

'Him!' He sounded dismissive.

'Look, I know you're worried sick about Issie but that man is a threat to young women everywhere and you owe it to them to be as concerned about finding him as you are her!' Nightingale noted the change of expression and added too late, 'Sir.'

Fenwick looked away, obviously angry but she waited him out in silence.

'Go on, then. What's your idea?'

'When I interviewed Jenni she mentioned that she had been intending to stay with a cousin. It didn't work out and the way she said it I sensed she had been asked to do something she wouldn't, probably sexual. I wondered whether this cousin might be Flash Harry.'

Said out loud in plain words it sounded pathetic so she was not surprised when Fenwick shook his head.

'I'm thinking it's more likely Flash Harry is Daniel Mariner. There hasn't been an attack since he was discovered dead. Bernstein is running his DNA but isn't giving it enough priority. You've reminded me that I need to chase her. Thank you.'

He met her eyes and despite his abrupt dismissal of her idea she had to prevent herself from reaching out to touch his hand. Worry for Issie seemed to be eating him up.

'Are they likely to ask you back on the case?'

He squirmed in his chair but Bess's return gave him an excuse for avoiding the question.

'Can I help at all?' Nightingale asked as Bess sipped her milk through a straw. 'Does he have friends in Sussex I could go and interview?'

'That's been done already, more than once. They've also checked with every one of her friends and the homes of family members in case she persuaded him to go to somewhere familiar. Nothing; and as neither of the Mariner brothers had a garage or lock-up they're out of ideas.'

'And no sign of a . . . ?' Nightingale glanced at the top of Bess's head and stopped short.

Fenwick mouthed 'body' and shook his head.

'He said "body", Nightingale,' Bess chirped.

'Time for you to go home, young lady.' At least Fenwick was grinning. 'Come and give me a hug before you go.'

'Can I buy my dress first, Daddy, seeing as you and Nightingale are both here and you're my favourite people?'

Fenwick opened his mouth to reply but Nightingale was there first.

'Certainly not; do you really think your father or I would reward your behaviour?'

Bess's eyes filled with tears at the roughness of Nightingale's words.

'Don't try it, Bess. You know you've done wrong and it's too late to try soppy tactics.'

'But it's the party on Monday!'

Nightingale saw doubt on Fenwick's face; he was tempted to indulge her. She shook her head and he sighed in acknowledgement.

'I'm sure you have some lovely clothes in the wardrobe that will do very well,' he said. 'If you had only gone shopping with Alice when you had the chance you'd have something new to wear, but it's too late now.'

Bess turned huge, tear-filled eyes to her father whose face softened before he caught sight of Nightingale's expression.

'You heard, Bess. The answer's no. Now give me a nice goodbye.'

Instead his daughter burst into tears, causing Fenwick such obvious distress that it made Nightingale quite annoyed. She bundled Bess into her coat unceremoniously and shook her head at Fenwick in a sign that said *pay her no heed* but the poor man tried to give his daughter a hug, which simply made matters worse.

'I'll be home soon, Bess. Be a good girl, now; be nice to Alice and say hello to your brother for me.' He turned to Nightingale. 'Thank you . . . for everything. I don't know what we'd do without you.' And he bent forward to kiss her cheek in a gesture that left Nightingale too surprised to respond.

He was gone before she could say anything, leaving her to find their hats, scarves and gloves in a state of emotional confusion. Given the unappreciative audience Bess stopped crying. By the time they were at the railway station she was actually in a good mood. It had started to snow again and they had to wait half an hour for a train that took over an hour to travel to Harlden. During the journey Nightingale spoke to Bess about her behaviour, or perhaps lectured would be a more appropriate word. She never told Fenwick or Alice what she said but by the time they arrived Bess was quiet, with no trace of her earlier sulk.

Nightingale had agreed with Alice that she would drive Bess home given the housekeeper's fear of the icy roads. Chris opened the door before she could knock and jumped into her arms as Alice hovered behind in the hall.

'Come in! Alice has made a special supper for you; you're going to stay the night and we can play a game and then you can read me a story in bed. It's only fair as Bess had you all afternoon.'

Nightingale didn't know what to say. It was almost seven o'clock and the temperature was far below freezing. She didn't fancy the drive back one bit but on the other hand . . .

'You're surely not thinking of driving home in this?' Alice gestured at the fresh snow.

'I have things to do.'

'So leave first thing in the morning. Come on, Louise. You're letting the warmth out.'

The children started to drag and push her over the threshold and she offered little resistance.

'Looks like I'll have to burden your hospitality after all then, Alice. Thank you.'

The children whooped as Alice locked the door for the night.

CHAPTER TWENTY-FIVE

After the incident with Bess, Fenwick decided he really did need to spend some time at home. Even so, he had stayed late with Bernstein. She agreed to have Dan Mariner's DNA analysis given more priority; her budget was virtually unlimited and no one would think to question it. In return Fenwick lingered in the major incident room with her, sympathising as she described the useless leads they were required to follow up as a result of Saxby's offer of a generous reward. Of course one of them might be for real but so far all it was doing was 'burning shoe leather', as she put it.

When Fenwick asked if he could look through some of them she had laughed and challenged him to get a life but left him to it. Fenwick found himself behind a cliff of paperwork in which he immediately immersed himself. By the time he had resurfaced and driven back to Harlden everyone was in bed. He stayed up late sipping a whisky and tried the Saturday crossword but he couldn't concentrate and gave up with three clues unanswered at three in the morning.

On Sunday he woke late and was annoyed to find that Louise Nightingale had been staying the night, leaving before breakfast to return to work. He was going to say something about it but Alice was in such a good mood, as were the children, that he kept quiet. What was left of the morning was spent with Bess and Chris playing games before eating a late lunch, 'like a proper family' as Bess said pointedly.

Alice was sent for an afternoon nap at his insistence, leaving him with the washing-up while the children disappeared to watch a film. He realised that he hadn't spoken to his mother for days. She had been let out of hospital after twenty-four hours, with nothing worse to show for her fall than bruising and a headache. The suspected fractured arm diagnosed in A&E had turned out to be a scar from an old injury. There was nothing to stop her travelling down to spend Christmas with them as planned. She was due to arrive on the twentieth and then return to her friends in time for Hogmanay.

When Fenwick called she was characteristically terse. He asked whether she might consider coming a little earlier, phrasing the idea lightly. His mother explained that she had already purchased her return rail ticket, well in advance to secure the best price, which left him in a dilemma. Should he admit that he needed her; that Alice was close to exhaustion?

No. Even if his mother wasn't badly hurt, she was recuperating and in no state to help. He said nothing except that should she decide to travel earlier, her room was ready waiting and the children would be delighted to see her. Something in his tone must have prompted her to ask after Alice. He replied briefly but his mother wouldn't let the topic drop.

'That poor woman is a saint. You're lucky to have her.'

'I know; I hope she realises that I'm grateful.'

'I wouldn't count on it.'

He bit back a retort that an inability to demonstrate appreciation was probably inherited.

After the call he went to sit in the conservatory with the Sunday papers. His subconscious was trying to tell him something that his conscious mind was busy suppressing. It was a feeling he was accustomed to. As he sat down he noticed an enormous pile of ironing in the corner. With a groan he set up the ironing board, suspecting that his motive was self-serving. He worked his way slowly through the pile with the radio on. As soon as it was finished he would try and have a nap. A car would be picking him up early the following morning and he wasn't a good sleeper at the best of times; hadn't been since his wife's death.

The steady repetition of the iron smoothing the laundry was therapeutic. His thoughts drifted with the sweep of the steaming-hot iron, from Flash Harry, to Issie, to his children, skirting the solitary hole in the middle of his life with accustomed ease; back to his fears for Issie, how he wished her parents had been smart enough to realise how damaged she was; to fear that he would mess up the same way with Bess, to baffled confusion as to how to reach her, how she needed a good role model; and so eventually, inevitably, to Nightingale. No matter how much he tried, whenever his mind emptied, thoughts of her would invade. Yet she scared him. The word brought his thinking to a shuddering stop and he raised his head, staring sightlessly at Chris's makeshift fort in the corner of the conservatory.

A whiff of scorching returned him to reality and he looked down to see that he had melted a brown patch on the knee of Bess's favourite glittery pink leggings. He had always hated them and part of him was pleased that they were ruined but then he remembered that she had planned to wear them to the school disco the following day.

'Oh no – she's going to go nuts!' Fenwick's breathing quickened; so much for helping out. There was only one thing for it.

In his bedroom at the back of the wardrobe was a bulging carrier bag. Fenwick was in the habit of buying gifts for his children whenever he saw something that he thought they would like. He would then keep them for Christmas or birthdays. This had two advantages; he spoilt them less than spontaneous giving would have done and it meant that he had a backup in case he didn't manage to buy them the special present he always meant to. At the bottom of the bag he found the pair of black jeans with embroidered peacocks on the legs and a matching sequined top that he had bought the month before and had been saving for Christmas. He would leave them for Bess to wear to the disco. There was a model thirteenth-century knight in armour for Chris to keep things fair.

Nightingale would have been furious that he was rewarding Bess's poor behaviour but there was no way he could leave Alice to face his daughter's fury at the destruction of the leggings.

At five he put the ironing board away and sent Chris to run his bath so that he could have a few minutes with Bess alone. She was making a model house for her brother's railway in an uncharacteristically sisterly gesture and they were assembling it together when the phone rang. He noticed Bess tense as he went to his study. It was Acting Chief Constable Harper-Brown. A teenage girl had been raped and it had all the hallmarks of Flash Harry.

'Thanks for letting me know, sir. I'll ask for the reports to be put on my desk first thing in the morning.'

'This is a very serious assault, Andrew. The girl is unconscious and may have brain damage. It could even be considered attempted murder.'

'I'm sure Jimmy MacDonald is handling the scene well, sir. He's a dependable man and I have every confidence in him.'

'That's not the point, Fenwick. Do I have to spell it out for you?'

'Apparently so, sir.' Fenwick was biting the inside of his lip.

He heard Harper-Brown exhale noisily and then grunt.

'Very well; you asked for it. It may have escaped your notice that you left the Mattias case with your reputation in less than first-class shape.'

'Isn't that a bit harsh? It was thanks to my line of enquiry into Mariner's past acquaintance that we found Annie Jones and then it was me that advised Superintendent Bernstein to call her immediately, leading us to the pump station in record time.'

'So you might say, Andrew, but that is not what the file records.'

'What?' He couldn't believe Deidre would have documented anything else.

'The official version is that Surrey found a Mr Knight . . .'

'Of course they did, but only after I sent Bob Cooper to the Bull and Drum to find him!'

'You did what? Unbelievable; you're lucky that isn't in the file! The man's retired. Are you running your own private detective agency now, Fenwick?'

'No, sir, but he has the best nose in the business and they were leaving the follow-up to that idiot Cobb. I couldn't just sit there and do nothing.'

'According to the files I've read that is exactly what you did do.'

'This beggars belief.' No way would Deidre stitch him up like this. 'Who wrote up the strategy and what came of it, sir?'

'Wait a moment,' there was the sound of keys tapping and then, 'a James Perkins. Do you know him?'

'He's CC Norman's stooge. So he's behind this confection of lies.'

'More like embroidered truth, I'm afraid, Andrew. And nothing you can do about it.'

'Why not, sir? It's my reputation and I don't understand why Norman would do this to me. He seemed straight enough.'

There was a pause and he heard Harper-Brown take a deep breath.

'I suspect Chief Constable Norman isn't even aware of any distortion in the report. Did you tell him anything directly?'

Fenwick thought hard. No he hadn't. Harper-Brown interpreted his silence.

'That's what I thought. Perkins is just doing what is expected of him.'

'Excuse me?'

'It will be tacit, Fenwick, if that's any consolation, and with no harm intended. He's just making his boss look as good as possible in the circumstances.'

'And hang the consequences?'

'Afraid so; and that is why I've called you. The Flash Harry investigation is your opportunity to put your reputation back on track. It has profile; it's very nasty and it needs a hero.'

'But—'

'For heaven's sake, Andrew! The hero should be you, not this stray sergeant you've borrowed from Harlden. Get off your butt and solve the thing.'

It was an order and he realised he had no choice. To ignore it would alienate H-B and might even make an enemy of him.

'I'm going to need a car, sir.'

'One is already on its way.'

Fenwick replaced the receiver and lowered his head, feeling exhausted suddenly. There was a change in the air behind him and he turned in time to see Bess swing away from the door. He heard feet pounding upstairs.

'Bess!'

He ran after her but she slammed her bedroom door in his face. He pushed it open to find her lying face down on her bed hitting the pillows.

'Bess I—'

'Once, just once I thought you'd be with us for breakfast on a school day. It's not too much to ask, is it? But yes, apparently it is!' She was sobbing into the pillow.

Fenwick sat down on the side of the bed and stroked her curly black hair, so like her mother's.

'I wanted that too, love, I miss it as much as you do.'

'Oh sure!'

'I do; not seeing you and Chris hurts a lot but I don't have a choice. Another girl has been injured.'

'Now, Daddy?' Chris was standing in the doorway, Alice hovering behind him.

'I'm afraid so; I'm so sorry. A car's coming to pick me up.'

Chris's bottom lip jutted out and Fenwick waited for tears but they didn't come. Instead Chris straightened his shoulders and gave a brief nod.

'You've been asked to go out personally again?' Fenwick nodded. 'That's because you're the best. This is probably a matter of life and death, isn't it?'

'It might be, Chris. I don't know at this stage.'

'Hmm.' His son walked over to the bed and prodded his sister none too gently on the bottom. 'Come on, Bess, it's like Nightingale said, we have to be brave and strong because Daddy needs us. There's no point sulking; show the Fenwick blood and spirit!'

Fenwick looked at his ten-year-old son in amazement. Behind him Alice covered a smile with her hand but Bess was unimpressed and they eventually left her alone to sulk. Alice made him a strong cup of tea and cut a slice of cake for the journey while Chris sat on his lap, his hair still damp from the bath. Just before the car arrived Bess graced them with her presence. Although she didn't say much, Fenwick realised it had taken a lot for her to leave her room and so treated her with respect. They all waved him goodbye.

He had almost reached Lewes HQ when his phone rang. His heart sank when he saw who was calling.

'Hello, Alice.'

'I just wanted to say thank you, Andrew. I went to iron those damned, excuse me, leggings of hers so that they'd be ready for madam tomorrow and I saw the mess you'd made of them.'

'Sorry, I—'

'No, never mind, that was going to happen someday and rather you than me! They were shoddy, cheap things and I've hated ironing them since the day she bought them. My heart sank but then I saw the package you'd left on the table. Andrew . . .'

'I know I shouldn't reward her behaviour but I couldn't leave you to . . .'

'Oh, I realise that but what was really sweet of you, dear, was the note you left on top. Letting me have the chance to give the clothes to her as a surprise present – that was such a kind thought. Of course I won't but—'

'You must, Alice. It's important.'

Fenwick spent some minutes arguing with his housekeeper and finally managed to persuade her that it would at least be a joint gift. When the call finished his mood for some reason was remarkably positive and it resonated in his voice when his phone rang again.

'Yes, good evening!'

'Andrew?'

He almost dropped the phone.

'Nightingale; this is a surprise. To what do I owe the pleasure?'

'I just wanted to explain why I was at your house last night. You see, by the time I'd taken Bess home it was late and the weather was bad so I . . . well, Alice . . .'

A memory of the irritation he had felt that morning rippled across the surface of Fenwick's good mood but disappeared quickly.

'Don't worry about it. I was sorry not to see you; I slept late. I don't normally, it was just that . . .' Why was he explaining himself? 'Anyway, it's good you called. I've asked Deidre to have Dan Mariner's DNA checked urgently against the database. We should have the results within the week.'

'Excellent.' There was another awkward pause. 'I rang your home first but Alice said you'd left because you'd been called out.'

'Did she?' The irritation was back. He did not like being discussed behind his back.

'Yes; don't be cross with her. She's worried about you.'

That didn't help his mood.

'You seem to be working so hard. If there's anything I can do . . . There isn't much to keep me busy right now, to be honest.'

'I can't believe that. Your resources have been cut just like all of us.'

'Yes, well what I mean is, there's plenty of work, it's just that none of it is particularly . . . demanding.'

'You were going to say interesting.'

That made her laugh.

'You're right. I wondered whether you needed any help with Flash Harry. I know the case backwards and I'm sure I could add value.'

'No help needed, thanks, Nightingale.'

'Oh . . . well I guess I should let you get on with whatever you're doing.'

After the call had finished he wondered whether he should have told her about the recent rape. No, he concluded. She would only have felt excluded. Better she knew nothing about it, given her unhealthy interest in Flash Harry. Still, it had been nice to hear from her.

Fenwick's driver concluded that his passenger's reputation for being a workaholic must be true. Why else would a man dragged away from the warmth of his family hearth on a bitter Sunday night be smiling?

CHAPTER TWENTY-SIX

Nightingale was heading for bed early when the phone rang. She listened as it went through to the machine.

'Louise, hi, it's Mac. Sorry to trouble you so late but I thought you should know. It's Jenni; she's been attacked again. She's in bad shape. Unconscious and this time the doctor's really worried. It happened in Cranleigh and she's been taken to A&E in Guildford. Your man Fenwick is here and has everything under control but seeing as you kind of took her under your wing I thought you'd want to know. Call me whenever you get this. I'm planning to stay with her all night.'

The machine beeped. Nightingale sat down hard on a kitchen stool and dropped her forehead into her hands. She was struggling not to cry, which was ridiculous.

'I have to go and see her,' she said to herself, startling the cat who had no doubt been expecting to slip onto her bed as soon as she was asleep.

He was a stray, adopted by several of the residents in the conversion where she lived and so never without a warm place to sleep and enough to eat.

'Sorry, Blackie. I have to go out.'

Fortunately she hadn't had anything to drink all day, and although the temperature was well below freezing, it wasn't actually snowing. She was glad of the winter tyres she had decided to have fitted.

It still took her well over an hour to reach the hospital so that it was gone ten by the time she arrived. Nightingale waved her warrant card and was directed to the ward where Jenni was being cared for in a side room. Walking towards it brought back memories of the first time she had seen the girl and her face was grim by the time she arrived.

Big Mac greeted her with a hug that was inappropriate but nice just the same.

'She's in there; out cold. The doctors are worried that a second blow to her head might have done some damage. She's due to have another scan in the morning.'

'What was she doing in Cranleigh of all places and how did she get there?'

'What we've found out so far is that a group of them – three girls all aged between sixteen and eighteen . . .'

'I still think she's under age, Mac. More like fourteen if you look at her.'

'Maybe, but we can't prove it one way or another and she insists she's sixteen if you remember. Anyway, these girls were given a lift from Harlden to Cranleigh by two lads. There's a club there that serves cut-price cocktails on a Sunday night and that's where they were headed. When they arrived Jenni received a call . . .'

'She has a mobile phone?'

'A cheap pay-as-you-go model, no bells and whistles, and no, we have no idea how she came by it. She took the call and left the others, saying that she had to meet someone. We've interviewed the two men and the other girls. None of them has any idea where she went or who called her.'

'And her phone?'

'Recovered but useless. The call to her came from another pay as you go and it's switched off.'

'How about CCTV?'

'We're gathering all the footage we can along the possible routes from where she left the girls to the location she was found. Some of the shops and offices are shut so we'll need to continue tomorrow but it's a start and we have traffic surveillance. That's where the boss has gone, to Guildford HQ. He says their technical facilities are first class.'

Nightingale didn't answer. She couldn't help but doubt his motives. He'd take any excuse to go close to the Mattias case. Would he even be thinking about Jenni right now?

'I'd like to look in on her, Mac.'

'Of course, go ahead. I need a cigarette anyway. I'll be back in ten.'

She set her jaw and opened the half-glazed door to Jenni's room, blinking hard as she caught sight of the still, slight form under the bedclothes.

Chief Constable Norman met the superintendent from Sussex MCS in his office. He was there late on a Sunday night to host the end-of-day briefing on Operation Goldilocks. Fenwick was shocked to see how much he had aged in a week and wondered whether he now regretted elbowing him out of the way. The strain of the operation must be horrendous.

'Sit down, Andrew. It's good to see you, though I doubt you're too pleased to be here.'

He must have read Perkins' report and realised the hatchet job his man had done in a vain attempt to shore up his boss's reputation. Fenwick wasn't about to give him the satisfaction of acknowledging the reason behind his greeting.

'Acting Chief Constable Harper-Brown told me you were good enough to allow MCS to take on the rape in Cranleigh in case it is connected to the series we are investigating. Thank you.'

Norman paused and then gave a brief nod as if appreciating the line Fenwick had chosen to adopt.

'The so-called Flash Harry attacks; it made sense. Rapists don't acknowledge our thin blue borderlines. Do you think it's the same man?'

'Too early to say, sir. If it is, then it destroys one theory we've been pursuing.'

'Which is?'

'That Daniel Mariner might have been Flash Harry.'

At mention of Mariner's name Norman's face darkened.

'Superintendent, there is no connection evident between the disappearance of Issie Mattias and Flash Harry and I don't want you contriving to find one. Understood?'

Fenwick squirmed under the look from Norman that seemed to penetrate even his defences.

'Understood?' the chief constable repeated.

'Yes, sir; understood.' Fenwick mentally crossed his fingers. 'However, I would like to ask your permission to use the technical facilities you have available to review the CCTV tapes we are securing in connection with the latest attack in Cranleigh. It will be more convenient than going to and from our facilities in Sussex.'

Norman appeared to relax and even managed a weary smile.

'Of course; happy to help. You'll need an officer to act as liaison and I have just the man for you. Detective Sergeant Jeremy Tate. He's just been made up and is a good chap, one of our best young talents.'

'Thank you, sir, if you can spare him?' Fenwick wondered why such a talent hadn't been deployed to help find Issie.

'You'll find him in the detective room. Can't miss him; has a shock of red hair.'

The open invitation to wander the corridors of Guildford HQ was more than Fenwick had hoped for and he set off with high expectations. After a prolonged prowl, however, he concluded that Bernstein wasn't around so he decided to find Tate without further delay. As he entered the detectives' room there were a few raised eyebrows but no one said anything. Tate was seated at a desk in the corner, back bent over a computer keyboard.

'Sergeant Tate?'

'Sir?' The man stood up and Fenwick realised he was as tall as he was, a rare occurrence. He had a northern accent, Lancastrian he thought.

'You're to work with me. Come along, I'll brief you in the canteen over a coffee.'

There were a few shaken heads as they left and Fenwick thought he even heard a muttered 'good luck'. He didn't care. He brought Tate up to speed on the essentials of the Flash Harry investigation and of the role he was to play. The man seemed enthusiastic, possibly over-keen. Again Fenwick wondered why he'd been available but there was no point speculating. He would find out soon enough.

'You're to liaise with Detective Sergeant Jimmy MacDonald, Big Mac to his friends. He's still with the girl while CST are working the scene where she was found. CC Norman has agreed to extend help to MCS so I'll base myself here for the next couple of days.'

'Will you and Sergeant MacDonald need accommodation, sir?'

'Yes, I suppose we will. Where I stayed before will be fine.'

'I guess that's the Travelodge, sir. It's usually where we put people up.'

'That's the one.' Fenwick glanced at his watch. 'Have the tapes worked on overnight and if there are any developments call me. This is my mobile number. Doesn't matter what time.'

Tate smiled as he wrote the details down in his notebook, obviously enjoying himself.

'I'll do that right away, sir! And then I'll go over to the scene to see if there is anything I can do there. Unless you have more for me?' He looked up expectantly like a dog waiting to be thrown a stick.

'That will be all, thank you, Tate.'

Fenwick watched him go. Such youth and enthusiasm! It was enough to make him exhausted. He summoned his driver and headed off to the motel, where they welcomed him back as a regular.

It didn't take him long to unpack his overnight bag and he was heading for the shower when his mobile rang. Expecting it to be Tate or MacDonald he answered immediately.

'Fenwick.'

'It's Nightingale, Andrew.'

'What are you doing ringing me at eleven o'clock at night?' Enough was enough.

'I'm at the hospital with Jenni.'

'You're what!'

'Don't be angry, please. I got to know her after she was attacked last time and I feel responsible for her.'

'For heaven's sake, Nightingale. That's no excuse.'

'She should have a friendly face here when she wakes up, Andrew, and I'm the only one she knows.'

She sounded upset. With difficulty Fenwick forced himself to calm down.

'Exactly why are you so interested, Nightingale? It's not like you to go soft.'

'She needs someone; we all do. And if we could get a good description of her attacker, then surely that's worth it. I'm probably the only person she'll talk to. Even Big Mac thinks so.'

'So you've spoken with him already.' He puffed out his cheeks in frustration.

She really was impossible, but on the other hand, she was bloody good and if he could rely on her personal attention he would be able to spend a bit more time at HQ. Bernstein was bound to be there in the morning.

'Won't you be missed at Harlden?'

'Not if you ask for me to spend a bit of time here, sir. A call to Superintendent Whitby in the morning is all it would take. Or an email, even. I could draft it for you if you like.'

'Stop, Nightingale. Enough; you've made your point and I'll see what I can do.'

'Oh, thanks! You've made my day. I didn't want to say so before but you'll also make Bob Cooper happy. He was working on one of the assaults just before he retired. We hadn't connected them and he was handling it as an isolated incident but I know he resented leaving the case unsolved. I feel I owe it to him.'

Fenwick smiled at the memory of the old team. Those days seemed so long ago.

'I can't imagine him being retired. He must be bored silly,' she continued.

'Quite the contrary. He's working privately for the Saxbys and I saw him recently. He must have gained a stone.'

'He can't afford that. Maybe I should stop by; he hates my nagging.'

'Good idea; why don't you call Dot?' Fenwick thought Mrs Cooper would welcome some help in her losing battle to control her husband's girth.

'OK, after all this is over.'

After he finished the call Fenwick wondered exactly what she had meant by her last remark.

An hour later as he tried in vain to fall asleep Fenwick heard a clock nearby chime midnight. Another day over; another day with no sight of Issie; another day in which a young girl had become the victim of an assault. It was hopeless. He felt a dark cloud of negativity settle over him and shut his eyes to try and keep it out. If even he doubted the ability of the forces of law to keep the peace, what hope was there? He shook his head, angry at himself. This wouldn't do.

Fenwick got up, shivering in the cool of the room, and pulled on his dressing gown. There was no point lying in bed getting depressed. He had all the Flash Harry files on his laptop and it was never a waste to reread the evidence. He switched the desk light on and booted up his computer. When the date and time came up on the screen he noted the eighteenth with a sense of relief.

What had it been about the date of seventeenth of December that his subconscious had been worrying at and why was he glad it was past? He frowned in concentration as he went through all the memorable dates associated with his late wife but there was nothing there. If anything, Decembers had been happy times. Fenwick shrugged his shoulders and gave up. It didn't matter.

It was only as he typed in his new password to access the files that the significance of the date hit him. As he pressed the keys for 'ISSIE=1' the realisation hit him. Yesterday had been Isabelle Mattias's eighteenth birthday.

CHAPTER TWENTY-SEVEN

She woke with a start and her eyes went immediately to the bed, which was empty.

'Jenni!' Nightingale was half out of the chair before Big Mac's restraining hand eased her back.

'She was taken for a scan a few minutes ago, don't worry. Here, have some coffee.'

He handed her a takeaway cup with a plastic lid.

'Black with sugar, right?' he asked hopefully.

She didn't have the heart to correct him and sipped cautiously through the hole in the lid, trying not to grimace.

'I must have fallen asleep; sorry.'

Mac smiled at her and she noticed his eyes creased at the corners in a way that was infectious.

'You saved me a numbing-night so don't apologise.'

'Numbing-ni . . .' Nightingale's brain was struggling to wake up.

'As in "rear-end" numbing. You slept in the chair. How's your neck?'

Nightingale twisted her head in a circle and winced.

'Want a massage?'

'Ah, no but the coffee will help, thanks. When's she due back?'

'In about half an hour, they said. Shall we stretch our legs?'

'Why not.'

They were back inside within fifteen minutes, driven in by the biting easterly wind.

'Phwoar! Why did my grandparents emigrate to this godforsaken isle when we could have enjoyed tropical sunshine?' Big Mac was stamping his feet to return the blood flow.

'Employment?' Nightingale hazarded. 'Betterment for their family?'

'Hmm. Cummon, let's grab breakfast while we can.'

He laughed at her choice of porridge; she scoffed at his fry-up. Both were content in their choice but Nightingale didn't want to linger. They returned to Jenni's room moments before she was brought back by an orderly. Nightingale studied the girl's innocent sleeping face and her anger rekindled.

'I'm going to find someone to tell me how she's doing.'

'I'll do that, you wait here,' Mac insisted. 'Just in case she wakes up.'

Once he had gone Nightingale bent over the bed and stroked Jenni's bruised forehead with the tip of a finger.

'Who did this to you, Jenni?' she whispered and saw the girl's eyes move under closed lids. 'Can you hear me? Are you in there, Jenni?'

More eye movement and one of Jenni's fingers twitched. Nightingale took her hand and held it gently, murmuring words of encouragement. After a few more minutes Jenni's eyes opened. She saw Nightingale and there was a flicker of a smile.

'Hello you; welcome back.' Nightingale forced a smile.

Jennie opened her mouth but there was no sound.

'Say that again, dear, I couldn't hear you.'

Instead Jenni shut her eyes and breathed out deeply.

'You can tell me later, don't worry,' Nightingale sighed. 'I'll still be here.'

Big Mac returned with a white-coated female doctor in tow, carrying a file.

'There's some good news, Nightingale,' Mac said.

'Indeed; I'm Doctor Williams.' Nightingale nodded a greeting.

'She woke up briefly just before you came in but has drifted off again.'

'That's good; she has one of the thickest skulls I've ever seen, and lucky for her that she has, otherwise the blow she received would have done some serious damage.'

'Would you say it was intentional?' Nightingale asked.

'I'm not an expert so my opinion isn't worth a lot, but I would say yes. Someone smashed a hard, tubular object down on her head. I can't imagine it could have been accidental. If she'd had a thin skull it might have killed her. As it is she's going to get away with concussion. If she's woken up once, even briefly, that's good news and she'll probably do so again.' Nightingale opened her mouth but Williams forestalled her, 'I'm sorry, I can't say when. It could be in minutes or, just as possible, hours.'

They thanked her and promised to alert a nurse should Jenni regain consciousness.

'So what's the plan?' Mac asked.

'I'm going to wait here. Superintendent Fenwick is asking Alison if I can stay on the case for a few days.'

Big Mac's face lit up.

'Wicked! That will be great. They haven't got anywhere with it, you know. MCS would have been better off leaving it with us.'

Nightingale noted he hadn't gone native and was relieved. She was still 'us'.

'Still, I should update Quinlan on Jenni's condition.'

'What time is it?' Nightingale looked at her watch. 'Eight-twenty. I thought it was much later.'

But Mac wasn't listening. He was staring at the bed.

'She's awake again,' he hissed out of the side of his mouth.

Nightingale spun around and greeted Jenni's open eyes with a big smile.

'Hi, you're back.'

Jenni moved her lips and Nightingale leant forward to hear.

Big Mac went to the other side of the bed and crouched down, out of Jenni's line of sight but close enough to listen.

'. . . n.'

'Can you say that again for me, love? I couldn't catch it.'

'S . . .'

Nightingale looked up briefly at Mac but he shook his head. He couldn't make it out either.

'Try again, one more time,' she encouraged.

'S . . . tann . . . st . . . n.' Jenni's eyelids fluttered closed and she was gone again.

'Did she say what I think she said?' Big Mac asked.

'Go on.' Nightingale didn't want to influence him with her own conjecture.

'I think she was trying to say St Anne's.'

'That's what I heard too.'

'We need to tell Fenwick at once. I'll call him.'

'Better still, go to Guildford and see him; there'll be a briefing soon. I'll wait here.'

Nightingale passed a tedious hour at Jenni's bedside. The girl didn't wake up again and she began to realise that she was wasting her time. Shortly before ten she was surprised to see the Milky Bar Kid turn up.

'Hello, Roy, what are you doing here?'

Constable Rogers beamed at her. She was the only one other than Whitby who paid him the courtesy of using his given name.

'Superintendent Whitby sent me, ma'am. She remembered that I'd been with Jenni before and thought that I'd be a familiar face if she woke up.'

It was typical of Whitby to recall such a detail.

'That's really helpful because there are things I should be doing but I was reluctant to leave her.'

Nightingale was already in her car when her mobile rang. It was Fenwick.

'Are you still at the hospital, Nightingale?'

'I'm just leaving; don't worry, there's a reliable officer with Jenni.'

'Good; unless you have other plans, can you meet me at St Anne's? Given what Jenni said, I think we have to pay them a visit immediately.'

'On my way.'

Tate dropped Fenwick off at exactly ten-thirty. Fenwick saw Nightingale locking her car and look around before heading in the wrong direction, exactly the mistake he had made when he had first arrived. He jumped out of the car and called out to her while Tate recovered his spilt papers from the snow.

'Nightingale; over here!'

He waited for her before taking the brick path into the main building. He had his hand ready in case she slipped but her boots made her sure-footed and it wasn't needed.

'We can agree how to proceed over a coffee, if you like. There's a machine on the second floor makes a good one.'

Fenwick walked up the stairs ahead of her feeling uncomfortable. Only when they reached the upper landing did he realise he hadn't said a word of greeting. Mind you neither had she.

'Do you want one?'

'Please, if there's some milk; oh and no sugar.'

'There's a fridge over there; usually there's some inside.'

Nightingale smiled as she brought the carton over.

'You certainly made yourself at home while you were here.'

For some reason her words made him blush and he glanced upwards subconsciously. As soon as he had poured their coffees he suggested they go downstairs.

'Why? This is private and there's no incident room here any more.'

Fenwick looked around and sat down on the edge of the sofa furthest away.

She seemed remarkably relaxed but he could feel himself sweating inside his winter suit. He gave her a short recount of the morning's briefing while she listened without interruption. When he finished she reached into her bag.

'Here's a copy of the additional work I did on Flash Harry since it went to MCS.' She handed over a surprisingly large plastic wallet of papers and he frowned. 'It looks more than it is and most of it is conjecture. The notes on the top are from this morning, after Jenni spoke. I outlined a few strategies and ideas.'

Fenwick pulled out two handwritten pages and read them in silence while Nightingale drank her coffee.

'So, essentially you have four theories: One: Dan Mariner and/or Jenni's cousin was one of a group of men who indulged in casual, sometimes forced sex, with underage girls. Two: That could have included disturbed girls from St Anne's like Issie, but was probably more focused on underprivileged teenagers with little family protection. Three: When Dan was killed, another member of the group – possibly the cousin – decided to lure Jenni to a meeting where he attempted to intimidate or kill her to secure her silence. Four: St Anne's was either the location of the meeting – which you doubt – or Jenni suspected that other girls here might have been abused and was trying to tell you.'

'Yes, that's about it.'

Fenwick shook his head reluctantly.

'You're convinced Daniel Mariner isn't Flash Harry, particularly now, given the recent assault on Jenni?'

'Yes, or as I say, Flash Harry could be more than one person.'

'But there has been one consistent DNA recovered. Doesn't that suggest one man?' He became aware that he was interrogating her.

Nightingale stared at him, obviously irritated.

'I agree that the attacks stopped when Dan died but now Jenni's been hurt. It could be unrelated of course but . . .'

Fenwick stood up and paced forcing Nightingale to continue.

'What I'd like to do is show Jenni's picture to teachers, staff and pupils to see if anyone recognises her. Do you agree?'

'That makes sense,' Fenwick acknowledged.

'May I ask what you'll do? I wasn't quite sure why you suggested meeting here, that's all.'

Neither was he any more, though it had seemed a good idea at the time.

'That's not really any of your business, Nightingale.'

She took a long swallow of coffee, looking at him directly, her expression inscrutable. She opened her mouth to say something and then shrugged, reminding him of Bess.

'Do you have alternative theories you'd like to share on Flash Harry, Andrew?' Her words were icily polite.

Fenwick pulled his A4 blue casebook from his briefcase and flicked through until he found the page he had completed for the next briefing.

'The only other theories are that she was attacked by a stranger or by someone she knew from her past, who caught up with her.'

'Like her cousin.'

'Fair point,' Fenwick closed the file sharply.

'Do you think there's any possibility of a connection with the Mattias girl's disappearance?'

Fenwick tensed.

'Sorry, that sounds harsh. I realise it must be very difficult for you to have been so close to finding her and then . . .'

'We were just hours behind Mariner.' He looked away. 'Now Surrey can find no trace of him, yet they know what he looks like, his car index and there's a nationwide search, but all the leads – and there are hundreds of them – have turned out to be dead ends. He's vanished. Issie's cash card hasn't been used for a week and her mobile is turned off, as is Mariner's.'

'Might he have killed her and then himself? They may only be found after the weather clears.'

She had voiced his worst fear, the one that kept him awake at night and invaded his dreams whenever he managed some sleep.

'Who knows; but Surrey is still treating the investigation with highest priority. Every place they might have gone has been searched at least twice; all deserted farm buildings or empty houses are being visited in a widening radius. There are posters up nationwide, particularly in garages and service stations because if he is still on the run and not in a bolt-hole somewhere he'll have to buy fuel. Interpol are alerted, and the French, Dutch and Belgium police, though there is no evidence that they've left the country, just in case he managed to stow away on a lorry or ferry and crossed the Channel. They're doing a televised reconstruction tonight and another press conference tomorrow.

'Saxby called me only last week to tell me I should re-involve myself in the hunt for his daughter. You can imagine how that was received at Guildford HQ! Meanwhile he's employed an army of private investigators.'

'And Surrey let him?' Nightingale sounded surprised.

'There's no such thing as "letting" Bill Saxby do something. He's his own man, with wealth and resources enough to do what he wants.'

'Not to mention his connections.'

'Indeed.'

'Poor you.' She hesitated and Fenwick feared what she was going to say next.

Fortunately his phone rang, cutting her off. He spoke his name then listened in silence before muttering a terse 'Very well.'

'I have to go, sorry, Nightingale. Chief Constable Norman wants me back at HQ.'

He frowned and muttered to himself 'I wonder why' as he

stood and picked up his coat and scarf. Nightingale bent to pick hers up at the same moment and their heads nearly clashed.

He left her in the hall, turning to watch her walk across the tiles towards the headmistress's office. He realised belatedly that he hadn't asked how she was; in fact he had shown no interest in her whatsoever. He closed his eyes for a moment, then shook his head and pulled his collar up against the wind that bit into him as he opened the front door.

CHAPTER TWENTY-EIGHT

After an uncomfortable meeting with CC Norman, Fenwick headed down to the canteen for a coffee. Somehow the chief constable had heard that he was at St Anne's and had summoned him back for a brutal interview. He had told him if he ever went there again without his permission he would make a formal complaint against him.

Fenwick had had his share of tough conversations in his life and weathered the onslaught calmly, so much so in fact that Norman had started to look uncomfortable towards the end.

'Do you have anything to say for yourself?'

At the invitation, Fenwick took the chance to explain why he had been at St Anne's. The latest girl attacked in the Flash Harry case had regained consciousness and named the school to the two officers attending her, one of whom was still there.

'And who might that be? Oh, don't tell me, I think I can guess. Alastair told me that before MCS took the case over it was with Harlden division. The SIO was a new inspector there. Has a name like a bird – Nightjar, or something. He's very good, apparently, has the pit bull instinct. I bet he leapt at the chance to become involved when the girl was attacked a second time. Well, as long as he's under your control I suppose you'll welcome the input.'

'It's Nightingale actually, sir . . .'

'That's right.'

Fenwick thought about Nightingale and frowned.

'And it's a she, not a he.'

'Really? The description I was given doesn't fit a woman. But she's quite good?' He looked at Fenwick quizzically.

She's exceptional, one of the best detectives I've ever worked with was what he wanted to say but he contented himself with, 'Extremely competent and utterly dedicated; we worked together in Harlden. I think she'll add a lot of value and if there is a link between Flash Harry and the Mariners,' he ignored Norman's frown and continued, 'she'll help us avoid the risk that we miss something.'

'No harm having another senior woman around, I suppose.'

Fenwick then had to listen to another lecture on keeping his nose out of Operation Goldilocks before being dismissed. It was midday but he didn't have much appetite. He found a spare room and called MCS to be brought up to date on other cases. Then he had a conference call on some necessary but dull administrative matters followed by a budget meeting that set the seal on a tedious day.

Just before five o'clock, Bernstein popped her head in.

'Here you are! I wondered where you were hiding. Any luck with Flash Harry?'

'Nothing new since this morning. Bazza will have updated you, I guess?'

'He did. He also mentioned that you charged off to St Anne's because the girl muttered something that sounded vaguely like it. It would have been nice if you'd mentioned it.'

Fenwick shrugged an apology.

'I got to hear as soon as Operations received Tate's call in . . .'

'So that's how Norman found out.'

'Of course. He's all over this case. There's nothing about it he doesn't know. I can barely breathe.'

'But still no progress?' He asked kindly but his question obviously hurt.

'Why don't you come along to the briefing now? It's about to start.'

'Won't that irritate Norman even further?'

Bernstein's grin in reply was pure malice. *What the heck*, he thought. *As long as I keep quiet.*

When he walked in he saw Nightingale and Big Mac perched at the back. Bazza along with several others were ogling her and Fenwick experienced a spurt of irritation. CC Norman had apparently wasted no time in inviting her to sit in. Instead of feeling grateful Fenwick was surprisingly uncomfortable. What would she expect from him? He knew she was desperate to find the person who attacked Jenni but it was even more important for him to avoid his tendency to become obsessed by theoretical connections.

The briefing lasted until six-thirty. Bernstein gave an update about the continuing hunt for Issie and Mariner. It was depressingly short. There had been hundreds of reported sightings, consuming thousands of man hours in front line work and record maintenance but so far none of them led anywhere. There had been no further ransom demand, no sight of Mariner's car. Issie had vanished.

After Bernstein had finished there was a heavy silence in the room. Even the most hardened officers were affected by the girl's disappearance and everyone knew that the case could be sliding towards a double-murder investigation.

'Thank you, Deidre. What's happening to the search teams; are they still out there?'

Thirty pairs of eyes looked instinctively at the sleet beating against the meeting room windows.

Bernstein scowled as if anticipating a reprimand.

'I've finally stopped the search, sir, at least for the on-foot teams. With the weather deteriorating they were wasting their time and would be risking their lives if the storm comes in as predicted. I've requested RTC to maintain their efforts in the area of intensive search in Kent, East Sussex, Hampshire and Berkshire on top of the nationwide alert. It's a huge area, of course, and there's some bitching and moaning because Traffic is really stretched with the weather conditions but everyone agreed to cooperate eventually.'

Norman nodded his support and Bernstein relaxed a little.

'And the fifth estate?' There were a few puzzled looks in the room so he added, 'The media?'

'Have turned their attention to the apparent reappearance of Flash Harry, other than Saxby's title. All eyes are on you again.' She turned to Fenwick and popped a piece of gum in her mouth.

He ignored the remark. There was no time to worry about the inevitable consequences for his career if he became associated with two failed investigations involving teenage girls. Norman gestured for him to give them an update on Flash Harry, just in case there was a connection to St Anne's. He did so quickly, asking Big Mac to report on Jenni's brief and only moment of consciousness that day, and Nightingale to feedback the results of her interviews at the college. No one had recognised Jenni's photo and there were no suggestions of any of the girls having been subjected to sexual coercion or abuse. He closed by asking when the results on Dan Mariner's DNA were due.

'Tomorrow,' Bernstein replied.

'Good,' Norman interjected, 'make sure you call Superintendent Fenwick personally as soon as they come in.'

The implication being that he really didn't need to hang around in Guildford and could be off back to Sussex and out of their hair. Well, that was as may be but he had decided to stay one more night in Guildford. If Mariner's DNA was a match to Flash Harry he was determined to take the chance to try and persuade Norman to let him continue as a passive observer on the Goldilocks operation. He knew his chances were slim but it would be hard for the chief constable to ignore the possible connection, and he had just heard that they had nothing else to work on.

He had one more call to make with his team in Lewes before calling it a night. After it finished he loosened his tie and wondered where Nightingale had got to and whether she fancied a drink. The incident room was busy but she wasn't there nor could anyone tell him where she had gone. When he tried her mobile it was switched off. With a resigned sigh he pulled out the latest reports that needed his attention and tried to concentrate.

He called Nightingale twice more but didn't bother to leave a further message. When he was barely able to keep his eyes focused, he called it a night. It was ten-thirty when Fenwick slipped the key card for room 303 into the lock. He threw his briefcase on to the bed and dropped the carrier bag containing his meagre supper on the narrow desk that the room afforded, tucked under a single window with a view of the car park. Easing off his tie, he hung his jacket on one of the three hangers on the open rail in a recess that served as a wardrobe.

There was a trouser press and iron conveniently provided. Before settling down he removed his trousers and arranged them carefully in the press, then he put on some jeans and shook out a fresh shirt. It was badly crumpled and part of him was tempted to hang it up and hope for the best but conditioning from childhood stopped him. With a sigh he unfolded the ironing board and plugged in the iron, paying particular attention to collar and cuffs.

Finished to his satisfaction, he hung it up and put the iron away. Enough; the shoes could wait until morning. He had been up since before six and was almost too tired to eat but as he'd had nothing but a slice of cake since breakfast he knew that he must. Fenwick tore open the supermarket carrier and laid it out on the desk. On top he arranged the BLT granary sandwich, packet of plain crisps, can of chilled lager and slice of fruitcake he had bought in the seven-eleven near the hotel. There were tea- and coffee-making facilities in the room so he had all he needed. He had his mouth full of the first bite of sandwich when his mobile phone rang. With a muttered expletive he pulled it out of his jacket pocket and answered.

'Yesh?' He chewed hard and swallowed part of the lump of dough and bacon painfully.

'Andrew; are you OK?' It was Nightingale.

'Just had my mouth full.'

'Oh, sorry to interrupt your dinner; shall I call you back later? Is it going cold?'

Fenwick glanced at the sandwich and shook his head ironically; if only.

'No, it's fine, go ahead.'

'I saw that you'd tried to reach me. Was it urgent?'

'Not really; where were you?'

'I . . . well, if you must know Big Mac took me out for a bite to eat.'

'Oh.' The remaining mush of sandwich in his mouth was inedible and he spat it out.

'We were both starving. I had hoped to catch you but someone said you were on a call. Anyway, do you fancy a drink now? I'm staying at the same motel as you and I'll be there in ten minutes.'

Fenwick cursed silently. He wanted to be up early and he really needed to get some sleep.

'I'll see you in the bar.'

By the time he had eaten his sandwich and shaved his five o'clock shadow into submission she was due to arrive so he headed down to the unfortunately themed bar he had noticed on arrival. He bought them both large glasses of the only decent red available, a Faugères from the Languedoc, and was skirting a large plastic agave as Nightingale walked in and walked over.

'I know you prefer white but on a night like this . . .'

'Perfect, thank you.'

There was a sales convention of some sort at the motel and the

303

bar was noisy. They found a small sofa in a corner. Fenwick was intensely aware of how close their knees were.

'Cheers.'

'Cheers. How is Bess?'

'Miffed that I left on Sunday but she did deign to speak to me on the phone this evening so better than it might be. I'm still very grateful . . .'

'Don't mention it, that's not why I asked. I'm very fond of her – and Chris – that's all.'

Fenwick sipped his wine.

'So, did you want more of a briefing on what I found out today?'

'Not really; unless there's anything really interesting.'

'Oh.' She sounded surprised. 'So why did you agree to meet up?'

'I just fancied having a drink together, like old times. It's why I rang you.'

'I see.'

Nightingale looked puzzled. Belatedly he realised she would have seen that he had called her three times. Oh well, that was too bad. He found he was struggling to find something to say. Nightingale came to the rescue, talking shop about his old division.

While she rabbited on about Harlden he watched her, noting the way her eyes creased at the edges when she smiled and the small frown line between her eyebrows. Why did he always think of her as so young?

He looked up and caught one of the salesmen staring. When their eyes met the man winked and nodded, sticking his thumb up. Fenwick looked away.

'. . . don't you think?'

'Hmm, what? Sorry I missed that last bit.'

'I said I really think you should be allowed back on Operation

Goldilocks. I just don't understand why Norman is so determined to keep you out.'

How had they landed on that?

'Oh, it's understandable. He's taken charge and asking me back would be tantamount to admitting failure.'

'But he's allowed you to explore the possible connection to Flash Harry. Surely that's hopeful?'

'Don't read too much into it. As soon as Dan Mariner's DNA results come through and he's confirmed as Flash he'll bid me a speedy farewell.'

'I really don't think Dan Mariner is Flash Harry, Andrew. Or at least, not acting on his own. Why else would Jenni be attacked? In that file I gave you, there were other possibilities . . .'

Fenwick shook his head in frustration. She was so damned stubborn once she latched onto an idea.

'Let it be, Nightingale. There's no point us arguing about it. Tomorrow we'll know for certain one way or another and with luck Jenni will wake up and you'll be able to secure a description of her attacker.'

'But what if—'

He raised a hand.

'Please, enough for one night. Let's just relax and finish the wine.'

'So all the talk about working together as a team is bullshit?'

Fenwick blinked at her language. She drained her glass and frowned.

'You know, Andrew, you're beginning to sound like the top brass you've always struggled to respect. If I didn't know you better I would say that promotion has got to you.'

'Would you like another?' He had drunk only half his glass.

'It's late; I should be getting to bed.' She stood up.

'OK. I'll just finish this, then. Goodnight, Nightingale.'

''Night, Andrew, sleep well.'

After she had gone he took his glass back to his room to finish with the crisps. Fenwick tried not to think about her final remarks, but as he nibbled fatty saltiness with fading appetite, he was forced to acknowledge that maybe she was right. Why was he warning her off when her intuition told her to plough on? It's what he would have done . . . once. Before his promotion he would never have counselled compromise.

He pushed the uneaten fruitcake away – perhaps he would fancy it for breakfast. He should head for bed with a calming warm drink, another sign that he was changing. Time was he would have been able to drink a double espresso and still sleep but now the bouts of insomnia that had plagued him since his wife's death were habitual. It was midnight; he was hesitating between the sachet of instant coffee and a herbal tea bag when he said to the empty room, and to his great surprise, 'Fuck.'

He picked up the camomile tea bag and sniffed it suspiciously before throwing it into the mug with disdain and pouring on boiling water. By the time he was ready for bed he had forgotten all about it and the tea went cold as he tossed and turned before sinking into a restless sleep.

CHAPTER TWENTY-NINE

Nightingale rubbed her eyes and arched her back, trying to ease the stiffness away. She had been sitting in the same position for hours, hunched over her laptop in the cramped motel room oblivious to time. Had she dragged her eyes from the screen to the window she might have marvelled at the icicles hanging in a beautifully defined sculpture from the gutter above but she was blind to the stark beauty of the bitter dawn.

She had woken abruptly at five o'clock thinking about Flash Harry. Her laptop lay open on the bed next to her, reminding her of the unanswered questions that had dogged her sleep. Fenwick was so sure Daniel Mariner was the perpetrator of the sexual assaults that she had started to believe him until Jenni had been attacked. His instincts were usually reliable but now she cursed the fact that she had trusted him and lowered her guard. She should have kept a closer eye on Jenni. Somehow the fact that the girl was lying injured in hospital was her fault.

Stretching out to her bag, Nightingale had pulled out a heavy jumper and dragged it over her pyjamas before rebooting her computer. The next two hours were spent working through every case file yet again, making careful notes as she went.

As a detective constable Nightingale had earned a reputation as an obsessive investigator, paying attention to every detail and doing her own research even when she should have left it to the specialists. The habit had never left her. Now as an inspector she read everything, sometimes correcting details in reports submitted to her by junior officers. She had an almost photographic memory and an uncanny ability to spot an error. It was a characteristic that irritated most and downright annoyed some but it meant her investigations were meticulously prepared for the Crown Prosecution Service, who – unknown to her – breathed easier when she was SIO.

Her knack for research and discerning patterns was being tested; there was nothing to find. In desperation she went back to her first interview with Jenni. She knew it almost by heart but she opened the file and forced herself to review it as if it were a cold case.

It was difficult to read her own part of the story and she skimmed it, but then forced herself back. She had run away from home, so had Jenni but because she hadn't given them her real name neither Harlden nor MCS had been able to find and interview her parents. Jenni had expected to stay with a cousin in Harlden but had ended up on the streets when that hadn't worked out. She and Big Mac had tried to find out where Jenni had been sleeping rough but had failed. No one admitted knowing her. She was a newcomer and hadn't made any friends.

Poor lonely kid. Nightingale sighed, rubbed her eyes and stood up. It was time for a shower and breakfast. Hours of backache and she had nothing to show for it. Maybe it had all been a waste of time. The DNA results on Dan Mariner would be through soon and then she and Fenwick would know one way or another. But that still wouldn't explain the second assault, which might have been intended to kill her.

Nightingale frowned. Would Fenwick really concentrate on finding Flash Harry or would he take the opportunity of his stay in Guildford to meddle in the hunt for Issie? Her mental image of him had long been as a rebel; a front line detective forced into promotions he didn't want but accepted out of a sense of duty and a desire to provide for his children; he challenged authority, broke the rules . . . once he became fixated on something or someone he never let it go. If only he'd felt as deeply the need for justice for Jenni as he did for Issie she would have been more relaxed about leaving him alone with the case, but he didn't.

'Surely he'll do a thorough job,' she muttered out loud, 'or have I idealised him?'

The Fenwick she remembered was another man in another time. As she shampooed her hair Nightingale turned over ideas for what to do next. Bazza had volunteered to take her around St Anne's if she wanted, though she couldn't think of a legitimate reason to go there again. What she could do was discover every detail of what Jenni did while in Harlden, her activities and relationships while in the shelter.

Whitby wanted Big Mac back in Harlden, particularly as Nightingale was now involved in following up the second attack on Jenni. She would have breakfast with Mac and agree how best he could dig into Jenni's activities. It was a plan! The more she thought about it the more she realised that Fenwick couldn't be relied upon to include her, even if Whitby did allow it.

'Sod it.' Nightingale shook her head at her reflection in the steamy bathroom mirror as she rubbed on face cream with unnecessary vigour. 'Your language is getting worse, madam.' She pulled a face. 'And they do say talking to yourself is the first sign of madness.'

Despite her frustration, Nightingale laughed. As soon as she was dressed she rang Mac. He had already left the motel so she arranged to meet him at a greasy spoon close to the hospital. She was starving.

They were tucking in to full English breakfasts when Nightingale's phone rang. She recognised the number immediately.

'Hello, Andrew.'

'Nightingale, good morning. I wanted you to be the first to

know. Dan Mariner's DNA matches that of Flash Harry. He was responsible for all the assaults except for the most recent, which must be unconnected.'

'I see. Thanks for letting me know. So this means you'll be closing the file?'

'Yes. I just need to have the final paperwork done. MacDonald can do that for me.'

'And how will the attack on Jenni be dealt with?'

'No idea.' His apparent indifference really annoyed her. 'That will be for Guildford and Harlden to argue over but it's nothing for MCS to be involved in.'

'I'll advise Superintendent Whitby, if you like; save you the bother.'

'Perfect. Thanks. Well, I'd best be going . . .' She could hear him breathing and waited for the goodbye. 'It was good to see you last night . . . I, ah, thought maybe we should try and do that again sometime.'

'Nice idea. You know where to find me.'

'Yes. Well I'd best be going.'

'You've said that once.' She bit her lip; that wasn't very friendly. She should have been kinder but with Big Mac sitting opposite listening she felt constrained, and anyway, he'd been so dismissive of Jenni! But still . . .

'Bye, then.'

Too late; he was gone.

'Dan Mariner is Flash Harry,' she confirmed.

'So where does that leave us with poor old Jenni?'

'Back to square one.'

'Will we be able to take it on, do you think? Or is Surrey going to claim jurisdiction?'

'Right now both you and I are allocated to Flash Harry so that gives us the scope to work on it.'

'For how long?'

'Well, until Whitby knows the case is closed . . .'

'And you've volunteered to tell her,' Mac said with a chuckle, but then his face sobered. 'Except that she'll see the closing report.'

'Which Fenwick is going to ask you to write.'

They grinned at each other, fellow conspirators.

'I reckon that'll take me most of the day, at least,' he suggested.

Nightingale nodded, mock-serious.

'It would do, a complicated file like that. And of course there are the loose ends to tie up.'

'There are? Oh yes, indeed there are.'

'And I happen to have a list of them here.' She passed him a handwritten page of A4, the result of her late night/early morning toil.

He scanned it quickly, his brow furrowed in concentration.

'This makes sense,' he said eventually. 'I guess the ones with an "N" next to them are the leads – that is, loose ends – that you'll be doing personally.'

'Exactly. They're the ones that can be done by phone. I want to stay here for when she wakes up.'

'I'm not sure Miss Whiplash would approve someone of your rank wasting their time like that. She sent Milky to save you from just that.'

'I know, but she also gave me today free to work with you and Fenwick on Flash Harry.'

'What if she finds out we knew it was Dan Mariner all along?'

Nightingale shrugged.

'That's a risk I'm prepared to take. Look, if it makes you feel any easier, we didn't have breakfast together and I assumed that Andrew Fenwick would give you the news. OK?'

Big Mac looked embarrassed.

'There's no need for that. We're in this together, for Jenni's sake.'

Nightingale suppressed the urge to kiss him.

* * *

The rest of the morning was uneventful. She sent Roy Rogers off to have a shower and something to eat as he'd stayed with Jenni all night. She told him to have a few hours' sleep as well but he said he'd managed enough in the chair and declined. Nightingale doubted it. It was most uncomfortable, too low at the back to rest your head and with a sagging seat that provided little support. Still, it was better than standing.

While Jenni slept peacefully Nightingale tracked down the people she had met while staying in the shelter in case any of them could give her a name or anything else to follow up on. It was a frustrating few hours until, by chance, she spoke again to the woman who was in charge of the shelter.

'You're just not prepared to give up, are you?' she asked when Nightingale called her for the third time in an attempt to find the last of Jenni's known acquaintances.

'Jenni deserves justice. She could have been killed and it's only thanks to her thick skull that she's here recovering.'

'You're with her still, are you?'

'Yes. Someone's here day and night for when she wakes up and I'm doing my share.'

'Well, all I can say is that you're unusually diligent for a policewoman. My charges don't normally count for anything with you lot.'

Nightingale bit back an angry retort, too aware that she was relying on the woman's cooperation.

'In the circumstances there might be one thing that could help you.'

Nightingale sat upright and tried to keep her voice calm.

'Go on.'

'Jenni was scared of someone called Stanley. A relative, I think.'
Stan not *St Anne's!*

'Any idea who he is?'

'No, I'm sorry I haven't. I overheard her talking on the phone to someone a few days ago and she said something like "please don't tell Stanley where I am, I'm begging you." I put it down to boyfriend trouble at the time but you've made me wonder.'

'Thank you. That could be helpful. And this was the pay-as-you-go phone she had on her when she was attacked?'

'Can't say, I'm afraid. Look, normally I respect their confidences – I have to otherwise they'd never trust me.'

'Understood; if this comes to anything, I will need an official statement but thank you,' she hurried on, sensing increasing reticence at the end of the phone, 'you might just have been an immense help to Jenni.'

Nightingale closed the call and looked at the girl lying on the bed in frustration. Behind her eyelids her eyes were moving furiously: right to left, up and down. She must be dreaming so vividly and yet she wouldn't wake up. Perhaps her fear was keeping her unconscious? Nightingale realised she couldn't rely on Jenni to help them and that she was probably wasting her time waiting.

Outside the window it was growing dark early as it started to snow again, which would make her journey back to Harlden difficult given the poor state of the roads. Still she was reluctant to leave. She'd have a cup of tea in the canteen and then call it a day. On her way to the lift she rang Mac to tell him about Stanley in case it helped. Roy was dozing in the waiting area and she woke him up.

'I'm just going for a tea break. Could you sit with her?'

'Yes, ma'am. Sorry, I didn't mean to be asleep.'

His hair was ruffled into a Tintin-like coif and his acne was bright in the cruel fluorescent light. Maybe if Jenni woke up she would identify more with him as someone of her own age!

CHAPTER THIRTY

With confirmation that Daniel Mariner was indeed Flash Harry Fenwick felt that he had at last achieved something, though his good mood didn't survive his call with Nightingale. It deteriorated even further after an unsettling meeting with CC Norman.

Overnight he had worked out several arguments in favour of him rejoining the search for Issie Mattias and not one of them was based on Norman's investigation being a failure. He rang Norman's office and asked for a meeting to be told that the earliest opportunity would be midday as the chief constable was out. That gave him an excuse to stay at Guildford HQ, which suited him.

Bernstein was pleased to see him and they spent the morning rehashing theories of where Mariner might have taken Issie. None of them was new, and though Bernstein didn't say as much, Fenwick could tell that their meeting had been a welcome distraction more than anything else. She hadn't expected a miracle, not even from him.

Norman offered him coffee and congratulations on resolving the Flash Harry case.

'This is good for you, Superintendent. Just what you needed. A nasty, serial case resolved – and with very little manpower! Alastair will be delighted.'

'Yes, the ACC will be relieved to see the case resolved. I was wond—'

'So what do you plan to do now? Take some well-deserved leave before Christmas, I shouldn't wonder.'

'Well actually, I was wondering whether I could rejoin Operation Goldilocks, sir.' The look on Norman's face made him hurry on. 'It's just that, with one brother a known sexual criminal, it might help to bring that angle into the search for Mariner junior.'

'We have done so already, Fenwick, and there is nothing you can add to my investigation.'

'With Flash Harry successfully out of the way, wouldn't it look good, sir?'

'Meaning things don't already. Forget it. And you can stop pestering the Saxbys as well. Asking them to lobby for your involvement is poor behaviour. I haven't taken action on it so far but if you persist . . .'

'I haven't done anything of the sort, sir. The last time I spoke to them was over a week ago, when I was still working for you.'

'Then why do I receive a daily call from them advocating your reinstatement in the inquiry?'

'I don't know, sir, but I can promise you it has nothing to do with me.'

Norman looked as if he wanted to call him a liar but satisfied himself by bringing the meeting to a close abruptly with a warning.

'If I find that you continue to take an interest in this operation, Superintendent, I will take it as an act of insubordination. Do you understand?'

'I only want to help, sir, in any way I can. I feel somehow responsible . . .'

'Sentimental twaddle, Fenwick. Grow up and grow a thicker skin. Now I suspect you have some tidying up to do before you take your leave, so I'll bid you good day. Oh,' as Fenwick stood up, 'and of course a happy Christmas with your family.'

Fenwick muttered a reciprocation and left, crushed by the

absolute dismissal of his legitimate interest. In his office he picked up his briefcase and called Tate to ask him to have his car brought round.

'It's been a pleasure working with you, sir. If ever there is anything I can do for you, please let me know.'

'Thank you, Tate.'

As he made his way to the outside of the building his mobile phone rang.

'Fenwick.'

'Superintendent? It's Lulu Bullock; I'm sorry to trouble you but I heard you were at the school yesterday and I wanted to speak with you. As you're back on the case again, I'd prefer it was you.'

'Is there something you need to share with the investigating officers, Miss Bullock?'

'I don't know. It's probably nothing but I thought I should mention it to you.'

'Mention what, Miss Bullock?'

'It's something I've found of Issie's, some background notes with her A-level sketches and they are . . . odd. I might be interpreting things but, well, I think they could link to the pictures she was working on.'

'The ones that suggest she might have been sexually abused?'

'Yes,' there was a rustle of turning pages, 'here; I'll read part of it to you: "*at the cross roads which path to take away from the past? My own straight on to the future I will shape despite the attempt of others to shape me. Or to the right, following my mother's determined ignorance and false peace of mind. Or do I go left, along my tormentor's path? Into the shady underworld of his obsession and power? Three ways, one choice; unless I take a fourth. Oblivion.*" It goes on like that, all a bit melodramatic and full of teenage mystery. But the way she was talking of a choice and her tormentor . . . It made me think of what you saw in the paintings she was working on.'

'You should share these with the chief constable, Miss Bullock. I can't judge whether the notes are relevant or not but neither should you. They need to be considered by experts.'

'I've sent your colleagues a transcript already. They are inclined to dismiss the paintings and the notes as unconnected. But you've been working on other cases of sexual assault. What if there's a link to your investigations?'

She was tempting him. If he could tell himself this was about Flash Harry then it would be a loose end and quite legitimate for him to take a look at what she had.

'Can you be sure that what you've found is recent enough to be relevant?'

'The notes are on the back of a test paper I gave them only three weeks ago. And it isn't just notes. There's something else as well, Superintendent.'

'The best thing is if you could send everything to me at my office in Lewes.'

'I don't want to trust them to the post and I won't be able to find a courier today as the secretary's away and her office is locked.'

'Hmm.' He looked at his watch: two thirty-five. He could be at St Anne's within half an hour, pick up the notes and still be in Harlden in time for the children's return from school. 'I'll come over now and pick them up.'

'Really? That would be great; what I mean is, good, I'll have them ready.'

Of course he could send Big Mac and not go driving off himself but what else had he to do? He stopped himself thinking about how stupid he was and suppressed the flicker of thought that it would be pleasant to see Lulu Bullock again.

CHAPTER THIRTY-ONE

Fenwick's car was four-wheel drive and he was glad, even though municipal gritters had readied the main roads for the forecast snowstorm. As he steered through the college gates the first snowflakes started to fall in a gentle patter on his windscreen.

He parked his car in the visitors' car park some distance from the building where Lulu Bullock had rooms. As he stepped out he pulled his coat collar tight against a biting wind that was whipping the fresh fall of snow into needles that stung any exposed skin. He stuffed his free hand into a pocket and concentrated on not falling over.

He was curious to know what Lulu Bullock had found among Issie's papers. As soon as he had them he told himself that he would leave. The front door was unlocked and he walked in, looking around for someone to whom he could announce his arrival. The place was empty. Feeling like an intruder, he made his way up the stairs.

On the second floor he walked past the staffroom and found the back stairs he remembered. They rose steeply into a gloomy space for which he couldn't find a switch. As he climbed he considered Lulu's way of life; on top of work in an isolated flat that must surely be lonely once school was over, almost spooky. He felt his way up the stairs, his fingers brushing the wall as he climbed away from the light. The small hairs on the back of his neck rose and he became aware of a presence on the stairs above.

She was dressed in a long black fur coat with leather boots tight to the knee.

'I was just going to check the art block,' she explained. 'I hadn't expected you to come so soon.'

'Do you need to go to the block now or can it wait?'

'I'll go later; come on up.'

He hesitated, wondering whether it would be better to talk in the staffroom below.

'I have coffee brewing and you're shivering; it will warm you up.'

She turned and started to climb. As the stair turned, a light came on suddenly, illuminating her profile and the shimmer of her long hair.

'Is there any news about Issie?' she asked. 'On the radio they just mentioned that the man who'd been killed near here was involved in Issie's abduction. Is that true?'

Fenwick carried on climbing the stairs. Norman and Bernstein had decided to go live with news of Dan Mariner's death and connect it to Issie's abduction. He didn't agree with their decision. If Mariner heard he might become desperate and harm Issie. To risk the publicity they must have run out of other ideas but there was no way he was going to confirm or deny anything to Miss Bullock.

'I'm afraid I can't comment.'

'Oh, I see; am I a suspect now?' She turned and smiled but Fenwick didn't respond.

He was regretting his impulse to come to the school. What had made him do it?

'I only need a few minutes of your time. I'm sure you must be busy.'

'Hardly! Everyone is at the carol service. The girls who are not Christians are allowed to spend a couple of hours in town while it's on but for teachers there's no such tolerance, which I object to. As I am resolutely agnostic I refuse to go. Over the years various heads have tried to enforce my attendance but each one has eventually realised the futility of their efforts. So there's only me and the caretakers here.'

'Oh.' He felt foolish. 'You should be more careful with your security then. I was able to walk straight in.'

'Everywhere is locked up. I'd just released the front door from my flat – I can do that – so that it wouldn't close and lock me out while I was in the art block. They'll be back by seven provided the weather doesn't get any worse.'

They had reached the landing from which the final set of stairs went up to her flat. Instead of continuing to climb, Lulu Bullock moved back one step.

'Aren't *you* worried sick about Issie, Superintendent?'

'Of course I am.'

When Lulu opened her front door a blanket of warm air enveloped Fenwick, infused with spices of some kind, tangy and rich at the same time. In the small hall he struggled to take off his scarf and coat.

'Here, let me help you.'

Lulu reached her arms behind his back and removed his coat in one smooth movement.

'It might be a good idea to take off your jacket as well; it's warm in here.'

He felt it taken from him.

'Go and sit by the fire; I'll get coffee.'

There was a fierce blaze in the glass-fronted fireplace. He watched the flames billow as the wind roared its way down the chimney. He could hear it screeching around the chimney as gusts surged over the school roofs. Instead of sitting down he looked properly at the paintings that covered the walls. Many of them were signed with dedications to her but the most accomplished of them bore no name. They were abstracts, mainly in waves of aquamarine or with deep, hypnotic green swirls that made him think of enchanted forests without end.

Looking at them increased his sense of displacement so he turned to the bookshelves as he had done on his first visit. This time, though, he dared to look at the sculptures. There were about a dozen of them: mostly bronzes but also a few in dark green marble. They glinted in the lamplight, throwing back reflections of the flames in their depths.

'Do you like them?'

She was behind him and when he turned he knew that she had been watching him.

'Very much; who did them?'

'I did; they're part of a series I've been working on. When it's finished I hope to exhibit. I only do small pieces these days because I don't have the space or money to work on larger ones any more.'

'Wouldn't the school help you?'

'Probably; but actually I like the excuse – working in miniature is new to me. It brings its own challenges and intensity.'

She passed him a large mug and their fingers brushed as he took it. He felt a rush of electricity as he had the first time that he had seen her but stronger. Lulu smiled at him and he saw the fine lines of her face that disappeared in repose. Her hair was silver in the firelight, loosely caught back in a tortoiseshell clasp. It gleamed and he had to suppress an urge to reach out and stroke it as if she were some luxurious cat; just to hear her purr.

'Try your coffee.'

How long had he been standing there like some dumbstruck teenager? He suddenly felt extremely hot, as if his face and ears were on fire, and took a sip of coffee. It was very good. An expert, he could taste Arabica beans freshly ground, and something else that was new to him.

'A hint of cinnamon, that's all,' she said, reading his thoughts, 'just enough to be different without spoiling the taste. Sometimes I use star aniseed but you don't strike me as the liquorish type.'

It made him uncomfortable that the coffee had been brewed with him in mind, as if the whole episode was anything but spontaneous. Lulu laughed. It was more like a man's chuckle; infectious.

Lulu placed her coffee on a small table and took a step towards him. He took a quick breath and stepped back. Just as he thought he was going to be forced to do something to create more distance between them there was a loud crash from above their heads that made them both jump. It was followed by a deafening grating as if a convict were dragging a ball and chain across the roof.

'What the devil . . . ?' He looked at her enquiringly.

'I've no idea; I've never heard anything like that before.'

The noise continued, became a scraping and then there was a metallic twang before something smashed against the window so loudly it made Lulu scream.

Fenwick pushed past her. One of the small panes of glass was cracked but otherwise the window was intact. Outside, a tangle of metal was swinging in the wind, threatening to curve back and finish its work.

'It's an old aerial; the wind has torn it loose. Do you have something I can cut the cable with? Otherwise you're going to lose your window.'

She was back in seconds with a pair of sharp secateurs.

'Hold the curtains out of the way; I'm going to open the window.'

As soon as he loosed the latch the wind jerked the frame from his grasp and swung it back hard against the outside wall.

'Damn!'

He had no choice but to lean out and try to catch the aerial.

Snow and ice particles flew into his face, half blinding him. It took him several attempts to reach the swinging mess of wire tubing and he was losing all sense of feeling in his arm by the time he finally grasped it with his left hand. The freezing metal immediately burnt his fingers but he had the presence of mind not to try and pull away. With his right hand he reached to cut the cable before trying to pull the aerial towards him. It was cumbersomely heavy. With great difficulty he managed at last to angle it inside. His left hand was by now welded to the metal and he still needed to close the damned window.

Dropping the secateurs he reached out with his right hand to try and find the edge of the window frame and pull it closed. As he did so he became aware of Lulu hanging on to his belt as he leant out further and further. At last he could feel the lower edge of the window frame and he pulled hard against the force of the wind. It was no good. The frame was flat to the wall, held there by the strength of the gale. He was just about to give up when Lulu passed him a cast iron toasting fork with curled prongs. Without speaking he gripped it firmly and managed to put enough of the tincs under the frame to lever it away from the wall but he didn't have a free hand to pull it in the rest of the way as his left was still stuck to the aerial.

Without being asked Lulu reached past him, head and shoulders out of the window, and grabbed the side of the frame with both hands. Together they managed to pull it closed and as soon as it was shut she locked it. They rested their heads against the glass for a moment, breathing deeply, before looking at each other with relief.

'That was fun,' he said, noticing his sodden shirt in surprise. His left hand was starting to hurt like hell. The metal had thawed out but as he prised his fingers away he could see dark-red burns on three fingers and a bloody graze on his palm where a sharp edge had ripped away skin as he had pulled it into the room.

'Let me look at that.' She took his injured hand in both of hers and turned it over, palm up. 'That must be painful; it needs to be cleaned and dressed properly. Come with me.'

He followed her into a small bathroom dominated by an old-fashioned, three-quarter-size claw-foot bath. Lulu found ointment, gauze and plasters as well as a spray of some sort.

'Iodine,' she said. 'It will hurt but it's better for the burns than a cream. Put your hand over the sink and I'll see to the fingers first.'

The spray attacked his injured flesh like stings from a swarm of wasps and he bit his lip.

'Brave boy.' She patted his arm. 'I think we should leave those burns open rather than cover them up. The skin is blistered but not broken and they'll heal faster that way. I'll try and make you a sort of gauze glove as you have to drive back, but as soon as you get home, take it off and just keep your hand clean, dry and open to the air. As for the cut on your palm, it's nasty. You've lost quite a bit of skin. That needs proper attention, maybe even a trip to casualty.'

'I haven't got time for that.'

'In which case, I have a dressing that I can put on but it will make it tricky for you to use your hand as you won't be able to bend it fully.'

He watched as she cleaned the wound and applied the dressing. She had small, neat fingers that didn't hesitate as she covered his palm in a strange, plastic-coated plaster.

'Were you ever a nurse?'

'No; just a first-aider.'

'Well, I feel in good hands.' Fenwick immediately regretted his words. 'Let's look at the window and see if you need to do something about that broken pane.'

They decided that it needed taping up, which she did quickly and effectively. She caught him staring as she did it.

'I'm good with my hands, always have been.'

'So is sculpture your favourite form of art?'

'Oh yes, though my style has changed a lot over the years. When I was Issie's age until my thirties I was into a sort of pagan, art nouveau style: naturalistic, heavy in symbolism. But now I take a pared-down, more abstract approach.' She smiled at him, pleased that he was interested. He noticed the lilac of her eyes, so deep as to be almost purple.

His breathing felt strange; his throat was too tight, his tie an encumbrance. He took another sip of coffee but it had gone cold and he grimaced.

'Let me pour you a fresh one.'

'No thanks; once I've looked at Issie's papers I'll be on my way.'

She handed him a beige folio tied with ribbon so that it resembled a solicitor's brief, which he struggled to undo.

'Here, let me.' She unpicked the knot and opened the file for him.

As he read, Fenwick's assessment of Issie as a disturbed young woman was confirmed. The trouble was it would be hard to prove whether anything had really happened to her or if the writings were some sort of teenage fantasy. They referred, usually obliquely, to 'torments'. Even making a case that these were physical rather than psychological would be a challenge.

At the back of the folio were a series of sketches for the paintings she had been working on, etched in black and red charcoal. One showed the face of the girl being raped on the stone altar. It was clearly a self-portrait. Next to it was a scrawled *NO!* In another there was an intricately worked detail of the gold pendant, which would be good enough to help them match it to Rodney Saxby's should they ever have sufficient evidence to charge him. Unfortunately, though, there wasn't enough here for him to begin to make a case.

'Not enough?' Lulu asked, reading his mind.

'If we had other evidence, then possibly. I'll take them with me anyway,' he noted her expression, 'and make copies.'

'But on their own they are insufficient?'

'Probably.'

Without speaking she stood up and left the room. When she returned she was carrying a crumpled, thin, supermarket plastic bag.

'I found this too. It was stuffed at the bottom of her bag of brushes and pens.'

She thrust it at Fenwick who flicked it open with his right fingertips. Inside was material of some sort. He didn't want to touch it unnecessarily in case it proved significant.

'What is it?'

'A T-shirt; hers, I think.'

'So?'

Lulu blushed.

'It's stained down the front and on one shoulder.' She looked away. 'It might be semen.'

'Why didn't you give it to me immediately?'

'I didn't want it to make you think that maybe Issie had gone away of her own accord with a lover.'

Fenwick suppressed a surge of anger towards this most irritating woman. For someone so intelligent she could be remarkably stupid.

'I need to get this to Surrey immediately. They'll have the lab run tests and we'll know what we're dealing with. Do you have a clean paper bag I can put it in?'

As he waited Fenwick studied the carrier bag. It was from a Greek supermarket. He remembered Jane Saxby telling him the story of the sailing trip that had gone so disastrously wrong. When Issie had run away . . . to be found by Rodney Saxby. His mind leapt ahead to possible conclusions. Did they still have the man under surveillance or was he off their suspect list? He took the offered bag.

'Thanks for the coffee and first aid.'

'Thank you for your help. Who knows what I'd have done if you hadn't been here.'

She didn't follow him down the stairs but released the lock of the front door remotely when he buzzed to be let out.

CHAPTER THIRTY-TWO

Fenwick had put on his coat, right glove and scarf before venturing outside but nothing prepared him for the force of the storm he walked into. He struggled to keep on the path and had difficulty opening his car door against the wind. Once inside, he left the engine running for several minutes until the windscreen started to clear, but the wipers were frozen solid to the glass and he had to step out again to ease them away. They scraped across the glass grudgingly, catching on stubborn ridges of ice that refused to melt.

Slowly the windscreen cleared and the interior of the car warmed. Fenwick eased the car out of park, regretting that he was no longer in an RTC vehicle with winter tyres but glad he had an automatic. His left hand hurt like hell, a distraction he tried to ignore as he steered one-handed into the snowstorm. He almost made it to the road but when he braked as he approached the gateway the rear wheels skidded and the car started to slide. His left hand reached the steering wheel too late and there was nothing he could do as the rear of the car slipped inexorably into the ditch at the side of the road.

'I don't believe it.'

Fenwick clambered out of the car, which had come to rest at an angle so that the driver's door pointed upwards and the front offside tyre was off the ground. He looked at the snow that was settling already on the skid marks and the roof of his car, and concluded that there was no way he was going to be able to get the car out of the ditch without help. He checked his watch; four twenty-two but it was already dark.

He opened his mobile and pressed autodial. The screen flickered and flashed: 'no network coverage'. There was nothing for it; he would have to go back and call for a car. After a moment's hesitation he put Issie's T-shirt, securely tied, under his coat. He wouldn't risk leaving it in the car.

Fenwick tried to remember how far the school was from the front entrance. Not far, surely; a matter of minutes in the car but he couldn't see any lights and the snow blew horizontally into his face , limiting his perspective. In the boot he had a Barbour, which he put on over his winter coat before starting back up the driveway. His shoes were heavy, thick-soled leather lace-ups but in minutes they were soaked through, as werc his trousers below the coat.

It was hard to see and at times he couldn't be sure he was still on the tarmac but the ditch either side guided him. Twice he almost fell as he pushed his way forward against the storm.

By the time he reached the school buildings his trousers were starting to freeze and his face was completely numb. The only fccling in his fingers was in his injured left hand, which throbbed with his pulse and had grown heavy as lead as he walked. When he reached the partial shelter of the porch at the old schoolhouse he leant against the half-glazed door too tired for a moment to do anything, then he pressed Lulu's number.

'Yes?'

'It's me. I didn't make it beyond the drive. Could you let me in? I need to call a car.'

The door buzzed. He climbed the stairs with difficulty, feeling light-headed and confused for no reason. Her door was open and he pushed inside gratefully. In the tiny hall he slipped off his shoes, which were soaked through, and walked in sodden socks into the living room. The fire glowed with an orange-red light; jazz was playing softly, a Bud Powell number he recognised.

'You look awful; are you OK?'

'Just a bit cold; I'll be fine in a minute.'

She looked at him sceptically and reached out to feel his face. He recoiled slightly from her touch but was too tired to resist.

'You're perishing cold. Where did you walk from?' Her tone was accusing.

'Just before the gates.'

'What? That's almost two miles. You're bloody lucky you're not lying out there freezing to death!' She sounded really angry.

He knew he should explain it was only a short walk, just the snow had made it more difficult, but his lips somehow were not connected properly to his mouth, and anyway, it was warm in the room, why have an argument?

'I just need to call . . . they'll send a car.'

He had the number in the mobile phone in his jacket pocket but it was quite hard to find and after a moment she flicked his hand away and reached in herself to retrieve it. He dialled Tate's number as he needed someone who wouldn't blab about where he was. The man answered quickly. When Fenwick asked for a car to come on the quiet and pick him up from St Anne's he sensed a moment's surprise.

'I think it will be better if I do that myself, sir. We've got a real blizzard blowing but leave it with me.'

Fenwick broke the connection with a sigh and tried to think. Who else did he need to call? Struggle as he might he couldn't remember.

'. . . I said, you need to get out of those wet things. Come on, Superintendent, you can't stay like that, you'll catch your death of cold.'

'Hmm?' Fenwick struggled to concentrate. Lulu Bullock was standing in front of him holding a pair of men's trousers, corduroys in a particularly nasty brown.

'Don't look at them like that; they were my dad's, God bless him, and they're all I've got. Come on, into the bathroom with you and you can change your shirt as well – it was soaked before and I doubt it's dried off.'

She thrust a bundle of clothes at him and virtually pushed him into the bathroom. He closed the door and sat down on the closed loo seat. He felt so tired and couldn't understand why. All he had done was walk from the school gates back to the main house. How could he feel like this? The clothes were warm and dry and he lowered his head into them, closing his eyes.

Knocking on the door roused him.

'Coming.'

He opened it to see Lulu holding a phone out for him. It was his mobile.

'A man called Tate needs to talk to you.' She looked him up and down, shook her head and walked away.

'Fenwick.'

'I'm really sorry, sir, but RTC are advising no travel unless absolutely essential. Roads are closing and I won't be able to reach you until the blizzard passes.'

Fenwick realised that if he insisted on Tate trying to reach him he might be putting him in danger, as well as asking him to draw attention to himself on an errand they would both rather keep quiet.

'Understood. If you could just call me if and when you set out? Oh, and text me the details of a haulage firm to help with my car?'

'Of course.' Tate sounded relieved.

Fenwick broke the connection and looked around for Lulu Bullock. She had gone off somewhere so he returned to the bathroom and changed into the dry clothes. They fitted quite well, even the trousers were long enough, and he started to feel warmer apart from his feet, which remained stubbornly numb.

When he stepped back into the living room she was there on the phone.

'—yes, don't worry. I've already spoken with Peter and Winston. They're double-checking all the buildings and a cousin is coming in to provide backup in case we have an emergency, so we're all right. I'm more concerned about all of you.'

Fenwick realised the school party must still be in Guildford.

'Well that's a relief. Hopefully the girls will think of it as an adventure . . . if there's any problem at all I will call, don't worry.'

'They're stranded?'

'Yes; the staff at the cathedral have arranged accommodation for the girls and housemistresses in their hall and found spare beds for the other teachers.'

'So you're on your own here – with the caretakers and cousin.'

'And you,' she said, 'at least I assume you'll need somewhere to sleep tonight?'

'I, ah, well, yes, I suppose . . . er, thank you.'

'No problem; pass me those wet things. You need socks but I want to check your feet first. You were gone an hour and I'd rather be sure they're OK.'

'I was only out there thirty minutes.'

'An hour, Superintendent, and that's bad.'

He insisted he could check his own toes and did so quickly. They were fine, though it was a bit worrying that he still couldn't feel them. Just as he finished Lulu came in with a bowl of water.

'It's only just warm – too hot and it would be agony for you. Once you get the feeling back I'll heat it up. It will hurt like hell for a while but then they should be back to normal. With luck you'll escape with chilblains.'

Thus it was that he spent the first part of the evening sitting with his trousers rolled up and bare feet in a galvanised bowl of water that was steadily made warmer by the ever attentive Lulu. He tried not to think what he looked like and closed his eyes for a moment.

He needed to think. There was a call still to make . . .

'Superintendent . . . Mr Fenwick? . . . Andrew!'

Someone was interrupting his briefing; he wanted to tell them to be quiet but he didn't know their name so he said, 'In a minute; let Big Mac finish.'

The shaking continued and he half opened an eye to see a strange woman looming over him. She reminded him of someone he knew very well but the realisation only served to confuse him further.

'What?'

'I've cooked some supper. It's eight o'clock. I probably should have woken you earlier but you were fast asleep so I left you.'

He managed to open both eyes and at the same time remembered to close his mouth. Recognition triggered memory and he struggled to sit up straight. His feet were no longer in the water but covered with a dry towel.

'What time did you say?' He sounded even to his own ears as if he were castigating reception for forgetting his wake-up call.

'Eight; you've been asleep for two hours. You're staying here at St Anne's, remember?'

Of course he did. He glanced down at the unfamiliar trousers, eased the collar that was scratching his neck and tried to smile. He should be grateful.

'I don't know if you're hungry but I was cooking supper for myself anyway; it's coq au vin with sautéed potatoes and spinach. I hope that's OK?'

'It sounds wonderful, thank you. I hadn't expected anything.' That was true. 'Have I time to call home?'

'Of course; I'll be in the kitchen. Come through when you're done.'

He used his mobile to call and forced himself awake as the number rang. Alice answered. She had expected him for supper but annoyance was soon replaced with concern for his safety. He was sorry to have worried her. The children were in bed early having misbehaved and, no, she wasn't inclined to go and get them so that they could say goodnight to their father. When the call finished he wandered towards the kitchen, hovering at the door.

'Here,' she passed him a glass of a red Burgundy. 'Don't look like that. You're not on duty and you have absolutely nowhere to go tonight so you might as well relax.'

Of course she was right.

The wine was a bit light for his taste but he didn't care. Suddenly he felt hungry. There was a small table against the window, which she had set for two. Mercifully there was no candle.

'Can I help?'

'Just put the bread and wine on the table and then we're all set.'

There was a moment's embarrassment when she had to cut up his food for him because of his injured hand but after that the meal was fantastic. Maybe it was because he was so hungry, or perhaps his experience in the snow had made him sensitive to simple comforts. He ate a second helping and relaxed back in his chair, too full even to contemplate the cheese she offered.

He felt more comfortable than previously. Lulu was keeping her distance; the perfect hostess but no more. There was something about her that intrigued, attracted and repelled him in equal measure but if she felt the same she gave no hint. The evening had become a pleasant interlude and he felt more relaxed than he had done in weeks.

They moved into the sitting room for coffee. She served brandy because the wine was finished. It was quite a large measure and he thought he wouldn't finish it but as the fire died down he noticed that most of it had gone. When he returned from a trip to the bathroom his glass looked rather fuller than when he had left.

Lulu sat in a chair by the fire, leaving him to relax on the sofa on his own. She was easy to talk to and didn't ask awkward questions, though she was naturally curious and asked about his family. As the level in the brandy glass ebbed he found himself sharing his concerns about Bess.

'She's obviously missing her mother,' Lulu said. 'It's a pity she doesn't have a role model to look up to; it might help as she navigates puberty.'

'Oh, but she does,' he said, feeling the warmth of the brandy expand to meet the heat of the fire on the soles of his feet. 'There's this police officer – a woman – that she really likes and looks up to. I'm sure that Bess sees her as a big sister, someone she admires and wants to impress.'

'Well that's good. And this young woman – I assume she's young' – Fenwick nodded – 'is she special, I mean to you? Are you and she . . .' Lulu sipped her brandy, not meeting his eye. 'I don't know why I'm being coy. Are you and she lovers?'

Fenwick almost spilt his drink.

'No way! She's a colleague, that's all. I respect her deeply but no, that is, never.'

Lulu was looking at him with a half smile, not mocking exactly but not kind either.

'So is there anyone special for you?'

'Other than Bess, Chris and my mother, no.' It had seemed a smart line before he said it.

Lulu stood up and came to sit beside him.

'Good; that makes things a lot simpler,' she said as one of her elegant fingers traced the line from his temple, down his jaw and back up to his ear. The delicacy of her touch made him shiver.

'I only have one bedroom. Of course I could make up a bed for you here on the couch but there's no need when you can as easily share mine.'

He knew what he wanted; more than anything at that moment: he wanted her, with a dry heat born of abstinence and denial. It would be so easy; no implications or obligations, just a simple night of pleasure with no regrets. But there was a nagging voice at the back of his mind: she's connected to the case, a witness at the least, maybe even more.

'Don't worry. I'm not guilty of anything,' she said and closed the gap between them, 'except of being unbelievably attracted to you.'

Her kiss was sudden and he found himself responding automatically. His lips parted and her tongue slipped in, licking his teeth, drawing a groan from deep inside him. Her hands went around his back and pulled his chest onto hers. Her fingers were strong, hungry, stroking down from his shoulders, along his spine to his belt.

She nibbled his lips; tiny little bites that made him gasp and kiss her back, like a drowning man sucking in air. Her fingers travelled round to the front of his belt and his hand flew to grip hers tightly.

'No, I can't.' He almost shouted and she moved her hand.

'There's no such thing as can't, didn't they teach you that at school?' Her fingers played with shirt buttons.

He pulled back, suddenly aware of what he was doing.

'No,' his voice was hoarse, 'this isn't right.'

She stared at him in surprise and tried to kiss him again but he turned his head.

'What is it? Are you married; engaged; committed somehow?'

'No.' He shook his head but his heart was saying yes to her words, to all of them.

'So what's the problem?'

The table lamp behind her made her hair shine in a halo around her shoulders. Her face was beautiful; her figure a slender silhouette, utterly desirable. He was a widower of four years, an eligible bachelor; so what was it that was holding him back?

'You're not attached,' she repeated with a smile and leant towards him again.

'I'm a widower,' he said and felt a fraud at the look of sympathy that settled on her face.

'Oh, I'm so sorry. Normally I'm sensitive to grief, I pick up on emotions, but I had no idea.' She backed off and picked up his cup. 'Straighten yourself up while I go and fetch you a nightcap.'

Fenwick smoothed his shirt with trembling hands and did up his belt, easing himself into a more comfortable position, painfully aware of how aroused he was. What was holding him back; why had he lied? Because it was a lie. Yes, Monique had died but that was years ago and he had been in relationships since. It was unworthy of him to dissemble in this way.

'Here, it's camomile tea, good for you.'

Fenwick took the mug from her and put it on the table. She looked at him expectantly, almost as if his resistance had been for show and now he would behave as he truly wanted to.

'Goodnight, Lulu. Thanks for a lovely dinner. I can sleep here; it won't be a problem.'

She shook her head but brought him a pillow and blankets, casting one last look over her shoulder as she went into her bedroom.

The storm blew itself out around four in the morning. He was awake and heard it die but fell asleep shortly afterwards. At eight his phone rang.

'Yes?'

'Good news, sir, I should be with you in less than an hour. The A3's open again and I've asked the highways agency to clear the route to St Anne's as a priority because of Goldilocks.' Tate's enthusiasm was as bad as a cold shower.

'Thank you.' Fenwick broke the call and looked around to find Lulu staring at him from the doorway with her customary half smile.

'Return to reality?'

He was drinking coffee and chewing his way through toast

337

when his phone rang again to alert him to the fact that Tate's car would arrive in ten minutes. He could hear the shower running and took his coffee into the living room.

He tried to study the sculptures; anything to distract his thoughts from the shower. He looked at the first piece without seeing it; his eyes moved on to the second and then the next. By the time he was looking at the fourth he realised that there might be a theme to the series that he could sense but not name. The shapes were abstract; voluptuous but also hard and purposeful. He walked slowly along the shelves, struggling to find the word to connect them and was about to give up when he spotted another bronze almost hidden behind a large book on Berthe Morisot.

He pushed the book to one side and gasped in shock. The statue was a perfect portrait of Nightingale.

'What is it?'

Lulu had walked in behind him wrapped in a bathrobe, hair in a towel. She came and stood beside him, looking over his shoulder.

'Oh that. It's an early piece. Do you like it?'

'It's . . . I . . .' Fenwick's mind was reeling from shock and the confusion of guilt that had ambushed him. 'An early piece . . . but then . . . who was the sitter?'

Lulu smiled at him.

'Why me, of course. It's a self-portrait.'

She just managed to steady the mug as it tipped from his hand.

PART FOUR

'It is the cause, it is the cause, my soul.
Let me not name it to you, you chaste stars.
It is the cause. Yet I'll not shed her blood,
Nor scar that whiter skin of hers than snow
And smooth as monumental alabaster.
Yet she must die, else she'll betray more men.
Put out the light, and then put out the light.'

William Shakespeare,
Othello

CHAPTER THIRTY-THREE

Mariner had almost forgotten that detectives were battling through atrocious weather conditions trying to find him. He had even lost track of the date until a letter had arrived that made him look at his watch for the first time in days. The nineteenth; this was their two-week anniversary!

He stared at the blizzard outside, mesmerised by the chaos of snowflakes. It was his sort of storm. It covered all tracks, including the twisting path to the recently abandoned cottage. The previous owners had been evicted because of mortgage arrears – he knew from the letters left behind. Not killing the albatross had changed his fortune, he was sure of that. Before he would have been captured within hours, but now, he leant back with a small grunt, anything was possible.

There was no furniture in the cottage but it had an old-style solid fuel Aga that kept the kitchen warm and provided the means for hot food. That was one of the reasons he had picked it out along with several others from the dozens listed on the agent's particulars, all due for auction and a quick sale. It had been third time lucky finding it. The first two hadn't been suitable. One turned out to be a semi and the other was at the end of a cul-de-sac. This one was just right. Although both gas and electricity had been disconnected the water was still running. There was a downstairs WC, brutally freezing but he didn't linger, just did his business and left sharpish. With the camping gear and food from home, plus what he had bought after leaving the pump station, they'd had enough to last for several days.

When that ran out he had risked the short walk to an all-night cheap and cheerful shop that had a decent frozen-food cabinet, fresh bread and milk and budget-price whisky. He had been twice and each time there was a different youth serving who was more worried about the kids pinching stuff than a quiet, cash-paying customer.

He was careful with the torch after dark. So far no one had stopped by except the postman from time to time, but he knew his routine and made sure the house was silent before he arrived. He remembered the estate agent's brief description: 'secluded' they'd called it. Bloody remote more like. Still it had suited him fine . . . until now.

Steve sighed. It was time to leave. The letter crushed in his palm told him that. The house was to be auctioned before Christmas according to the notice the bank had sent to the previous owners. Why? They were long gone but perhaps the lenders were required to send it by law, or it was an administrative screw-up. Whatever, it had been another piece of luck that warned him there could be visitors before long. So best be gone. He pulled his eyes away from the storm and took in the immediate view: camp bed, two sleeping bags, camping gaz, empty cardboard boxes, the girl slouched against the Aga.

'Wake up.' He tapped her cheek lightly in an attempt to rouse her.

There was a bruise by her eye that made him feel embarrassed but he told himself she had deserved a little bit of correction. The girl groaned and turned her face away.

'Wake up! Issie,' he whispered, stroking her greasy hair back in a gesture that made her eyelids flicker but underneath all he could see were the whites.

'Come on, darlin', wake up.'

'Ngh?' A frown line appeared then cleared as her eyes cracked open.

'It's Badger, come on Issie.'

A look that was something like terror flashed across her face, making him angry. Behind the anger was something else that he wouldn't identify. He lifted her up carefully, keeping his face out of reach of those sharp little teeth but it was an unnecessary precaution as her head lolled away from him and her eyes closed again.

She was so light. It had been two days since she had eaten. The hunger strike was her latest attempt to force him to let her go. As they had been low on provisions he'd left her to it but now he needed her strong. He hugged her, used to the stale smell of her filthy clothes and the feel of gritty skin.

'We're going to leave, darling, and you must eat something before we go.'

Issie's eyes opened wide, the hope in them more than he could bear.

'Don't say it!' He let her go and she fell to the floor, banging the back of her head. He ignored her and leant over to make some tea. 'You aren't going home yet; we just need to find somewhere else.'

While the water heated he searched in the box for some food to tempt her with. There were cheese and onion crisps, a chocolate bar and the last of the milk. That would do. He opened the carton.

'Here.' He poured milk into the top of a thermos and held it to her mouth. Issie drank greedily and he rewarded her obedience with a pat on her head. Then she started to choke.

'Whoa, you'll make yourself sick. You can have some more later. Hungry?'

'No.' It was a tiny whisper.

'You've got to eat. Come on, chocolate or crisps?' She shook her head. 'If you don't you'll get more than another slap. I'm not kidding.'

Issie cringed away from him and said, in the voice of a five-year-old, 'Choc'late.'

He broke the bar into tiny pieces and fed her patiently, cupping the back of her head with his palm as she chewed. When she'd had enough she closed her eyes and lay back on the floor.

'Issie.'

She shook her head but he needed her help.

'Where shall we go?'

Her expression turned to one of confusion.

'We have to leave; where shall we go?'

'Home?' The pleading in her voice was pathetic.

'Don't be stupid. I'm talking about you and me. Home's not going to work now, is it? We need somewhere to stay that's warm and quiet.'

He could see her struggling to think and it sort of amused him. She was meant to be the smart one. Issie mumbled something.

'What?'

'Nana's,' she repeated and opened her eyes with effort, trying to concentrate.

'I told you, don't be stupid.'

But she insisted.

'Nana's.'

'She'll be there, won't she?'

'No. In Australia for Chris'mas. House's empty.'

'Where is it?'

'South Downs, near Alfriston, not far.'

'And you're sure it will be empty?' She nodded briefly then winced. 'Neighbours?'

'Not close. In countryside.'

'Give me directions.'

'Too difficult. I'll show you.'

He slapped her for being stupid; how could she direct him from inside the boot of the car, which is where he would have to

343

put her. She barely flinched. After she had drunk her milk Issie asked for more chocolate. The food seemed to do her good so he made her a cup of tea. This time, she was able to hold the cup herself and when he asked for directions again her voice was stronger.

'It's difficult,' she insisted, 'but I can take you there. I know the way.'

'Do you promise to sit on the floor and do nothing?'

'What can I do like this?' Issie gestured with her chin to her bound hands and feet.

'OK, but nothing funny or you'll be back in the boot. Have you got keys to the place?'

'Nana keeps a spare set in the bird feeder by the porch. We'll be able to get in, don't worry.'

It took only minutes to pack the car despite the snow. The blizzard would make driving difficult but it was perfect cover for his journey. Just to be on the safe side he double-checked that the oily mud he had smeared on the number plates hadn't washed off. When everything was ready he bundled Issie into the footwell of the front passenger seat from where she could give him directions while being out of sight. The lane to the cottage was overhung with trees that had protected the ungritted surface from the worst of the snow; just as well, really, or the postman wouldn't have delivered the letter. When they reached the A272 the driving conditions improved a little, though the dual carriageway was reduced to narrow single lanes in both directions. He turned east. There was hardly any traffic and they managed to drive past Billingshurst without incident. Mariner stayed on the main highway not daring to risk the minor roads.

A police patrol car passed in the other direction south of Haywards Heath and he put his foot down instinctively only to feel the rear tyres start to slide. Easing off immediately he stared in the rear-view mirror at its tail lights, waiting to see the red flash of braking that would tell him it was all over, but they just carried on and he started to breathe again. A short while afterwards they came to the A275 where he turned south towards Lewes and the A27. The road was in worse condition so he slowed to around twenty miles an hour, to the annoyance of the female driving a Range Rover behind him. As soon as she could she pulled out, hooting her horn as she passed. Mariner didn't care; let her risk her neck, stupid cow.

The roads around Lewes were busy and he became stuck in a traffic jam. He checked that he had locked the doors and stuffed a rag in Issie's mouth in case she was tempted to try something. After thirty minutes they reached the main junction with the A27 and he was able to speed up a little, but no sooner had he done so than the low fuel warning light started flashing.

'Shit! How much further?' He reached down and yanked out the gag.

'Five to ten miles.'

'Can't you be more precise?'

'That's my best guess.'

He couldn't afford to run out of petrol so that meant buying some. Would his card work; would hers? He didn't have much money left; what was he going to do? He decided to pull over into a lay-by to give himself some time to think. As he did so he saw the Range Rover that had overtaken him parked at the far end with the woman standing beside it glaring. She started walking over immediately. If he drove off she might suspect something. If she came close to the car . . . he shoved the gag deeper into Issie's mouth and wrapped his scarf up to his nose. He opened the glove compartment and found a heavy metal-cased torch. Mariner stepped out, pulling his hood down almost to his nose.

'It was making a noise and now it won't start,' the woman said without ceremony. 'The repair people said it will be an hour before they can get here and I'll freeze to death in that time. Could you give me a lift as far as Beddingham, I can wait at a friend's there.'

Not even a please or thank you but that didn't surprise him. No way was she getting near his car. He gripped the torch harder, testing its weight.

'Let me have a look for you.' His voice was muffled by the scarf.

'I doubt you'll do any better than I did,' she retorted dismissively, but at least she was no longer heading towards his vehicle but was retreating to her own, taking silly little steps.

Mariner reached the car before she did and opened the driver's door. The key was still in the ignition so he climbed in and turned it gently. The engine spluttered and almost caught. A little less fuel this time he thought and tried again. It started on the third attempt, just as the woman opened the passenger door.

'Oh! Well why didn't it do that for me?' She glared at the offending dashboard. 'Well never mind, thank you.'

She waited for Mariner to vacate the driver's seat and slid over. He watched her go feeling very pleased. Not only had he been the hero of the moment, he hadn't needed to hurt her and he had also been able to help himself to a bundle of notes straight from the cash machine that she had obligingly stuffed in the side pocket of her handbag, between the front seats. He jumped into the Mondeo and set off at once in case she noticed the money was gone.

There was a petrol station with a car park in Beddingham, east of Lewes. Mariner pulled in behind an articulated lorry absent its driver. In the shadow cast by the truck he removed enough from the boot to make room for Issie and then pushed her inside, taped her mouth shut and bound her feet tight with a loop around her neck.

The cold went straight to his bladder and he decided he needed to pee before filling up. He was still wearing the scarf around his face and his hooded sweatshirt with the thick, brown sheepskin coat. The money was in his pocket, all two hundred and fifty pounds of it. With only his cheeks and eyes visible he walked into the shop adjoining the petrol station looking for the gents. There was a television on above the counter tuned to a local news channel. He ignored it and followed the signs to the back of the shop.

'It's that poor missing kid, isn't it?' a woman said to the man next to her standing by the freezer choosing a pizza.

'Terrible. But it looks like they know who done it. See there.'

Mariner froze. Although he had assumed the police would be looking for him, so far it hadn't been real. He didn't dare turn towards the screen but shuffled past with his back towards them, his shoulder blades crawling. Should he just leave? But that would look suspicious. The lad behind the checkout looked as thick as two short planks and was busy chatting up a girl who had come in pretending to buy a lottery ticket but was really only after attention. He picked up some milk, biscuits and two sliced loaves at random and walked quickly to the counter where he asked for forty Marlboro. All the while he kept listening to the news report.

'. . . *More than two weeks after the disappearance of Isabelle Mattias the police are reminding the public that anyone seeing a cream Ford Mondeo registration ST EV 77 should get in touch with the incident room at Surrey Constabulary. Do not approach the car or the man, Steven Mariner, aged thirty-five. If you see anything suspicious call the number on the screen immediately. The police advise extreme caution.*'

He thought he was going to be sick, right there on the floor with all of them looking but he managed to swallow, take his change and leave the shop. Once outside, he ran to the car and threw the shopping on the back seat. He relieved himself in the bushes, lit a cigarette with shaking hands and inhaled deeply before starting the engine. He had put the Mondeo in gear before he realised it would be stupid to drive off. The police had the registration number and he had almost no petrol. Shit! What could he do? Mariner looked around the car park. He would've been able to break into anything once, in the days when the Mariner boys had learnt to drive at the expense of the neighbourhood car owners, but that was years back and security was more sophisticated now. He scanned the cars nearby, looking for older models. Nothing . . . no wait, there, a Land Rover parked at the far end on its own. What better for these conditions?

He drove up next to it and tried the driver's door; it was locked, of course, but it took him less than a minute with a bit of thin wire from his toolbox to open it. After that it was easy to load up his gear and dump the girl on the floor in the front, still gagged and bound hand and foot. All he had to do now was park the Mondeo away from where the Land Rover was so there wouldn't be an immediate link.

He was driving along the A27 less than seven minutes after hearing the TV broadcast. His hands were shaking but he kept the speed steady and slowly his heart stopped its ridiculous hammering. It was easier driving the old Land Rover, with its four-wheel drive. Although the steering was heavy he didn't mind as it was feather-light compared to the wreck that was Dan's van. He pulled into a small lay-by and untaped her mouth. She didn't ask him why they had changed cars; in fact she said nothing at all other than to confirm directions when asked.

There was a tattered Ordnance Survey map of the area in the car and she located the farm for him. It was as she said, less than ten miles away but the last part of the journey would be on B roads and single-lane tracks and he realised they would never have made it in the Mondeo. As they turned off the A27 onto a minor road signposted Berwick he felt ice beneath the snow under his wheels. There was no other traffic. Even though the snowfall was lessening the conditions were treacherous and it was growing dark.

'It's on this side of the Downs; there's only a bit of a hill to climb before we turn off onto the track and that's fairly level so far as I can remember,' Issie said as if reading his thoughts. He didn't like that and taped up her mouth.

It took him half an hour to do the last two miles, crawling along on roads thick with packed ice. Twice he had to steer around abandoned cars, his heart hammering in case their occupants were still inside and needed help. Both times they were empty and his panicked breathing slowed to rapid as they neared their destination.

'You said it's called "Abbott's Farm"?' He didn't want to stop and consult the map in case the car wouldn't start again.

Issie replied with an affirmative grunt.

'And the turning's on the right just after the sign to Well's Farm?'

'Ngh.' Yes.

He switched the lights to full beam and scanned the hedgerow.

'Here it is!'

He couldn't believe it; on his left was a signpost for Well's Farm; to his right twenty yards further on a hand-painted board read 'Abbott's Farm'. He had been convinced that she would try and trick him but she hadn't, bless her. He manoeuvred into the turning but the way was blocked by a five-bar gate. Snow piled deep round it and he could see a chain looped through to the gatepost padlocked shut.

'How do we get in? It's locked. You never said it would be locked.'

Issie shrugged her shoulders.

Mariner pulled on his hat and scarf and stepped into the night, locking the doors out of habit. The snowdrift reached above his knees, soaking his jeans. It was very dark beyond the cones of light from the headlights and the trees moaned in the wind. He shivered but took comfort that he wasn't on his own. The girl was there, his lucky white albatross, and soon they'd be toasty warm inside. The toolbox with his bolt cutters was wedged between a spade and the sleeping bags.

Cutting through the chain was a piece of cake but there was no way of opening the gate without shifting the drift so he started to shovel. His gloves were soon soaked through and his back started to ache as he bent to shunt the snow aside. It was difficult work and he was soon sweating inside his coat. Very slowly he cleared the way.

He had almost finished when out of the corner of his eye he saw the beam of car headlights swing around the bend. A four-wheel drive Lexus eased pass at a snail's pace, the male driver merely glancing at him without curiosity, too intent on the road to pay him much heed. Red tail lights glowed as the car drove on and he relaxed slightly.

'BLAAAAAAAAR! BLAAAAAAAAAR!'

The deafening noise of a car horn shattered the silent night.

'Shit!'

He stumbled back, almost falling over, in a desperate attempt to reach the car and stop her. Down the road the other car's brake lights came on.

'Shit fuck!'

He unlocked the doors and pushed her away from the steering wheel, the force of his gesture knocking her head on the dashboard before she slumped back into the footwell on the other side.

'Everything all right?'

He backed out of the Land Rover, closing the door firmly, and moved a step closer to the car where the man had opened his window and stuck his head out into the bitter air. Mariner could see Issie scream against the tape and raised his voice in a shout.

'I'm fine, thanks. It's the snow; it's got into the electrics. Keeps shorting the horn; sorry. Terrible weather!'

'Awful. Well goodnight, then.' The man closed his window as Steve shouted after him.

'Goodnight! Thanks again.' He waved as the car pulled away.

He rested his shaking hands on the icy roof of the car, before returning to the back-breaking work of clearing the gate. After another ten minutes he was able to push it wide enough to drive the car through. He needed to shut the gate and regretted cutting the chain as he couldn't secure it properly to keep out intruders and nosy parkers but he looped it around the post anyway to give some semblance of security. Issie was crying noisily, almost choking into the tape as her tears blocked her nose and streamed down her face. He bent down and hit her hard on the back of her head.

'You little bitch,' he said, betrayal sounding thick in his voice.

The sobs turned to muffled screams as he hit her again. With the gate shut behind them he pulled Issie up roughly from the floor and pushed her into the passenger seat.

'Don't you ever do that again, d'you hear?'

She kept moaning so he shook her hard. The tears turned to hiccoughs. He held her face tight between his palms, squeezing until he could feel her teeth grate.

'We're in this together, you and me.' He pulled her close for emphasis, so close he could smell stale milk on her breath. 'What happens to me will happen to you, got that? Good luck, bad luck. What's mine is yours and you've no way out. Understand?'

She squeezed her eyes shut and turned her face as much as she could within his grip. He pressed her face harder.

'Answer me. Say, "yes Steve". Another hard shake. 'Say it.'

'Mmmh.'

'What? I couldn't hear that.'

'Mmmh!'

'You be a good girl, now.' He felt her nod between his palms and he smiled. 'Come on, let's you and me get inside.'

There was a long rutted track beyond the gate that forked sharp right under overhanging trees that screened the farm drive from the road. In five minutes the headlights picked out the side of a barn. He drove around to an irregular-shaped yard with a half-timbered, thatched house on the north side. Mariner opened his door and stepped into the night.

His legs were shaking, his back was on fire, his stomach a twisted acid mess but he had made it. Sanctuary. Slowly, careful of his footing through the deep-packed snow, he walked towards what appeared to be the front door. Bright lights flashed on without warning.

'What the f—?'

He dropped instinctively into a crouch and looked around but they were on their own.

'Bloody movement-sensitive lights,' he said to himself and ran the last few steps.

The keys were where she had said they would be and he relaxed. Not a trick, then; but as he breathed on them and waited for them to thaw so he could prise them out, he wondered. If there were lights there might be a burglar alarm. What if it was connected to the local police station? Dan had been caught like that once breaking into Mrs Beale's general store. Nothing had happened when he broke a back window. No way he could've known he'd triggered the contact alarm and hidden camera that had him on tape. It was only when he stepped into the backyard and found himself held fast by two uniformed coppers that he realised he'd been fooled.

A house like this; an absentee owner . . . Of course there would be an alarm. Little cow; that's why she hadn't bothered to try and trick him on the way here. If he opened the door even with the keys but didn't punch in the security code in time it would automatically set it off. There would be a pad to enter the code somewhere. Question was, where would it be and what was the code?

Mariner strode back to the car and yanked the passenger door open.

'Ow!' Issie yelped as he ripped the tape from her mouth.

'That's the least you'll get from me if you don't tell me how to turn off the alarm.'

'What alarm?' But her eyes slid away and he knew at once that she was lying.

'If you don't tell me I will beat you, d'you hear? And if you still don't, I'm going to dump you here, tied and taped up and leave you to freeze to death. We either turn off the alarm and go in that house together or you die here. Your Nana will find you in a month when she comes home. Won't that be a nice late Christmas present!'

Issie started to cry; it sounded pathetic so he clipped her round the ear. He wondered briefly if she would get the smarts eventually and learn how to stay silent the way he had but he pushed the thought away as soon as it surfaced.

'I'll leave you to die. Lucky bird or not; I mean it.' And he did.

Two hours later he lay in a hot bath full of muscle-relaxing bubbles sipping a glass of red wine from the well-stocked wine store he had found in a room off the kitchen. Issie was washed and retied in the master bedroom, a clean gag in place. The idea of her waiting for him, lying helpless and naked under the duvet, was incredibly arousing. He stroked himself lazily as he thought back over the previous hours.

Once he had deactivated the alarm he had prowled around, leaving her tied up on the hall floor despite her protests that she needed the toilet. He had found a bathroom upstairs with no windows that could be locked from the outside. Once he had checked it for potential weapons he had locked her in there, untied, with instructions to do whatever she needed and have a shower while he unloaded the car.

In addition to the little food he had brought at the petrol station, the kitchen had a well-stocked store cupboard and a full freezer. There was a fireplace in the lounge laid ready, no doubt to welcome the owner after Christmas. He had found matches and lit the fire, putting a guard around it from habit, and then searched upstairs until he found a dressing gown that would fit Issie.

She was still in the shower when he unlocked the door. The wet pure white slipperiness of her body, clean and shiny like a virgin's, was too erotic to resist so he'd had her on the floor, her wet back slip-sliding across the tiles. At one point he thought she might be crying and he was about to smack it out of her but he realised it was more likely water from her wet hair. Afterwards he told her to take another shower while he made them supper. This time when he came back she was wrapped up in the dressing gown, the pink frill tight at her neck. She looked so cute he had kissed the top of her head.

They ate baked beans on toast in front of the fire with no lights on, just some candles he found, so that was romantic. She asked for second helpings so he had tied her hands up with the dressing gown cord and pulled her behind him into the kitchen. Once there he secured the free end of the cord to a radiator next to a pine table, as far away from the working end of the kitchen as possible. She had sat down and laid her arm carefully on the table, easing away the fabric of the dressing gown.

He glanced over as he buttered the toast and was shocked by the sight of her wrist. It was a real mess, making him feel sick to look at it. There was no way they'd be going to A&E so he realised he would have to sort it. There was a first-aid kit in the main bathroom and memories of bandaging up his mother's various self-inflicted wounds guided him through disinfecting and cleaning Issie's injury with a level of practice he hoped impressed her.

'Thank you, Steve,' she said quietly after he had finished.

'Do you want some painkillers?'

'Yes please.'

He gave her two and a cup of hot chocolate with a shot of whisky. Then he led her up the stairs, regagging and binding her to a king-sized brass bed, before covering her with the duvet and running his bath. As he lay now in the water, savouring the wine, thinking of her waiting for him, his mind went over the day: receiving the warning letter; starting that woman's car; taking her money; ditching the Mondeo; finding this house; fending off the do-gooding driver; remembering that a place like this would have an alarm. It had been a great day!

He couldn't afford to lose her now. Looking back he realised that she had come close to being really ill, what with the cold, lack of food and septic wrist. He had probably saved her life he realised, smiling. Now she owed him everything. Her stepfather was still there: loaded, waiting for his next call. As long as he had her with him, everything was going to be all right. She really was his lucky charm.

CHAPTER THIRTY-FOUR

During the tortuous drive to Surrey HQ Fenwick rang Bernstein to let her know he had some evidence for immediate processing. She was in a meeting but Bazza answered and recognised his voice immediately.

'It's good to hear from you, sir,' His words dropped to a whisper. 'The chief constable is away at a police authority meeting all day.'

'I'll bring the item in personally, then. And Deidre; is she around?'

'No, sir. There's a coordination conference with Sussex and Hampshire but she's due back this afternoon.'

'Thank you, Bazza, very helpful.'

As he finished the call he caught Tate observing him from the rear-view mirror. He broke eye contact immediately but Fenwick said, 'Are you curious?'

'Yes, sir!'

'One of the teachers has found something of Issie's that might be evidence of the abuse we suspected on viewing her A-level artwork.'

'But that theory's been dismissed, sir, as low probability.' Tate frowned.

'Has it? Well I always have the option of including it in the wrap-up of Flash Harry.' He scratched his cheek, realising he hadn't shaved. 'Yes; that would work.'

Tate escorted him up to the detectives' room. It was almost empty and the few there did an amazing job of not seeing him.

'I can arrange to have the item sent securely to the lab if you like, sir,' Tate volunteered and Fenwick accepted gratefully.

Only later did he think to ask him what case reference he had given it.

'Both, sir; and I've made sure the receivers on Goldilocks noted the shirt before it left here.'

'Thank you, Tate; that was smart.'

The lanky red-head beamed.

'Your car will take a few hours to get here, I'm afraid, sir. I could have had it sent to Lewes but then I thought you'd need a driver.'

'You did the right thing, thanks.'

That gave him time to go out for a decent coffee during which he could think how best to introduce the meeting with Lulu Bullock in his case file and call Big Mac to chase up his report. He downed a double espresso while making sketchy notes of inquiry thinner than the napkin he was writing on. He ordered another espresso and called home on the spur of the moment.

Alice was pleased to hear from him but that was all that could be said for the call. His mother was due later and as the children had finished school for the Christmas holiday he asked Bess to make sure her room looked nice. It was a monosyllabic exchange.

After his call with Big Mac he started to feel restless. He would be missed at MCS soon. He felt disorientated but he told himself sleeping over at Lulu's was innocent – well, all right, not entirely but nothing had happened really. He had been obliged to stay at the school anyway so it wasn't as if he had wasted any time and as for their almost encounter . . . it didn't mean anything.

That wasn't what was really eating him, though. It was the morning after; that statue, the self-portrait with an unnerving resemblance to Nightingale. As he replayed each fragment of the evening he became increasingly uneasy. He drank the espresso at the counter and walked back, oblivious to the eerie quiet of the streets.

In the small waiting area by the lifts on the ground floor he recognised Jane Saxby and his unease vanished in a wave of remorse and sympathy.

'Lady Saxby, what are you—?'

'Jane, please Superintendent, I've told you before.'

She tried to smile but her face collapsed on the effort. She had aged even more since he had last seen her.

'Are you waiting for someone?'

'Yes, you.'

'I'm not involved any more; surely you're aware of that.'

'I know, but Bill's decided you're the only man for the job and I agree with him.'

Despite the tragic circumstances Fenwick was embarrassed. How had she known he was still at HQ? He glanced around; one of Saxby's private detectives must be watching the place.

'I'm sure it would be better to see Chief Constable Norman when he returns.'

'I've come to see you,' she insisted as he hesitated, 'please?'

He sighed. This was very risky. At least he had to find somewhere out of sight. He asked and was buzzed through to an empty interview room on the ground floor.

'Please sit. Would you like something to drink?'

'No thanks. You're wondering why I'm here taking up your time.'

'No, it's just that . . .'

'I know there's no news of Issie. If there were, Tony would have told us. He's a godsend, even Bill appreciates him. I realise that he must be due some leave by now but still he stays. Are all family liaison officers the same?'

'It sounds like you have someone special.' Fenwick scribbled a note to mention Tony to Bernstein. 'So . . . ?'

'Why am I here? Well it's simple; I had a dream about Issie last night. Please don't look like that; I know I sound pathetic . . .'

'I didn't mean to appear dismissive.'

'You didn't, Superintendent, dismissive I can cope with. Pity is more difficult.' Her voice caught.

'I'm sorry.'

'Don't be. Bill said I was stupid to come but when we heard you were here I just had to. This wasn't an ordinary dream. It was as if I was in the room with her, right there, really strange. Can I tell you about it?'

'Of course.' He took out his notebook and found the day's page, so far with little noted.

'Firstly, I know she is still alive. She's being held by that man Mariner. He hasn't hurt her exactly,' Jane Saxby's face twisted with the effort to remain calm, 'but he has abused her. She's tied up a lot of the time but it's somewhere warm – at least now it is. At first I think she was very cold, in fact I'm sure she was, that's the only reason I can think why I was freezing all the time. Now it's better and she's fed too.'

'Do you have any idea where she might be?'

'No, I'm sorry. In the dream all I see is her face. She's been crying, I can see that, but she looks more determined now and – what's the word? – resourceful, like she knows how to cope. That's good, isn't it?'

She looked at him hopefully. Fenwick took a moment to finish what he was writing.

'It was a dream – I can't really comment on what it might mean.' If he wasn't allowed pity then honesty would have to do.

Jane Saxby gave him the collapsing smile again that made his heart ache.

'The point is, Mr Fenwick . . . Andrew . . . the point is that I want you to think of her as very much alive. If anyone could survive this it's Issie. Just because it's been over two weeks doesn't mean she's dead. You have to believe me. When she was just a little girl she ran away into the forest – playing survival games that made us sick with worry – but she turned up the following morning, not even hungry.

'This is a girl who never left home without her emergency kit and iron rations; who went with her father into central Africa at the age of eleven and came face to face with a bull elephant that wandered into their camp. She thought it was "cool". When she came home she decided she would adopt a whole herd and started a collection at school to fund their protection. She is the most amazing child, Andrew, someone special. She will not give in to this – so please, don't give up on her.'

Fenwick kept his eyes on the notebook until he was confident of his expression and then looked Issie's mother square in the face. He was rewarded with a proper smile.

'I can see you feel it too,' she said, 'that's good.'

'She's the first thing I think of every morning and my last thoughts at night are of her.' He said the simple truth without emphasis but now it was her turn to look away.

'You must keep looking for Issie, Superintendent.'

'But I—'

'You're a resourceful man and the investigative team sits in this building. I'm begging you, please get involved. I know you'll find her. You're the only man who can.'

He heard himself explain to her that the chief constable had taken the lead; that there were seventy officers still working around the clock looking for Issie; that there was a nationwide hunt . . . but as he saw her out he knew that, somehow, he would do as she asked.

The major incident room for Goldilocks was on the same floor as the detectives' room. Fenwick strolled down and found only the receivers and a researcher there.

'I'd like to see the listing of all reports of sightings of Mariner and Issie following the offer of the reward.' His remark was met with looks of astonishment. 'There may be a link to an unresolved aspect of the Flash Harry case.'

'But there are hundreds, sir,' one of the receivers objected.

'Today would be good.'

He settled himself at a desk out of sight from the door and started to read. After the first half-dozen the reading changed to scanning but he had developed a system. There was a large-scale map of Surrey on one board and of Sussex on another, with smaller maps for the other counties dotted around. By referencing the maps he started to put the sightings in order based on a widening geographic circle with the caravan at the centre. After thirty had been placed in that way he ran out of space and removed them to another desk before starting on the next pile. He lost track of time.

'I said excuse me, sir, only I noticed what you were doing and it's just . . .' The young woman clerk standing above him had flushed an unattractive pink that made her neck blotchy.

'Go on, out with it.'

'Well, the system you're using, sir, I've done it already. I've got a computer program that can simulate the pattern of the sightings by any noted criteria.'

'Noted criteria being?'

'Time and date of receipt; location; details of the witness; notable features . . .'

'Such as?'

'As prioritised by DC Bernstein, sir,' she saw him open his mouth and rushed on, 'those include petrol stations, lock-ups, garages, anywhere close to a cashpoint, food shops; plus any of the known addresses that Issie might have gone to.'

'Can you show me?'

Once seated at her terminal the researcher relaxed into her role as helpful educator. She brought up screen after screen of data, then maps showing plotted sightings. Fenwick's knee started aching and he pulled up a chair.

'Go back to the beginning again, would you? I'd like to look at the maps based on sightings from the first two days after they left the pump station.'

When the first map came up Fenwick took time to study it carefully. Despite receiving more than a hundred calls in the first twelve hours after the reward was offered, not one sighting came from the same place. The same was true for the next twelve hours, but as the maps moved into Sunday the tenth, a cluster of four points appeared along the A272 between Midhurst and Billingshurst.

'We looked into that one especially, sir. DS Bernstein sent two officers together to interview the witnesses.'

'Can I see the statements?'

'Of course!'

With a flourish she entered a few keystrokes and three documents appeared on her screen, linked by unique reference numbers to the location reports. Fenwick read them quickly.

'Can I see the fourth one, please?'

A look of confusion filled her face.

'Ah, could you just give me a minute, sir?'

Fenwick leant back and watched the increasingly frantic taps of her fingers as she searched the electronic files. After five minutes he stood up and walked over to the map, realising that breathing down her neck probably wasn't helping. Within a minute he was back, patience not being his strong point. The receiver and second researcher had given up any pretence of working and were offering helpful advice to their colleague whose face was now crimson.

'And?'

'It's not here, sir. I have the call reference linked through to the map but the witness statement isn't logged.'

'Maybe it's because the call came more than a week later?' the other researcher suggested. 'Perhaps it's filed elsewhere?'

'That's what I thought, but I still can't find it.'

'Who was the call from?' Fenwick asked.

'It was from . . . a Ms Nicholls from Engleworth and Rodgers, a firm of estate agents. Ms Nicholls rang on the sixteenth on her return from a week's holiday – she had missed the original media coverage but recognised Mariner when she saw a reconstruction this weekend.'

Fenwick had a vague memory of Bernstein saying something about a call from an estate agent. Surely she would have looked into it?

'Bring up the record of the call would you?'

The researcher opened the document and Fenwick read it out loud.

'It says Ms Nicholls rang to report seeing a man answering Mariner's description hovering outside the estate agents the previous Saturday . . . that would be the 9th. He picked up one of their flyers from the rack outside before walking away. She didn't see the announcement about Mariner being wanted in connection with Issie until she returned.'

'What sort of flyer was it the man picked up?'

'Sir?'

'It's not a difficult question.'

'I, ah . . . if it doesn't say, then I don't know, sir.'

'Could you give me Ms Nicholls' number? Now, please.'

In the privacy of the farthest desk in the detectives' room his hand hesitated over the handset. Then he dialled.

'Yes?'

'Deidre? It's Andrew. Are you somewhere you can speak privately?'

'Hang on . . .' He heard the sound of footsteps and a door closing. 'OK, what is it?'

'Deidre, I don't know how to say this but . . .' He paused

and took a deep breath. 'I'll be blunt. I think there's a sighting of Mariner that needs looking into ASAP.'

'And this would have come to your attention how, exactly?' The weather outside had nothing on her frostiness.

'Does that matter? Look, this isn't easy. Jane Saxby came into Guildford HQ this morning.'

'Oh great, and you took the chance to see her while I was out.'

'No; she came in looking for me. I can't help that, Deidre; I tried to avoid it and persuade her to talk to someone else but she wouldn't.'

'So nothing to do with your ego, then.'

'For God's sake, just listen, will you? I'll grovel and apologise some other time but right now surely our shared priority is Issie's welfare.'

'A *shared* priority, Andrew? I thought I could trust you, but it just goes to show I should have known better.'

Fenwick bit his lip hard.

'We can deal with all the personal baggage some other time, right now I need you to listen, goddamit! I had a choice before making this call – several, actually. Norman is in charge – I could have called him; or I could have followed up on the lead personally – I nearly did to be honest; but then I thought, no, call Deidre, it's what you would expect if roles were reversed. I'm beginning to wonder whether I've made a mistake.'

'Lead; you said "lead". What lead? What did Jane Saxby say?'

'It wasn't from her.' Fenwick tensed his left hand, the pain from his burns a welcome distraction. 'It's something you said, actually – last Saturday when we met up.'

'Me?' Her disbelief made him swallow hard; some people just wouldn't be helped.

'You mentioned a call from an estate agent, Ms Nicholls.'

'So what?'

'Well, she's based in Petworth, on the junction between the

A272 and A283 where it runs south from Haslemere – that's one of the likely escape routes we plotted for Mariner, if you remember.'

Silence; he could hear Bernstein chewing.

'She came back from a week's holiday and reported seeing someone resembling Mariner before she left.'

'I remember; there's no need to lecture me with my own case, Andrew.'

Why was he bothering to be diplomatic?

'Who did you send to interview her?'

'What?' Ice down the line.

'You heard.'

'I . . . it will be on the file if you're so damned interested.'

'It's not.'

An audible gulp, then, 'It must be, but from memory it would have been Bazza, or perhaps Cobb . . . they did most of the follow-up.'

'Have you got your notebook with you; it would have been the sixteenth?'

It was a dumb question; he could already hear pages turning.

'Yup, found it; it was Cobb.'

'There's no record of an interview on file, Deidre.'

'So he's a bit late posting. For heaven's sake, Andrew, this was sighting number two hundred and sixty-three! What's this all about?'

'It was in Petworth. That makes it sighting four in one location on one day, the ninth. You took the other three seriously enough to send a team of two; and I bet neither of them was Nutty Cobb.'

'Tell me what you think.' No more bullshit.

'I'm not sure but I have a theory based on nothing more than a loose end and instinct.'

'That strong?'

Fenwick didn't laugh.

'Ms Nicholls says a man matching Mariner's description picked up a flyer in front of their agency. What if there were house details in there including properties available for immediate possession? That means some of them could have been vacant.'

'Mariner's not that smart.'

'I've looked up the address for Engleworth and Rodgers while we've been speaking. It's away from the town centre and close to a petrol station with a food outlet, the sort of place Mariner could have stopped.'

'Does it say on file what the flyer was?'

'No; someone needs to call Ms Nicholls and find out. It will look better in your casebook than mine.'

'And I'm checking because?'

Fenwick shook his head. Did the woman need spoon-feeding?

'Forget I said that. I'll call you back.'

And she was gone; just like that. He waited twenty minutes for her callback then couldn't stand it any longer and went for a walk, collar up, scarf obscuring his face in case Norman returned unexpectedly. The driving sleet forced him back inside and he climbed the stairs to the detectives' floor. On his temporary desk was a note saying that Lulu Bullock had called. He screwed it up and tossed it in the bin.

CHAPTER THIRTY-FIVE

Nightingale arrived early in Harlden. Superintendent Whitby had insisted she return despite her request to stay with Jenni. The girl remained unconscious and the doctors could give no indication of when she might wake up. In the circumstances Nightingale had no choice but to do as ordered. Her confidence in Milky, who would stay at the girl's bedside, was small consolation.

Nobody in the detective room showed the least curiosity for her visit to Guildford but were pleased to find out that Big Mac was on his way home. She was just settling at her desk when her phone rang.

'DI Nightingale.'

'Louise! Oh, thank goodness,' Nightingale felt a spurt of indigestion, 'I hoped I'd be able to reach you. Superintendent Whitby has come down with the flu . . .'

So her meeting was cancelled; she could sneak back to the hospital!

'. . . She was due to speak at a career's conference to young women this afternoon and wondered whether you would mind standing in for her rather than letting the organisers down. Her speech notes are all typed up.'

'I'm sorry, did you say a speech?'

'Yes, she'd be so grateful and I could drop the notes down to you.' Nightingale's silence prompted her to up the offer. 'And her personal driver is available, if that would help. I know it's quite an imposition.'

It was an order couched as a request. Naturally Nightingale agreed. She would need to change into her dress uniform, and to be at the venue in time meant leaving before lunchtime. It was to be held in Dorking Hall at two, which might just give her time to pop in and see Jenni on her way as long as nothing came up before she left. Unfortunately, the fates were not kind and she was running late by the time she met the driver, who waited while she changed and drove them out of Harlden in professional silence.

Nightingale opened the file Brenda had delivered and started to read. The talk was part of a panel presentation to an audience of about one hundred and twenty students. As well as Superintendent Whitby there were going to be speakers from other professions, all of them successful women with something to say about making choices and pursuing a career.

Well I'm not a good example.

The more she read Whitby's notes about her impeccable career, the more Nightingale realised she would feel a fraud presenting them. She tried to tell herself that the audience would be pre-programmed to ignore the advice anyway, and hearing it third hand would give them even more excuse. What a mess. By the time they arrived she was wondering whether it would have been better to decline.

'Oh, thank you so much.' The organiser looked like a stuffed Christmas turkey, with wattled neck and feathery red hair above a full chest swathed in a bacon-coloured shawl. 'When we heard that Alison was ill we thought we'd have a problem. One of the other speakers has already cried off because of the weather and another is sending a substitute too. Still, I'm sure what you have to say will be most edifying for the girls. I think you have time for a cup of tea before we start and that way you can meet the other panellists.'

Nightingale was led down a short flight of concrete steps to a windowless room, overly hot after the frigid walk from the car. Inside there were four other women, all considerably older than she was. The turkey gabbled rapid introductions.

'This is Professor Downey, a consultant neurologist who is researching Alzheimer's and did that marvellous paper you probably read about.' Nightingale shook hands, noticing that she wasn't introduced in return, probably because gobble-gobble had forgotten her name. 'Lady Helen Sanders, was a prominent civil servant, as you must know, and now chairman of our board of governors, among her many other responsibilities – we are really so grateful, Helen, that you could spare the time.

'Wendy – I'm sorry, dear, I can never remember your last name – Evans, yes of course. Runs a successful investment company and also set up a charity that provides used books to underprivileged children in Africa. And this lady is another kind substitute for her headmistress who was unable to come. We are lucky, as she is, of course, famous in her own right for her art. Lulu Bullock, may I introduce . . . sorry, dear, your name again?'

Nightingale's mouth fell open but fortunately Lulu was looking down to place her empty cup on the table and missed it.

'I'm Louise Nightingale,' she said and stuck out her hand not knowing what else to do.

'Hi, Louise,' the woman said calmly but when she looked up her face was a picture of – what?

The detective in Nightingale watched to see if this woman had any idea that she was meeting her own child, the daughter she thought had died twenty-nine years before. No she didn't. There was confusion, a frown, the head tilted to one side as Lulu searched her face.

'I'm sorry, did you say your name was Nightingale? It's just that I knew a Nightingale once; it was a long time ago and in a place far away, as they say.' She gave a twisted smile.

Nightingale couldn't speak. She gulped down tea.

'My father, perhaps,' she managed at last.

'Oh dear, I hope you're not losing your voice,' the Turkey remarked. 'I say, excuse me for being personal, but are you two related? The resemblance is uncanny – you could be mother and daughter. Ha, ha! Silly old me.'

They were saved from answering by a call from the doorway.

'Miss Wright says it's time to go onstage and everyone's here.' The girl who threw in the prompt was gone before anyone had a chance to argue.

Nightingale followed the line of eminent ladies onto the platform in a daze, noting the clip of their heels on the wooden stage and the different variations of smart that they had chosen to wear, all except Lulu who looked the artist she was, in a long woollen skirt, peasant blouse and loose-knit cardigan. Her clothes were loose and shambolic. She should have looked untidy but somehow the soft jades and heathers went together perfectly. In Nightingale's opinion, she was the most elegantly dressed of the lot.

There was nothing onstage to hide behind, just a semicircle of seats with a low table in front for water glasses. Nightingale put Superintendent Whitby's notes down carefully. She was to speak last. One by one the other women stood and delivered their advice eloquently, sometimes with humour that raised polite laughter. Nightingale barely heard them. She would have to stand up soon and say something.

To her chagrin she had stage fright. Until the point her foot stepped onto the platform she had been all right but now she was terrified. She had faced down rapists and murderers, ended up in hospital for her pains and come very close to dying once in the line of duty but never had she felt as frightened as she did at that moment. Her hands trembled when she sipped from her glass, spilling water onto her notes. Helen Sanders passed her a tissue and smiled reassuringly.

When Lulu Bullock stood up Nightingale paid attention for the first time. She wasn't as tall and wore her grey hair long but otherwise, the Turkey was right, they looked like the same person with just the passage of years between them.

'I shouldn't be here at all,' Lulu started, 'I'm only a stand-in; sorry for that. I'm a really bad role model for any of you; I've been in trouble with the police – in fact I'm nervous even being on the same platform as the inspector there!' Pause for laughter; Nightingale felt mortified – she was a figure of fun and she hadn't even spoken – worse, it was Lulu who mocked her.

'I was arrested I think six times before I was twenty,' that caused a ripple, 'mainly for drugs but also for breaches of the peace.'

The Turkey was sitting in the front row. Nightingale watched her face change from white to pink to bright red as Lulu continued. Despite herself, she found that she was laughing with everyone else and she could see that all the girls were paying attention for the first time, even at the end when she became serious.

'The one thing I want you all to remember is that the only reason I am here, with the benefits of a great job and the ability to pursue my art with passion, is that I have been incredibly lucky. When I was arrested my family found me excellent lawyers – we could afford it because both my parents had worked hard. I had no gratitude, of course,' a sardonic smile, 'but the reality is if I had been the daughter of someone else my life would have been a complete mess. Instead I have few regrets – other than the fact that I don't have a child of my own to be as kind and supportive to as my parents were to me.

'So if you are going to remember any advice from what I have shared with you it is to value your family, not trust to luck but be true to yourselves.'

She received a genuine round of applause that continued even as Helen Sanders stood up. Nightingale felt a bit sorry for her – how do you follow such a popular speaker? – but Helen was equally entertaining, making government work sound not just an important public service but also interesting and influential. As she concluded her talk Nightingale's butterflies threatened to overwhelm her. She stood up on automatic pilot, then realised she hadn't picked up her notes, half turned to go back and then decided on the spur of the moment to ignore them.

'Good afternoon everyone, my name is Louise Nightingale and, as you've heard already, I am a detective inspector in Sussex Constabulary, based at Harlden. Like Lulu Bullock I'm a stand-in as well, for an amazing woman who is the superintendent in charge of Harlden and my boss. She is ill today, which is why you've ended up with me.

'What am I going to say to you?' She paused and looked at the one hundred and twenty faces staring at her with a mixture of anticipation and indifference.

As she waited she noticed that, curiously, her silence was having more effect than her words. She held the moment a fraction longer. From the corner of her eye she watched the Turkey shuffle in discomfort and smiled.

'You see I have a choice and I need your help. I could either read out the superintendent's notes – and they are really good,' she gestured back at the table, 'or I could tell you how I ended up in the police, became a detective and as a result have come face to face with rapists and murderers. Which would you prefer?'

There was another silence but she didn't break it and eventually one of the girls sitting close to the front called out.

'Your story, of course.'

Nightingale nodded; the moment of theatre had given her confidence. If she treated this as a performance and not a speech she would be all right.

'Very well; I must start by saying that, like Lulu, I too have

372

been arrested.' That caused a ripple. 'It was after I ran away from home for the fourth time. The first three were uneventful, though I managed to get to France once before I was deported back.'

Beneath her the Turkey appeared about to faint.

'On the last occasion I made it as far as Glasgow. Don't ask me why I went there, it just happened to be where I ended up. I stayed for two months, sleeping rough and eventually doing drugs.'

There was a soft cry of dismay from one of the teachers that Nightingale ignored.

'I only tried crack once. I had a terrible reaction to it and nearly died. That's my first piece of advice: don't ever do drugs because they can kill you. I was in hospital for a long time but considered myself lucky. Another girl who had been with me also had a bad reaction; she almost died.'

She continued with the story she had shared with Jenni; just the plain facts, no embellishment.

'There was a female police constable that kept coming to see me. I didn't have any visitors and I was miserable and lonely. She didn't want anything and she certainly wasn't stupid enough to try and give me advice. I ended up looking forward to her visits and – to cut a long story short – she persuaded me to go home. She was really great. I don't know what she said to my father in private but he started to treat me differently – like a grown-up – from that point on.'

Nightingale went on to describe how she had scraped into her father's old university thanks to his contacts but decided while she was there that the only thing she wanted to do was police work, much against her parents' wishes.

'This is my second piece of advice; if you have a vocation, no matter how unpopular it might be, go for it – but don't assume it will be easy. I had to work really hard to gain the degree I needed to be accepted onto the police graduate entry scheme, plus there was the physical fitness side of it to master as well. Before uni I wasn't in good shape but knowing I needed to be fit to pass the entrance tests was a real incentive.'

She kept the description of her career short, not mentioning that she had been promoted quickly or that she had received a commendation for bravery before she was twenty-five, but she did mention how tough it was to progress in a male-dominated world.

'That's my third and last piece of advice; unfortunately there is still some passive discrimination out there – not just against us women but against all minorities – and not only in the police. Be ready for it; don't accept it and be confident enough that you will be good enough to succeed despite it. There are some tremendous women in the force; my boss, Superintendent Whitby, is one of them, a real inspiration.' As she said it, to her surprise, Nightingale realised it was true.

After she sat down and the applause finished, Helen Sanders said there was time for questions. At first there was silence but then one of the teachers asked Helen about her own role models and mentoring, a nice safe topic that put the afternoon's agenda back on track. This was followed by a question to Lulu about how difficult it was to be successful as an artist. After this there was a flurry of hands in the air with sensible questions, until at last there was one for Nightingale from the back of the hall.

'Could you tell us why you ran away from home, please?'

Helen whispered to her.

'That's a bit personal; you don't have to answer if you don't want to.'

'No, it's all right.' She raised her voice. 'I left home because I didn't get on with my parents, simple as that.'

'But four times, you said you ran away four times!'

'Yes, well I *really* didn't get on with them,' she laughed, turning the whole thing into a joke but she could feel Lulu's eyes on her and her cheeks coloured.

The afternoon drew to a close with the usual vote of thanks and finally Nightingale could escape. She didn't know whether she wanted to talk to Lulu or not. Part of her was consumed with the need to reveal everything but something held her back. It was the same caution that had prevented her from trying to find Lulu after discovering that she was her father's love child and cuckoo in his matrimonial nest.

Telling Lulu would be admitting the truth, that her past life was a lie. Was she ready to do that and deal with the consequences? They were walking back to the little box room where they had left their coats. The other women were chatting easily, exchanging compliments about each other's talks.

'I think you two were the stars,' Helen said generously, smiling at Lulu and Nightingale. 'Like mother like daughter, eh?' The look on their faces must have alerted her to a faux pas. 'Sorry, I thought I heard earlier someone say that you were related and, well, looking at you both I assumed . . . I didn't mean to cause offence.'

'None taken,' Lulu recovered first.

They lingered as the other women gathered their belongings and left. Finally they were on their own.

'It is strange,' Lulu remarked, 'we do look similar, though you have your father's eyes.'

'Yes I do.' If she was meant to be surprised by the comment, of course she was not. 'You know that he – that they are both, ah – that there was a car accident?'

'I read about that; I was truly sorry for you and your brother. It must have been terrible.'

'Yes it was; in fact it contributed to me taking leave of absence from work and I went to stay at Mill Farm. While I was there I saw the statue you did for my aunt's grave. It's beautiful; so is the font.'

'So you knew about me?' Lulu looked concerned.

'Not until I went to the farm but there were letters you'd sent my father and a photograph that my aunt had kept.' It was now or never, if she didn't tell her it would always lie between them. 'Look, would you like a drink? I have a police driver because I'm standing in for my boss and I could give you a lift back?'

'I have my car but why don't you follow me and we can have a drink at my place?'

That's what they did. For Nightingale it was a long drive.

At St Anne's she followed Lulu up the stairs to the top of the old house while her driver went to beg a cup of tea somewhere. Nightingale sat on the sofa where Fenwick had rested the night before. Lulu lit the fire and offered coffee.

'Actually, do you have anything stronger? I think we're going to need it.'

Lulu frowned.

'It wasn't that bad! I thought we both did quite well.'

'Please?'

'I can add a splash of brandy if you like but I'm out of wine; I had an unexpected visitor last night and haven't been able to go replenish my little rack.' An unconscious smile played across her face.

'That's fine, thank you.'

Lulu was relaxed in her own home. Nightingale felt slightly sick. She drank half the coffee quickly and looked so longingly at the brandy bottle that Lulu topped it up.

'I suppose it's not every day that you meet your father's mistress,' Lulu said with a sad smile. 'You are so like him in your ways that I'm finding the familiarity a bit difficult to deal with, if I'm honest.'

Nightingale couldn't look at her. She put down her mug and started talking at the fire.

'In the year after my parents were married, in the August, you gave birth to a baby girl while staying with a family friend,

Angela, who acted as midwife. She told you your baby died.'

She glanced up to see Lulu staring at her aghast and looked away quickly.

'What the . . . how do you know that? Angela, of course; she told you?'

'I met her when I was staying at Mill Farm; she decided that I needed care and attention. When I discovered the photos and letters my aunt had kept I confronted Angela with them and she told me.'

'Damn the woman! She promised me she would never tell a soul. So now as a policewoman you're going to tell me I broke the law by burying my baby on the hillside.' Lulu's anger at Angela's betrayal spilt into her reaction to Nightingale. 'Well it's none of your business. That baby was buried with love' – she was crying but seemed unaware of it – 'and if anyone wants to prosecute me now, let them!'

'I know she was laid to rest with love; I found the grave by the spring and the carving you put over her. I cleaned it up and ever since I go there once a year, on the anniversary of her death, with flowers. She was my half-sister after all.'

Lulu stared at her with brimming eyes, shocked but still angry. She poured them both more brandy and swallowed hers in one gulp.

'So you know.' Her voice was hoarse. 'I'm sorry, that must have come as a terrible shock. Your father knew that I was carrying his child but I had no expectations that he would help me look after her; and when the baby died . . . well that resolved the problem.'

'Your baby didn't die,' Nightingale whispered.

'Oh she did, I held her and she was quite cold. She did die.' Lulu could barely speak.

'A baby died, yes, but she wasn't yours. My father's wife had twins the day before you were delivered of your child . . .'

'I know; I read the announcement that Angela kindly sent to me. So sweet of her.'

'Wait, let me finish.' Nightingale took a deep breath. 'It was a boy and a girl. The little girl died shortly before you gave birth; a cot death probably. Mary, her mother, was asleep and completely unaware and my father didn't know what to do. He carried the baby through the night to Angela – perhaps hoping that he was mistaken and that the baby was alive after all, but sadly she wasn't.

Lulu put a hand to her mouth as she shook her head in denial.

'Please listen. Angela persuaded my father that it would be best for everybody if he took your daughter as his own and left his dead child behind. It was that baby she carried into the bedroom where you lay waiting, while your daughter was taken back to the farm and slipped into the empty cot. Your baby never died. It was Mary's daughter you buried, not your own.'

Lulu was staring at her with a look of incomprehension.

'No, that can't be right. I held my baby; she was white and cold. There was blood on the blanket she was wrapped in, my blood. She was dead. I saw her.'

'You saw Mary's child, wrapped in the bloody delivery sheet.'

'No, that can't be! That means Angela lied to me. Why would she do that? Why put me through so much pain? She never liked me, I know, and only looked after me because she was besotted with your father, but to deceive me like that . . . ? It's inhuman.'

'She did, Lulu. You're right, she was obsessed with my father and would have done anything for him, but she was also eaten up with jealousy towards you – so much so that I think she hated you. This was her chance to please him, hurt you and injure Mary.'

'Injure Mary; how?'

'Don't you think my mother realised at some point when that little girl was growing up that it wasn't her child – as she grew older and became the splitting image of you, a constant reminder of her husband's mistress? Oh, believe me; she was injured that night, with a deep invisible wound that festered.'

Lulu rubbed her forehead.

'I can't think straight. This is crazy; it makes no sense. I'd have known if my baby were alive . . . what sort of mother do you think I was? If my daughter had been alive I would have gone anywhere to find her!'

'You can't blame yourself for the conspiracy. You thought her dead so you didn't look for her . . .' Nightingale paused and smiled for the first time. 'But she has found you.'

CHAPTER THIRTY-SIX

The sound of a toilet flushing woke her. She tried to stretch to ease the ache in her shoulders but the restraints were too tight. Issie struggled to remember where she was. The room was familiar but somehow from the wrong perspective; and her thinking was fuzzy. It looked like Nana's bedroom, but how? Slowly her mind cleared. The long journey the previous day; her attempt to alert a passing motorist with the horn while Steve shovelled; Steve's attack on her later . . . her mind sheered away from recollection but thoughts ambushed her anyway.

She was still captive, in a comfortable bed, with her wrist bandaged and she had been fed but she was a prisoner. And she needed the bathroom.

'Hello?'

Her voice sounded weak and scratchy and she couldn't reach the water glass by the bed.

'Hello!' Louder, more insistent. 'I need to go to the bathroom.'

There was a noise of somebody knocking over a chair and then footsteps in the hall. As always, his imminent presence made her shudder but she forced herself to look calm. The door banged open and she saw him silhouetted against the light.

'Steve, please can I go to the toilet?'

He stumbled towards the bed and half fell onto it, lying there with no apparent intention of moving. The smell of alcohol was overpowering. He had discovered the wine store immediately and she suspected he would sniff out the spirit cupboard in due course. Her Nana liked a tipple so there would be plenty for him to enjoy. With luck he'd be half-cut or asleep most of the time they were here. Disgusting maybe but it was preferable to Steve Mariner sober because she had learnt that when under the influence he rarely consummated the sex he started. Instead he would fall into a heavy sleep, often lying across her on the chill kitchen floor of their previous hideout so that her legs slowly went numb.

She had never told him he passed out. It was far better that he thought they had had another night of 'amazing love' as he called it. He was living in a dream where he was Casanova and she his kept mistress. Issie encouraged the fantasy, aware that reality would overwhelm him eventually and then her life would become even more precarious.

It was now sixteen days since he had abducted her, over two weeks since he had killed his brother. Steve had adjusted to this bizarre reality by denying it and she had gone along. After the first week he had grown bored with sex, sometimes preferring to masturbate in front of her as he fantasised about what they would do next.

When this happened the first time, she had been disgusted and had bitten the sleeping bag as tears of shame soaked her cheeks. Then, when he had fallen asleep, she realised that she had been spared sex with him. Subsequently, when he started to feel himself as he stared at her or read from a small supply of pornography she encouraged him so that by the time he reached her it was over almost as soon as he touched her. Slowly as the days passed his attentions had reduced.

Her grandmother had a satellite dish so Steve would have all the TV he desired. The place was centrally heated, with a microwave and luxury bathrooms. She would have a chance to regain her strength. Her malnourished fever was better already after a decent meal and good night's sleep. Lying next to him last night under clean sheets with her head on a soft pillow, Issie had prayed and said a silent thank you for being alive.

Steve untied her and pushed her gently towards the shower, an internal room with no windows where she was allowed to use the toilet unsupervised. After she'd been to the loo, Issie did her exercises: sit-ups, push-ups, jumps – until her muscles burned. She took a long time showering and washing her hair, noticing that she was skin and bone but that the cut on her wrist was no longer as inflamed. She had to grow strong again, like her old self, although that was ridiculous of course. Her old self had vanished the second she had stepped into Steve Mariner's Mondeo. Nevertheless, it was time to start thinking again. She needed a plan.

The previous day, when he hit her after the incident with the horn, she had realised that he was only just in control. She had almost choked on her own blood and might have died. He was unstable and prone to losing his temper at any time. At some point the food in the freezer would run out. Worse, so would the alcohol and Steve Mariner sober was a more dangerous prospect than when under the influence.

He might treat her as he would a valuable, semi-domesticated animal but that was deceptive. Issie knew never to complain and was always grateful, that way Steve stayed calm. Otherwise he was as stable as an unexploded bomb. Now that she was on familiar territory she decided she needed to find a weapon to use against him if he finally snapped.

'Oi, have you died in there or something?'

'No, Steve, just enjoying a long shower. Sorry, I'll be right out.'

She opened the door, her short hair wet and spiky, her skin flushed, her grin so impish her cheeks ached from the strain.

'Shall I do lunch?'

Steve regarded her cautiously and then shook his head.

'Do you think I'm daft? Let you loose near all those knives. Uh-huh.'

'I just thought you might like a change – I can cook.'

'My cooking not good enough for you?' He scowled.

'No, nothing like that, it's just that it doesn't seem right to let a man like you do all that domestic stuff and I'd like to help.'

He scratched his head with the hand that wasn't holding a can of lager.

'What're you up to, young lady?' He grinned and aimed a kiss at her lips.

Issie forced herself not to turn away and met his mouth with her own, kissing back; accepting but not enticing. She didn't want to appear so willing that he would become excited, which seemed to happen more when she was subservient.

'I'm not up to anything. It's just that I'm feeling better thanks to all your care and it's only right I play my part.'

'I know what part I'd like you to play right now,' he reached out and squeezed her left buttock hard. Issie forced a bigger smile.

'Aren't you hungry? Better to eat first. Everything will last longer that way.'

'You saying I don't last long enough?'

His fingers tightened on her flesh and it was all she could do not to cry out in pain.

'Of course not. I just *want* you to last a long time that's all. Come on, Steve; let's have a plate of bacon and eggs, or a pizza, if you like.'

At the mention of pizza Steve turned away, a look of real pain on his face.

'Not pizza; not yet.'

'OK, sure.' His changes of mood worried her but he hadn't tied her up again – the first time ever that she had been left unrestrained. 'I know where the eggs are and if you open the bacon packet I won't need to touch a knife.'

Issie walked confidently towards the stairs, her back tensed for his hand on her shoulder. It didn't happen.

She took the eggs, bacon and tomatoes out of the fridge and asked him to pass her the frying pan and cut some bread for toast. He did as he was told but watched her like a hawk.

'Can we eat it together here in the kitchen?'

He said nothing so she carried on, little Miss Domesticity. She found two large red wine goblets and placed them on the table.

'Look at these!' she said triumphantly, 'we need a decent wine to do them justice. What have you got there, Steve?'

He showed her two bottles that he had taken from the rack.

'The Médoc, I think.' She apologised silently to her nana. 'The corkscrew's—'

'I know where the sodding corkscrew is.'

'Of course.'

As he turned his back to find it Issie managed to slip a paring knife up her sleeve.

'Put it back,' he said without turning around. 'The knife, put it back. Now.'

Steve swung at her without warning, his fist hitting her shoulder and almost knocking her to the ground.

'Ungrateful bitch! Do you think I'm stupid or something?'

He loomed over her, the red wine bottle gripped in his hand like a club. She remembered what had happened to his brother and cowered against the fridge, her arms raised protectively.

'Sorry, Steve. I was tempted to be independent, to cut up the tomatoes myself. It was a stupid thing to do, I know that.'

'Going to try and run away from me were you?' His fist came down onto her arms but he had put the bottle down somewhere so only his knuckles connected. Issie bit back a cry of pain and pleaded.

'No, Steve! Please don't. I was only trying to help; I wouldn't do anything, honestly.'

'Anything like sticking me with that poxy blade, you mean?' He hit her again.

Issie rolled away and stumbled out of the kitchen in a half

crouch. She made it as far as the shower room and was trying to bolt the door as he slammed it open.

'Don't try to hide in here.'

He pulled her up by an arm, wrenching her shoulder, and aimed a kick at her backside. The tip of his boot caught her coccyx and she moaned as the pain spread up her spine.

'Enough, Steve, please, you've done enough.' She tried to keep her tone reasonable, to reach through his rage.

He shoved her back against the landing wall and let go of her arm.

'Don't you ever do that again or I'll kill you; got it?' His face was inches from hers. She could smell his breath, thick with lager and onion crisps.

'I won't, Steve.' Issie could feel tears of capitulation in her eyes and blinked. 'I'm sorry.'

'Why should I believe you? You stuck up little piece of shit? Every time I think I can trust you off you go, trying it on. You pretend to like me but behind it all you're just as bad as the rest of them: looking down on me, hating me, laughing at me behind my back because you think you're so much better. Well, you're not, you hear!'

He leant back and slapped her face, forcing the brimming tears on to her cheeks.

'And don't you fucking cry at me.'

Issie tried to swallow a sob but couldn't. Now that the tears had started she couldn't control them. They drove Steve wild.

'Shut up! I can't stand poxy crying; shut it!'

But she couldn't. The dam had burst. The effect of days of fear, loneliness and the pain of abuse had accumulated inside her, kept under control by her determination not to give up hope. Mariner kicked her as she crumpled to the floor. Before Issie blacked out she finally realised that maybe she was going to die.

CHAPTER THIRTY-SEVEN

Fenwick drove away from Guildford slowly, feeling the pull of the case at his back. After two miles he had to stop. He stopped in a lay-by and, on impulse, pulled on his boots to go for a walk through woodland along a footpath deep with snow. His body virtually ached with yearning to turn around, confront Norman and demand to be allowed back on Operation Goldilocks. No matter how hard he tried to divert his thinking, his mind was crowded with action plans for follow-up on the estate agent lead that he had left with Bernstein.

As he walked, he checked his phone every few minutes in the hope that she had called but it remained stubbornly inert. It would take at least a day for the DNA analysis of Issie's T-shirt to be completed, even supposing it was hers. He blessed Tate for linking the evidence to Flash Harry, at least that way he would be informed immediately the results arrived. It was growing dark. Time to acknowledge there wasn't going to be a miracle summons for him to return to Guildford. With a sigh he returned to his car and took the road to Harlden.

When he arrived at his house he was shocked to see a foot of snow in the drive, broken only by a narrow beaten path to the porch. He parked carefully, making sure not to block Alice's Fiat but it looked as if it hadn't been driven for days, judging by the snow that had accumulated around and on top of it.

It was only a short walk to the front door but by the time he reached it his fingers were numb. He fumbled with the key and let himself in. Warmth, light, the smells of baking and Bess's strawberry bubble bath engulfed him. Ivy had been woven inexpertly along the length of the banisters; the holly he usually cut from the ever-fruitful tree in the garden already bedecked the top of picture frames and the hall mirror. He was suddenly engulfed with gratitude that they were all here, alive, waiting for him. Inexplicably he felt like crying.

'Bess you've been in there an hour and Chris needs his bath. What are you doing?'

His mother's words carried down the stairs. He could hear the television in the living room; Chris must be enjoying a delayed bedtime as his sister monopolised the bathroom. Fenwick opened the door soundlessly and gazed at his son as he lay on the rug in front of the fire, engrossed in a nature documentary about polar bears rather than his usual cartoons. He sneaked up behind him and bent down swiftly to gather him about the waist.

'Gotcha!'

'Daddy! Daddy! You're home.' Chris twisted in his grasp and threw his arms about his neck, hugging him so that he could barely breathe.'

'You're choking me!'

Chris didn't care. He was overjoyed to see him.

'Are you here for tonight?'

Fenwick managed to smile back.

'All night and for breakfast tomorrow morning.'

'Yay! That means you can help with the Christmas tree. It *still* isn't decorated because Alice refuses to put the lights on until you've checked they won't burn us to death in our beds.'

'I'm sure she's quite capable of looking at them herself.'

'Oh no I'm not, Andrew. They need a man's touch, and before you say it, Christopher, you are not old enough yet, my boy.'

'I'll look at them before dinner. Just let me get changed first.'

Chris hung on his father's arm as he climbed the stairs. Fenwick's mother was waiting at the top, looking older than he remembered and with a spectacular black eye.

'I know, I look terrible but it's all show and doesn't hurt.' He bent down so that she could peck his cheek in her customary greeting. 'But you're nay picture yourself. And *what* have you done to that hand?'

Fenwick was overcome with self-consciousness. He hadn't looked at himself for days, other than shaving in the tiny hotel mirror. His left hand slipped behind his back out of sight.

'Just a small accident; my way of getting out of the Christmas washing-up!' His mother frowned and didn't return his smile. 'I'll be down in a minute. Chris, go and unwind the lights would you please, carefully? Oh, hello Bess.'

His daughter was in her dressing gown, her hair damp and half its normal volume.

'Oh, it's you; hi.'

She walked past him and into her room, closing the door. Fenwick raised his eyebrows.

'At least she spoke to you,' her brother remarked, 'you're lucky. Most of us have to make do with a grunt.'

'Chris.' The warning tone in his mother's voice brought back memories and Fenwick put a finger to his lips behind her back to encourage Chris to silence. 'And I saw that.'

He changed into thick dark-brown chinos, a brushed-cotton heather shirt and a cream jumper that Monique, his late wife, had bought him. Dressing proved somewhat difficult but there was no way he was going to ask for help. Downstairs he noted that the table had been reset for three, the children already having been given their supper, and there was a mug of strong tea waiting for him. His eyes drifted to the wine rack.

'I'll open a bottle with the meal,' his mother said, placing three wine glasses on the kitchen table, which surprised him as she rarely drank.

He could hear Chris running his bath and singing a pirate song.

'He had a solo in the school pantomime,' Alice said, beaming proudly.

'Aye, a pity you couldn't make it, Andrew,' his mother finished for her.

Fenwick retreated to the sitting room where the Christmas tree stood naked in the bay window. The lights worked perfectly first time and he wound them around the tree with practised care, leaving a cluster at the top to illuminate the angel. He sensed a change in the air behind him and turned to see Bess sitting on the sofa opposite the fire.

'Could you put on a Christmas CD, love, please?'

'Which one?'

'Your favourite, of course.'

Ever since she was a little girl, Bess had been enchanted by a Kings College choir's arrangement of carols. With the opening verse of 'In the Bleak Midwinter' issuing from the speakers he lifted the lid off the first box of tree decorations.

'Want to help me?'

Bess started to place the ornaments on the coffee table, laying them carefully in order: angels together, then the soft toys, baubles, stars, some unfortunate glittery doves that should have been thrown away but were special because Monique had bought them for her when she was three years old. Then very carefully, as if it were the most precious of icons, the angel she had made with her mother the year before she became ill. One of the wings hung at an angle.

'Oh!' Bess dropped her head into her hands and burst into tears.

'There, there, love, we can fix that easily. Don't worry.'

Fenwick wrapped his arms around his daughter's shoulders but she continued to sob disconsolately.

'Ssh, it's OK.'

'But it's not OK. Everything's going wrong; nothing stays the same. It's all horrible.'

Fenwick rocked her to and fro, as he used to when she was little, at a loss to know what was making her so sad or what to do to make her pain go away.

His mother walked into the room, sat down in the armchair closest to the fire and took out her knitting.

'This is a lovely CD,' she said, as if her granddaughter wasn't distraught on the sofa. 'We should play this again on Christmas Day. Fifteen minutes to dinner, Andrew. Will you be doing any more of the tree before we eat?'

She looked at him calmly over the top of Bess's shaking shoulders and gave her small, tight smile. Fenwick gestured to Bess with his chin as if to say *what do I do?* She mouthed, 'Let it be.' He didn't know what that meant but after a moment, the crying eased and he heard Bess sigh.

'So, Bess, bring the angel through and I'll find the glue we need to fix her.'

Amazingly, the pragmatic suggestion was rewarded with a nod. As he had expected, the decoration was easily mended. Bess smiled as the injured wing was arranged into place.

'I wonder whether we should repaint her smile; what do you think?'

'No! Mummy did the smile. You'd never get it the way she did.'

'You're probably right. Come on, you can help me put her on the tree.'

'And me too, Daddy!'

Chris had finished his bath in record time, evidenced by the soap suds still in his hair.

'You can do the doves and the polar bear, Chris. Remember the bear protects the angel so you have to put him in the right place.'

During supper, which fortunately was shepherd's pie and peas so he could eat with just a fork, the children were allowed to stay up and watch the end of a Disney film. School had finished so there was no need to worry about one night's short sleep. Afterwards he went to finish decorating the tree. Chris was asleep on the sofa before long and Bess was not the best helper, dropping one bauble so that it shattered, but it wasn't a special one so no one really minded.

Fenwick carried Chris upstairs and laid him in bed, kissing the top of his head before going to Bess's bedroom to tuck her in. There was a new poster on the back of the door. The lead singer's thrusting pelvis made him shudder.

'Story?' she asked in a voice so small she could have been five again.

'It's gone ten-thirty, love. You're almost asleep.'

'Story,' she repeated and handed him a battered copy of *The Wind in the Willows*. Sight of the familiar cover made him wince. Before Toad could even get into his car Bess was fast asleep. Fenwick decided he would follow her example, explaining to Alice and his mother that he was almost asleep on his feet. As he went to switch off his mobile phone he noticed a missed call from Bob Cooper but it was too late to ring back tonight. There was no message.

He stood under the shower until his skin glowed, his injured hand resting on the wall outside the stream of water in a vain attempt to keep the dressing dry. Then he wrapped himself in his dressing gown as an easier option than trying to button his pyjamas. Outside, a rising wind buffeted the window finding a gap in the frame that puffed out the curtains. Fenwick felt exhausted but far from sleep. Details of the hunt for Issie flickered into his mind and vanished before he could focus on them, and all the time, running beneath the surface, was the sostenuto of his night at Lulu's and, for some reason, his last conversation with Nightingale.

Fenwick didn't want to think about it. He was ashamed of his behaviour, embarrassed every time he recalled it. He groaned in the empty room and bit his lip, attempting to block out an overwhelming sense of guilt. As a distant church clock struck eleven he stared at the darkness of the ceiling and reached out his left hand to the cold empty sheet by his side.

Cooper opened the front door and tiptoed into the darkened hall. Without turning on the light he eased off his shoes; he wasn't about to add ruining the carpet to his other crimes. He had promised to be home by the time Fred and Marjorie arrived and he had failed. Even worse, he hadn't turned up for dinner. He was starving and hoped Dot had left something he could microwave.

He crept along the hall and into the kitchen, surprised as he opened the door that the light was still on. Dot was sitting at the table in her thick winter dressing gown reading.

'Oh, er . . . hello, love.' Cooper made a show of looking for his slippers, not sure what sort of greeting he was about to receive.

'Hello, Bob, are you hungry?'

'Starving; is there anything left, look I'm sorry it's so late . . .'

'Hush up; wash your hands and get yourself some bread and spread. It's steak and ale pie with swede and carrot mash; and there's a glass of red wine left from the bottle Fred brought, if you fancy one.'

Cooper couldn't believe it and cut some bread as directed. He was about to add butter but thought that would test Dot's patience and used the good-for-him spread instead.

The food appeared quickly and he ate while his wife watched in silence. When he had finished she poured him the last of the wine.

'Tell me about the investigation, Bob, and why you're so obsessed with it.'

'I wouldn't say I was obsessed, it's just . . .'

'Stimulating, exciting?'

'Well yes, I suppose it is.'

'That's what I thought. You've had more spark in you the last two weeks than in the previous six months. Oh, I know you like the free time but you can't deny sometimes you find retirement a bore.'

She was smiling as she said it and Bob decided he had to be honest. Dot listened carefully as he spoke and then made them both a cup of tea.

'And what's so compelling about this investigation? You can share with me now that you're no longer in the force, can't you?'

'I suppose so. Well, for a start I have to help the Saxbys find their daughter alive or dead – the uncertainty is killing Jane, her mum. She's skin and bone and she doesn't sleep. It's terrible to see her shrink and age. And Bill, Lord Saxby, is almost as bad. I have to help them, Dot. I helped to identify Mariner and then I found someone at the Bull and Drum who led Andrew to the woman who knew about the place they'd been hiding away. They missed them by hours. If I'd only found that bloke earlier, Issie would be home safe and sound by now.'

Dot reached out and held his hand.

'That's not your fault, love. You can't blame yourself.'

Cooper looked away, blinking.

'But what if it had been our Maggie at that age? How would we have coped? She's made us grandparents – so much love . . .' His voice caught. 'It's not *right*, Dot. It's bloody well not right that their daughter's been snatched away like this.'

Dot stood up and stepped around the table to cuddle his head against her comfortable bosom.

'I know, Bob, I know,' she said, rocking him gently.

'Here.'

She passed him a piece of kitchen roll and he blew his nose noisily.

'Thank you,' he sighed. 'This isn't doing anyone any good is it? I'm ashamed of myself. I was never like this when I was in the force.'

Dot was perhaps too diplomatic to answer and went to fill the kettle.

'I think we'll have camomile tonight.'

Bob came up behind her and hugged her around the middle.

'I love you,' he said into her hair.

'I know, and I love you too. Now go and have a shower. I'll bring up the tea.'

CHAPTER THIRTY-EIGHT

The flat wasn't as warm as she expected when she walked in. She had forgotten to change the central heating timer before leaving. The hall thermostat read eighteen degrees. There was a pathetic meowing from the top of the cupboard housing the boiler.

'Hello, Cat; what are you complaining about?'

The black moggy jumped down and wrapped himself around her calves. Nightingale scratched the top of his head between the ears but didn't attempt to pick him up. Blackie was independent, untrusting and had very sharp claws. She gave him some fresh milk and filled his bowl with dried food. He glared at her for failing to remember that salmon was his favourite, which almost made her laugh as she filled the kettle. She would have hated a grateful pet.

Sorting out his supper occupied her mind, befuddled with the brandy and a swirling mess of emotions. One moment she was euphoric that she had finally met her real mother. The next she was vulnerable and terrified for no reason. No sooner had she got to grips with her paranoia than she plunged into despondency. Bizarrely there was a sense of anticlimax underneath it all, which she didn't understand. It made her feel guilty and that made everything else so much worse.

No sooner had the cat finished eating than he demanded to be let out. It was late, time for him to prowl his territory and for her to go to bed. She made a mug of herbal tea and checked that everywhere was locked up tight, checking obsessively as if fearing an invader. If she was lucky she would be able to find a few hours' sleep.

An hour later she was still lying awake listening to the wind moan around the chimney. Another slate had worked loose but there was nothing she could do about it. Slipping on her dressing gown she made another cup of tea, wincing as she caught sight of the time. Tomorrow was a big day; she was determined to take advantage of Whitby's absence to visit Jenni and she wanted to read the final report on Flash Harry from cover to cover. She shut her eyes briefly and her thoughts turned to Fenwick. This was no good. She needed to sleep. Blackie was scratching at the door so she let him in. He followed her to the bedroom and plonked his weight down on her feet. She fell asleep almost immediately.

At five o'clock she jerked awake, sweat from a nightmare chill on her chest despite the cool of the bedroom. Her iPod earphones were still in but the stream of calming Gregorian chants that had lulled her had finished long ago. There was a persistent pain behind her eyes and her mouth was dry. She drank what was left in her water glass and squeezed her eyes shut, willing herself back to sleep, but her mind immediately struggled to recall her dream.

Flash Harry had been telling her the identity of his victims. There were hundreds of them, he'd said, two a week stretching back years. '*Should've caught me sooner*,' he'd gloated and she had picked up a knife . . .

How many victims had there been? Were there really hundreds of them? Had Fenwick and Big Mac done everything to find them and would they work assiduously to notify them of Dan Mariner's death? Possibly not, given Fenwick's obsession with the search for Issie. What about the ones who may never have come forward? They would be living with psychological damage that might be healed if they knew the perpetrator of the violence against them had been brought to account. It had been rough justice, nothing to do with the force of law but still . . .

Nightingale sat up and winced. It was important that they were told that their attacker had been dealt with. She needed to think through a plan of how to contact the known victims and a way of finding any they were as yet unaware of. There was no chance she would sleep again. Nightingale switched on the bedside light and swung her feet onto the floor, finding her slippers in an automatic movement. Tea; that would be good.

As she waited for the kettle to boil, Nightingale wondered how to tackle the conflicting tasks ahead of her. The easiest thing to do would be to ask Big Mac for help. No point trying to speak to Fenwick . . . A strand of conversation with Lulu came back to her. As they had talked she had found herself mentioning her unrequited love for an older man. Lulu had given her firm advice. Should she follow it?

Nightingale shuddered. The day ahead was going to be complicated enough! She needed to concentrate. First things first, she needed to track down Big Mac. He should be in Harlden today; they could work together on Flash Harry before she went to Guildford to see Jenni. They would need to go through the Home Office database, HOLMES, and make up a list of victims. She poured boiling water onto the detox tea bag she had persuaded herself tasted all right then threw it away and made herself an espresso. She was expecting a demanding day.

Mac was already in the detectives' room when she arrived before eight o'clock.

'Morning, early bird,' he said cheerfully.

'Good morning, Detective,' she replied with mock severity. 'How's the report coming along?'

'With his nibs for review. He said he'd be back to me by lunchtime.'

'So you're free this morning!'

Big Mac looked cautious.

'What are you plotting, ma'am?' He touched his forehead in mock subservience.

She told him of her worry for Flash Harry's victims, known and anonymous. He looked guilty.

'I should have thought of that. There's a list obviously in the report but I haven't initiated contact. I assumed MCS would organise that. I'll get onto them.'

'Hang on; before you do, let's identify those on our patch so that we can cover them ourselves. And we should speak to the PO at Lewes. Publicity on Dan Mariner may bring others into the open.'

'Leave it with me.' Big Mac was already scanning his computer while reaching for the phone with his other hand.

'So you won't need my help?'

'No,' he looked up and winked at her, 'not for a couple of hours, anyway; enough time for you to get to the Royal and back.'

'Mind-reader.'

He shrugged modestly, making her laugh.

Nightingale decided to stop by one of the hospital cafés to pick up something for Constable Rogers before seeing Jenni. She stepped out of the lift bearing a takeaway tea and slice of cake when she saw him walking fast down the corridor towards her. As soon as he saw her his face lifted into a look of relief.

'That man there,' he whispered, pointing towards someone on the far side of a pillar with his back to them talking into a mobile phone despite the notices. 'I saw him hovering outside Jenni's room yesterday but when he saw me he wandered off. This morning he came back, even though it's not visiting time. I was in the toilet next to Jenni's room and he was about to go in when he saw me. I didn't know whether to follow him or stay with her, but now you're here . . .'

'Well done. Go back and call this in while I keep an eye on him. Your uniform will scare him off.'

Nightingale walked to one side of the pillar to gain a better look at the man. He was shorter than she was, about five ten but thickset, with long, curly brown hair, a flash leather jacket and heavy boots. His face was obscured and he hadn't noticed her with Rogers. When a registrar passed the man stopped her, presumably to ask about Jenni, but he had his back turned and was talking so quietly that Nightingale couldn't hear. The registrar's reply though carried clearly.

'. . . no telling, I'm afraid. She's being hydrated and fed intravenously so there's no immediate need for concern, though we are becoming a little worried about how long she's remaining unconscious.'

'Will she recover fully?'

'The scans we took of her brain suggest that she will but we'll have to wait to be sure. But do tell her mum when you see her that we're optimistic. By the way, you should really talk to the police while you're here. They're keen to trace her relatives. What was your name again?'

'Fred; I'm a cousin but I see her mum all the time.'

'Right, a cousin you say?' The registrar sounded confused. 'I thought you told the nurse yesterday you were her brother and on the file she noted your name as Stanley.' The registrar's pager buzzed and she looked at it with a frown. 'Look, I have to deal with this but I want you to wait here while a nurse goes and finds the officer waiting with Jenni. We need to sort this out.'

He agreed but as soon as the registrar was out of sight, the man calling himself Fred walked quickly to the lift. Nightingale followed, picking up a magazine from a coffee table as she passed. As they waited together for the lift to arrive, she turned to a page at random and learnt the best way to ice a Christmas cake. She continued to study it while descending to the ground floor.

Her plan was to follow the man to his car rather than accost him straight away. That way she would discover the index number, as a contingency against him providing a false name and address. Unfortunately, he turned away from the car park and headed for the main entrance so she was obliged to follow. She hunched under her umbrella, walking slowly to allow him to get far enough ahead so that she could ring Big Mac. Her call went straight through to messaging.

When she looked up the man was no longer visible through the falling snow. Cursing, she increased her pace, only to come to a halt abruptly when she spotted him at the bus stop immediately outside the hospital. Nightingale darted into the meagre protection of the bus shelter. The man looked at her suspiciously but she ignored him and started to text Mac. Eventually he turned away.

The bus arrived after five minutes. Just before it did so, she realised she didn't have a ticket and couldn't show her warrant card. She hoped it was one that allowed you to pay the fare on board. It was and she breathed a sigh of relief.

The bus was almost full but she found a seat from where she could keep the suspect in view. It was overheated and the tips of her ears and fingers tingled as they thawed, a strange, comforting sensation. Her boots had rubber soles and her hooded coat was well lined; *No such thing as bad weather, just inappropriate clothing* – her father's words came back to her. She loosened her scarf.

The man was on the phone two rows in front. She could hear the murmur of his voice but not the words. As the bus neared the next stop she tensed in case he was getting off but he didn't move. There was a buzz and she noticed a text from Mac: 'You rang. Problem?'

'Following suspect on #37 Arriva bus from hosp to town centre.'

She pressed 'send' and then immediately typed out a further

message: 'male, white, 5.10. long brown hair. Age c25. Distinctive leather jacket. Need backup. Cant call.'

The bus stopped again and the man remained seated. By now people were standing in the aisle and Nightingale relaxed a little, realising that it would take time for him to disembark.

Mac's reply was brief and to the point: 'Stick with him. Help on way.' When she put the phone in her pocket her hand brushed against a ski lift pass that brought back a snapshot of memory: of ex-boyfriend Clive insisting he could handle the challenge of a black run on their first morning in Kitzbühel and then the hours waiting for him in the hospital as his wrist was set. She had skied alone for the rest of the holiday. He hadn't appreciated her independence or the fact that she was the better skier. His snapped wrist turned out to be the start of the break in their relationship. Nightingale had been relieved.

She had no idea where their route was taking them and minimal knowledge of Guildford. The street outside was as anonymous as any suburb so she pressed 'present location' on the i-map app. It showed them nearing the Friary where she had met Bess earlier that month. If he left the bus there it would be hard to follow him unobtrusively but there was no other option.

All was quiet; around her other passengers read, listened to music or dozed in an atmosphere that was surprisingly soothing. A sudden shout disturbed the calm. Three seats ahead an Asian lady in her sixties was arguing with the man she was trailing who had put his wet boots on the seat beside her.

'Somebody's going to sit there.'

'What's it to you?'

The man leant into her space, clearly expecting her to back down. She didn't.

'Please take your feet off the seat. I've had enough of people like you messing up public property.'

'Fuck off.'

'Don't speak to me like that.' The woman was furious but powerless to do anything.

Other passengers looked away with expressions of incredulity or indifference as they puzzled on what had prompted someone into such public-spirited but inherently stupid behaviour. The man started laughing, victorious, but the woman was not prepared to give up that easily.

'I'm going to report you; that's criminal damage. There's CCTV on this bus, your face is on camera and when I make an official complaint they'll be able to find you.'

There was a soft groan as the other passengers exhaled. *Why couldn't she just leave it alone?* The demeanour of the man changed from belligerent to threatening.

'You're asking for trouble,' he said, leaning until his face was almost touching hers. 'Shut up.'

'I will not.'

The sound of the slap reverberated through the bus. Nightingale was on her feet and moving forward instantly.

'Leave her alone, now!'

'Who do you think you are? Fuck off.' The man turned his attention back to the public-spirited woman.

'I said, leave her alone.' When he ignored her Nightingale realised she had no option.

'Police.' She waved her card. 'You're under arrest. Anything you—'

The punch he aimed at her arm almost connected but Nightingale's reactions were faster. Her other hand came up and grabbed his wrist, twisting sharply so that the shock travelled up his arm and he howled in pain. Then the bus braked hard and she almost lost her footing. Her grip weakened and he was able to jerk his arm free. He swung around and squared up to Nightingale as the bus driver brought the vehicle to a halt.

'Keep the doors shut,' she called out. 'Call your control and tell them to send traffic police to our location.'

'No way!' The man sprang towards her, his fist clenched around the handle of a knife that had appeared without warning.

There were shouts of alarm but Nightingale merely shook her head.

'Don't be stupid. Threatening a police officer doesn't do your situation any good at all.'

Her calm confused him. She was meant to panic at the sight of the weapon. His mouth dropped open as he tried to think what to do next. Nightingale saved him the trouble.

She closed the distance between them in one step, locked her hand about the fist that held the knife, squeezed, rotated and pulled back sharply in a classic self-defence move, neatly stepping on the knife as it landed on the floor. In the same motion she twisted the man's arm up behind his back again and grabbed his other hand with her free one.

'I need my scarf to secure him,' she said to the Asian lady who obliged with alacrity.

Nightingale secured both his arms to a support and addressed the rest of the bus.

'I'm sorry to delay your journey but we're going to have to wait for my colleagues to turn up and take this gentleman away.'

There were a few murmurs but most people appeared resigned or relieved. The lady beside her was glowing with accomplishment.

'I knew it was the right time to make a stand,' she said with satisfaction.

'Madam, we never advise having a go. Please don't make a habit of it.'

Nightingale managed to hide her delight at having an excuse to arrest the suspect without having to prove any connection to Jenni. It would give them a full twenty-four hours with him in custody. She was feeling very pleased with herself when an RTC blue and yellow turned up. The uniformed officer took in the scene, with the knife on the floor and the burly man struggling against his restraint. Nightingale smiled at him triumphantly as she announced her name and rank but he scowled back.

'You could have been badly hurt,' he hissed. 'He's a big man; you should have left it to us!'

'Things didn't work out that way and don't fuss. He was no bother at all, were you?'

She smiled at the man who had ceased to shout and swear but looked prepared to do murder.

'Watch out!' The officer pulled her back just in time to avoid a gob of spittle that smeared the collar of her coat.

Nightingale looked at it in disgust.

'I saw it all,' the Asian lady said, 'and I'm very happy to be a witness to everything.'

'I'll find out where you live,' the man growled, adding to the list of potential charges against him.

The look the lady gave him was majestic in its contempt.

'Thank you,' Nightingale said, smiling. It was turning into a really good day!

They had a suspect in custody who might have assaulted Jenni and enough to hold him on to give them time to hope the girl regained consciousness and could make a statement. On top of that, she had had a virtually risk-free opportunity to test a little of her self-defence. Years before, she and a colleague had been attacked by a knife-wielding teenager high on drugs. Ever since then Nightingale had attended regular refreshers on self-defence and joined a kick-boxing class. She still ran at least three times a week but the kick-boxing had added muscle tone and quickened her reflexes.

It was sweet of the officer to be concerned, she thought, wriggling her toes inside her boots, but that man hadn't stood a chance!

She accompanied the suspect to Guildford HQ where she handed him over, reluctantly, to a detective there. The assault on Jenni had happened in Cranleigh; the man had tried to get to her in the Royal Surrey based in Guildford; and she had arrested him minutes from the Friary. No matter how hard she tried she couldn't find a way to insinuate herself into the case as anything other than witness and arresting officer.

She gave a full statement to a young detective constable with red hair who seemed diligent and asked the right questions. Afterwards she shared everything she knew or suspected of Jenni and her background, including the idea that Stanley was the man in custody and could well be the cousin Jenni had been planning to stay with when she had first run away from home. When she asked if he would keep her informed the officer was only too pleased to oblige.

Nightingale left Guildford HQ on a high and paused for a coffee, selecting by chance Fenwick's neighbourhood favourite from his short involvement on Operation Goldilocks. As she sipped a long Americano her thoughts swung first to him and then to her conversation with Lulu the day before. Her mood shifted. It was time, she knew. What she had to do could no longer be put off. She shut her eyes briefly in resignation then picked up her handbag and left.

CHAPTER THIRTY-NINE

If Acting Chief Constable Harper-Brown was pleased to see Fenwick after his resolution of the Flash Harry case he did a good job of concealing it. Their meeting took longer than the normal hour as H-B listed the problems that had accumulated during Fenwick's absence but which remained unresolved despite his return.

'The department is clearly missing decisive leadership, Superintendent. And while I am relieved that the so-called Flash Harry case has been resolved it barely starts to return your solve rate to a respectable level.'

Fenwick didn't bother to remind the CC that his detection rate was now merely in line with that of the county.

'I'll put a task force together to tackle the priority cases, sir, just as soon as I have finalised the Flash Harry reports and organised the necessary FLO follow-up with his victims.'

'You're surely not going to get distracted into that personally, are you?'

'The officer seconded from Harlden is doing the heavy lifting but the sign-off will obviously be my responsibility.'

'I meant the victim follow-up; don't be obtuse.'

'I need to make sure it's well organised, that's all. The work will be managed in the relevant divisions.'

'Good. Are you planning to take any time off over Christmas?'

The abrupt change of subject confused him. He thought quickly.

'With your permission, sir, I was hoping to. I haven't seen that much of my children these past weeks.'

Harper-Brown studied him over the top of the half-moon glasses he had taken to wearing recently, perched low down on the bridge of his nose. His icy expression softened.

'I imagine not. And they probably need to see you, don't they, particularly at this time of year, with their, ah, not having a mother at home . . . at least, that is still the case?'

'It is.'

'Very well; so today's the twenty-first. Why don't we agree that you put things square for the New Year today and then take a week off? That will give you a long weekend to get ready for Christmas on Monday, what?'

He's watching too many old WWII movies, Fenwick thought but he appreciated the kindness.

'Thank you, sir. And may I take this opportunity to wish you and Mrs Harper-Brown a very happy Christmas?'

'Indeed you may; likewise.'

If this was to be his last day in the office Fenwick realised he needed to buy some presents for the civilian staff that supported him and his team. As there was a pause in the sleet he went out immediately and bought his customary mix of chocolates, scent and flowers, remembering at the last minute that he needed Christmas cards too. On his way back he stopped for a double espresso and another to go.

The tokens were received with surprised thanks, which was a bit unfair as he did the same each year. On his desk was a gift-wrapped package from the secretarial assistant and several envelopes that he stuffed in his briefcase. No one remarked on his bandaged hand, though one of the older constables was bold enough to remark that he was glad the boss was going to get some rest over Christmas.

Fenwick knew he looked tired and he had lost weight but the man's solicitude still wasn't welcome.

Big Mac's report was waiting in his in-box and he downloaded it to print. An hour later he realised he hadn't drunk his takeaway coffee and he was missing it. As it was almost noon he decided to head for the canteen. Just as he was leaving his office, his mobile rang.

'You were right!' Bernstein shouted before he could even say his name. 'Bazza's had the locals checking every house on that estate agent's flyer. He prioritised any that were vacant and in remote locations. He thinks we've got something.

'There's a house in a village called Dragon's Green, east of Billingshurst on the A272 with signs of recent occupation. It could be where Mariner holed up with Issie after he left the pump station.'

'Is an operations unit on the way?'

'Already there; Bazza and I aren't far behind but the house looks unoccupied according to the report, so don't get your hopes up.'

'If they've been there since the Saturday before last how on earth did no one see them?'

Even though it was his lead that had led to the discovery, Fenwick found it hard to believe that Mariner would have been able to stay in an inhabited area for so long.

'The house is on the outskirts of the village at the end of an unmade road. The electricity had been turned off so there wouldn't have been any lights to give them away, but there is an Aga that would have been enough to keep them warm.'

'But what did they do for food? The supplies Mariner had taken from his wife's store cupboard would have run out long ago.'

'He could have walked into the village so no one would have seen his car, and in this weather it wouldn't raise suspicions if he muffled up to conceal his face. Anyway we'll find out soon enough. As soon as we've checked out the location I'll start a door-to-door while CST do a fingertip.'

'That makes sense.' Fenwick tried to keep the longing out of his voice.

'Look, Andrew. This call is off the record. OK?'

'Of course.'

'And the postcode I'm about to text you from my private phone didn't come from me.'

'You mean . . . ?'

'Don't be obtuse, I'm asking if you want to join us there.'

Norman had made it clear if he ever went near the Goldilocks operation again he would have his head, and H-B expected a master plan for MCS before Christmas. But the A272 . . . he could just head west out of Lewes and keep on going.

'I have a few things I must do but as soon as they're finished I'll be over. Thank you, Deidre, I appreciate this.'

Fenwick spent his most productive two hours ever clearing the Flash Harry report and outlining the New Year strategy to get MCS back on track. At three he bid a cheerful farewell to his team and left. He would drive himself and no one would ever know officially that he wasn't going straight home.

Bernstein walked Fenwick to just inside the back door, which opened directly into the kitchen. It was lit by battery-operated spotlights allowing the crime scene technicians to work through the dusk and into the night. There was rubbish everywhere, left in untidy piles. A short woman called Partridge, dressed as they all were in head-to-toe white coveralls, took Fenwick through what they had found so far.

'That's a sleeping bag over there. As soon as the photographer has finished in that corner we'll be sending it off for forensic tests. Fingerprints already confirm that Mariner and Issie Mattias were here. They are widespread about this room, in a hall back there and a bathroom. There's no sign of where they might have gone on leaving.'

Fenwick walked with Bernstein on raised aluminium steps across the room, to prevent them from contaminating the scene. Thick litter was evidence of a long period of occupation. Plastic bags bearing the logo of the local convenience store bore witness that Mariner had ventured out for supplies and hadn't been recognised. Partridge passed them a bagged till receipt dated the eighteenth. They looked at each other and grimaced. So close yet again.

Every item was being meticulously numbered and photographed *in situ* before bagging and sending to the lab. Less than half the room had been cleared, with the bags stacked ready for despatch. Against the far wall the sleeping bag lay in a crumpled heap. Even in the damp cold it stank of urine and sweat. Beside it was a girl's blouse, torn and bloody.

Bernstein knelt down and used the tip of her pen to lift it from the ground. It had been photographed so she could move it. There were spiky auburn hairs matted in a clot of blood. Fenwick closed his eyes briefly and then crouched down beside her, noting the label at the neck; women's size small, the same as his daughter Bess wore. He was suddenly consumed with a rage so fierce his sight blurred.

Without saying anything the two detectives rose and walked away to find somewhere warm to wait for the CSTs to do enough for them to have a proper look at the scene. It would take at least another hour.

'Bloody Cobb.' Bernstein was eating a quick sandwich with Fenwick and Bazza in the near-empty village pub.

Other than the three of them the rest of the team was continuing door-to-door enquiries. There was no street CCTV but the shop had a camera and the film had been requisitioned. Another officer had been despatched to secure and check camera coverage of the A272. The POLSA, police search advisor, had advised them on the search of the premises. First priority had been a sweep of the house and grounds with dogs in case Issie had been left there, alive or dead, but it had come up empty. Now the immediate focus was on the only room with heat, though the rest of the house would be pulled apart in due course in case a body had been well hidden, as had happened in the past.

'I should have known not to trust him.'

Fenwick said nothing.

'At least we know that Issie was alive when she arrived,' Bazza volunteered.

'Do we?' Bernstein looked gloomy.

Fenwick took a small sip of beer but he wasn't enjoying it; too bitter for his taste.

'What do you think? She *was* alive at the house, wasn't she, sir?' Bazza seemed determined to be optimistic.

Fenwick wanted to agree with him but he was worried it was hope not insight and so he was careful in his reply. The blood on the T-shirt was human, that had been determined with a presumptive test, and the good news was that there wasn't a lot of it. The spatter pattern was consistent – in his inexpert opinion – with a nosebleed or cut lip, nothing more.

'If she was held there, the really good news is that: one, he didn't panic and abandon her after the failed ransom demand; and two, they had somewhere to shelter out of the weather.'

'Exactly,' Bazza insisted.

Fenwick understood; the man was compensating for his guilt about the length of time it had taken them to locate the second hiding place but that wasn't what really mattered.

'So where did Mariner go next?' Fenwick asked, pushing the half pint aside.

Bernstein shook her head in frustration.

'We don't know. Just like we have no idea whether he's dumped Issie's body rather than cope with the fact that he's a kidnapper.'

'And murderer,' Bazza added.

'As if we need to be reminded. The problem is that we don't understand Mariner. The profile we had done is only good for toilet paper.'

Fenwick agreed. According to the profiler, Mariner was basically an ordinary bloke. Except that he had abducted and abused a young girl and murdered his brother in the process; so much for ordinary! In less trying circumstances Fenwick might have meditated on how easily a man could find himself so far from the life he thought he was going to follow; how he had taken small but irreversible steps towards a doom that condemned him as society's pariah. But he didn't have time to waste on that.

'We do know Issie,' he said. 'Maybe we should be profiling her.'

He said it to be provocative, to lift them out of their gloom but as the words left his mouth he realised he meant them.

'Supposing Issie is still alive . . .'

'You hope,' Bernstein said.

'So do you. Listen; Issie's smart, athletic, resourceful and creative – compared with Mariner she's Einstein. Why are we assuming she has no influence after two weeks together?' He was waving his arms around and Bazza rescued his glass. Over by the bar a lone drinker turned to stare.

'OK,' Bernstein whispered, 'it's an idea; where are you going with it?'

Fenwick didn't know.

'Well,' Bazza ventured softly, 'let's think: what would Issie do? She's held by a guy who has no idea what to do with her but hasn't killed her. Her main motive will be to stay alive. So how will she do that?'

They all knew.

'Sex,' Bernstein said at last for all of them.

'And drink,' Bazza added. They both looked at him. 'We know from his friend that Mariner enjoyed a tipple.'

'Let's hope he drinks enough to be incapable.' Bernstein shuddered as she downed the last of her lemonade.

Fenwick found himself liking her more.

'My round,' he said and headed to the bar for a change of ale to the guest brew of the month, Black Cat.

He was served quickly and managed to carry a tray back without spilling any despite his bad hand.

'So, where is she?' Bernstein asked as soon as he sat down.

Fenwick concentrated on placing the drinks down carefully.

'Well?'

'Good beer this,' he said after a slow mouthful during which he managed to mask his resentment at her expectations.

'For heaven's sake, Andrew, screw the beer!'

Now even the barman was listening.

'You smoke, don't you Bazza?'

'Yeah, but—'

'Let's take these outside.'

It was freezing and the promised sleet had started.

Bernstein shivered, chewed and looked enviously at Bazza as he inhaled.

'Well?'

'Assuming that Issie's alive but realises Mariner isn't going to let her go, she'll try and help him find somewhere warm. Let's assume she has some influence; where would she take him?'

Bernstein and Bazza looked at him as if he were mad.

'Bear with me; we're treating her as a victim but what if she's managed to build a relationship with him – it may only be sexual – but supposing she's managed to take them somewhere familiar and safe?'

'You're crediting her with a lot, Andrew.'

'Mariner hasn't many choices left and he might be desperate for an idea. Why don't you see her parents again and collect all the addresses of anywhere she might have been as a child?'

'We did that day one,' Bernstein said, stamping her feet to encourage circulation, 'and we checked them thoroughly, twice.' It was said with emphasis.

'You should revisit them all now we know he's on the move again.'

Bazza nodded and stubbed out his cigarette. It was a plan and it was better than nothing.

'We have the addresses,' Bernstein acknowledged. 'Redistribute them, Bazza, and send Henderson to reinterview the parents to make sure we have everything. Better yet, get Tony to do it.'

'Have you told the Saxbys about here?' Fenwick asked as soon as Bazza had gone.

Bernstein shuddered.

'I'm meeting Norman at the Hall in an hour so I'd better check on the latest at the scene.'

Fenwick wished her luck before returning with his unfinished half to the warmth of the pub. He enjoyed the tingle as feeling returned to his ears. Their seats had been taken but there was a table for two free in the far corner and he squeezed into it, keeping his coat on against the draught from the window. He had almost finished his beer when his mobile rang. It was Nightingale.

'Hello?'

'Andrew, I'm sorry to call but I need to see you.'

She sounded strange. If he didn't know her better he would say she was drunk.

'I see; what's going on?'

'Nothing's going on, Andrew; I just need to see you, now, this evening. I can't explain, not over the phone, but it's important.'

'You've found something out about the case?'

Her sigh was definitely emotional.

'Look, where are you? I'll come to you if it's more convenient.'

'I'm at the Map and Compass in Dragon's Green, it's just outside—'

'I know where it is. I'm less than seven miles away. I'm coming right away.'

'Well . . .' He glanced at his watch. It was gone six o'clock and it was starting to snow, but before he could say anything the call disconnected.

She saw him as soon as she walked in, oblivious to the turned heads and stares as always. Pushing through to the bar, Nightingale bought herself a drink, a Scotch and water to Fenwick's surprise. When she sat down in front of him it was obvious that she had been crying. For a slow minute they sat opposite each other in silence, tucked into the corner like illicit lovers. Eventually Nightingale swallowed her drink in one and sighed.

'I've made an amazing discovery, Andrew,' she said, her words slurring slightly. 'I found my mother.'

Now he was really worried; her mother and father had died in a car accident years before.

'I know what you're thinking; my mum died, well you're wrong. My father's wife, Mary, died. At the time I thought she was my mother but I found out the truth while I was staying at Mill Farm. I was swapped with Mary's real baby daughter when she died almost immediately after birth. Please, Andrew,' she held up a hand, 'let me finish this, it's important.

'My father knew; he was my real father, by the way. I was his daughter by the lover he had right up until he was married. He and a friend conspired to swap me and my dead half-sister so that my birth mother thought I had been stillborn.'

'If true that's despicable.'

'Yes it is and yes it was. She had to deal with all the pain of losing a child.'

Fenwick nodded as the first stirrings of unease uncurled inside him. Why should that mention of a dead baby trigger a recent memory? He observed Nightingale with growing disquiet as she told him the rest of her story, including finding her half-sister's grave and discovering the identity of her real – as yet unnamed – mother.

'I couldn't bring myself to search for her. There was all the trauma at the farm . . . when Smith . . . when you saved my life,' she looked at Fenwick properly for the first time, her eyes shiny with unshed tears, 'but the real reason was that I was too scared to risk being rejected. Then yesterday I met her by chance, on a stage in front of hundreds of schoolgirls.'

'At St Anne's?' Fenwick's breathing constricted as he realised what he was dreading.

'No, in Dorking,' he exhaled in relief, 'but she is a teacher at St Anne's. You might have interviewed her, Lulu Bullock?'

He thought he was going to be sick.

'Yes, I believe I did.'

'After I told her the truth and she finally believed me she was wonderful.' Nightingale beamed at him as a tear trickled unnoticed down her cheek. 'We talked for hours. She's really kind and so wise. So I decided to tell her about us.'

'What about us? You mentioned my name?'

'No, as it happens, I didn't, only that I have been in love with the same man for seven years and that he didn't seem to want to acknowledge my feelings for him and the possibility that he had feelings for me.'

She looked at him expectantly but Fenwick was giving his glass his undivided attention.

'I can't deal with this now, Nightingale. I don't have time for . . . you, us, oh I don't know!'

'I expected you to say that. I told Lulu how you would react but she advised me to tell you anyway.' She pushed her empty glass away.

He could feel the intensity of her gaze burning the top of his head.

'Andrew, I have my pride. It's hard for me to come here and tell you that I'm still in love with you. Why did I risk that? Because I think somewhere inside that impervious hide of yours is a decent, kind man who deserves a second chance at love.

'I know I sound like a soppy woman's magazine but I can't think how to tell you in a more sophisticated way. You are incomplete on your own, Andrew, and I think you know it. Your children certainly do and at least they would approve.' She hesitated and shook her head. 'I didn't mean to say that. This shouldn't be a decision you make based on anything but your own feelings.'

Fenwick didn't have any words. He was angry with her for daring to come and confront him and disappointed at her lack of professionalism. And she seemed drunk; how was she going to drive home? He was damned if he was going to give her a lift.

'I need to get going.' He pushed his empty glass away.

'Of course you do. Don't let me keep you!'

She waited, her eyes drilling into him. He could see her hand lying next to the empty glass, inches away, and yet he was frozen, with indecision, anger, fear, even embarrassment. Thoughts of Lulu flicked across his synapses . . . Nightingale's mother! He really was going to be sick. Perhaps that first beer had been off. If Nightingale ever found out about the night he had spent at St Anne's would she believe that nothing had happened? And Lulu, he still hadn't called her, hadn't known how to deal with the confusion of his feelings towards her, the way she attracted and repelled him in equal measure. He took a deep breath, struggling to find words that wouldn't form.

Nightingale stood up suddenly, knocking her chair so that it banged the wall. She tugged on her overcoat and picked up her handbag. Without another word she was gone.

He raised his eyes to study the space where she had been sitting. The cushions still bore the imprint of her weight. On one of them was a glossy black hair that had escaped the untidy ponytail he had noted without realising. The growing noise in the

417

pub continued but he felt empty, surrounded by silence. The lump in his throat was threatening to choke him. He should leave and go home.

Five minutes later he was sitting in the same position when his phone rang.

'Yes?'

It was Bernstein.

'Issie's a clever girl, isn't she? She wrote a message – possibly in her own blood – on the floor under the sleeping bag where Mariner wouldn't have seen it.'

Fenwick was instantly alert and focused.

'What did she say?'

'"*Issie alive 13th*", and then she's added "*17th*".'

'Clever girl. Has Bazza got that list of places?'

'He's already on it. Are you going to risk coming back to Guildford? I should warn you that Norman will be there.'

'No, there's nothing I'll be able to do except make things more complicated so I might as well go home, but you will let me know if anything happens?'

'Of course; I'll call you as soon as we have anything new.'

He was finally accepted as a partner; had he been in a better mood he would have smiled.

CHAPTER FORTY

Issie realised that she had been left untied since Steve had carried her to the bedroom unconscious from his beating the previous afternoon. She had been aware of him looking in on her from time to time. At some point he had given her a cup of sweet tea that made her feel sick and some aspirins. She had swallowed them and then wondered whether there were enough left for her to kill herself. The pain was intense, particularly in her head and down her right side, which had taken the brunt of his kicking as she had turned her back into a huddle against him.

She had no idea what time it was, only that it was going dark again and that Steve had slipped into bed beside her at some point when she had been asleep. Now she was wide awake. She listened carefully to his muffled snores and the grunts that he made when he was in his heaviest sleep. His left arm was outside the bedclothes. Very carefully she eased herself up so that she could see the watch face. It had a digital luminous dial and read 20.52. Beneath it was the date: 21.12.

Tears filled her eyes without warning. It was the anniversary of her dad's death. He had been dead five years and would have been forty-eight on Christmas Day. Issie wept silently, utterly forlorn. Her poor mum, suffering the anniversary on her own, worrying about where she was. And here she was wondering how to kill herself. She wiped her eyes angrily on the sheet. This would not do!

She was behaving like a helpless victim. Her dad would have been shocked; her grandfather furious. She had always been the tough one, a survivor, not some sex slave to this pathetic creature. She hit Steve on his arm, filled with a sudden murderous intent. He stirred in his sleep and opened one eye. She froze.

'Go back to sleep, baby,' she crooned. He could snap her spine in a few blows if he chose.

As Steve's snores resumed Issie laid her head back down carefully, biting her lip as stars crackled in front of her eyes. He could have killed her. She had been stupid to think that a pathetic little knife would protect her from one of his rages. They didn't happen often but she had learnt that the frequency grew when he felt frustrated. How much food and drink were left from her nana's supplies? And fuel? Did they have enough logs and oil in the tank to keep the place warm?

It dawned on Issie that, even as she stayed at the farm, the risk of being killed or badly injured by Mariner increased every day. It wasn't a place of refuge; it would be her tomb. The idea made her realise that she no longer wanted to die. With the acknowledgement came a decision that she would not!

She was on home territory, had known the surrounding countryside since she was born, walking the footpaths that crisscrossed the Downs with her grandfather since she was able to toddle beside him. If there was a break in the weather she would find a way to walk away from here – provided she was strong enough.

Issie felt the sharpness of her hip bones, the ache deep in her right pelvis and along her side. She counted her ribs, circled her wrists and was shocked at how thin they had become. No way could she manage the walk she needed to do in this condition. Food and exercise were essential.

She slipped out of bed, careful to put a pillow beside him so that he didn't feel the void she left. In the bathroom she closed the door, put on the light and studied her face.

'Oh my God,' she breathed, unable to comprehend that the image staring back at her through a half-closed right eye was her own. Her jaw was yellow; her right eye blackened. One side of her neck was covered with bruises from his fingers; she hadn't remembered him strangling her and shuddered. Her right shoulder had dark-red contusions as if from being beaten with a stick; her breasts were covered in sooty marks that must have been impressions from his fingers as he had squeezed her.

Issie turned and looked down her side. As she had feared, the worst bruising was over her right hip and buttock, which had taken the brunt of the beating. There were painkillers in the cabinet and she swallowed two more, noting that there were only four left. She couldn't have killed herself that way anyway! The thought brought an ironic twist to her lips.

Tomorrow she would start to think about escape. The sanctuary of her grandmother's home was a trap and she needed to get away as soon as she could. Her physical condition, the weather and isolation of the cottage were serious hurdles but Issie was not daunted. Her beloved grandfather, Pappy, had drummed into her the six Ps of backwoods' man survival: 'perfect planning prevents painfully poor performance', though she had long ago learnt that 'painfully' was a euphemistic replacement to save a child's sensitivities.

She would need to stretch and exercise carefully if she was to recuperate enough to make her walk to freedom. The cuts, though painful and ugly to look at, were irrelevant. Rebuilding her fitness and stamina was what mattered, and quickly, before Steve's fantasy world collapsed.

As she tiptoed back and hovered outside the bedroom doorway,

Steve coughed in his sleep in the way he sometimes did before waking up. Issie dropped to all fours, muffled a yelp of pain and crawled back to bed, easing herself beneath the covers as he shook his head, rose up slightly and mumbled her name. She stroked his arm reassuringly and he rolled back into sleep. Sometime after ten o'clock she joined him.

CHAPTER FORTY-ONE

There is a common assumption fuelled by TV crime dramas that DNA analysis takes no time at all but that is not true. Although the test itself can be completed in a matter of hours, unless a request is flagged as urgent it can take weeks as the analyst works through the backlog of submitted samples in strict 'first come first served' order. In the case of the T-shirt Fenwick had Tate send off they had asked not only for the semen to be analysed but also for tests to be run to try and confirm that the article had belonged to Issie.

Even though Tate had flagged the sample he submitted as potentially linked to two important cases, given that Issie's abductor was known Fenwick had not expected priority treatment. So he was surprised to see a message from Detective Sergeant Tate when he switched his mobile on Friday morning. He called back at once.

'The results are through, sir! It is definitely Issie's shirt, or rather she had definitely worn it, and you'll never guess who the semen samples match to.'

'That's why I'm calling, Constable.'

'Yes of course; sorry, sir. Well they come from Rodney Saxby. It's what you suspected from the beginning when you found those paintings, sir: Issie has been abused.'

Fenwick remembered Octavia Henry's scorn at the idea Issie would have run off with a lover because she hated the idea of sex.

He shut his eyes and could see vividly the sketches Issie had made in preparation for the painting, where the face of the girl being abused had not yet been obscured. They had been self-portraits.

'. . . has gone to arrest him.'

'Sorry, who has?'

'Sergeant Holland, sir.'

He should have been concentrating on following up on the addresses where Issie might have gone with Mariner.

'Why him?'

'Excuse me, sir, but I wouldn't know that.'

Of course he wouldn't. Fenwick thanked Tate for his help and congratulated him on securing the results so quickly. As soon as he rang off his mother tapped on the door of his study and asked if he was going to join them on a shopping expedition into Harlden.

'I won't thanks.'

'We can wait if you need to make another call, Andrew. That's nae bother.'

'No,' Fenwick shook his head, 'you go without me.'

'Well, will you at least come and join us for lunch? You did say you were off now until after Christmas, didn't you?'

'Yes, yes. I'll see what I can do. Just let me know where you'll be going.'

As soon as she had left he rang Bernstein.

'Deidre, it's Andrew. Look, I was wondering . . .'

'Whether you can join the interview with that bastard Rodney Saxby? Sorry, Andrew, I've already suggested it to the Conqueror and he's against it. Thinks you'll use it as an excuse to interfere in Goldilocks. Can't think where he got that idea from!'

'But he's put Bazza on it and he should be concentrating on checking possible places where Mariner might be hiding with Issie.'

'I'm aware of what he should be doing, Andrew, and I don't need you making matters worse. Look, try and back off a bit, can you? We're still processing the scene in Dragon's Green and I have a team working through every possible address linked to Issie. It's unlikely that Rodney Saxby's assault is connected to her abduction . . .'

'Other than driving her into the arms of an unstable, insecure predator! If Saxby junior hadn't assaulted her there's no way she would have been so vulnerable.'

'Possibly.' He heard Bernstein sigh and knew he was testing her patience.

'At least let me tell you my theory.'

'Go on, then, you'll do so whether I like it or not.'

'Thanks; in my first interview with Jane Saxby she told me about a sailing holiday somewhere in the Greek islands. Issie ran away following an argument with her stepfather after Saxby junior joined them on the yacht.'

'Yes, I remember. You have a habit of doing very detailed notes, Andrew. And I have a habit of reading every statement.'

'I'm sure you do. In that same interview you'll find reference to the fact that Rodney Saxby was the one who found Issie on Cephalonia and brought her back. Her mother said that afterwards she retreated completely into herself and was in a terrible mood. What if that was when Saxby assaulted her? Semen on a T-shirt suggests oral sex or masturbation rather than rape. He might have forced Issie into either.'

'Surely she would have accused him immediately she saw her mother?'

'You know what abuse can do to adult/child relationships and she would have been insecure because of her mother's new relationship. Perhaps Rodney Saxby said he would tell them it was consensual, that she was a slut. Or maybe he threatened to hurt her mother. Who knows? We need to find Issie to understand why she kept quiet about something so odious.'

'Meanwhile, we'll bring Rodney-boy in and see if we can't

crack him. I'm good at interrogation, Andrew. It's one of my strong points, trust me.'

'And the hunt for Issie?'

'Goes on! With full and utter dedication. You're not the only one consumed with guilt, goddamit.'

There was a catch in her voice.

'I'm sorry, Deidre, that was shitty of me. I know there couldn't be a better officer dedicated to finding Issie.'

'Except for you, perhaps,' Her voice was broken. 'I'd have you back in an instant, y'know. You are bloody brilliant and I don't have any issue admitting that. Both breakthroughs have come from your work and yes, that does make me feel inadequate but I can get over that because I don't suffer from penis-envy, despite what my detractors might think.'

He didn't know how to respond.

'So; we'll bring Saxby junior in,' she coughed and continued more strongly, 'interview the bastard to breaking point, while continuing to devote hundreds of man hours a day to finding Issie with relentless determination worthy of you.'

'I know; as I said, I didn't mean to imply anything else.'

'Noted; and don't worry as soon as anything breaks you'll be the first to know.'

'First? Before the Conqueror?'

'Yes.'

After he finished the call Fenwick made himself a coffee and rang a number he had on autodial.

'Holland.'

'Bazza, it's Andrew Fenwick. I realise you're on your way to arrest Rodney Saxby but if you could just give me a quick update on where you've got to checking known locations for Issie.'

'It's well on track, sir. We're looking into every address Issie might have known, focusing on the South East.'

'How many are there?'

'More than forty. To speed things up we are asking local forces to help with the visits and searches.'

He itched to tell him not to rely on anyone but their own team but he knew such advice would be as unwelcome as it was impractical given the condition of the roads. Bernstein and Bazza were making a trade-off between speed and absolute reliability. In her position he would probably have done the same thing.

'Thank you. Good luck with Saxby.'

'Have to find him first, sir. He wasn't at home just now when we called. His housekeeper says he's at his club. That's where I'm heading now.'

Fenwick finished his coffee, deeply frustrated not to be directly involved. His home phone rang and he answered it on the first ring.

'It's your mother, Andrew. We're going out to the Dog and Bacon for lunch as there's a play area for the children there they've kept clear of snow. Will ye be joining us? It's such a lovely day after all the weather we've had.'

Fenwick glanced outside. He hadn't noticed but it was a beautiful morning, with a Wedgewood-blue sky. In the emptiness of his kitchen he shrugged. Why not? There wasn't anything else for him to do.

CHAPTER FORTY-TWO

Issie was awake before Steve on Friday morning. Carefully, a fraction of an inch at a time, she lifted his arm off her waist sufficient to slide out from beneath. She had a pillow ready, knowing that he was acutely aware of her presence even when he slept. Gently, she lowered the arm on top of it and slipped out of bed without so much as disturbing the quilt.

It was still dark. Her body ached; the right leg had stiffened and it took some time before it would bear her full weight. Her arms felt better though, despite the beating. She had woken with an idea and knew she must act on it before her nerve failed her.

She had gone to sleep worried that they were about to run out of painkillers and trying to think where else she might be able to find some. That led her to remember the first-aid case and that inside it she would find more than pills.

She crept along the landing to the laundry room where she remembered that her grandmother kept the case. Without switching on the light she found it and pulled if off the shelf. Back on the landing, there was just enough illumination from a half-closed curtain for her to make out the door to the shower room that had become 'hers' during her captivity. She went inside, turned on the light and tried not to look at herself but it was impossible not to notice the bruises. He had made a real mess of her. Issie swallowed a burst of anger; this wasn't the time to indulge in emotion – she had things to do before he woke up.

She knelt down by the side of the toilet, keeping the sole of her foot against the door as Steve had the key with him at all times. There was an inspection panel beside the toilet underneath the sink that her grandmother never replaced securely because she couldn't manage the screws once they were done up tight.

Issie found tweezers in the first-aid kit. She bent one arm to ninety degrees and gripped the lopsided T formed by the other at the join to improvise a screwdriver with which to remove the panel screws. It took several minutes for her to manage all four and by the time she had finished she was covered in sweat, not only from exertion but also fear.

Although the case was too big to fit inside the inspection void she was able to hide scissors, tweezers, some safety pins, bandages, dressings and plasters; the start of her escape kit.

At the bottom of the first-aid box she found a paper bag inside which were some pills that had been prescribed to her grandfather. She saw his name and the date and blinked back tears; he had been taking them just weeks before he died. So what were they? She muttered the unfamiliar name to herself in the silence of the dark: *procarbazine*. The other packet contained an old prescription for well-known sleeping tablets. She hid the packets as well before putting more painkillers in the bathroom cupboard and returning the first-aid box to its place.

First task complete, Issie looked in on Steve, avoiding the creaky floorboard immediately outside their bedroom door. He was snoring heavily. There was a decision to be made; should she risk going downstairs or not? She wasn't sure she would be able to walk quietly enough after the beating. Her right hip flared with pain every time she put weight on it. The other cuts and bruises, though painful, weren't hampering her movement too badly.

As she hovered outside the doorway, Steve coughed. He could wake at any time. The most important thing now was to avoid being tied up. Any risks she took had to be weighed against that, including not being there when he woke. She bit her lip in anticipation of the pain and crouched down to creep back to bed.

Issie lay awake beside Steve for another forty minutes. By his watch it was seven twenty-three when he turned from her, taking his disgusting early morning breath with him. He smelt of alcohol and over-spiced 'chilli con carne'. It was one of his 'specials': baked beans, chillies, fried onions and mince. Issie loathed it.

After he turned onto his back Steve started to snore heavily. He wasn't about to wake up soon. Issie closed her eyes and struggled with what to do. She needed time to prepare but if he woke and found her gone he might overreact. But if she just lay here and then he tied her up anyway when he woke up she would have missed her opportunity. There wasn't a choice, really. Issie placed her trusty pillow next to him and slipped out of bed.

This time she put on a dressing gown. The house was cold and she needed to go into her grandfather's study. As Steve had cut the phone lines and disabled the computer she would have to revert to old-fashioned methods to find out the effect of the drugs he had been taking. She was convinced that her grandfather would have researched the disease that killed him, and its treatments.

It took her a while to find the folder in his desk but as soon as she opened it she saw a print out on procarbazine. It was used to treat brain tumours and lymphoma. She shuddered and forced herself to read about its side effects. They were many and thoughts of Pappy's discomfort were quickly replaced by images of Steve Mariner suffering. She was particularly taken with the rare side effects: itchy rash, flushed face, difficulty breathing. Even some of the common side effects would be disabling: fatigue, effects on nerves, fever, and flu-like symptoms. Steve was a hypochondriac. If he succumbed to a fraction of these he would retreat to the couch, and if she gave him an overdose . . . Issie smiled.

She read the rest of the page noting that alcohol was to be avoided. Excellent! The sleeping tablets shouldn't be mixed with the chemo according to Pappy's notes. That was good; she could prepare a nice little cocktail for him if only he would trust her in the kitchen.

Issie crept out of the study and looked in on Steve. He was muttering to himself and moving beneath the bedclothes. Soon he would be awake. It was time for step two of her cunning plan: she needed him to trust her around food. She eased herself downstairs and switched on the radio in the kitchen to show she wasn't being secretive. They were down to the last frozen pack of bacon and there were just five eggs left. Issie realised time was running out. She needed to strengthen her right leg, exercise, bulk up and complete her escape kit, after which she would be ready to leave whenever the weather allowed.

As she cooked she thought about what she would need. The nearest village was less than two miles away. If it had been summer she would have risked going with nothing but good shoes and clothes despite her weakened condition. Unfortunately it was the depth of winter, with snowdrifts around the farm over three feet deep. Even a short walk in such conditions if unprepared would be dangerous. Issie thought back to the survival manuals she had devoured as a child.

As a minimum she would need food, liquids, something to provide heat in an emergency, the right clothes and a torch. Ideally she should have a safety blanket as well, that's what the manuals advised, lightweight, metallic, they could be a lifesaver but she didn't have one. As the bacon started to sizzle Issie opened kitchen cupboards, listening all the time for his footsteps. There was a roll of black plastic sacks that would provide waterproof storage as well as the means to improvise a sleeping bag or foul-weather protection. She pulled off ten quickly and stuffed them behind the rubbish bin where they wouldn't look out of place. In the drawer under the oven she found extra-wide aluminium foil for roasting. That could serve as an emergency blanket at a pinch. She would need to pull off a large length and fold it when she could be sure Steve wasn't about to walk in.

Later she would have to raid her grandmother's chest of drawers in the hope that she had silk and wool or cashmere that could be layered beneath a heavyweight woollen jumper of her grandfather's that she was already wearing during the day. Her cotton T-shirt would be completely unsuitable for a winter hike; the last thing she needed was material that would evaporate her body warmth efficiently.

But what was she do to about weatherproof trousers? The snow would be a problem. She could see it lying in great drifts across the yard. If she couldn't keep her legs dry she would succumb quickly to hypothermia. Had her grandmother kept any of her husband's endurance gear? Possibly, but where and how would she ever find it?

While the snow didn't create perfect escape conditions it would probably stop or slow Steve from following her. He was a real townie and hated the cold. She tuned the radio to BBC 4 to catch the *Today* programme in case there was any news about her. When the headlines came on at eight she stopped what she was doing and listened but there was nothing. Today's weather forecast was interesting; it predicted a clear day with only light snows –a perfect day for an escape but she couldn't risk it in her present condition. Tomorrow there would be heavy snow in the South East, but then they expected an improvement in conditions for Christmas Eve before the arrival of what could be the worst blizzard in a decade on Christmas Day.

Listeners were warned not to plan to travel on Christmas Day and to take advantage of the relatively calm conditions the day before. Well, that was exactly what she now intended to do. Depending on how quickly she could recover, particularly the muscles in her hip and legs, she would escape on the 24th. It would be a wonderful Christmas present for her mum!

Issie pulled back the curtains and stared into the yard. It was still dark but she could see the snow deep against the barn and outbuildings. As she made toast for Steve's bacon sandwich she ran through the route she planned to take. She would find the track at the bottom of the drive and turn east along it. Within two miles she would find the village of Alfriston. There was a particular pub there that she remembered and a church. Even if the wind was blowing she would be sheltered for part of the journey.

In what had been the gunroom in her grandfather's day and was now a store for anything her grandmother didn't want to leave in the barn, there was an old Barbour, complete with lining, with mittens in the pocket and a scarf stuffed down one sleeve, plus several pairs of wellington boots, including her spare pair for when she came to stay. The socks and long johns she needed would be in the airing cupboard. She would take spare ones with her in a plastic rubbish bag to keep them dry.

Now, what about a candle in a tin, a compass and a whistle? She was trying to remember where she had kept them as a little girl when there was a step immediately behind her.

'What are you doing?'

'I wanted to surprise you with breakfast in bed.' She decided she couldn't afford to be scared of him any more.

'Really? Oh, that's nice! Is that for me, then?' He pointed at the toast and gently browning bacon. He was wearing her grandfather's dressing gown and that made Issie angrier than anything so far.

'Well, it's for both of us, actually. As you're up would you mind laying the table? It will be ready in five minutes – unless you'd like an egg as well?'

'No, a bacon sarnie will do me, thanks. Got to be a bit careful, haven't we?'

As soon as the food was ready he grabbed the plate with the sandwich and took a bite as he walked over to the heavy pine table in front of the Aga.

'Tha's good,' he said with his mouth full. He smiled through crumbs and a smear of tomato sauce but he couldn't meet her eye and she realised that he was feeling guilty about the beating.

Issie forced a grin and started eating. She wasn't hungry but that was irrelevant.

'Weather's not getting any better,' she said. 'Radio forecast says there won't be a thaw this side of New Year.'

'That doesn't bother us, does it, little Is? In fact it's all to the good. The road is already blocked so no one can come nosing around, and if it's really bad there will be fewer travellers.'

'As long as the electricity doesn't fail,' she said, smiling inside.

Steve shuddered. He didn't like the dark or the cold. The other evening when there had been a brief power cut he had huddled on the sofa by the fire until the lights returned. The house could be spooky in the dark. As a little girl she had been scared of its shadows and creaks but by the age of eight she had mastered her fear and now thought Steve's pathetic.

'There's a generator, you said, didn't you?'

'Yes, in the shed next to the barn. Shall we go and check on it after breakfast in case we need it?' Steve glanced at her suspiciously then nodded.

As soon as breakfast was finished she dressed warmly and then found him boots and a thick jumper to put on under his jacket. Everything she needed was in the gunroom and she was delighted that she was able to try it on openly. When she opened the back door, she was confronted with snow piled to handle height.

'Bloody hell, will you look at that!'

'There's a spade in the gunroom, Steve; hang on.'

She was back quickly and passed it to him.

'You want me to do it?'

'I don't think I'm up to it, Steve.' Issie was having to rest against the wall as her injured leg spasmed.

He looked at her battered face, the way she had one hand pressed to her side and his eyes filled with tears.

'Does it . . . does it hurt a lot, Is?'

'A bit, Steve, yes.'

'I'm s . . . Look you shouldn't have riled me, should you?'

'No, Steve, and I've learnt my lesson but it does hurt and I don't think I'll be able to help shovel. It's man's work, anyway, but if you start I'll come behind and widen the path.'

For thirty minutes Steve worked in silence with Issie doing her best to sweep snow as he shovelled. It was at least some exercise, though it made her back and arms ache. The heat of their labour kept the freezing cold at bay but their noses and ears were soon tingling. The path they cleared ran to the right from the back door to a shed by an old barn. The door was locked, so Issie had to go back for the key. As she did so, alone in the kitchen, she stuffed a bar of chocolate and a pack of biscuits into the inner pocket of the Barbour.

'Here,' she passed him the key but no matter how hard he tried the lock wouldn't open.

'It's frozen solid,' he complained. 'Only one thing for it!' Without further ado he unzipped his flies and peed on the lock.

Issie burst out laughing and he looked at her in surprise.

'Never seen that before?' He shook himself and rezipped. 'Bloody hell that's cold; I'm the amazing shrinking man! But it's worked, see.' The key turned and they stepped into the freezing shed.

It was dark inside and the light bulb didn't work so again Issie was sent back to the kitchen to find a new one. This time she hid the remains of the loaf of bread and the end of some cheese in the cupboard in the gunroom before returning.

'Will this do?'

For answer Steve twisted the new bulb in and switched it on. They could see the Honda generator sitting in the corner. It was more complicated than Issie remembered.

'You reckon that thing still works?' Steve sounded sceptical. 'Looks fit for the junk yard if you ask me.'

'I haven't seen it used since I was a little girl but we should give it a go.'

The motor was only a little bigger than a lawnmower's, but try as he might, Steve could not get it started.

'I told you, it's buggered.'

Watching Steve had brought back memories of Pappy demonstrating the best way to start the generator. He had explained that she was '*a cantankerous girl, old Jessie*' that needed tenderness not brute strength, otherwise the engine flooded. He had a way of fiddling with a little valve when *Jessie* had a sulk.

'I've just remembered something my grandfather used to do.'

Steve shrugged; if he couldn't start it there was no way a bit of a girl would be able to. Issie crouched down with difficulty because of her hip and rubbed the nose of the valve until she could feel diesel trickle out. Then she took the cord toggle and pulled back in a long, strong motion that didn't jerk. The motor coughed and died. She repeated the action, careful not to go too hard. There was another splutter, longer this time before it failed. On the third attempt the motor caught and the generator kicked into life. Issie let it run for a minute and then switched it off.

'So, we're ready if we need it,' she said, pleased with herself.

Steve stepped forward and hugged her. She winced at the pressure but he didn't notice.

'Well done, little Issie!' It was as if he had taught her himself. Issie forced a smile.

'Let's get back inside, it's freezing. I'll make us some coffee, if you like.'

'Just tea for me, Is.'

Issie made sure that she emphasised her limp, moving slowly. It was essential that he didn't tie her up again. If she could make him think her physically weak as well as docile maybe he wouldn't bother, particularly given the snows that had cut them off. She filled the kettle and put it on the Aga. There was half a fruitcake frozen in the freezer, probably put there when her thrifty grandmother had left for Australia; she never wasted anything. She put it on top of the Aga to thaw out. Steve was watching her carefully.

'We deserve a treat, don't you think?'

He nodded.

'I'm going to light the fire in the lounge. You come straight in and join me as soon as that tea's made. OK?'

'Yes, Steve, I just need the loo first.'

In the shower room Issie found the sleeping pills and the ivory chemotherapy capsules. The packet said 50mg. Would they dissolve in tea? Worth a try, and a sleeping pill definitely would.

She checked on Steve as she came downstairs. He was watching a rerun of a John Wayne western on television, lying on the sofa with a blanket over his legs. The fire he'd made was a small one, to ration the logs.

Issie made his tea. She opened a capsule carefully with a knife and ground up a sleeping tablet, stirring them both into the teapot. She added extra sugar to Steve's mug and made herself a cup of instant coffee.

'Tea's up,' she called out cheerfully and took the tray through to the sitting room.

CHAPTER FORTY-THREE

The sun disappeared behind clouds and a sudden blast of arctic air sent the Fenwick children scurrying back inside the Dog and Bacon just as the adults were ordering coffee. Fenwick had been in good form, to the delight of Alice and surprise of his mother, who kept looking at him suspiciously. He found her scrutiny unnerving.

They decided to visit Father Christmas at a garden centre after lunch rather than try to do any more shopping, given the weather. As they were in two cars the children insisted on going with him. They spent forever in Santa's grotto, which didn't bother his mother or Alice as they had a lovely time wandering around the Christmas displays and taking ages to choose seasonal knick-knacks Fenwick knew were superfluous while they waited for the children to emerge. When they finally left it was dark and the roads were treacherous. Alice decided to leave her car to pick up the following morning in daylight. They all crammed into his for the short journey home, with the children fighting over who was to sit where. So when his mobile phone rang he answered hands-free and said immediately, just in case, 'Fenwick; I'm just with my children right now.'

'Oh, right.' He heard confusion in Bernstein's voice and then realised she probably didn't even know he had any. 'When would it be good to call you back?'

'In half an hour, thanks.'

* * *

He was waiting impatiently for her call with a cup of tea in his study when it came through after four-thirty.

'We have Saxby in custody. You won't believe this but the chief constable has relented and says you can join the interview with him.'

'That's brilliant, but why?'

'Well I suspect it's because the first attempt has been an abject failure. In fact, it was worse than that; I would say it was a disaster. Instead of calling a solicitor with his one call he rang big brother who stormed down here, solicitor in tow and demanded the immediate release of junior. Norman said no and took him into his office to explain why. They almost came to blows.'

'Ouch. So how are things now?'

'Lord Saxby has left in high dudgeon threatening press coverage of the, I quote, "abject effing failure of the police to find my daughter" in the *Sunday Enquirer*. Rodney is in with his brief, who is a Mr Box . . .'

'Oh, I know Box; money doesn't buy better.'

'Exactly.'

'So I'm the last hope?' he said, whereas what he was thinking was *I'm to be the damned scapegoat again*.

'You're being kind.' So she was thinking the same.

'How long has he been in custody?'

'We arrested him at thirteen forty-five.'

'And you'll be holding him for the full twenty-four hours?'

'Too right.'

'Very well; I'll come over early tomorrow morning. I had a drink at lunchtime and the roads are really bad. That way you can continue to work on him and I really will be the last hope.'

'I don't blame you.' But she sighed. 'See you, then.'

He was watching Bess put the finishing touches to a Christmas cake she had made when she said out of the blue, 'Will we see Nightingale before Christmas, Daddy? Only I've made her a card.'

He felt his mother's eyes on the back of his neck. Chris stopped playing his computer game. The silence grew.

'It would be nice, Andrew,' Alice said. 'She's been such a sport. Why not invite her over for a drink with us all tomorrow?'

'It's very short notice; she's bound to be busy.'

'An attractive girl like her, yes possibly, but if you don't ask you won't find out, will you?'

'Go *on*, Daddy,' Bess insisted, sounding exactly like her mother had done when she nagged him.

'I'll think about it.'

'Don't procrastinate, Daddy,' Chris chimed in, switching off his game and coming over to jump on his father's knee.

'That's a good word, Chrissy.'

'I can spell it too, Alice, P . . . R . . . O . . . C . . . R . . .'

'A–S–T–I–N–A–T–E! It's not that difficult.'

'Bess!'

Fenwick breathed a sigh of relief as his mother took his daughter to task. While they were distracted he disappeared to his study and shut the door firmly. He concentrated on doing the paperwork he had been putting to one side for too long. Then he decided the keyboard and screen needed a good clean and was in the process of sorting out the pens in his drawer into size order when he threw the last one down in disgust.

Without giving himself time to rethink he dialled and Nightingale answered immediately.

'Oh,' she said when she heard his name. 'It's you. What do you want?'

'Nightingale, how are you?'

'Fine; busy.'

'Of course, I won't keep you long.' He ran his free hand through his hair. 'Look, Nightingale, last night . . . I didn't react very well and, well, I'm sorry.'

Nothing.

'I was – am so worried about Issie and the timing wasn't the best . . . I . . . look . . . I heard what you said, I mean I really heard it and we should talk. It's just that right now . . . well, I'm in a mess, quite honestly.'

He heard an intake of breath but she didn't speak.

'What I mean is . . .' God this was difficult, 'well all I can think about is finding Issie and sorting my home life out. I'm messing up with Bess. If I'm not careful she could end up as damaged as Issie.' He had to look up and blink. 'This isn't working. I'm just sorry; OK?'

'OK,' she said at last. 'At least you called; that's something.'

'It wasn't easy.'

'Do you want a medal? Neither was going to see you last night.'

'Sorry; I know . . . can you just give me some time? To clear my mind?'

'To find Issie, you mean.'

'Yes.'

'She's not your case any more.'

'I know but . . .'

'And after all this time the chances of her being found alive must be slim.'

'She was alive on the seventeenth, we know that for sure.' His jaw was aching with the effort to keep his voice level.

'I wasn't aware; there's been nothing on the news.'

'Norman has a news blackout. So please keep it to yourself but we have hope. And Mariner isn't a cold-blooded killer.'

'Despite the brother?

'That was an accident, I'm sure of it.'

'I don't know what to say, Andrew.'

'All I'm asking for is the chance to spend time with Bess and Chris and to think things through.'

'Will you really give yourself that time? You seem to know an awful lot about the hunt for Issie, given that you are no longer involved. Does CC Norman know you're being kept so well informed?'

'I'm helping them, Nightingale, on the quiet I admit, but I found something—' he stopped himself; he couldn't mention Lulu not now.

He heard her sigh.

'Very well, let's talk again when you're ready but don't mess me about, Andrew. That would be unkind.'

'I promise. Thank you. I'll be in touch after Christmas, then.' Relief was making him light-headed.

'All right . . . oh, and Andrew.'

'Yes?'

'I hope Issie is found soon, really I do.'

'Thank you,' he said, so he didn't hear her mutter, '*For your sake as well as hers.*'

CHAPTER FORTY-FOUR

Issie had a very good day. Late afternoon brought a power cut but by then Steve was oblivious. He hadn't moved from the sofa since drinking Issie's doctored tea. His snores were so loud she could hear them wherever she went in the house, relishing the freedom to move and to prepare.

There was a dusty backpack in the spare room, which she cleaned and lined with one of the plastic sacks. After that she gathered her essential kit and packed it tightly in the bag, thinking through the most efficient way to stow the contents in case of emergency. Issie discovered her old schoolgirl compass by chance, less impressive than she remembered. She made a lantern for the pack by punching holes with a skewer in an empty, washed baked bean can and then securing a length of candle inside on melted wax. It was unlikely she would ever need it; the two-mile walk would be nothing, even in the snow, to a girl who used to hike all day but Pappy had impressed on her from a very young age the need to be prepared.

After she finished packing some plastic-wrapped sticks of dry kindling she went to check on Steve. He was still fast asleep. The fire had dwindled to glowing embers so she put on one of the smaller logs and a precious lump of coal. It flickered back to life but it was hardly a blaze and the house was starting to become cold as the electric pump no longer circulated hot water from the Aga. She should go and start the generator.

The idea was daunting; to venture outside on her own with her dodgy hip would be risky. On the other hand it would be good to see how her body coped with the icy conditions. It was such a pity that she wasn't yet fit, otherwise she would have tied Steve up and left as soon as he had fallen asleep, but she wasn't yet ready. She needed to build up muscle strength and eat more before she ventured out. As soon as she had hidden her pack, she would eat some soup, wrap up tight and tackle the generator. At that moment she heard Steve groan.

Andy Parker zipped his quilted jacket up to his chin and pulled the hood tight. It hadn't snowed all day but the wind cut into any exposed flesh, flaying it to painful redness in seconds. His glasses protected his eyes but were almost useless as they steamed up with the humidity as he breathed cautiously through a barely open mouth.

The instruction from Operations to the RPU to check out Abbott's Farm was as unwanted as his Auntie May arriving for Christmas. He had been in the canteen when the call came, hoping for a couple of hours out of sight before sliding home for the Christmas weekend. Unfortunately, the duty sergeant had other ideas and seemed to take particular pleasure in giving this road policing officer the assignment; sadistic bastard.

It wasn't even his job; but apparently Operations considered road traffic best suited for the dreadful driving conditions he would face on the Downs. That was a new one to him and way beyond the call; he'd have a word with the Federation rep when he next saw him.

It had taken Andy over an hour to travel the short distance along the A27 from Lewes to Wilmington. He now faced the problem of finishing the last mile to the farm. Ahead, the single-track road was virtually impassable, even for his 4x4. The council had decided not to waste precious grit on keeping such a minor road open. He radioed in, expecting to be told to abandon the job, but was told to get off his arse and walk it, but not to approach if there were signs of occupation.

Andy tried the usual health and safety line; it was nasty out there and would be dark early; if he slipped and hurt himself there would be hell – and a lot of money – to pay. At that he had been told to make sure he took his radio with him so he could call for help if needed. He thought he could hear laughter as the transmission closed. Of course he had all the necessary gear in the car; it was standard winter issue. That wasn't the point.

As soon as he opened the car door, the wind flung needles of ice against his cheeks and nose. His boots were a tight fit over extra socks but he managed to squeeze into them, then it was a matter of stowing the torch and radio while balancing the spade on his back. The snow was packed deep and even higher along the verge where the wind had whipped it into crested waves through which black-fingered hawthorn scratched to the surface.

'Bloody hell! I'm never going to make this.' Andy struggled to push through the snow. Every hundred yards was taking forever; he thought again about turning around.

Steve Mariner was doubled up in agony on the toilet with only the torch for company when its battery died.

'Issie! Issie!'

Another spasm gripped his insides. Whatever had upset him was vicious; he had never felt so ill.

'Issie! For God's sake I need you. The torch has gone out.'

He heard her footsteps outside on the landing.

'There's a candle here just to the left of the door, Steve. Shall I bring it in?'

'No, agh, just leave it there. I'll be out in a minute.' More cramps, a disgusting rush and a smell that made him nauseous. He felt clammy and weak. She mustn't see him like this.

445

'I'll find new batteries and then go and see if I can start the generator.'

'Be careful,' he whispered in the darkness.

Issie knew where the spare batteries were but Steve was scared of the dark and he deserved to be isolated in there feeling like death. She couldn't believe that he had had such a bad reaction to the procarbazine already. She waited in the hall for some time, listening to him groaning.

Andy had developed a routine: ensure left foot is securely placed, pull right foot out of snow leaning on shovel for support, place down firmly, test, lift left foot and repeat. It was a slow, muscle-aching rhythm but he was making progress. Although dusk was falling early the snow gleamed sharply, lighting the path ahead. He must almost be there. There had been a house a long while back but it wasn't the one and its lights had disappeared in the dip of the hill. The smell of woodsmoke in the wind was comforting. An anthropologist might have suggested atavistic feelings were the source; deep memories of the safety of the open fire in the cave, surrounded by the rest of the tribe. For Andy it just made him think of his gran.

A signpost loomed up in the gloom. Andy shone his torch on it and read out loud 'Abbott's Farm ¾ mile'; there was an arrow pointing down an even narrower track.

'At last.'

Andy walked down it and found that the snow wasn't as deep. The gnarled limbs of ancient oaks hunched above him. Even bare of leaves they were dense enough to provide cover but it was harder to see. The clear sky was being invaded from the east by swollen grey clouds, lit by the setting sun. He switched on his torch, trying to trace the curves of the path ahead. At least he felt warm, in fact he was sweating inside his parka but his face under the scarf was numb and his hands painfully cold. The track started to climb and he was soon panting. On the breast of a hill the trees fell back and he had to work extra hard.

Why was he doing this? His shift was almost over and he should have been on his way home to Amanda, warm and welcoming; the smell of dinner tempting him as much as her soft curves. Bugger this for a lark! Another waft of woodsmoke, sweet and fragrant; it made him miss her more. He was tempted to give up. What were the chances of that girl being out here anyway? Zero. Look at this road; no one had driven down here for ages. He might just as well turn around now and tell the sarge the house was empty, but he didn't.

It wasn't a sense of duty that pushed him on but thoughts of his wife. The missing girl looked a bit like Amanda when he had first met her in the sixth form. The photos had affected him, not that he'd shown it, of course, but inside he had been angry and scared for her. With thoughts of Amanda on his mind he struggled on, swearing when his legs spasmed or the wind drove dirt in his face. He reached the crest of the next hill and looked down into darkness beyond. He could see nothing, not even the track as it dipped away. He pulled out his torch but as he flicked it on the clouds parted and he was granted a view of the wide valley below, crossed by bands of rose light and sharp black shadows cast by the setting sun. He could see the farm over half a mile away, dark against the surrounding pink-grey fields. It looked deserted: no lights, pitch-black. The track leading to it was covered in thick virgin snow. Andy nodded to himself; sorted. He had done his job and now he could go home.

He reached the car in half the time and turned the key in the ignition in trepidation but the engine started first time and the headlights came on. He sighed and felt deep relief. In fact, it was exactly the same feeling that Steve Mariner was experiencing as his body finally stopped cramping and the light in the bathroom came back on.

CHAPTER FORTY-FIVE

On his way to Guildford Saturday morning Fenwick telephoned Saxby Hall. He was in luck; the butler answered and told him that the master was out but Lady Saxby was at home. When he was put through Fenwick wasted no time and told her what he needed and why. She understood at once. By the time he drew up in front of the marble columns of the Hall she was waiting for him at the top of the steps, outside despite the cold.

She thrust a large envelope towards him.

'Here; I think it's what you need. I hope it helps you nail the bastard!'

'I intend to do my best.'

She reached up and kissed his cheek quickly, then turned away without another word.

The drive into Guildford town centre took a long time as the roads were solid with shoppers making the most of the pause between snowstorms. When he arrived he went straight to the detectives' room and found Bernstein with Bazza and Cobb.

'At last! I thought you'd never get here. We have precisely three hours left to crack the bastard or he walks.'

'You have a DNA match.'

'He now claims it was consensual and Issie was seventeen; so it's disgusting but not a crime.' She passed him a folder.

Fenwick read the interview transcript quickly.

'I'm amazed his brother is funding the best lawyer money can buy given what he's said he did with Issie.'

'He only admitted having sex with her late yesterday evening. I doubt Lord Saxby knows.'

'Interesting,' Fenwick started to smile. 'You made him rattled enough to get a lot of detail from him. That's going to be helpful.'

'Glad you think so; it hasn't done us any good. He's all yours, in interview room three with Box. We're going to observe.'

'I'd like one of you with me for continuity, don't mind which. And I want photos of all the evidence numbered and ready in a folder.'

There was something in his tone that made Bernstein ask, 'Ready for what?'

Fenwick grinned and tapped his nose.

'Never you mind, but I think you're going to enjoy this.'

He squared his shoulders and swung out of the room. Behind his back he heard Cobb ask, 'Is he on something?'

Bazza sat in while he started the interrogation in a slow, polite manner that annoyed Saxby junior, who had clearly been looking forward to an aggressive encounter given that the police were running out of time. However, Fenwick was doing everything by the book. He did not expect answers, let alone the truth, but the interview was visually recorded and he was confident that Saxby would reveal the sort of man he really was. When that happened the prosecution would receive a gift; no jury would be unaffected by his arrogance and disdain for Issie or the law.

'So when did you first have sex with Isabelle Mattias?'

'I've told you lot this already.'

'Tell me, please.'

'It would have been about two months ago.'

'And that was the first time; you are quite sure?'

'Yes.'

'Where did you have sex?'

'I've told you, in my car.'

'Where was your car parked at the time?'

'I can't remember. In woods somewhere.'

Fenwick continued to ask questions, forcing Saxby to elaborate on each time he had what he claimed was consensual sex with Issie. When what he said didn't match his previous answers Fenwick drew attention to the differences. Saxby became increasingly irritated. When he stopped talking Fenwick turned his attention to the folder of photographs on the table between them.

'I am showing the suspect a photograph of a painting labelled Exhibit A.3, by the missing girl, Isabelle Mattias. It shows a man with a gold medallion, matching one worn by him when he was arrested.'

'So what? The girl's clearly obsessed with me.'

Box leant over and whispered in Saxby's ear.

'I am showing the suspect a second painting, Exhibit A.4, by Isabelle Mattias that depicts her being raped by the man who, in the previous photo was wearing the medallion. Do you dispute that the man in this painting looks like you?'

'The girl was fantasising. I can't help it if she's got a warped imagination.'

Box whispered again. Saxby looked irritated and shrugged.

'I am showing the suspect a third photograph of a T-shirt, Exhibit T.1, from which we extracted DNA matching the suspect's own. Do you recognise this T-shirt, Rodney?'

'No.'

'Wouldn't you say it is a summer item of clothing, not really suitable for a winter's assignation in a car?'

'She must have worn it under her jumper. I don't know.'

'I am now showing the suspect a printed album, which will be entered as evidence after this interview, obtained from the Saxby family containing photographs of a sailing holiday in July last year. They were taken by one of the crew who had been charged with making a photographic record of the holiday.'

Saxby twitched and looked away as Fenwick opened the album at a marked page and placed it on the table. The double-page spread contained seven images. The date, time and location of the photos were printed across the top of the pages. In the first picture Issie was sitting alone at the bow of a yacht; in the second she was glaring mutinously at the camera. In the third and fourth she was sitting at a lunch table with her mother and both Saxbys. On the table between them was a meal of prawns, Greek salad, bread, ouzo and wine. In the fifth picture she was in a tender with Rodney Saxby coming towards the yacht; the sixth had her climbing aboard and in the seventh she was standing rigid, eyes wide, staring at the camera.

'You will note, Rodney, that Issie is wearing a T-shirt in the photos I am showing you that is visually similar to the Exhibit T.1. In fact, if you look carefully at the right side on the hem you will see a small tear that is identical. That would suggest it is the same T-shirt.'

Saxby continued to look away but the vein at the side of his forehead was pulsing.

'When we asked our forensic facility to analyse the T-shirt, they not only recovered your and Issie's DNA, they also isolated the following trace evidence: suntan lotion; a breadcrumb fragment; microscopic drops of olive oil and juice from a prawn; specks of charcoal from a barbecue and a splash of tomato juice.

'Please would you take a look at the last photograph in the sequence and then compare the T-shirt Issie is wearing with Exhibit T.1? No, you won't? Then I'll tell you what a comparison shows. A stain in the photo taken on the yacht is identical to that on the T-shirt we have in evidence.'

'This is a stitch-up! That bitch has framed me and you're in on it. You told her what you needed and she Photoshopped it. That's what they've done! Box, get me out of here. This is a travesty of justice.'

'The original SD card for these photos is with all the others at your brother's house, in a safe in his private office. Issie's mother does not have a combination to that safe, only to the family one. Your brother had the album printed immediately on return from the holiday by a supplier they have used for the past two years. A detective is taking a statement from them, which will confirm exactly when the album was commissioned, printed and paid for.

'Every day has a section dedicated to it. When your brother suggested they should skip over the record of when Issie ran away and you found her, his wife disagreed. She needed to work out what had happened to Issie on that holiday, when she turned from a happy, confident teenager to a virtual recluse who hardly spoke. Jane Saxby recognised something had happened on that day and wanted the record of it preserved; mother's instinct you might say.

'Based on the evidence we have in front of us I think we can solve that problem for her. Issie ran away from the yacht, probably as a result of unwanted sexual advances from you. You pursued her to the island where she was hiding and forced her to perform a sexual act, thereby asserting control over her in a way you could use without her mother knowing.'

'Nonsense; this is bullshit. Why would I do that?'

'I can think of reasons. Perhaps you were motivated by desire for Issie, a beautiful, virginal sixteen-year-old; or by the need to hurt Jane Saxby because of your intense jealousy towards her. Having abused Issie sexually, you then brought her back to the yacht.

'This last picture shows a girl in shock, the evidence of abuse fresh on her T-shirt. Here!' Fenwick slapped his hand down over a stain on the front of Issie's shirt.

'NO!'

Box put a restraining hand on his client's shoulder.

'Yes, Rodney. You have lied about when, where, how and why your semen ended up on a seventeen-year-old's clothes and these photographs are categorical proof of that. I am going to leave the pleasure of charging you to my colleagues while I go and inform her parents.'

'You can't do that! These are unfounded allegations, twisted lies concocted by that bitch of a mother.'

'I think we can safely leave that to a court to decide, Rodney.'

As he stepped out of the interview room Fenwick found that he was shaking. Bernstein leapt out of the observation room and hugged him.

'Have I ever told you you're brilliant?'

'No.' He tried to smile but the tension was too much.

'Are you really going to Saxby Hall now?'

He shook his head.

'That's for you and Norman to do. I only said it for effect so that he realised his lifeline to his brother was about to be cut. Go in and charge him. It has to be you. Every detail of this must be done by the book, everything. We cannot let that bastard walk. He abused Issie, virtually driving her into Mariner's arms.'

Bernstein opened the door to the interview suite and walked in, head high.

Cobb was hovering outside the observation room. As Fenwick passed he said, 'Well done, sir.' Fenwick nodded an acknowledgement. 'But if you don't mind me saying, you don't look very happy.'

Fenwick turned heavy eyes to the sergeant briefly before turning away.

'We're no closer to finding Issie, are we, Cobb? No closer at all.'

And with that he walked away.

PART FIVE

'A cold coming they had of it, at this time of year; just the worst time of year to take a journey, and a specially long journey, in. The ways deep, the weather sharp, the days short, the sun farthest off in *solstitio brumali*, the very dead of winter.'

Lancelot Andrewes, 1555–1626

CHAPTER FORTY-SIX

Nightingale was at her desk even though it was the Saturday before Christmas. Big Mac had done a good job of tracing and talking to all the Flash Harry victims in Sussex and had been sweet enough to leave a thank you card from one of them on Nightingale's desk with a yellow Post-it note attached, which read: *This should have been sent to you. You did this. Fancy a celebratory drink sometime? M.*

It was a nice idea. Maybe he was free that evening. She was looking up his mobile number when Alison Whitby walked into the detectives' room unannounced and headed straight for her desk. Nightingale stood up.

'Sit down, sit down.' Whitby's voice sounded as if she still had a cold and she looked pale. 'I came to thank you for standing in for me on Wednesday.'

'It was no problem, ma'am.'

'It's Alison, remember? Have you got a minute? There was something I wanted to talk to you about.'

'Of course.'

Nightingale stood up and walked towards the stairs. As she opened the fire door, Whitby said.

'Let's go and have a bite to eat, shall we?'

Harlden no longer ran to a fully staffed canteen but there was a kitchen to which hot food was delivered two or three times a day, depending on demand. As they walked in, Nightingale smelt pies, pasties and soup. Whitby chose a sausage roll while Nightingale put a carton of tomato soup in the microwave. A uniformed constable waltzed in whistling, did a double take and about-turned.

Whitby grinned and closed the door.

'As soon as they know I'm in here we won't be disturbed.'

Nightingale smiled uncertainly.

'I've had Acting Chief Constable Harper-Brown on the phone,' she said, peeling the plastic wrap off the roll.

'Oh yes?' Nightingale fussed over finding a spoon.

Whitby waited patiently for her to sit down, chewing quietly.

'He's impressed; it doesn't happen that often.'

'By what, ma'am . . . er, Alison?'

'You; why else would I be talking to you? The way you insisted on following up on Flash Harry, even when it went to MCS; your attention to Jenni as a witness—'

Victim, she thought.

'—and the fact that you've had MacDonald following up to inform the victims on our patch. The chairman of the PCC had a call from one family to thank him, and the victim support group is impressed for once. It all reflects very well on the boss.'

'That's good to know, but Mac did all the hard work.'

'That's as may be but you were the SIO.'

'Original SIO,' she corrected.

'Yes, well poor old Andrew hasn't come out of it too well.'

Nightingale pushed the remains of over half her soup to one side.

'You should eat some more, Louise; you're losing weight.'

'I'll eat properly later, thanks. Why is Superintendent Fenwick not being credited with Flash Harry?'

'Because you made the arrest and insisted the girl Jenni was watched day and night.'

She hadn't put that last part in her arrest statement. Someone must have told H-B.

'Big Mac was working for him when he did all the legwork with the victims,' she insisted.

'Yes, but Andrew made sure H-B knew it was you who had ordered him to do it, just as he mentioned having Rogers stay with Jenni had been down to you as well.'

'That's decent of him.'

'It is; particularly as he needed the kudos himself.'

Nightingale felt uncomfortable talking about Fenwick. And why was Whitby on first-name terms with him?

'I can see I'm embarrassing you so I'll stop, but I thought you should know and I wanted to say well done in person.'

'Thank you.'

Nightingale stood up.

'There's one more thing.'

She sat down again.

'I know you're prepared to work across Christmas, Louise, but I honestly don't think there's much point. Stanley Turner is in custody pending his trial. The paperwork for that is well advanced, as it always is with you, and Jenni is out of hospital.'

'She is?' Nightingale raised her eyebrows in surprise. 'Milky was meant to call me. That's great.'

'Don't be hard on him. He's probably at home getting some sleep. He was the one who persuaded her to talk.'

'Will she be going home now?'

'The shelter is prepared to let her stay there over Christmas and no one from social services was around to disagree. After Christmas things might change but for now she's where she wants to be, or so I'm told.' Nightingale smiled with relief. 'So you might as well take the chance to have some time off. There's simply no reason to wreck your Christmas. I have sufficient cover for the period without you.'

'It doesn't feel right. I'd volunteered to come in.'

Whitby nodded.

'I know; I would feel the same but take my advice: when you have a lucky break seize it because there'll be plenty of times when it works the other way. If anything comes up or a new lead develops on Stanley, Operations will let you know. In the meantime, go home and be with your family.'

Nightingale decided not to argue. There was just one errand that she had to do and then she would go back to her flat and let her brother know the good news. After that she'd see if she could track down Big Mac.

The front door of the shelter was brightened by a holly wreath and there was a decorated Christmas tree in the hall. The woman who ran it recognised Nightingale and shook her hand warmly.

'Jenni's not here, I'm afraid. She went out as soon as she had washed and changed, even though I told her she should take it easy.' She sounded resigned rather than angry. 'Is that present for her? That's a kind thought; I hope she appreciates it.'

Nightingale placed the gift under the tree and left with a heavy heart. Jenni should have been recuperating but she was so headstrong – literally! Despite her best efforts, she suspected that Jenni did not want to be saved and, if anything, resented her continued interest. Her only hope was that common sense would eventually prevail. Nightingale made a determined effort not to think about Jenni and by the time she reached home had almost succeeded.

CHAPTER FORTY-SEVEN

He woke to the smell of cooking bacon and faint noises from the kitchen. It evoked an amazingly satisfying and contented feeling that lasted until reality returned. He pushed it away, eyes shut tight against the day. For once he had slept well and woken naturally and he willed the moment of contentment to last.

'Breakfast in ten minutes!'

There were worse summons to the day.

The forecast was for sunshine and continued bitter cold. Fenwick showered quickly and dressed warmly with vest, brushed-cotton shirt and jumper, long johns and thick cord trousers. He might have been preparing to help Chris with his snowman as his son undoubtedly hoped but his motives were unclear, even to himself.

'It's on the table!' His mother's voice took him back thirty years.

It didn't do to be late but he was last to arrive. Even Bess was there, looking rumpled.

'For what we are about to receive may the Lord make us truly thankful, amen.' There was a ripple of 'amens' around the table and then the clatter of knives and forks as five hungry people tucked into a cooked breakfast.

'So will you be coming to church with us? Andrew?'

'Church?'

'It's Sunday, Daddy; Christmas Eve,' Chris reminded him with a smile embellished by tomato ketchup.

'I may have to do a little work, I'm afraid.'

'Today?' Bess looked at him appalled.

'It's only a maybe,' he prevaricated.

'Well that's something, at least,' his mother remarked and raised an eyebrow.

Alice, bless her, concentrated on dunking toast in her fried egg.

'What time is the service?'

'Ten o'clock but we'll be leaving early as it will be hard to park if we're late. The church is bound to be full. So we'll need to leave in an hour. You'll be taking us, son, to save Alice that miserable drive.'

He retreated to his study while they cleared the breakfast things away and logged on to view the newspapers online. For some reason he decided to look at the *Sunday Enquirer*, not a paper he normally bothered to read.

'FAILURE!'

The headline screamed above a full-width picture of Issie. Fenwick tasted egg at the back of his throat and swallowed hard. Saxby was wreaking his revenge against the investigation as he had promised. He opened the next page, holding his breath, to see an unflattering picture of Bernstein with CC Norman. The tone of the reporting was overwhelmingly critical. Despite himself, he felt some relief that he wasn't criticised. In fact, the one passing mention of his name was in the only positive paragraph in the full-page piece.

There was no way Norman would ever forgive him, let alone allow him back on the case. He might as well accept it and move on. Except that, of course, that was impossible with Issie still missing. There would be no peace in his life until she was found. With a shudder he realised that she might never be and that he would have to live with that. How?

'Come on, Andrew,' his mother's voice penetrated the closed door, 'time for church!'

Peter Wilson felt terrible. On Tuesday afternoon he'd taken to his bed with flu and only now did he feel well enough to try and get dressed. His wife hadn't been around to look after him as she was staying with her mother for a week in lieu of the old bat coming for Christmas. She hadn't been in the least sympathetic to his moans and coughs down the phone as he complained that he was ill, no really, not just a cold but with a proper temperature, aches, everything. In response she had directed him to paracetamol in the medicine cabinet and told him to drink plenty of fluids. Five miserable days later he had lost half a stone and his tongue felt like dried out chamois leather.

He was in glazing: repairing and replacing, the latter being the most lucrative. Fortunately business was pretty quiet this close to Christmas so he had been able to postpone the few appointments he had until January but he was worried about his car. The Land Rover was parked over the road by the garage as his cottage didn't have a parking space. When the snow had returned on Wednesday he had been even more concerned for it, left for days now in freezing temperatures.

Peter had rung Wilf, his mate who ran the petrol station, to ask him to check on his car but he was off sick himself and there was only the Gormless Kid on duty. As well to ask a snowman as that boy; if he had anything between his ears it had melted long ago.

So Peter was worried and maybe he was starting to feel just a little bit better. For the first time in days he was peckish but the fridge was on hunger strike. What he really fancied was a toasted bacon butty, with brown sauce, and perhaps a fried egg. At eight o'clock, after a brief chat on the phone with the missus who clearly thought he was well enough to fend for himself,

Peter had a shower, found some warm clothes in the airing cupboard and made himself a cup of tea with long-life milk. He hated the processed flavour but it was better than nothing. His knees felt wobbly and his head was inclined to spin if he moved too quickly but he had good shoes, a proper fleece-lined coat, and it was only a couple of minutes across the road to the garage and their well-stocked cold cabinet.

Outside the air froze his tonsils.

'Bloody Norah!'

He wrapped his scarf around his face and held on to the fence as he eased his way down the path and out of the gate. The road had been gritted but there was a pile of snow over a foot deep at the kerb that he had to clamber through in order to cross, repeating the exercise on the other side.

'If I fall over and die it'll be on your head, Mary,' he muttered as he slid his way towards the petrol station with its twenty-four-hour promise of service.

As he skidded to a halt in front of the window he saw the Gormless Kid behind the till chatting to some overweight teen who should have been at home exercising or helping her mum.

'Hello, Mr Wilson,' the GK boomed as he entered, the bell announcing his arrival. 'Did you see the storm last week? Me and Avril was saying it was like being in the Arctic – so cold, and the wind . . . it was terrible, wasn't it, Avril?'

Avril's indifference to conversation with anyone outside her generation was world class.

Peter grunted in reply and headed for the refrigerated cabinet. There they were, the beauties: smoked back rashers still within their sell-by date, butter and some eggs. All he needed now was fresh milk, bread, some tomatoes and maybe a Mars bar for later. He carried the pile to the checkout and waited while Avril decided to move her bulk to one side.

'Nine pounds and ten pence, thanks, Mr Wilson.' The GK

placed the breakfast collection into a plastic bag with care as Peter found a note and coin.

'Don't suppose you noticed if my car is all right, did you?'

The GK looked at him dumbly.

'My car, the one I always leave in the car park?'

An expression close to guilt flickered across the GK's face; Avril frowned.

'He's not a bleeding parking attendant, y'know.'

'I know, I know.' Peter's head was starting to ache. All he wanted was to get back home. Thoughts of breakfast had been replaced with an aching tiredness behind his eyes, but still, he was here and if he didn't check on the car he would only worry about it later.

'Only, I've been ill with the flu. Would you mind, I mean . . .'

'Sorry, Mr Wilson, I can't leave the till, not allowed to.'

Peter turned towards Avril who regarded him with twelve stone of contempt.

'No way; I'm delicate, I am.'

He searched her face for irony, found only belligerent sincerity and suppressed a shudder.

'OK, it was only an idea. Hang on to this lot, would you?' He contemplated suggesting they should check on him if he wasn't back in five minutes but took another look at her face and thought better of it.

He stepped out of the side door that led to the parking lot. It wasn't that big and he knew where he had left his car: two rows to the left under the hedge where it would have some protection from the weather. The surface of the car park hadn't been gritted and Peter had to concentrate to keep his balance. The first row was empty; the second had a trailer parked across two bays and a Ford, thick with snow beside it. His Land Rover should have been just beyond that.

Except that it wasn't. The space where he had left it was empty apart from three inches of pristine snow, as were the spaces to the right and left. There was no car to be seen.

'I don't believe it, who'd pinch a ten-year-old Land Rover?'

Peter plodded closer, stopped on the edge of the space where he was sure he had left his car and turned a full circle. No; the car had gone. In fact, other than the trailer and Mondeo the lot was deserted. Peter groaned and trudged back to the garage.

'My car's gone.'

'It's not his fault!'

'I know, all I'm saying is it's gone. Can you call the police? I need to report it, otherwise the insurance is invalid.'

In the end he called himself, the GK and Avril having decided that it was none of their business and not interesting enough to text their friends about. Peter went home while he waited for the police to arrive. Fortified by a strong cup of tea with a tot of rum in it, hunger took over again and he had a fry-up while he waited, which was just as well as it took almost an hour for the lazy buggers to bother to turn up. What he didn't realise was that if Surrey constabulary hadn't put a notice out asking for all reported vehicle thefts to be treated with priority in case they were linked to Isabelle Mattias's disappearance he could have been waiting until after Christmas.

Peter led the lanky constable into the front room and made some fresh tea out of habit; his wife was always nice to visitors and he had been with her long enough to wear away some of his misanthropy.

'So you're sure it's gone, absolutely sure?'

'Course I am, otherwise I wouldn't have called you.'

'No way you could have parked it elsewhere?'

'No.' Peter bit his tongue.

'And you parked it over there?' The constable gestured with his notebook towards the garage opposite. He looked bored and keen to be gone.

'Yes, always in the same space.'

'So it couldn't be somewhere else, maybe round the corner or behind other cars?'

Peter sighed, loudly.

'No, like I said, it wasn't where I left it and apart from Walter's old trailer and a Ford Mondeo the car park is empty.'

'Ford Mondeo?' There was a flicker of interest in the lad's eyes for the first time.

'No, my car's a Land Rover.'

'Four-wheel drive, I expect.'

To Peter's surprise the constable actually wrote something in his book.

'Yes, and in good nick.' He decided not to mention the rust, thinking of the insurance.

'Can you show me exactly where it was parked, sir?'

'What, go outside again? I've not been well, you know.'

'If you could just point me in the right direction, then?'

Peter pulled back the lace curtain and watched the policeman cross the road.

'Well that's more than I expected.' He was almost impressed.

After forty minutes waiting for him to return Peter cleared the tea things away and found his Mars bar. The sound of a siren disturbed him and he jumped up in time to see an unmarked car skid into the side of the road beside the garage, lights flashing. Ten minutes later another one appeared together with a white van.

'All this for my car?' Peter scratched his head; something wasn't quite right.

There was a knock at his door and when he opened it he stepped back in surprise as three people crowded on his step.

'Mr . . .' A woman about his wife's age paused in the act of remembering his name.

'Wilson,' he said. 'It was only a Land Rover, you know; not that I don't miss it, of course, and I'll have to claim for another.'

'Might we come in, Mr Wilson? My name is Superintendent Bernstein, Surrey Constabulary.' She was inside the hall before he could ask her to remove her shoes.

'We'll only take a few minutes of your time, sir. Can you tell me when you last saw your car?'

'I parked it like normal on Monday evening.'

'You're sure it was Monday?'

'Positive. My wife left for her mother's on Tuesday morning and I started to feel rough right after. I haven't been out of the house since until today.'

'Thank you.' She finished writing a brief note in her book and snapped it shut. 'That fits,' she said to the man who had come in with her. 'Cobb, you start things off at the garage, I've got a call to make.'

She headed off without saying goodbye and the others trailed after her. Peter looked at the wet grit on the carpet and went to find the vacuum cleaner.

Fenwick was sitting on his own at the back of the coffee shop, a copy of the *Sunday Enquirer* in front of him. They had arrived ridiculously early at the church and he had refused to wait inside when he could be enjoying a proper espresso. He had thirty minutes before he should join them, which meant he could fit in a dash of Christmas shopping if he forewent another espresso.

He descended on the first department store he came across like a locust and bought all but his mother's present before moving to the shop next door, where he was queuing at the checkout when his mobile rang.

'Fenwick, it's Deidre. We've located the Mondeo.'

Fenwick almost dropped his purchase but the helpful young lady on the till caught it and scanned the code.

'Where?' He rummaged in his wallet for his credit card, phone jammed beneath his jaw.

'On the A27 west of Lewes.'

'Lewes! What on earth was he doing there? Never mind, tell me what you have so far.'

He punched in his pin and mouthed thank you to the assistant.

'It is definitely Mariner's car and he could now be driving a Land Rover that has just been reported missing. He might have swapped cars anytime between last Monday and Wednesday, when we had the very heavy snow. There were no tracks or footprints other than the owner's around the Mondeo. Unfortunately the CCTV tapes are reused every forty-eight hours so although we're checking them we don't anticipate much.

'The crime scene manager is already on site and I'm expecting him to report back soon. In fact, hang on . . .' there was a rustle and the sound of her muffled voice.

'Sorry about that, he just came in with a receipt from the garage that they've found in the boot of the car. It's dated and timed for three twenty-two last Tuesday. He bought petrol, a few groceries . . . some cigarettes, nothing else.'

'So the Mondeo's been sitting there since and no one spotted it. You wait until I speak to Sussex RTC!' He was walking out of the store fast, oblivious of the curious looks around him.

'Andrew, the car is parked behind the garage; no one could have seen it from the road.'

'Exactly the sort of place they should have checked.'

'You can't expect them to search every parking space between Guildford and the coast.'

'That's precisely what I would have expected. Five days that bastard has on us and we've no idea where he went after he swapped cars.'

If Bernstein noted his proprietary interest she ignored it.

'The Land Rover index is already with ANPR and we have a team reviewing highway CCTV footage from Tuesday onwards. We might be in luck if he went east, as the A27 has some of the most sophisticated cameras around the junction with the A26 to Newhaven; it's considered a high-risk junction.'

'I appreciate the call. If there's anything at all I can do . . .' Fenwick had walked back to his car while talking.

'It's Christmas Eve, Andrew. You have young kids. At least my mum's at her sister's.'

'This is the first break in over a week, Deidre . . .'

'And if the Conqueror knew you're still hanging around Operation Goldilocks he'd have a fit.'

'He still doesn't know?' Fenwick was struggling to open the hatchback one-handed. 'Hang on a sec.'

He loaded the bags inside and opened the driver's door, immediately switching on the ignition and slotting his phone into hands-free.

'Back again; you were saying, Norman has no idea that we're in touch? How did you keep it secret for this long?'

'I have my methods, and anyway, he's not someone people confide in.'

'Does that mean I could come and join you and still be under the radar?'

'Anything you choose to do in your own time is your affair so far as I'm concerned. Young Tate has asked me the same question. He seems to have caught your bug and is as obsessed as you are.'

'I am not obsessed.'

'I'm only repeating popular opinion. Look, I'm going to text you where we are; what you do next is up to you.'

After he had rung off, Fenwick noticed he had a missed call and pressed redial.

'Good morning, sir!' Tate's excitement was like a jolt of electricity. 'Have you heard? I've just been speaking with Bazza and—'

'Yes, Tate, I have. Good news, isn't it!'

'Absolutely; it's why I'm on my way to you now. I thought

maybe we could take a drive over Lewes way.'

'Did you indeed, and where are you?'

'Less than five miles north of Harlden, sir.'

'Perfect, come straight to the town centre main car park, you'll find me there.'

Fenwick locked the car, sent Alice a text and walked quickly to the church, where his housekeeper was waiting at the rear door looking concerned.

'I have to go, Alice,' he explained. 'Take the children and mother home. Here are the keys and this is where I parked the car.'

He handed her the parking ticket with the floor and bay number written on it. Without letting her ask any questions he kissed the top of her head and left. As he waited in front of the car park Fenwick called Bazza.

'Do you have the list of addresses connected with Issie's disappearance? The ones you were rechecking?'

'Yes; they've all been revisited and nothing's come up; why?'

'I want you to identify those closest to Lewes; go out in an expanding circle around the town and call me back.'

Tate pulled up and Fenwick jumped in with barely a hello.

On the A24 south of Harlden traffic was reduced to a single lane because of ice and snow. Bazza called him as traffic inched forward.

'There are five addresses within ten miles of Lewes, sir. Two are the homes of friends Issie has stayed with or visited. Both can be ruled out as the families are at home and there's no way Issie could be hidden there, unless they were in cahoots with Mariner and that is very unlikely. One address belongs to the uncle of a friend who travels a lot and is away. The house was checked yesterday and is empty.'

'It needs to be revisited anyway.'

'Really . . .' There was a hesitation and then, 'Yes, of course.

As for the other two, one is a centre for music where Issie sang in the county choir. It's a sprawling country house, with a lot of outbuildings and it's shut for the holidays. The local police say they did a thorough search but I guess you'll want that redone also?'

'Yes; and the last address?'

'Issie's grandmother's; she's away in Australia visiting her other daughter and family. Again, the place was rechecked on Friday but we'll have someone sent again just to be sure.'

'Good; can you email me the addresses?'

'They're on the way.'

As Tate made his way southwards Fenwick opened the maps application on his phone and entered the location of the garage where Mariner's car had been found, then, one by one, the postcodes of the addresses Bazza had just sent him but it was painfully slow.

'Have you got a map of east Sussex and Kent, Sergeant?'

'No sir.'

'Stop at the first garage and buy one, would you?'

Fifteen minutes later Fenwick had marked the garage and all the locations on a large-scale map of the area around Lewes. None of them looked more promising than the others. Bernstein rang to say that a POLSA team from East Sussex had arrived and were organising a full search of the area surrounding the garage in case Issie's body had been dumped when Mariner changed car. An incident room had been set up in Lewes and the acting CC of West Sussex was extending every help to Surrey.

'We're doing a house-to-house in case anyone saw Mariner or the car. So far there's no CCTV that's useful. I have unlimited officers available to do whatever we ask of them, but where to begin? Oh, and the weather forecast has changed; we're due snow. Apparently the Met Office underestimated the speed the bad weather would hit us. That's going to be a big help.'

'As you have the resources, you might as well follow up on the addresses Bazza has.'

'That's already in hand and I've also got the team back in Guildford double-checking whether Mariner or his wife has any connection with this area. Where are you?'

'About to join what looks like a horrendous traffic jam on the A272. No idea when we'll be with you but I'll keep you posted.'

Tate turned on the blues and twos as they forced their way onto the main road. Their speed edged up to thirty, and then forty as a path cleared. Ahead of them clouds started to appear on the eastern horizon.

CHAPTER FORTY-EIGHT

The patient was tucked up in bed with a towel and bucket handy just in case he was sick, though he had eaten nothing since the previous day's breakfast.

'Issie!'

'Yes, Steve, I'm here.' Issie walked into the bedroom carrying clean bedding. 'If you can manage to get to the bathroom I'll change the bed. We can't have you sleeping in it messed up like that.'

Steve flushed, whether from embarrassment or anger she couldn't tell but that no longer mattered as he was incapable of violence. Still, she reacted as if cowed, head down, shoulders shrugged in protectively; she absolutely could not afford to be tied up, not now.

They were without electricity as the generator had just run out of diesel but so far the house was warm enough thanks to the Aga and open fire. Steve hobbled to the main bathroom where Issie had already run him a bath, topping up the tepid water in the tank with kettlefuls from the kitchen. On the chair were clean pyjamas and a new dressing gown her grandfather had never got to wear.

By the time Steve was back in the bedroom the bed was made and there were two hot-water bottles warming the sheets. The more warm and comfortable he was the less likely he would be to get up and prowl. Steve hugged a bottle to his stomach and groaned.

'Still bad?'

'Cramps, all the time.'

'Do you want to take some painkillers? Maybe a hot water and whisky would help?'

'I'll try anything. Just want it to stop.'

Issie brought up a hot toddy and two junior aspirins; he wouldn't know they weren't full strength and she was worried about giving him anything stronger. In the drink she had mixed another sleeping tablet. As he swallowed she forced herself not to stare.

'Let's hope that helps. Come to bed, Issie. We'll keep warmer the two of us.'

'I just need to have a wash and I'll be right back.'

Outside the bedroom Issie changed into the layers of clothing she had prepared for her journey: a silk camisole; long-sleeved woollen vest of her grandfather's that was too big but exactly what she needed. Over that went a high-collared shirt. A cashmere cardigan and fleece were hidden downstairs. She stepped into the long johns she had found; then she pulled up long hiking socks. Her only real problem was trousers. None of her grandmother's were the right material and the best she could find were some thick jeans. If it started to snow, not that the forecast had predicted any, her legs would soon become wet and she would run the risk of hypothermia.

She looked in on Steve. He was lying on his back snoring loudly. If he was sick like that he would choke on his own vomit. Despite everything he had done to her Issie didn't want to be responsible for his death. She knelt on the bed and rolled him into the recovery position, making sure his head was at the right angle to keep his airway open. It was time to go but she hesitated. He was sleeping deeply; his face relaxed into a half smile. Disgusted at herself, she left the room without looking back.

Outside the house Issie made slower progress than she had expected. Her muscles were sore from the beating and stiff from a fortnight of inactivity. With gritted teeth she pushed herself to find the stride and a rhythm that minimised discomfort. It wouldn't be for long, she told herself. According to Steve's watch it was half past twelve when she left, later than she had hoped but she had been forced to wait until she persuaded him to drink the toddy. She wasn't concerned. The sun was still shining despite a distant smudge of cloud; there was plenty of daylight ahead and she had known the footpath since childhood. There was a slightly shorter route north, along a narrow track that would have taken her to Alciston but she would have to navigate a steep slope down Bostal Hill, which was tricky in anything but good conditions. Looking at the snow piled high along the South Downs Way she made an easy decision to stick to the path she knew.

As she walked Issie kept an eye on the purple-black clouds gathering along the north-east horizon. This wasn't the weather they had promised on the radio before the power cut and Issie was uncomfortable. If it hadn't been for the blizzard warning for the following day she would have considered going back and keeping Steve drugged for another twenty-four hours, but knowing conditions the next day would only worsen she pressed on.

She forced herself up the steep slope of Bostal Hill. This would be the worst part of the journey so better to push on through it. Her legs continued to ache and her shoulders were soon sore from the backpack but she ignored the discomfort and concentrated instead on keeping the path markers in sight, her only means of finding and sticking to the South Downs Way. The snow was deep, sometimes over wellington boot height and she started to worry that her jeans were getting wet. No matter how carefully she stepped, the fabric about her knees grew damp.

The change of weather announced its arrival gently with a whispering rustle, a teasing patter of sleet against brittle branches.

Issie was too intent on keeping her footing as she walked downhill towards New Pond to notice. The sun was still free of clouds, making her squint against the blinding white snow and casting disorientating elongated shadows wherever a tree or fence post poked above its pristine purity. She paused and looked up. Heavy clouds were massing to blot out the sun. They hadn't yet arrived above her so that she had the sense of being suspended between two worlds of chill light and dark cold.

Issie returned her eyes to the track, barely a subtle depression in the snow. She couldn't afford to become distracted by the eerie beauty of the Downs around her. The first icy gust of wind on her cheek went unnoticed, though she pulled up the collar of the Barbour unconsciously. It was the persistent rattle that made her stop and look around; there it was again, an irritated rustle that demanded attention. Her eyes tracked the sound to its source: to the north side of the track a solitary, stunted beech was shaking the remnants of its wizened foliage at her. The shock of burnt chocolate-brown in the otherwise monochrome landscape made Issie smile with pleasure, her artist's inspiration engaged despite her vulnerability.

'Silly old tree.' She reached over and patted its bark as she passed.

Twenty yards later she came across a footpath sign, one finger pointing back over her shoulder towards Bostal Hill, the other down the path she was following, directing her to Alfriston in one and a quarter miles.

'I can manage that.' She spoke out loud and with conviction; it made her feel better.

All the precautions she had taken: the rucksack on her back packed with first-aid kit, change of clothes, food, warm drink, water, wax-dipped matches, candle tin, kindling, pre-cut lengths of string – even bin liners against the wet – all of it banging insistently between her shoulder blades as she marched onwards would be unnecessary, she told herself. She was a drama queen to prepare like that when her goal was so close.

She was fifteen minutes into her journey already and would reach safety soon, well before the weather turned really bad. It was freezing cold, to be sure, and her nose and cheeks were stinging from the wind but it was nothing to worry about dressed as she was. Issie took a bite of chocolate and adjusted the shoulder straps to settle the pack more comfortably. Behind her the beech leaves' death rattle was whipped away on the stiffening breeze and she retreated into her own world.

Her toes were warm inside the wellingtons but her legs were starting to be a problem. Her jeans were soaked up to the bottom of her jacket. Despite thermal long johns her knee joints were achingly cold and the wet wool scratched the sensitive skin of her inner thighs. Issie stepped carefully through a particularly deep drift as the path descended, keeping her legs slightly apart to reduce the chafing that was making her sore. Ahead of her the tops of fence posts were still visible above the snowdrifts, guiding her way. The sight should have been comforting but something about it disturbed her.

As she tramped forwards she puzzled. What was worrying her; what was wrong? When she reached the next post she paused and touched it to make sure it was really there. Any excuse to rest her legs. They were tiring quickly as she had to step so high through the deep snow.

'No shadows,' she said at last and looked up.

The sun had finally been swallowed up and with it the landscape lost perspective, lacking both depth and sense of distance. The clouds seemed to brush the top of the tumuli on Bostal Hill. Issie took a deep breath and set off again. Never mind the wet jeans and discomfort, she would be warm and dry soon. Alfriston wasn't far and if she remembered correctly there was a hotel to the west before the village, close to the South Downs Way.

Even if that was shut, there were other houses and the church, St Andrew's, clustered around the green that her grandfather had always called the Tye.

Thinking of him and the church brought back memories of the midnight service with her parents and grandparents before her father had died. It made her smile even as the snow started. She stopped to catch her breath and looked behind her. The new fall was beginning to cover her tracks. If by some bad luck Steve had woken up and decided to venture out in search of her, very soon there would be no trace left for him to follow.

For a while after the snow started Issie managed to maintain the same pace but then the fall became so dense as to almost suffocate her and she found it hard to breathe. It was driving straight into her but she had no option other than to keep going. When she tried walking backwards to protect her face from the skin-flaying wind she almost fell over and had to turn back, reluctantly, into the storm, scarf pulled up high over her mouth and nose.

The snow was settling fast, adding another layer on top of the existing covering. Black clouds darkened the day to premature twilight, making it hard for her to see and keep to the path. Should she turn back? She must be near the midpoint of her journey and to return would take almost as long as to press on. Alfriston had to be less than a mile away now. All she needed to do was keep on the track between the fence posts and she would be fine. There was no need to panic. Yet she felt a cold worm of apprehension twist in her stomach. This weather could kill even so close to safety.

'Stupid.' The sound of her own voice gave her courage and she straightened her shoulders ready to confront the next blast in her face. She recalled Pappy's advice culled from his service days: '*Do you know what the most important survival tool is?*' he had once asked her. She hadn't been able to guess and he had tapped his head in answer: '*This, your brain; mind, willpower, call it what you will. To survive you must first* decide *to survive.*' She was definitely going to survive!

'*Good King Wenceslaus last looked out / On the feast of Stephen / When the snow lay round about / Deep and crisp and even . . .*' Issie sang in a true contralto, marching in time to the verse. '*In his master's steps he trod / Where the snow lay . . .* Ow!'

Without warning she found herself twisted uncomfortably on the ground. She raised herself up on an elbow, shaking her head to clear it.

'What the . . . ?' Her left foot was tangled in something that had been concealed beneath the snow, strong enough to snare her. She sat up, feeling icy water seep through the seat of her jeans and brushed the snow clear of her trapped foot. Twisted around it was a long strand of barbed wire angry as a bramble. The thickness of her boot had protected her from its barbs but she couldn't free her foot no matter how hard she pulled.

Reluctantly she removed her right glove and started to tease the wire away from the rubber ankle. It took several minutes and her fingers had gone numb but at last she managed to lift her foot away and stand up. She tested her ankle carefully but nothing seemed to be damaged. At least she hadn't hurt herself, but from the waist down she was soaked through and quickly losing all sense of feeling.

The change of clothes she had with her didn't seem so stupid after all. Issie looked around for somewhere to shelter but the wire fences offered no protection. At least she had had the presence of mind to put the bin liners on top to keep everything else dry. She pulled one of them out and placed it on the ground in the depression made by her fall. The wind whipped it away before she could catch it so she had to use a second one, planting her foot on top quickly and then the heavy rucksack. Dry jeans, long johns, knickers and socks were together in a plastic bag. She didn't take them out in case they too blew away but sorted them into order within the pack.

She managed to pull off her boots without falling over. The jeans and socks came next. Her legs were an alarming colour, a sort of blotched scarlet that contrasted with the bleached white of her toes. Despite the cold, Issie knew she had to dry herself and used a spare shirt to do so. Her teeth were chattering alarmingly by the time she pulled on layers of fresh clothes as fast as her fumbling fingers would allow. She grew desperate as she tried to cover up quickly before the snow soaked her new clothing. The soft dry wool of the long johns was comforting; the jeans when she dragged them on blissfully warm. She managed to slide her feet into her boots while keeping the new socks dry and she immediately felt better.

Issie was bundling the wet clothes into the bin liner but then thought; why bother? They were useless now and would weigh her down. '*Never discard clothing.*'

'But Pappy, they're heavy.'

Still, she did as his silent urging insisted and packed them away, making sure to keep the bin liners on top. As she was about to lace up the pack she had an idea; why not use two bin liners like puttees about her knees? It took her several minutes but Issie managed to wrap the liners into eighteen-inch protective barriers from mid wellington boot up to mid thigh, securing them with some of the lengths of string from her kit.

She slung the pack on her back and squared her shoulders ready to stride out . . . but which way? In the confusion of the fall and re-dressing she had lost her direction of travel . . . and her footprints had vanished. Her schoolgirl compass was in her pocket and she pulled it out to find north. The direction finder pointed behind her but that couldn't be right. She changed position and tried again. The pointer didn't move and she realised it was stuck fast, useless. Issie threw it away in disgust.

There were no shadows to guide her, only the biting wind that had previously been in her face, hitting the left side more than the right. Using it as the only means of navigation she set out. After a few minutes she realised she was going up hill; was that right? Hadn't the track been descending before she fell? But if she turned around how could she be certain she was going in the correct direction? She was on the South Downs Way after all, famous for its undulating meander. No, it was better to keep going.

It was hard to see the path and the fence posts no longer stood out clearly from the snow. Had she lost so much time freeing herself and changing? Surely not, it was just the bad weather closing in. She had no watch because she hadn't dared take Steve's in case he woke up. Thinking of him made her feel uneasy.

The wind was really moaning now, a melancholy howl like a lost dog seeking company. It buffeted her hood and isolated her from all other sound so that it was some time before she heard the rattling. Looking up into the gloom Issie could see a shape on the path ahead and her stomach flipped. Had he come to get her? She almost turned and ran but what was the point? Instead she stood her ground and waited. The shape didn't come any nearer so she walked forward cautiously until she could see the outline of a stunted beech – not any beech tree but the one she had passed before.

'No! NO! That's not fair!' Issie wiped angry tears from her cheeks before they could freeze.

She set her mouth in a thin line and turned one hundred and eighty degrees. Even allowing for an hour of wasted time if couldn't be later than two o'clock. Despite the growing dark, she had less than a mile and a quarter to go. She *would* do this.

The snow was falling as thick as a curtain as she walked and slipped back down the hill, staying near the fence posts to avoid the snare of barbed wire. The drifts were deeper but it was preferable to falling over again. Issie tried singing another carol but her heart wasn't in it so she started counting her paces silently, muttering a satisfied *yes!* every time she passed another one hundred. There was a sudden extreme gust of wind that blew off the hood of her Barbour, forcing her to stop and refasten the soaking cord. She looked up at the sky as she did so, tilting her head right back.

Above her black clouds were spreading like an angry bruise from the north-east, tracking fast and low, carrying yet more snow. This wasn't meant to happen until tomorrow! The weatherman had said light snow showers with the *threat* of blizzard conditions in the north. He had been explicit: '*If you have to travel get it out of the way,*' he'd said, '*and make sure you have plenty of provisions in your store cupboard!*'

That was why she had made her plans for today; there was meant to be a break in the weather but they had been wrong. This must be the predicted blizzard; the worst of the winter so far, arriving twenty-four hours early. Why had she trusted the Met Office? She would have to speed up. Alfriston might be less than an hour away but so was the worst of the storm by the look of it and when that arrived she might be forced to seek shelter. The thought made her shiver despite the sweat of exertion and fear on her back.

Woodsmoke. Andy Parker was dozing on the sofa in front of the fire dreaming of woodsmoke. Except that his fire was electric and his cold – which was flu, really, whatever the wife said – meant that he couldn't smell anything, but still the memory of woodsmoke woke him.

'Feeling better?' His wife looked up from the present she was wrapping far more elaborately than was necessary.

'Ndoh, feel awful,' and he coughed wetly to prove it.

'You could have another Lemsip if you want; it's been more than four hours.'

'I dink a whisky and ginger would be bedder.'

'It's too early for Grandma's remedy!'

'Whad dime is id?' he asked looking at the gloom outside.

'Two o'clock.'

'Oh?' He looked at her in confusion.

'It's the blizzard, it's arrived early; that's why it's so dark. Have a Lemsip now and you could still have a whisky later.'

But he wasn't listening. As he settled back on the cushions he felt a deep unease and guilt for no apparent reason. He closed his eyes and within a minute was asleep again.

CHAPTER FORTY-NINE

The really heavy snow started as Fenwick arrived at the mobile incident unit that blocked access to the garage car park. The satnav told him they were on the A27 east of Beddingham, which was as well as there was no view of anything from within the car. Tate had been smart enough to find a four-wheel-drive vehicle and had navigated the stationary traffic and icy conditions, siren blaring, with consummate skill.

Bernstein had decided to keep a core team on site as they had no idea in which direction Mariner had gone and roads in and out of Lewes were bound to be congested. As the van was bitterly cold most of the team were in the garage itself, squeezed into the storeroom at the back. When he opened the door he saw Bazza Holland hunched over his phone, his nose an inch from the screen.

'You'll wreck your eyesight, Baz,' he said as he poured some coffee from a thermos and picked up a fruit biscuit. They hadn't stopped for lunch.

'Look at this,' Bazza was too excited to worry about formality, 'here; I think it's the Land Rover. It's just been sent over from traffic surveillance. The image is timed at sixteen-o-two last Tuesday on the A27 three miles to the east of Beddingham.'

'Which is where exactly?'

'Here.' Bernstein stood up and pulled out one of several 1:50,000 scale Ordnance Survey maps that were stacked on a box of digestive biscuits.

Fenwick could feel the sour taste of adrenalin on his tongue.

'Where does he go after that?'

'Don't know, sir,' Bazza flinched at the look he received, 'that's the only sighting so far . . .' he hesitated, 'and in the bad weather we can't be absolutely sure it's the same Land Rover. The number plate is partially obscured.'

'Have someone enhance the image urgently,' he instructed.

'Already happening,' Bernstein remarked with surprising calm. 'Good that you're here.'

He looked at her in silent apology and she responded with a one-sided smile. Bazza seemed gobsmacked at his boss's apparent calm.

'That's the first and only sighting we have of him so far,' she continued. 'All footage from the time the Land Rover was last parked is being scrutinised within a radius of twenty-five miles.'

Fenwick took a swallow of coffee, frowning.

'Let's assume that the sighting is of him – what was he doing there? It's past the turning for Newhaven and the ferries, so what's out there?'

'There's no connection here with Mariner; we've triple-checked.'

'And the addresses you told me know about, Bazza? Wasn't the grandmother's house around here somewhere?'

'It's on the Downs, just about . . .' Bernstein pointed a yellow-tipped finger at the map. 'Here: on the hills outside Alfriston. The location has been checked twice, the second time this week but they promised to go out again today.'

Fenwick frowned in concentration at the map.

'It's not that far from the possible sighting.' Unnoticed behind them Bazza picked up his mobile and turned away to make a call. 'Exactly.'

Fenwick's thumbs tingled.

He studied the map again and put a black cross on the location of the farm, sipping lukewarm coffee.

'Sir!' Bazza sounded excited. 'I've just spoken to the Highways Authority. To reach the grandmother's place he would have followed the A27 as far as Alciston but that road was closed on Tuesday because a fallen tree had smashed an electricity substation. The other route is via Alfriston, and then on minor roads across to the farm. They were doubtful a vehicle could have made it but in a Land Rover – well they said it might have been possible.'

Fenwick's throat went dry.

'You said the farm was "checked" Deidre, not searched.'

'Did I?' Bernstein was reaching for the report.

'Was it searched or wasn't it? We need to know!'

He heard Bernstein's intake of breath and cursed his impatience. She would point out that he was a meddling micromanager who should remember he was an unofficial guest. Instead, 'You're right, it just says "checked"; there's nothing about a search.'

'If the roads have been in bad condition and they thought he was driving the Mondeo . . .' Bazza ventured.

'I'll get the status confirmed immediately,' Bernstein said quietly.

Fenwick turned back to the map, keeping his face turned away, his thoughts to himself.

'Andy, Andy! Wake up! It's HQ; they say it's urgent, about that missing girl.' His wife looked scared.

Andy tried to focus, shook his head and picked up the receiver. 'Dyeah?' He was poorly. 'Whad? . . . I send in my report . . .'course I did . . . Search? Well nod exactly. It wasn't necessary. The road was blocked with snow so thick it was obvious no one was there . . . yes, I know it's been falling all week but the house was pitch-black, no lights, nothing . . . well if you pud it like thad but no car could've reached the place, I had to shovel my way through . . . Unusual? No, it would've been in my report wouldn't id . . . wouldn't id, sir. Nod again, nod tonight; I'm on leave, and anyway, I'm very sick. Be careful, sir, or I'll have the federation on this, I will—' The call ended abruptly.

'Everything all right, love?' She was white as a ghost.

'Just work,' Andy shrugged and turned his gaze to the artificial flicker of the fire.

'I'll get you some Grandma's remedy, shall I?' She kissed the top of his head and padded to the kitchen.

Anything unusual? Woodsmoke . . . Oh shit! Woodsmoke. Andy picked up the receiver as if it was red hot then put it down again and stared at it. His wife's voice reached him from the kitchen.

'They said that poor girl might be around here, that's why I had to wake you, otherwise they wouldn't have troubled us. Poor little thing; I worry about her. Do you think she might still be alive, love? I do hope so.'

Andy didn't reply, just stared at the phone and bit his fingernails.

CHAPTER FIFTY

Just after two o'clock the sky went black. There was a lull in the wind and the countryside sank into muffled silence. Huddled inside his cashmere overcoat Fenwick sniffed the air and shivered.

'We should press on.'

'To where?' Tate frowned and tugged his scarf up higher.

He would have been quite happy to wait with the others at the garage but his boss had given in to an urgent need for action and insisted on leaving ten minutes before, much to the amusement of Bernstein and Bazza, who had shaken their heads at him in sympathy. More fool him for attaching himself to an obsessive.

There was a map open in front of the windscreen. Tate's gloved finger hovered over it.

'We're here; the Mondeo was found two miles back there.'

'And the grandmother's house is where exactly?'

Tate peered at the large-scale map.

'Around about here.'

'We might as well go straight there. If he's gone somewhere else then it will show up on camera and Bernstein will call us, but this way we can double-check ourselves faster than HQ will be able to despatch someone.'

Tate bit his lip, put the car into gear and pulled out of the lay-by. He was unnerved by Fenwick's mood. The superintendent was always quiet but the current aura of – what exactly? – not detachment, more absence, was unnerving. Half a mile back he had insisted Tate stop the car and had stepped out into the frigid afternoon. Tate had assumed it was for a call of nature and politely looked away but Fenwick just stood there, glaring at the sky and sniffing like a damned bloodhound. Then he had come back into the car as if nothing had happened and they drove on until the next demand to stop.

'What makes you think they went to the grandmother's, sir?'

'Nothing; they could very well not be there. Mariner might have found another empty house at random, probably did as it worked last time, but if I'm right about Issie . . .' He stopped talking and gazed out of the window.

'Two days ago the local force checked it out and confirmed the house was empty, sir.'

Fenwick rubbed the fogged glass with his gloved hand.

'Why else would he be in the area? Issie knows this place. Her mother says she stayed with her grandparents given the slightest opportunity.'

'You think Mariner would listen to Issie?' Tate subconsciously shook his head as he pressed 'Go' on the satnav and watched the route being calculated.

'They've been together for nineteen days. I think she'll have worked out how to manage him.'

Tate hoped that his involuntary snort of disbelief was covered by his cough.

'We must hurry.' Fenwick finally deigned to snap his seat belt shut and the pinging alarm died. 'There's heavy snow coming.'

'They said on the radio the blizzard would arrive overnight.'

'Well, they're wrong; can't you smell it?'

Fenwick glared at the sergeant who maintained a diplomatic silence. They were forced to travel slowly even though the roads were virtually empty and they had four-wheel drive. Every now and then the front or back wheels would lose their grip, but Tate managed the car confidently and they progressed without incident.

Fenwick's mobile rang making them both jump.

'Yes? . . . Hello, Bazza . . . You what?' Fenwick leant forward suddenly, his free hand braced against the dashboard, listening intently. 'And you've already told the chief constable? Good. Well Tate and I are already on our way there. We're probably half an hour ahead of you. It's essential that a search team is despatched at once . . . good.'

Fenwick broke the call, muttering to himself. Tate opened his mouth but his boss raised a hand, silencing him.

'Let me think.' He was trying his phone. 'It's hard to get a signal out here.'

'I can use my radio.'

Fenwick shook his head. The last thing he wanted was to be on the record. No one knew he was here except Bernstein and Bazza.

'I, er . . . it sounded as if Bazza had news.'

'He did. The materials recovered from the last house Issie and Mariner stayed at are still being processed at the laboratory. In the rubbish they found a paper bag with a single word daubed on it in tomato sauce; "NANA".' Fenwick looked at Tate triumphantly.

'Maybe Issie was lonely and missing her grandmother,' Tate suggested and winced in the face of Fenwick's scowl. 'But of course the most important thing is that she's still alive.'

'Indeed,' Fenwick sounded mollified. 'The thing is how am I going to explain to Norman that I'm involved in Goldilocks?'

Tate was surprised that Fenwick should be confiding in him.

He screwed up his face in thought, but then had to return his concentration to a particularly difficult corner. Once he had navigated it he said, 'There's no obvious reason, sir, but maybe I could have received a tip about one of Flash Harry's undiscovered victims that led us there.'

'You would do that for me?' Fenwick was staring at him.

Tate squirmed in discomfort and remained silent.

'That's very decent of you, Tate, but it's tenuous and I'm not going to let you.' Fenwick stared out at the blank, white landscape. 'I'm simply going to have to admit that I decided to use my day off to help Bernstein.'

'Even though you are off the case, sir?'

'Even though I am off the case.' Fenwick gave a twisted smile. 'And stop calling me "sir". We've worked together long enough – it's Andrew. What's your first name, by the way?'

'Jeremy, sir . . . Andrew.'

'Good.'

Tate said nothing more. They both knew that Fenwick had stepped so far over the line that he would be facing disciplinary action if . . . when . . . CC Norman found out. Yet the superintendent didn't seem to care. He was more worried about the weather and reaching the grandmother's farm than his career. It wasn't his place to judge, he decided. Belatedly he realised that Fenwick had dragged him into a mess that could also have implications for his own career.

'I'll tell Norman that I ordered you to keep silent and just do what I told you, Jeremy,' Fenwick said as if reading his mind. 'For now let's keep focused on getting to this damned village. How much further?'

'In about a mile we turn right.'

Fenwick nodded and went back to staring out of the window.

As they neared the turning Tate eased to the crown of the road, feeling compacted snow beneath the tyres.

'What's that?'

The side road had a red triangle in the middle with bollards to either side.

'It says "road closed", sir. I'll go and check to see what's going on.' Tate parked the car by the left verge with hazard warning lights on and clambered out.

He was back quickly.

'A fallen tree has brought down the power line. It's lying across the road and there's a hazard warning from the electricity company saying "danger of death". We shouldn't risk it.'

He saw Fenwick start to button his coat.

'Hang on a sec, sir. According to the map there is another way to the farm. If we continue about a mile on this road we should be able to turn right and still get there. In fact there are two options: either we can go via Berwick or on to Alfriston.'

'Let's go, then.'

The road to Berwick was also closed but a few yards further on the turning to Alfriston was clear and the surface seemed to have been gritted. As they started down the hill to the village a heavy swirl of snow battered the windscreen. By the time they reached the village limits Tate had turned on the windscreen wipers. As he did so, Fenwick's mobile rang.

'There's a signal here. Pull over for a moment so I can take this.'

Tate turned into a car park on the left just before the village proper.

'Fenwick.'

'It's Deidre, Andrew. Where are you?'

'Just entering Alfriston.'

'On the way to the grandmother's house?'

'Yes; the route via Alciston is still blocked. Why?'

'You're not going to like this,' she warned. 'Some stupid bugger has screwed up big time and deserves to be fired, except of course he won't be because he'll claim stress and go sick.'

Fenwick's good hand clenched into a fist.

'Just tell me.'

'A lazy sod of a flat-footed constable has just admitted that he didn't actually check physically inside the grandmother's house. He says he had to struggle through more than a mile of undisturbed snow just to reach the gate and that the track beyond showed no signs of a vehicle having travelled down it. He had a good look around, saw solid snow more than a foot deep and the house dark without signs of life.'

'Stupid bugger! We've had so much snow what he saw meant nothing.'

'Exactly; but Shit-for-Brains insists he went far enough down the track to check the place out. As there were no lights and no other signs of life he concluded no one was there, turned around and reported it empty.'

Fenwick uttered an obscenity that shocked even Tate and hit the dashboard with his fist.

'When was this?'

'Two days ago.'

'And we think Mariner stole the car on Tuesday the nineteenth. So if they went straight to the grandmother's they would have been there. There are power lines down so the place could well have been dark because of no electricity. What made him admit his mistake now?'

'His wife. Apparently she confronted him and it all came out.'

'You know what this means.'

'Yup, we've gone from hunch to probable in the last half-hour. I'm on my way to you now with some of the team from the garage. Lewes has already despatched a Local Support Team. So with the eight of them, us four and you two we'll have fourteen officers to deploy in no time. Pretty stupid of Mariner to choose somewhere so close to Lewes. Fancy hiding out on Sussex HQ's home patch!

'The ambulance service has been notified and should be with us by the time we enter the farm. If there's any chance that you and Tate can get some visuals before we arrive – without being seen, natch, then that will be a big help.'

'Will do. The mobile signal is irregular around here so you may need to reach us by radio.'

'Shouldn't be a problem.'

'It would help if you could remember in your notes for today that you detailed Tate to be here so that when you radio him there's good reason.'

There was an awkward pause as she realised the mess Fenwick was in.

'Of course. See you soon.' She hung up.

'Thank you, si . . . Andrew.'

'Don't mention it. Just get me down this hill into the village in one piece.'

CHAPTER FIFTY-ONE

Issie was relieved to be in dry clothes again but the exposure of bare flesh to the wind-borne snow had chilled her until her teeth rattled.

'Movement,' she said to herself, vigorously stamping her feet. 'It can't be far now.'

She looked up but immediately had to screw her eyes tight as the wind drove snow into them. Visibility was deteriorating fast. She could only just make out the fence to her left, its posts black against the grey of the snow. Issie walked over until it was within touching distance, lifting her knees high to wade through the drifts along the path. Head down, she ploughed on. The cold soon ceased to be a problem as her body warmed with exercise, except for the exposed flesh above her scarf, but tiredness was creeping up on her.

After three weeks of poor treatment in captivity she wasn't fit despite her surreptitious attempts at exercise whenever Steve wasn't looking. Her muscles were aching across her back and down her legs, and there was an ominous pain in her right hip where Steve had kicked her that made her catch her breath when it flared. She pressed her right hand against it.

'Not long now,' she muttered and started to count into her moist scarf.

'. . . five hundred and six; five hundred and seven . . .'

Other than her whispered, determined words, all she could

hear was the sound of the wind. It was howling in rage against the cowering countryside. Issie thought of dormice and hedgehogs hibernating safe in their nests. If they could survive this then so could she. She felt betrayed by the weather. The forecast had promised overcast skies and no snow, yet she was walking into the teeth of a storm worse than any of the winter so far. She wouldn't shape the word blizzard to herself but it was hiding there in the recesses of her mind waiting to scare her.

'One thousand six hundred and five . . . one thousand six hundred and six . . . one—Aah!'

Issie doubled over, her hand pressed against her hip, the pain momentarily more than she could bear. She tried a step forward but the snow was deep and the step she needed to take so high that the fire shooting through her hip was excruciating. Tears of agony and sudden exhaustion filled her eyes but she blinked them away, angry with herself at the sign of weakness. She would NOT fail!

'Just a moment,' she comforted herself, bent almost double to relieve the strain in her side. 'Just a moment.'

A strong gust almost knocked her over. Issie straightened up by inches as the pain faded back to an intense ache. She stretched straight and then twisted from the waist, first one way then the next. So far so good. Maybe she should ditch the backpack. After all, she must be close to Alfriston by now.

'Stupid.' She banished the thought. 'Come on girl, not far now. If you can't step over the snow then you'll have to wade through it. Now where was I? Oh sod it! One . . . two . . . three.'

The wind shrieked, laughing at her so that she could no longer hear her own voice except as an echo inside her head. Issie raised the middle digit of her left hand – the right was still pressed to her hip – and laughed back.

'Ha ha! Why don't you clear off and torment someone else. Go wreck some sheds and tear off some roofs and Leave Me ALONE!'

The wind howled. Issie ploughed on, following the path

with only her voice for company. She lost track of time but kept counting, even when she had to stop because of the fire in her hip. Around her, day darkened prematurely to night as the storm assumed blizzard intensity.

'Seventy hundred and twenty-something . . . seventy hundred and twenty-something more, oh I don't know . . . three. Seventy hun . . . hang on, is seventy hundred right?' Issie paused, favouring her injured side, her forehead corrugated with effort. 'Ten, twenty, thirty, forty, fifty, sixty, seventy! Yes, that's right. Seventy hundred and . . . something.'

She laughed but the wind whipped the sound away as it left her lips.

At least I'm warm, she thought, *and I'm not panicking*. It was remarkable how calm she felt. She was marvelling at her state of mind when she bumped her knee. Looking up she could just make out some planks of wood in front of her, set at odd angles and rising into a hedge that she realised was blocking the track. Very strange. Issie stared at them, trying to work out how to get around them. Behind her, she could just make out a few fence posts disappearing into the snow. To her left and right was a thick hedge. The only way over seemed to be these planks.

Something about them seemed familiar. Issie closed her eyes in an effort to concentrate and tried to think. As the wind buffeted her she remembered. It was a stile: it had been placed there to climb over; of course. She felt a little frightened. How could she have forgotten what a stile looked like? The concern subsided to be replaced by an uncomfortable reality: would she be able to manage? Her legs were as heavy as iron, her knees rusty with cold and her hip . . . locked in a spasm at the thought.

When it had passed she murmured '*Here goes*' and squared up to the obstacle.

Issie lifted her left leg first, then realised that was stupid because her right would have to do the hard work of going over the top, so she stepped down again and tried to raise her right leg. It wouldn't go; even trying was agony. Biting her lip and refusing to cry, Issie leant her weight against one of the wooden uprights. Using both hands she grasped the underside of her right thigh and lifted.

The pain made her scream but she persisted until her right boot was placed on the icy wooden step at knee height. Now what? Blinking back tears she shrugged out of her rucksack and heaved it over the stile to land in a snow bank on the other side. Gripping the top she pulled her weight up until her left foot was on the same level as her right. Issie twisted, whimpering, and lowered her upper body on top of the stile. Taking her body weight on her chest and stomach she lifted her right leg, ignoring the shooting sharp needles that ran down the side of her leg as she did so. After a moment's rest she let it down the other side in a sudden fall that hurt like hell but was soon over. Now sitting astride the stile as if it were a horse, Issie twisted again and brought her left leg over and down to steady herself. Her right side from waist to toe felt as if someone was crushing every bone in a vice.

'Aargh . . . ah!' She was panting with exhaustion and she still had to work out how to clamber down the other side. She lowered her left foot carefully . . . and was saved the bother of any further effort as it skidded out from under, dragging her from the top of the stile. She tried to save herself but only managed to twist her back before gravity claimed her and she fell.

Her head landed on the rucksack but the snow was so deep that it cushioned the shock and it hardly hurt at all. She lay spreadeagled like a fallen angel, bolts of lightning pain shooting up her leg and into her pelvis. Had she broken anything? Gingerly Issie sat up. She wriggled her toes and felt them move. When she told her knees to rise they obeyed. She rotated her shoulders and apart from stiffness from carrying the pack they seemed fine. Nothing was broken. Groaning like an old woman, Issie brushed off the snow and stood up. Thanks to her jacket, the bin liner-puttees and boots she was hardly wet at all. She picked up her pack, settled it between her shoulder blades, ignoring the protest from tendons and muscles that had been appreciating the rest, and hobbled forward.

The storm shrieked towards its height but Issie limped on, straining her eyes to pierce the gloom in search of any sign of habitation that surely must be close by now.

'It's no good, sir . . . Andrew; we'll never get down the hill. It's sheet ice. Even with these tyres we won't be able to control the car and there's a tight turn at the bottom. We'll risk ploughing into the corner cottage if we try to go on.'

'Then there's no option but to walk. Grab the shovel and reflective jackets from the back.'

They stepped out into the blizzard and immediately hunched into themselves. Fenwick had his coat collar up to his ears and his scarf tight to his nose but he had no hat. Tate was better prepared with a puffy hooded jacket that looked enviably warm.

'Let's hope she's not out in this,' Tate said as he walked to the front of the car and Fenwick felt a rush of empathy. Those had been his thoughts exactly.

'God willing,' he muttered.

They started down the hill, hugging the wall, reaching out suddenly from time to time to steady themselves.

'So how far from here to the farm?' Fenwick asked but before Tate could answer his radio squawked into life and he answered, finding shelter in a doorway so that he could listen.

'The MIU's down there already. They must have passed us but I didn't see them, did you?'

'And they made it down the hill.'

The sergeant hung his head. 'Sorry.'

'Never mind, let's go and find them.'

At the far end of the village, beyond a pub/hotel that promised warmth and hospitality, there was a rutted car park and in it the MIU. It was identical to dozens Fenwick had seen before, even down to the backs hunched over the complexities of the communication system that greeted them when they walked inside.

A short, burly man in a thick quilted jacket and deerstalker hailed them as they entered.

'Jack Nesbit.' He stuck out a hand and Fenwick shook it. 'DCI from Eastbourne; we came in from the south. Almost didn't make it up that last hill – a bit hairy but we're here now. And you are? Sorry to be direct but HQ didn't say there'd be someone on the ground already.'

'I'm Superintendent Andrew Fenwick, head of Sussex MCS, and this is Sergeant Tate, Surrey CID. We've been involved in Goldilocks from the beginning and a connected investigation.'

Nesbit glanced at the proffered warrant card – standard procedure since a journalist had managed to infiltrate an MIU the year before – and nodded. Fenwick breathed a sigh of relief; his explanation had been taken at face value. Tate suppressed a grin.

'So where are we?' Fenwick asked.

A large-scale map of the area had been taped up in obvious haste on the back of the door. While Tate poured two large mugs of black coffee from a thermos without being asked, Fenwick and Nesbit studied it.

'We're here,' Nesbit pointed to a blue cross. 'The grandmother's house is there.'

Fenwick stared at a red circle.

'So close,' he muttered. 'Less than three miles as the crow flies.'

'Two point three exactly from where we are; less than two to the western outskirts of Alfriston.'

'What's the best way to get there?'

Nesbit broke eye contact, taking time to unzip his heavy jacket. 'Well?'

'That's the problem. The roads through Alciston and Berwick are impassable and the single lane road from Alfriston to the farm is under more than three feet of snow. The only way to reach the farm from here would be on foot along the South Downs Way. And in this weather we can't call out H900.'

'We have four-by-fours, we don't need the helicopter.'

'Lewes sent two of them out half an hour ago; they can't get through. I tried one from the south as well. It's stuck in a drift and we'll have to wait for a tow truck to pull it out.'

Fenwick sensed Tate's relief that he hadn't been such a failure.

'We have to get there.' He stared around as if the answer would materialise if only he knew where to look.

Tate suddenly saw his boss as Nesbit might see him – wild, deranged, maybe slightly crazy. He thrust a plastic mug of coffee into his hand. Fenwick took a sip immediately and then a proper, long swallow.

'There must be some way to reach her,' he said at last, more calmly.

Nesbit shrugged and seeing this Tate stepped forward.

'I, er . . .' He hesitated but Fenwick turned to him at once.

'Go on, Jeremy,' he snapped.

'What about tractors? There are plenty of farms about. Some of them will have heavy machines capable of getting through the snow, otherwise they'd be unable to feed their sheep in the depths of winter. We could commandeer them.'

Nesbit laughed but Fenwick turned on him.

'Have you got a better idea, Jack?'

The smirk disappeared.

'No, sir.'

'Then find out where the farms are. Look,' he pointed, 'there's habitation here and here and a farm there . . . plus possibly that one there.' He was jabbing at the map as Nesbit noted down the locations. 'As soon as you've made contact with the owners, deploy the vehicles as you think best and radio back.'

Nesbit looked at him as if he really was crazy.

'Not you? You're not here to direct the investigation?'

Fenwick blinked twice and looked away. Tate could see his jaw tighten.

'It's your MIU, and you have a direct order from Lewes, Jack. I'm leaving it to you. Consider me an advisor and an additional pair of hands but the lead stays with you until DS Bernstein arrives. Better not to complicate matters.'

Nesbit frowned and looked as if he would like to check Fenwick's warrant card again but he said nothing and soon left, asking Tate to go with him. Fenwick was alone with the MIU team, none of whom looked inclined to start a conversation, which suited him just fine.

A vicious gust of wind rocked the van, strong enough to shake a plastic coffee cup to the floor. Fenwick picked it up and threw it in the bin in the far corner. There was nothing to do except wait, keep a low profile and hope. Twenty minutes passed with only routine call-ins from the teams deployed around Alfriston. Then ten minutes later one of them checked in to say that they had reached one of the farms and within five minutes they confirmed that they had full cooperation from the owner and would shortly be leaving by tractor to try to reach the grandmother's house down farm tracks and single-lane roads.

Shortly afterwards the second team called in and Fenwick heard Tate's voice shouting above the gale that they were on their way to the grandmother's. Before he could intervene to say he shouldn't be part of the effort because he wasn't equipped for it, the signal failed.

The third team radioed a few minutes later with bad news; there was no qualified driver at the farm and their team leader wouldn't let them take the tractor because they hadn't had the necessary training.

'Then walk there!' Fenwick shouted loud enough for his voice to be heard by the unfortunate officer at the other end.

'I hope to do so, sir. We're just trying to persuade the inspector here.'

'Put him on.'

But Fenwick was interrupted by Nesbit's return and the communications technician handed him the headset with relief.

'If you don't have a qualified driver you are to return to Alfriston and meet us in the car park. We have two teams successfully on their way; that should be enough.'

Fenwick paced the short distance to the map and turned his back.

'Sorry, sir, but they really can't go on without owner permission and lacking training; particularly not in this weather.'

Fenwick said nothing. Nesbit passed him a fresh cup of coffee and they waited in silence. At seven minutes past three the second team was back on the radio.

'We are concealed twenty yards from the farm. There are signs of occupation and a Land Rover in the yard with an index number matching the vehicle stolen from the garage. What shall we do, sir?' The question was directed at Nesbit who looked expectantly at Fenwick.

'What's your name?' Fenwick settled a headset more comfortably.

'DC Aspen, sir. Sergeant Tate is right next to me.'

'Put him on.' There was a rustling that deafened him. 'Jeremy, how many are you?'

'Just the two of us and the farmer. That's all that could fit in the tractor cab and we didn't want to risk the trailer in case it slowed us down. Aspen and I were the smallest.'

'Wait where you are out of sight until I call you back.' He turned to Nesbit.

'Where's the second team; do we know?'

Nesbit had anticipated his question and was already on another radio.

'They estimate less than ten minutes away and there are eight of them. They did take a trailer. Where should they rendezvous?'

Fenwick radioed Tate back and asked for his exact location and then told him to wait until the other team arrived. It was twelve minutes before the next call but by then there were ten officers on location. Nesbit and Fenwick agreed that there was no chance to send more of the Local Support Team and to use the teams they had there. The senior officer on site was a Sergeant Mulberry. Nesbit gave him a good write-up including previous resisted arrests, so Fenwick decided they had to trust to him.

As official senior officer present Nesbit directed the operation: deployment of officers around the main house covering all exits with two to stay in the yard by the vehicle.

The signal was too weak and inconsistent for them to remain connected while the men entered the house so they waited in silence apart from the howling storm outside. Fenwick was chewing the side of his thumb and only stopped when it started to bleed. In a surprisingly short time Mulberry called in.

'We have him, sir! We've got the bastard! It's Mariner, for sure. He was fast asleep in bed! Piece of cake.'

'And Issie,' Fenwick bellowed. 'Is she all right?'

There was a horrible pause.

'Well, go on.'

'We can't find her, sir. We're searching the main house but so far nothing. There are signs she was here. There's damp ladies' underwear drying in one of the bathrooms and Mariner insists she must be hiding somewhere . . . but it looks as if she may not be here.'

Fenwick reached out to the wall for support.

CHAPTER FIFTY-TWO

It was impossible to breathe; he couldn't suck in enough air and his head started to spin. Fenwick clutched the door frame and struggled not to sink to the ground. She wasn't there. His insistence had been proved right; they had found Mariner and evidence that he had been holding Issie at the farm but . . . He gasped and Nesbit glanced at him with concern. By concentrating on his breathing he managed to calm down and the palpitations slowed. The black spots faded from his vision.

Had Mariner dumped Issie somewhere, alive or dead? Was her body hidden even now on the farm? He heard Nesbit ordering an immediate search of the premises while one of the radio operators was calling in POLSA.

'What is Mariner saying?' Keeping the panic out of his voice took effort but he thought he managed.

'He's incoherent, seems to be ill or on drugs or something. From what we can gather he insists Issie is there somewhere.' Nesbit was holding the mike and turned away to give another stream of instructions.

Fenwick continued to take slow, deep breaths.

'Ask them to put Tate on, would you?'

Nesbit handed him the radio.

'Jeremy, listen. You need to be my eyes and ears. I want you to search for anything that might give us a hint of any kind as to where Issie might be.'

'Will do; I'll call you back.'

As soon as he broke the connection Fenwick started to pace the van; long steps that meant he was turning constantly in the confined space. Nesbit passed him a fresh coffee and he took it without noticing.

Where is she? He pulled out the picture of Issie that Jane Saxby had given him, of her daughter hanging upside down by her knees from the branch of a tree, laughing, sticking her tongue out at the camera, belly button stud glinting in sunlight that filtered through the leaves. He felt his throat tighten. She wasn't dead; she couldn't be.

'It's Tate for you, Superintendent.'

'Put him on speaker.'

'Here's what we think has happened. It looks as if Mariner has been given a cocktail of chemotherapy drugs and sleeping pills. We've found empty prescription packets in the kitchen bin with Issie's grandfather's name on them. Our theory is that Issie spiked his food. There are the remains of a whisky toddy that we are sending back for tests.

'Mariner is still pretty incoherent but he says he felt fine until Friday. He can't remember anything at all about today other than the need to sleep or rush to the toilet. He swears that he has no idea where Issie might be.'

Fenwick stared at the photo. *Clever little Issie. You worked out an escape plan. But you're too smart to set out into the worst blizzard of the winter, unless . . .*

'Is there television, Internet or radio at the farm?'

Nesbit looked at him as if he had lost his senses but Tate answered immediately, as if expecting the question.

'Yes, sir—'

'Damn!'

'—but there's no power. According to Mariner the mains supply failed three days ago and they switched to a generator but it ran out of diesel this morning. So . . .'

'She wouldn't have heard the revised weather forecast. She didn't expect the blizzard until Christmas Day. That explains it. Issie planned to leave ahead of the storm, knowing that if she waited they could be trapped without power for days. And Mariner says she was there this morning?'

'Yes, he keeps repeating it; that is when he's not in the toilet. He's leaking almost constantly.'

'Spare us the details, Sergeant. With luck there'll be some permanent damage to the bastard, but right now we need to find out where Issie has gone.'

'He might have hidden her body somewhere and this is all a lie,' Nesbit volunteered into Fenwick's grimace.

'It's a possibility but we can't assume so. What if she's out there in this?' He gestured to the walls of the MIU just as a blast of wind reminded them of the storm raging beyond.

'How on earth are we going to find her?' Nesbit countered. 'In this weather, with the farm in the middle of nowhere. Even if we knew the direction she was heading in it would be suicide to send a team out in this!'

Fenwick glared at the DCI but he couldn't disagree. Nesbit continued, knowing he had the force of logic with him.

'And anyway, are you telling me that a seventeen-year-old abused, traumatised girl would have the courage and intelligence to plan something like this? To drug a kidnapper we know has been sexually abusing her? Studies show that a kidnap victim adjusts their behaviour to appease their captor. She would have been conditioned into submission long ago.'

'Eighteen,' Fenwick said. 'She's eighteen not seventeen and yes, that is exactly what I'm saying. You don't know Issie . . .'

'And with respect, sir, neither do you. You've never met the girl.'

'Her mother says . . .'

'Her mother! What desperate parent have you ever met who

doesn't idealise their child into some wunderkind as soon as they vanish?'

Fenwick had such a strong urge to punch Nesbit that he had to walk away. As he did so there was a discreet cough from the radio.

'We're still scouring the farm but if we are to mount a wider search we need to start as soon as possible. It's already growing dark and it will be pitch-black soon in this weather.'

'No way,' Nesbit shook his head, 'it would be like looking for a needle in a haystack.'

Fenwick had waived his operational authority, was already likely to receive a severe reprimand for even being there. He couldn't pull rank on the DCI but that didn't mean he was about to give up.

'You said when I arrived that your men were equipped for a severe-weather search.'

'Yes but—'

Fenwick held up his hand.

'Supposing I can find out where she might be heading; would you reconsider?'

Nesbit scratched his head, not bothering to hide his irritation.

'Perhaps, but how will you do that?'

'I'll call her parents. They might be able to help us.'

'For God's sake, Fenwick, I mean, sir. They're likely to say anything to get us out there. I don't think we can trust them, with the best will in the world.'

'Jane Saxby wouldn't lie to me. Look, I'll let you listen in so you can judge for yourself.'

Fenwick pulled out his phone but before he could dial it rang, startling them both. He answered.

'Superintendent Fenwick?'

'Yes.'

'It's Jane Saxby.' A shiver went down Fenwick's spine as he

put the call on speaker. 'Excuse me for calling you but I just had to.'

'Do you mind – you're on speaker so my colleague can hear the call?'

'Fine; I know this will sound crazy but you must listen to me. It's Issie,' Fenwick's heart leapt painfully, 'I think she's in terrible danger. I know I told you when I last saw you that I dreamt she was safe and warm—'

Out of the corner of his eye Fenwick saw Nesbit shake his head and he just hoped her mother wasn't about to blow any chance he had of persuading the man to risk his officers' lives.

'—but since lunchtime I've felt this increasing sense of dread. It's so real it makes me physically sick and, Superintendent – I'm so very, very cold.' He heard her voice catch. 'I think he might have given up on the ransom idea at last and dumped her outside.'

There was a rustle of the receiver being muffled and behind it the sound of sobbing, quickly stifled. Nesbit wasn't looking so sceptical any more.

'Issie has been missing for almost three weeks. Have you felt like this before?'

'No, never. I told you there was a time I knew she was terrified and that bastard has been abusing her but never anything like this . . . and it has nothing to do with it being Christmas Eve. I just *know* something is wrong. The last few days I've been feeling more positive for some reason, and this morning . . . I woke up feeling so sure you would find her. The day felt different somehow; I had real hope for the first time. But then around lunchtime it started. I felt cold, sick, so worried I couldn't even think and it has just got worse. So in the end I had to call you. Superintendent,' he heard her gulp, 'I think Issie is dying.'

He looked at Nesbit who gave an imperceptible nod.

'There has been a development,' he heard her gasp and

hurried on, 'we haven't found Issie but there has been progress. I'm passing you over to the officer in charge of this part of the operation.' Fenwick handed over his phone.

'This is DCI Nesbit, Lady Saxby; I organised a localised search for Issie at Abbott's Farm.'

'My mother's house! But why there?'

'We received information that led us to believe Mariner might be there with your daughter.'

'But you've had it checked several times. Why now?'

Nesbit looked at Fenwick as if thinking exactly the same question.

'I believe it was at Superintendent Fenwick's insistence, ma'am.'

'I don't understand.'

'We can explain in detail later but right now it is very important that we tell you that we apprehended the suspect Steven Mariner at the location in question.'

'You've found him?' It was barely a whisper. 'And my daughter?' Softer still.

'She no longer appears to be with him but there is evidence to suggest that she was staying there. According to Mariner she was there at breakfast but he has no idea where she might be now. We are searching the property and outbuildings but so far there is no trace of her.'

'She's been there, recently?' Fenwick could hear the fury building in her tone. 'And you failed to find her!'

'What's wrong, darling?' They heard Bill Saxby in the background, his voice becoming louder as he drew closer to the phone.

'They've found Mariner at Mummy's place. And Issie has been there! But she isn't there now.'

'*Give me that!*'

'What the fuck's going on? Why didn't you have someone

509

there guarding the place permanently? We told you day one that Issie might suggest they go there.'

Fenwick knew that he had in fact pooh-poohed the idea when Bernstein had insisted on a list of addresses for all Issie's friends and relations.

Guarding it permanently on the off chance she might persuade Mariner to go there was illogical but he could understand Saxby's insistence. Once a theory became certainty every fact, every action or lack thereof, was judged through a different lens. The inquiry that would inevitably follow this case would be horrible, would probably wreck his career, but he didn't care. That wasn't the point. They needed to find Issie.

'Now we know she was there,' Nesbit was saying, 'we need your help to work out where she might have gone. One theory is,' he looked at Fenwick and gave a sigh of capitulation, 'that she managed to escape from Mariner earlier today. We found him drugged and incapacitated.'

'But why would Issie set off in the middle of a blizzard? She's not stupid.' Lady Saxby had taken the phone.

'It's only one hypothesis, made more feasible by the fact that she might not have known the weather was due to change. There is no power at your mother's house and even early this morning the forecast was for the snow to arrive on Christmas Day, not today.'

'Oh God! You're right. If she thought the weather conditions weren't too bad it is exactly the sort of thing Issie would do. She was always having adventures when she stayed with her Nana and Pappy. She knows the Downs around there like the back of her hand. You have to find her!'

'For that we need your help. Is there anywhere in particular she would have gone?'

'I don't know,' there was despair in her voice, 'but she would have planned carefully, my father drilled that into her, and she would have chosen a route she knew well. That probably means sticking to the South Downs Way. The question is, in which direction?'

Fenwick marvelled that the woman could master her fear and put away her anger so quickly; to be so calm and focused. She was remarkable, just like her daughter.

'The good news is,' she continued, 'that she has proper outdoor clothes at the farm. She kept them in the boot room ready for when she visited. Check to see if they're missing. If they are gone then so's she. Meanwhile, do you have an Ordnance Survey map of the area?'

The two men walked over to it.

'You see the farm?' Fenwick stared at the red circle. 'There's a footpath that crosses the public byway where it meets the track to the farm.'

'Got it.'

'It's not the one to Alciston or Berwick.'

'No, understood.'

'Follow it south-east and you'll come to a village called Alfriston.'

The blue cross.

'That's where we are now.'

'Thank God; then there's hope. Issie is most likely to be making her way to Alfriston. She's been walking that route since she was a toddler. She would have chosen somewhere familiar. I'm certain that's where you will find her. Is Superintendent Fenwick still there?'

'I'm here.'

'I know the weather is atrocious; I suspect there are probably rules that say you can't send officers out when their lives might be at risk but you *have* to find her, Superintendent. Andrew, please. Don't abandon Issie now when you're so close. I'm begging you. If you'd only got there a few hours earlier we wouldn't even be having this conversation.'

'I know.' Fenwick looked at Nesbit. Was it enough to persuade this man to put lives at risk?

Nesbit was studying the map.

'It's barely two miles,' Fenwick said, acutely aware that Issie's mother was listening. 'If we send out a search team from here and another from the farm, we could cover the distance inside an hour, even in this weather.'

He could sense Nesbit trying to persuade himself that he wasn't breaking regulations. Fenwick held his breath.

'Very well, I'll authorise a search until we lose the last of the light.'

'Thank you,' Jane Saxby murmured just before her husband grabbed the phone.

'Find her, Fenwick, and you will never have to worry about money again. If you don't, your life will not be worth living.'

'*Bill, no!*'

'I don't need any further incentive – positive or negative – to find your daughter, sir,' Fenwick said calmly and broke the connection. He turned to Nesbit.

'Come on, Jack, let's go and find her.'

CHAPTER FIFTY-THREE

Issie wasn't sure any more quite where she was or in which direction she was walking. She remembered that she should be keeping the tops of wooden fence posts on her left for some reason but the snow was so deep that there would be minutes when she couldn't spot them. Still she kept plodding through the driving snow, sometimes unable to see more than the immediate space in front of her.

She was slow now, each pace a step of fire from her hip down into her knee but she was determined and almost welcomed the pain as something to keep her focused. Although she wasn't hungry Issie knew that she should eat and have some of her warm drink. Not that she was cold but she just knew it was what she was meant to do. The trouble was there was no shelter and if she stopped walking she feared she wouldn't be able to start again, that her muscles would finally seize up.

Her back was aching from being bent over to protect her face from the cruelty of the wind. Sometimes it was so strong she could barely breathe. The good news was that her face no longer stung and her hands and feet seemed to have become accustomed to the cold because they didn't hurt any more. Issie pushed herself through another drift, realising that she was wading rather than walking most of the time. Her knees were numb and damp despite the bin liner wrappings.

It was much darker now. She knew that she should be concerned at the rapidly dwindling light. It meant that she had been walking for longer than she had thought but she wasn't worried. Despite the hostile conditions and her isolation, Issie was managing to stay calm. If she thought about things philosophically, she actually had very little to worry about. All she needed to do was keep on; everything else would sort itself out.

She was unaware that each step was shorter than the last as every one was a mammoth effort. Issie yawned behind her scarf and realised that she was really tired.

A little bit further, we're nearly there, girl – her Pappy's words from when she was little, trotting beside him three steps to his one, determined not to be carried the last part of the way. She could almost imagine him walking beside her.

'I'm tired and a bit cold, Pappy.'

'I know, girl, but it's only a little way now and then you can have a nice mug of hot chocolate.'

'With cream and a flake on top?'

'Of course, only the best for my own special girl. Come on, just through the copse and we're almost there.'

Pappy would ruffle her hair then and her legs always grew stronger.

The copse . . . Issie screwed up her eyes. Why was that important? She almost stopped with the effort to concentrate. A copse was . . . what was a copse? Was it a dead body? No, that was a corpse . . . so a copse was . . . a stream? No, but she knew the river would be coming up soon so she would have to be careful. A copse was . . .

'TREES! A copse is trees!' Issie yelped with excitement.

Soon there would be enough shelter to pause and eat something. She quickened her pace . . . or thought she did.

There was a shadow on her left. Issie tried to identify it but the snowfall was too heavy to make out its shape. Was that a tree? She took another couple of steps and the shadow assumed the shape of a bent hawthorn, half drowned in snow on the windward side. A little further on was another, then a young ash and an alder sapling. This must be the copse! She turned and pushed through a deep drift towards them.

A scrappy cluster of brambles, hazel and more hawthorns had formed a hedge around larger stunted trees. The snow in the lee was light, barely a few inches deep, though it was piled hedge high on the windward side. Issie headed towards the shelter, relishing the bliss of being able to walk more freely at last. She used her boots to kick most of the snow away. On the cleared patch she put down a black bin liner and immediately weighted it with her pack. Crouching down with difficulty she ignored the shooting pains in her hip and breathed deeply in the relatively calm air. For the first time in what felt like hours she was out of the biting wind. She knelt down and forced herself to concentrate on what to do next but it was very difficult.

Issie opened her pack with difficulty as her right hand had no feeling and found a packet of chocolate biscuits, cursing that she hadn't thought to open them before leaving the farm. She used her teeth to pull off her gloves. The shiny wrapper was impossible to open with numb hands so she had to use her teeth to rip it open. The top biscuits fell out so she scooped them up with her palms and crammed them into her mouth, chewing hungrily.

Feeling returned slowly to her left hand in excruciating shots of pins and needles. She relished the pain and shook her other hand, willing some blood into her bone-white fingers. Nothing happened but soon she was able to use her left hand to eat with. Three biscuits later she tried to open the thermos flask of sweet tea she had brought with her just in case, never expecting to drink it. The plastic cup came off easily enough, but try as she might, she could not twist open the stopper. She remembered fastening it tightly that morning to make sure it wouldn't spill – too tightly, as it turned out, for her left hand to open now. She was thirsty, though, and the biscuits had made it worse. There was a small bottle of water in her pack but that would be cold. Not good, she told herself, though she couldn't remember why; but she was so thirsty and surely a few sips wouldn't do any harm.

She managed to open the bottle and took a mouthful of water. She shuddered as the cold hit the back of her throat and shivered violently but she had another gulp anyway, too thirsty to care and forgetting to warm it in her mouth before swallowing.

'Careful,' she told herself, shivering, but half the bottle had already gone. Her teeth were chattering uncontrollably.

It was time to move on. Issie put everything back in her pack and stood up slowly, favouring her good side. Shouldering her burden with difficulty, she took a step towards the posts marking the footpath. The blast of the gale as she left the shelter of the trees almost knocked her over. How had she managed to walk through that? Surely it had got stronger. Maybe it would be sensible to sit out the worst of it by the hedge. She could use a couple of the bin liners to make a sort of shelter and wrap herself up in the foil and sleeping bag, with the other bin liners over it and her spare jumper as padding.

It was a good plan; she would be able to rest for a few minutes. Maybe then the pain in her back, hip and legs would ease off. One-handed it took Issie a long time to sort herself out. While emptying the backpack she found her Swedish fire steel and candle tin, which she had forgotten about, and wax matches. She had even put a couple of firelighters and small sticks of kindling in there, though she had also forgotten about them. She lit the candle in the perforated tin with difficulty, using all but three of the matches but it was so good to feel its heat that she didn't care. For a full five minutes she squatted there, oblivious to everything but its warmth.

At last she looked up and around; noticed the blizzard conditions, the relative shelter in the copse, with the thick, insulating snow on the north and east sides. Issie stared at her dead-white right hand and took a deep breath. With the food, warmth and relative shelter she was starting to think straight again. If she couldn't make a fire, she would probably die.

The fire steel was a new one, the last present Pappy had bought her. It still had paint on the fire starter but that would come off quickly enough with her penknife. If she could find some fallen wood she could keep a fire going long enough to warm herself. Issie shuffled around the copse and found twigs and small branches among the floor litter. There were sprays of last year's leaves clinging to some of them. Of course, they were damp but she discarded the soaking ones and kept those underneath that seemed drier. With her precious firelighters, sticks of kindling and the steel it might just work. She would save the last matches just in case it didn't.

Clearing the steel of paint took time as she had to wedge it between her knees and could only use one hand but it was done eventually. She used her feet to clear out a square for the fire and laid most of the kindling sticks and some of the smallest twigs in a shallow pyramid over a crumbled firelighter. She had torn shreds of paper wrapping from a stale bar of mint cake in her pocket and a packet of paper tissues ready to keep the blaze going. She took a long, slow breath and concentrated.

The first attempt with the steel failed. So did the second and the third.

'So I'm not ambidextrous,' she laughed as her left hand tried to assume the dexterity of its useless right partner. 'Try again.'

A spark caught a twist of paper on the fifth attempt and a piece of firelighter puffed into flame. Issie let out a yelp of pleasure. The feeble flame almost died but she cupped her hand around it and then lowered her body to shelter it from the whips of wind that flew through the branches of the hedge. The kindling was dry and flamed quickly but even the small twigs took a long time to catch and steamed first before reluctantly glowing red and flickering alight. When they did she learnt that they would then burn fast so that she had to wiggle in another piece quickly. It was a delicate balancing act: too much and she would kill the flame; too little and the heat would be insufficient to dry the next twig for it to burn. But Issie had been making campfires since she was six and her instincts were still there, fatigued and drowsy, perhaps, but enough to guide her.

For more than ten minutes Issie nurtured and coaxed the tiny fire, watching as it smouldered, flared and started to die. She used a match so that the flare of sulphurous heat could kindle another firelighter. As she put the last fragment in, she prayed and added a slightly bigger piece of wood as all her twigs had gone.

The branch hissed and sizzled, moisture oozing out of the end furthest from the heat.

'Please, please, please . . .'

There was a splutter and a tongue of flame licked upwards greedily. Issie poked another piece of fallen wood into the middle of the flames and watched as it lay there, smoking, reluctant until it too started to sweat out its moisture and, finally, caught fire.

'Thank you, God, thank you, thank you, thank you.'

She kissed the next piece of wood and placed it very carefully on one side of the fragile, falling pyramid. She watched as it lay there, inert and unhelpful but then slowly it too started to smoulder and a spurt of gas ignited from one side. Issie had no idea how long it had taken – she had lost all sense of time – but finally she had a proper little fire going. It was no bigger than the size of a dinner plate but slowly she was able to enlarge it and soon had to go for more fuel.

There were plenty of fallen twigs, branches and sprays of dead leaves around her but to gather them she had to leave the fire exposed to the wind, which gusted through the hedge unpredictably. Issie took her backpack and propped it up carefully between two of the larger branches in an improvised windbreak. Then she moved as quickly as she could and gathered more wood, still handicapped by a useless right hand but at least she could wedge the sticks under her arm and keep the left hand free.

By the time she returned the fire had sunk low, so she added twigs first, some of the driest dead leaves and held her breath waiting for them to catch. The leaves took first, bursting into sudden flame that ignited the twigs. She added a stick about the width of her thumb. It was the driest she had found; would it take? It started to smoke, moisture bubbled, and then the underside glowed red and it finally caught fire. Issie laughed and added a few more twigs. Hissing, smoking, protesting, her fire had finally decided it was not going to die.

Satisfied that she could focus on something else for a few minutes Issie turned her attention to fixing one of the bin liners – split along one side and the bottom to open it out – across the thickest part of the hedge. She used the thorny hawthorn to spear it and then tied pieces of string from the puttees around convenient branches to hold it firm, using her teeth to do a lot of the work. After ten minutes she had one liner attached. It billowed and sucked as fingers of wind tormented it but by resting her pack against the bottom edge she took much of the stress off the bindings and it relaxed. So did Issie.

The shelter cut down the wind substantially. It was just two feet high, and draughts still whistled beneath the lower edge as she hadn't been able to get the plastic flush to the ground, but it was a huge improvement. Plus the more it snowed the thicker the drift became on the far side of the hedge and bizarrely that would help protect her. After tending her fire, Issie managed to secure a second liner in the same way, widening the windbreak.

The fire by now was the size of a large frying pan and able to cope with branches half the width of her wrist. It still hissed horribly with each new piece and some of the snow from the branch canopy melted in the heat and dampened the flames. Issie decided to attach a further bin liner to the branches above her, blown almost horizontal by decades of prevailing wind. It took her longer, much longer, to complete this task and by the time she had finished she could barely see what she was doing, even with light from the fire, but it made an enormous difference. Next she managed to fasten another liner to the hedge and pulled it down to the ground, weighted with stones and her bag of wet clothing so that her shelter was now just open to the lee side where the fire was.

There was now virtually no snowfall in her little den beneath the trees. She cleared what was left of it away with her feet and found a few more twigs, which she placed immediately on the fire. It was smoky but not too bad. She could afford to make herself comfortable. Issie crawled out and went foraging again, this time looking for as many branches as she could find so that she could place them as a frame to keep her off the frozen ground, with leaves and dead bracken to make a bit of a cushion. She couldn't spend as much time on the task as she would have liked because of the fire but she gathered enough for a thin layer. She unrolled her sleeping bag, slipping it inside the last of the bin liners from her pack before placing her remaining spare clothing – a shirt and two jumpers – underneath. Then she unwrapped the last puttee, ripped it along the seams and put it on top of the thin mattress she had made before laying the sleeping bag on top of it.

Feeling very pleased with herself but incredibly tired Issie wrapped the foil over her shoulders and sat back in her shelter, wriggling bottom first up against the hedge, with her feet and legs close around the fire. There was a small stack of branches within reach, enough for an hour or so, she thought, though she would have been unable to justify that conclusion had she been asked. It felt so good not to have to walk or to carry the backpack. Her legs felt burning hot but she knew they couldn't be. Even though her jeans weren't very wet they were icy cold but they should start to warm up now. She nibbled another biscuit and swallowed a sip of water. With no expectation of success she gave the top of the thermos another savage twist with her left hand . . . and felt it give! Two more attempts eased it free.

Very carefully she poured herself half a cup of sweet tea, replaced the screw top and sipped. Bliss! The sweet heat filled her mouth and she swallowed, feeling the warmth trickle down inside her. Another sip, then another and the cup was empty. She poured some more and drank slowly, savouring every micro-mouthful.

Slowly Issie's head cleared as her body warmed. She still couldn't feel her right hand but there was a strange tingling up and down her arm that made her hopeful. It had been stupid to hold onto her hip like that for so long, locking her hand in one position, exposed to the cold. Clenching her teeth, she prised the white, claw-like fingers back fearing they might snap. They didn't and all but her little finger stayed almost straight. In the gloom they looked skeletal.

'Maybe it's the start of frostbite,' she muttered and pushed her hand under her armpit.

Her gloves were soaked through and drying by the fire. She looked around her improvised shelter properly for the first time and saw it for what it really was. In her mind-numbed state she had been building a little nest without thought of purpose or consequence beyond an escape from the storm. The modest heat from her small fire and the inner warmth of the tea were clearing her mind steadily. She realised she would never survive the night, not even in this shelter.

At some point, maybe in a few hours at most, she would run out of fallen wood for the fire and she had nothing with which to cut more. She might just be able to break off smaller branches – and the exercise would do her good – but would it be enough to last the night?

Issie shuddered at the reality of her situation and bit back tears. What really scared her was the effect the cold had had on her mind. She had been sinking into a hypothermic state of calm stupidity, just like they said in Pappy's survival guides. It would have killed her. At least now she was thinking straight again but what was she to do? She needed a plan. There weren't that many options really: she could stay or she could go.

The survival manuals typically advised staying put unless the conditions you were in were dangerous or unsustainable, as it increased the chances of rescue; always assuming someone knew roughly where you might be. Was her starting point, direction of travel or current location known to anyone? No. Was her situation dangerous? Yes. Were her survival conditions sustainable? Probably not. Therefore there was no option but to move on. Issie's spirit shrank at the idea. She didn't know how far she was from Alfriston; night had fallen early; weather conditions were atrocious . . . but it was her only viable choice. If only she could stop the cramp in her hip and regain the use of her right hand she would be more confident of her chances.

As if the thought had power, a bolt of fiery pain exploded in her right thumb causing her to cry out.

'Dear God!' She was almost weeping but it was what she had asked for so she bit down hard on her lower lip.

Even so she couldn't stifle a whimper as a sensation like being electrocuted filled her index finger. Tears rolled unchecked and unnoticed down her cheeks as parts of her hand throbbed back to life.

'This must be good news,' she told herself through clenched teeth. 'I'll just wait here a few more minutes until the worst is over, then I'll pack up and be on my way.'

Issie yawned deep and long as she picked up another branch to add to the flames, noting with satisfaction that the fire was now hot enough for it to catch almost at once. As soon as it was burning she added another one on top. Her eyes focused on the flames, on their colour and brightness, the patterns and shapes, anything that would distract her from her own burning discomfort. When she was a little girl she had told herself stories about what she could see in the fire and she did so again to keep her mind away from the pain in her fingers. There, was that a little gnome running to escape a wizard's spell? Would he make it? Yes! And there . . . Issie yawned . . . was that another little man . . . a scurrying flicker in the flames . . . would he escape? . . . yes . . . no . . . oh dear. Issie yawned again.

CHAPTER FIFTY-FOUR

The newsagent sold a guide to Alfriston with a fold-out map. Fenwick and Nesbit had agreed that the best place to assemble the search party was the village hall close to St Andrew's church. They expected Bernstein and her team to arrive before they set off, boosting their numbers. The hill into the centre of the village was too steep for any vehicle to drive up, including the MIU, so that was left in the car park south of the village. Fenwick and Nesbit set off to find the keyholder for the hall. The third operations team that had remained behind for lack of transport would carry up portable equipment.

As soon as they stepped out of the MIU the wind punched their backs, almost knocking them over.

'This is crazy,' Nesbit shouted.

'You made a commitment to her parents,' Fenwick yelled back, hoping his words carried.

Any further conversation died as they concentrated on keeping their footing on the treacherous pavement. They hardly saw a soul and were about to concede that they couldn't find the hall when someone appeared from the doorway of the lower inn in the village and walked up to them.

'Hi, I'm John Pembroke, publican of this manor. One of your officers has just told me what this is all about. You'll never find the girl in this without local help. Which one of you is in charge?'

Fenwick pointed to Nesbit who introduced himself.

'Your man said you were bringing out dogs?' Nesbit nodded. 'Well, good luck with that. It's sheepdogs you'll be needing in this. They're trained to find animals in the snow. And yes, before you ask, I know where there are a few around here.'

'Thank you,' Fenwick jumped in.

'But we're not asking for volunteers,' Jack Nesbit insisted.

'They'll come anyway, as soon as they find out. You might as well get ready for them. Meanwhile, I'll show you the way to the vicarage; that's where you'll find the hall keys.'

They followed him through a gate and down a brick path to the front door of the vicarage. The door was opened by a round-faced, cheerful woman in her late thirties.

'Hello, John.' She smiled warmly and turned to the strangers. 'I'm Juliette Barber, the vicar's wife. How can we help you?'

They showed their warrant cards and her face clouded with concern.

'I'll leave them with you, Juliette; got things to see to.'

Pembroke left, no doubt to drum up volunteers, Fenwick thought and was relieved, though he could see that Nesbit was worried.

'Come in, come in. Let me take your coats. George! Two police officers are here.'

A boy of about ten poked his head out of a door on the right of the hall.

'Mark, go and put the kettle on. Anne, help your brother. Now please; jump to it, Miss Curiosity.'

The children were almost the same age as Fenwick's and he suddenly remembered it was Christmas Eve and they would be waiting for him. Guilt washed through him, almost as strong as his concern for Issie. He pushed it away. Juliette led them into a comfortable sitting room and was encouraging them to sit down when her husband walked in and shook them warmly by the hand.

'George Barber, vicar of St Andrew's, what can we do for you?'

He was perhaps a little younger than his wife and shorter, already balding on top, with pale-blue eyes and fair hair.

Nesbit explained why they were in Alfriston and what they needed.

'You think Isabelle Mattias has been held around here?' Juliette Barber sounded incredulous. 'And we didn't know? Oh my.' Her hand fluttered to her throat and she looked devastated. 'Poor, poor girl. You know who she is, George; you remember her. She used to come to church with her grandparents, all through the summer and sometimes at Christmas, until a year ago when her grandfather died.'

'Issie, yes, of course; lovely girl. Always kind and patient with the children, particularly Anne. So sad, to lose her father and then her grandfather soon after. They were very close. And she's been kept around here?'

'We have every reason to believe so and that she is trying to walk from her grandmother's house to Alfriston along the South Downs Way.'

'In this?' All eyes turned to the window. 'Oh no; may the Lord protect and guide her to us.'

'Amen,' his wife said.

'We're sending out a search team and need to use your church hall as a muster point.'

'Well yes, you could, but it's been set up for coffee and mince pies after the Christingle Service.'

'Of course you can.' Husband and wife spoke at the same time.

'I'll go over there straight away,' the vicar said, 'and ask them to make ready for you.'

'I'll do it, George. You need to get ready for Christingle; it starts in under an hour.'

'Is it that time already? Well yes, but don't go on your own, dear. Ah tea; you must have some, detectives. You need to keep up your strength and it will take us a while to clear the refreshments away.'

'Five minutes, then,' Nesbit said, remembering to add, 'thank you.'

Anne carried in a tray with a tea service and a plate of biscuits; her brother brought in two mugs as their parents disappeared to their various duties. Fenwick and Nesbit were left in the comfortable sitting room with two wide-eyed children. A coal and log fire crackled behind a fireguard.

'I put the star on the top of the tree this year,' Mark said proudly, breaking the silence.

'Did you, all by yourself?' Without realising it Fenwick had adopted the tone he used with Chris and didn't notice Nesbit's surprised glance.

'Yes.'

'No, Daddy helped you,' his sister insisted.

'Only a bit, just to hold the steps.'

'That's impressive, Mark.' Fenwick sipped the boiling-hot tea, eager to leave, and scalded his tongue.

'I made *that*.' His sister pointed to a coat hanger bent into a circle that had been decorated with tinsel and cut-out paper stars and angels. To the untrained eye it was a misshapen coat hanger but Fenwick recognised a Christmas wreath from years of receiving similar offerings. It had been given pride of place over the fireplace.

'*Very* good,' he said. 'I like that angel there in particular. The face is very lifelike.'

Anne beamed.

Fenwick's phone rang. He excused himself and took the call in the hall.

'Hello?'

'Andrew, it's Alice. Sorry to disturb you.'

'Is there a problem? Are the children all right?'

'Yes, yes, it's not that, it's just that . . .'

As always when embarrassed Alice could not finish her sentence.

'You want to know whether I'll be home tonight.'

'Well, yes . . . and that you're looking after yourself. Your mother and I were talking just now and we thought . . . well, that is to say . . .'

Fenwick swallowed his irritation. Could they think of nothing but their own trivial necessities?

'The simple answer, Alice, is that I don't know whether I'll be home before midnight or not. There's been a break in the case and we have an urgent search starting. God willing it will be over soon but . . .' he closed his eyes briefly, 'I just can't say. I haven't got a crystal ball.'

'Of course not, no.'

She sounded upset; why was she so sensitive all of a sudden?

'And tomorrow . . . is there any chance?'

'I don't know! Look, I have no idea. It will depend on how long the search lasts.' *And what we find.*

'It's Christmas Day tomorrow, Andrew. Had you forgotten?'

'Let me speak to him.' He could hear his mother's voice in the background, drawing nearer, and his jaw tightened.

'Andrew?'

'Hello, Mother.'

'I gather you're out searching for this poor wee girl.'

'She's eighteen but she is a wee thing and yes, we are.'

His mother's voice dropped so that he could barely hear her.

'Is she still alive do you think, son? Is there any chance?'

A shot of pure love for his mother tightened his throat without warning.

'I hope so, Mum; I really do but . . . she may be out there in this storm right now.'

'Oh, my dear. Does that mean you'll be venturing forth yourself, Andrew? Or will you leave that to the experts?'

'They are on their way and we have an operations unit here

already with winter equipment so they will start immediately.' *Is evasion a lie?*

'What time is it? Almost quarter of four but the daylight's already gone. Will you search in the dark?'

'We will continue for as long as it takes. Issie won't survive long in this.'

'Of course. So we should assume that you won't be home anytime soon. I'll explain it to the children somehow, don't worry. Better that you don't talk to them, you'll only upset them. You concentrate on finding that poor lassie. If you possibly can, try and give us a call tomorrow so we can wish you a happy Christmas and vice versa . . . oh, and let us know if you'll be home after all because we can always delay lunch.'

'Thank you, Mum.'

'Oh, and Andrew?'

'Yes?'

'You look after yourself . . . and . . . and I'm very proud of you.'

With that she was gone. Had she waited for a response Fenwick wouldn't have been able to give one. His mother never ceased to surprise him.

Juliette Barber walked in as Fenwick was about to return to the sitting room.

'That's all sorted. Oh, and you should know that there are seven big strong volunteers waiting there for you. Word has got around, thanks to John. Now, you both look famished, you must take a thermos of soup with you.'

Suitably provisioned, she led them to the village hall where the Christmas refreshments had been moved to one end and a space cleared large enough to accommodate the incident team and volunteers plus portable equipment from the MIU. A trestle table was being stocked by women Fenwick suspected were from the local WI with food, urns of hot drinks, torches and blankets.

A large platter of home-cured ham and mustard sandwiches appeared courtesy of the pub and disappeared quickly.

Nesbit split the incident team into four groups and evened up the numbers with volunteers so that each search party comprised four to five men. The female officers and volunteers were politely told that they could not go out. It was a tough call in an age of equality but Nesbit remained firm. 'Let them sue me', he muttered to Fenwick. Using the Ordnance Survey map, he allocated search zones and named them Matthew, Mark, Luke and John in deference to their location and the time of year. The team that had left the farm to walk the Way as far as they could before nightfall, he belatedly christened Andrew.

Shortly after the search teams left George Barber rushed in, his cheeks flushed as if he had been running.

'Oh, you've already started. I'm sorry to be late.' Fenwick stared at him, confused. 'I wanted to say a prayer to bless the search,' the vicar explained. 'I think it would make sense anyway, don't you?'

The people in the room bowed their heads while he prayed for God's help and guidance in finding Issie. Fenwick kept his head bowed until Nesbit coughed loudly and he looked up and realised that the vicar had left to conduct the children's Christmas service for all those too young to stay awake for carols and midnight Mass.

There was silence in the hall, broken only by the radio as the search teams reported back. It was always the same; no news. At five past four DI Bernstein arrived with Bazza, Cobb and half a dozen others. Fenwick stared at her in disbelief; she looked awful, haggard with great bags under her eyes and straggling wild hair. Bazza was no better; he'd clearly not had time for his second shave of the day.

'Good grief, Andrew, you look terrible.'

'Nice to see you too.'

'And you are?' she asked Nesbit, walking over with her hand stuck out.

'DCI Jack Nesbit.'

'Superintendent Bernstein and it's Deidre. So what have we got, Jack?'

It was clear that she had immediately assumed command and she pulled Nesbit to one side so that he could brief her. Bazza came over to where Fenwick was staring at the map.

'It's pitch-black out there,' he said, 'and the blizzard shows no signs of easing. If anything, I think it's getting worse. If we don't find her soon . . .'

'Don't waste your breath stating the obvious.'

'Yes, but we don't even know for sure that she's out there. This could be a wild goose chase.'

'Issie's there somewhere, I'm sure of it. She was at the farm this morning and managed to drug Mariner. It's just like her to plan an escape.'

'In this weather? You've always said she was smart.'

'She didn't know. The blizzard was forecast for tomorrow.'

'If she left after lunch, there's a possibility she's already dead.'

'Do you think I don't know that?' Fenwick snapped and then shook his head. 'She would have planned ahead. She's resourceful.'

'But not indestructible,' Nesbit countered, walking up behind them.

'We must go on,' Fenwick protested and looked at Bernstein. 'Deidre, please, we can't abandon her.'

'We're proposing the following, Andrew.' Fenwick held his breath. 'Each team will do forty minutes before coming back. We'll run them in cycles. My lot can go out now and relieve Matthew and Mark. They'll work the parts of the grid not yet covered.'

'And Luke and John?'

'We need them back here. Don't look like that. Once we see

531

what state the first two teams are in we can decide whether they can do another stint and for how long.'

Fenwick knew it was impossible to argue. She was right. Lives were at risk.

'What about calling in the army, or mountain rescue?'

Deidre patted his arm.

'A TA unit from Brighton was despatched over an hour ago so they should be here soon. We're lucky; some of them have had Arctic training. They'll start a search immediately they arrive, probably taking over from the police teams. The dog handlers are en route but stuck behind a pile-up and don't know what time they'll arrive. Meanwhile, there are several farmers in the parties already out there with their sheepdogs. By the way, when is Tate due back here with Mariner?'

'We were taking Mariner straight to Lewes, Deidre,' Nesbit interjected. 'There didn't seem much point dragging him through the weather on an unnecessary journey. He may have to go to hospital; he's in a bad way.'

'Good, I hope the bastard dies and saves us the trouble of a trial. It would be a lot less complicated.' She flicked a glance at Fenwick and grimaced. 'So Tate is with him?'

'I, er, hang on.' Nesbit checked his notebook. 'No, he's in team Andrew, the one that set out from the farm.'

'And they are where exactly right now?'

One of the radio operators looked up.

'They haven't checked in for ten minutes, ma'am. Perhaps they don't have a signal.'

'Call them; keep trying until you get through.'

She and Nesbit returned to the map while Bazza hovered over the radios and Cobb helped himself to tea and cake. None of them noticed when Fenwick slipped away.

CHAPTER FIFTY-FIVE

When Nightingale's mobile phone rang she thought immediately of Fenwick for some reason.

'Nightingale.'

'Oh good.' Try as she might Nightingale couldn't place the voice and its soft Scottish accent. 'Alice tried you at home but then thought you're probably out somewhere. Anyway . . .'

'Alice? What's happened; are the children all right, and Andrew? Is he OK?'

'Calm down, dear; nothing is wrong – at least, not right this instant it isn't. This is Andrew's mother, Gertrude Fenwick.'

'Oh hello, Mrs Fenwick.'

'Now, this will seem a strange request but I would like you to consider joining us for Christmas.'

Nightingale automatically looked at her watch as her brain seized up. It was four-thirty. She was at her brother's house where she was to spend Christmas, in the middle of helping Naomi before her family clan descended. It was her way of compensating for a planned early departure on Boxing Day. Twenty-four hours *en famille* was about all she thought she'd be able to handle. She became aware of a patient silence on the other end of the call.

'May I ask why, please?'

'I realise it is short notice and that it might be difficult for you; you're sure to have other plans. However, I think it very unlikely that my son will be here tonight and maybe even tomorrow for that matter and I am concerned for the children, Bess in particular. She has taken the news extremely badly.'

'With a tantrum and hysterics?' Nightingale sighed.

'Indeed. Now, I don't normally tolerate such behaviour but Alice tells me that the children haven't seen their father for more than a brief stay in three weeks.'

'Really?'

'Yes. Of course many children have to cope with absent fathers but having no mother either, and the uncertainty . . . never knowing when they might see him. All that exhausted hope and weary expectation. It's quite destabilising.'

'I'm sure Andrew doesn't realise. I mean, he cares for them so much, I'm certain . . .' Nightingale stopped, realising that she was defending the indefensible to the man's mother who probably knew him a darn sight better than she did. 'Anyway, um, why would my being there . . . I don't quite see?'

'I'm not one to beat about the bush, Miss Nightingale. The children adore you, Bess especially, but even Chrissy. I know you haven't done anything to encourage this . . .'

'I haven't, honestly, quite the opposite. The last thing I wanted to do was make their lives even more complicated.'

'I believe you. Alice has no reason to welcome their attachment to you but she is also a fan . . . yes, you are dear, you know you are. Where was I?'

'You've asked me to come and stay to help the children through a difficult Christmas, possibly without their father.'

'That's it exactly, well done. So, what do you say?'

Nightingale could see her nephew Barnabas staring in awe at the presents under the tree, old enough to know it was special but too young still to be spoilt. Her heart ached and she didn't know what to do.

'But what will Andrew say? He'll hate the idea.'

She heard his mother sigh.

'I very much fear that it may be my son who will need you most.'

Decision made.

Nightingale drove very slowly from her brother's house to Fenwick's home, sticking to main roads until the last possible moment. Gertrude Fenwick's last words were in her mind constantly. Fenwick had to be out there looking for Issie, even though it wasn't his case. He had been hovering on the edges of it ever since Norman had replaced him, encouraged she suspected by Superintendent Bernstein. A flash of anger made her grimace. It was irresponsible of that woman to endanger Fenwick's career just because she needed his help. No, that was unfair; Andrew would have been all too willing to remain involved.

If Issie Mattias died . . . she shook the thought away; it was too painful to contemplate. He had invested so much of himself into finding her. But what was he doing on Christmas Eve in the middle of a blizzard? What could be keeping him away from home other than a break in the case? She had to know. Nightingale rang her old boss from Harlden, Superintendent Quinlan. He would be able to find out; his connections were legendary. Ten minutes later Nightingale knew all she needed to and now she wasn't just worried for Fenwick's state of mind. She was scared stiff that he would be out looking for Issie personally. In this!

She called his mobile only to hear the automated voice tell her to leave a message.

'Andrew, it's Nightingale. It is now five o'clock on Christmas Eve and I need to speak to you. It's urgent, please call me.'

She closed the call and immediately said his name again to redial. This time the electronic voice informed her that the mailbox was full. Her pulse throbbed painfully in her throat as she drove. Part of her wanted to turn around and head east; out to where Quinlan had told her the search party was hunting.

'You fool, Andrew. Why can't you just, for once, leave it to the experts and come home? It isn't even your damn case!' Her voice caught and she punched the steering wheel.

It wouldn't do to turn up with tears on her cheeks. As she turned north-east into the teeth of the storm she had to turn the windscreen wipers to full speed but they could barely cope with the onslaught of snow and ice battering her car. Nightingale's heart constricted with fear. *If he really was out in this . . . if Issie was in this . . . they don't stand a chance. Someone was going to die.*

Would Andrew have had the sense to stay in the operations centre? Never; finding Issie had gone beyond obsession. She had seen him compelled to take risks on other cases; had experienced his willingness to do the unconventional in the heat of the chase, or sometimes out of sheer bloody-mindedness, but this was different. Somehow returning Issie alive to her mother had become his sole purpose in life.

No wonder his children felt abandoned. They had been. Nightingale composed herself and took a deep breath. After a journey of almost an hour she would soon be with them. They would look in her eyes and search her face for reassurance. They mustn't see the fear and desperation she felt. As she pulled into his drive she practised a smile in the rear-view mirror . . . and then tried again.

CHAPTER FIFTY-SIX

'You can't go out on your own in this!'

The shout barely carried through the howling gale.

'I said . . .' A heavy hand grabbed Fenwick's shoulder and spun him round. 'Oh, it's you, sir. I'm sorry, I thought you were some damn-fool volunteer heading off on their own. DCI Nesbit has given strict instructions not to let anyone past unless they are part of an official search party.'

'Yet you're here in this on your own.'

'We swap every fifteen minutes, sir, again the DCI's orders. There are three of us rotating this shift. The other two are keeping warm in the village hall. I'll be relieved in five minutes.'

'I see; good system.'

'Nesbit's like that, sir; always by the book.'

Fenwick's mood plummeted. The search could be called off any minute.

'Look, you head on back; I'll wait for your replacement as I'm here.'

He could see the officer straining not to ask him what exactly he was doing there.

'I'd better wait, sir. He gave strict instructions.'

'Look, Sergeant . . .'

'Constable, sir. Under all of this I don't carry any stripes.'

Fenwick smiled.

'Well anyway, what's your name?'

'Carlton, sir.'

'First name?'

'Eddie.'

'Well Eddie, I'm going to stay out anyway. I needed some fresh air and to get a sense of the conditions personally.'

'They're terrible; I've never seen anything like it. Even the TAs who are out there are saying this is worse than some of their Arctic training.' It was clear that Carlton thought the search a risky waste of time.

'Two minutes and your replacement will be here. Go on, head back. I'll cover for you.' Fenwick managed to keep his voice neutral.

'Well,' Carlton checked his watch, 'as you say, sir, only a minute to go and you're here . . .'

Fenwick watched until the officer's back disappeared into the swirling snow and then turned down the footpath that led out of Alfriston away from the Cuckmere River towards the South Downs Way. He could barely see his way, despite the orange tape that had been strung along the fence to help the search parties find their way back. He had to bend double against the wind that was blowing constantly from the north-east, almost strong enough to knock him over.

His thick overcoat was bare protection from the icy blasts and his leather driving gloves were inadequate for the freezing temperatures and penetrating cold. At least he had remembered to put on a hat before leaving. There had been a red woollen bobble thing on a peg by the door that he had borrowed. Every now and then he thought he could hear shouts above the bellow of the storm but no sooner had he concentrated on the sound than the wind whipped it away.

The snow along the path had been beaten by the search parties into a rutted ice passage about two feet wide with mounds of snow to either side, sometimes in drifts waist high. Fenwick kept to it, treading forward determinedly until he could make out the constant calls of the searchers and the occasional yelps of excited – perhaps terrified – dogs.

'Issie! . . . Issieee . . . Come on lass, where are you?'

There was a party immediately ahead of him and they soon converged. Fenwick recognised John, the big publican, by his orange puffed jacked.

'What are you doing out here, Mr Fenwick?'

'Thought I'd join in for a spell.'

'It's madness to come on your own; you're putting your own life at risk and that won't help the girl. We're just on our way back. Two of the volunteers are in a bad way so I've had to call it a day. I need to tell them at the hall to be more selective with the volunteers. Some of these old lads shouldn't have left their firesides.'

'Is there another group further on? I'll join them.'

John looked at him in exasperation and shook his head.

'You're not dressed properly and bluntly you're not setting the best example, if you don't mind me saying so.'

'I do mind,' Fenwick shouted above the wind, 'but as you're helping us I'll let the remark pass.' But he realised he had no effective authority over the man. They were equals in the eye of the storm.

They trudged back in silence, John in the lead catching most of the wind that was hammering into their faces.

'Was there any sign of her?'

John turned and cupped his ear for Fenwick to repeat his question.

'No.' He shook his head.

Fenwick realised that shouting Issie's name into the wind might be futile.

'If she's still some way away she'll never hear us,' Fenwick shouted in John's ear.

'I know, but let's hope the party coming from her grandmother's converges on ours and closes the gap.'

Tate! He hadn't given the young officer a moment's thought but he was out in this too and without the benefit of provisions, equipment and a relief pattern. Was Nesbit expecting him to walk the whole way?

'Give me a minute.'

'Cold already?'

'I need to check something.'

Fenwick pulled out his mobile and saw that he had a weak signal; one bar. Tate had rung him several times so the number should still be in the memory of the phone. He found it and pressed call back. It rang for a long time before an automated voice told him that the phone he was calling was out of range or switched off.

'What's the matter?'

'One of my officers; he's in the party that left the farm. I wanted to see how they were doing.'

'With luck they will have had sense enough to turn around,' John said bluntly. 'Come on, we need to keep moving or we're going to freeze.'

'You seem to know what you're doing, John,' he shouted.

'Before I came here I owned a pub near Scafell in the Lake District. I was a volunteer in the local search and rescue.'

Fenwick nodded. At least he was in good company in what even he had to acknowledge was a dangerous venture. John was wearing full alpine gear and Fenwick understood now that it wasn't because he was a skier. He could no longer feel his feet. The outer layer of his scarf was frozen solid where he had it wrapped around his face.

'We need to get warm and you into dry clothing. Come to the pub with me. You're about my size, a bit taller perhaps, but I've some togs that should suit.'

'Thank you.' Fenwick clapped John on the shoulder.

Fenwick kept trying Tate's number without success. He was becoming seriously worried for him. As they trudged up the main road they bumped into the vicar on his way to the church hall.

'Superintendent, John; how goes it?'

'Nothing so far, George, I'm afraid.'

The vicar hung his head and Fenwick realised it was for prayer and not in despair.

'Will you be going ahead with the midnight service?' John asked.

'Of course! I realise few will turn out – we only had ten families at Christingle and normally the church is packed – but for those who wish to take Communion and celebrate the day of Christ's birth the church must be open. In fact, there are people in there now praying for Issie and I expect that number to grow as the evening passes. Who could sit comfortably at home knowing she might be out there somewhere so close to us?'

'You're right, of course; I just hope a few of them will still need sustenance.' John immediately looked as if he regretted his words and shook his head to dismiss them. 'Never mind. Come on, Mr Fenwick, let's get you into proper clothes.'

The search was called off minutes after Fenwick arrived back at the hall, now dressed in John's spare winter gear. Chief Constable Norman had been receiving updates every fifteen minutes from Bernstein and it had been his decision finally for the search to cease when she told him they already had one officer on the way to hospital and three receiving medical attention locally from paramedics who had at last arrived.

At five-forty Tate's party had arrived in Alfriston on a tractor trailer. One of the officers was taken to hospital with suspected frostbite but Tate seemed to be all right. His safe arrival was the only light in what promised to be a bleak evening. Fenwick tried again to venture out but John and Nesbit forcibly restrained him, much to the embarrassment of those who witnessed it.

He felt stupid. There he was, dressed in full rescue kit of ski long johns, thermal vest and socks, shirts and jumpers which kept him warm but still allowed his skin to breathe, and they wouldn't let him out there. He even had a pair of rugged boots; old and scuffed but serviceable and far better than the wellingtons he had been wearing. Dressed for the weather he had reasoned that he could stand another couple of hours outside but the others disagreed. Even though the worst of the blizzard seemed to be passing and the wind was slowly easing to storm force, the conditions continued to be diabolical. Half the village had lost power and none of the roads were passable.

Jane Saxby had been calling every ten minutes, sometimes Bernstein, at others Fenwick. It was Bernstein who had told her that the search had been called off for the night.

'We will resume at first light, ma'am.'

'That will be too late and you know it! Why aren't you doing something now?'

'We have tried everything we possibly could . . .'

'What about helicopters? Have you tried them?'

'We attempted to involve our own, the air ambulance and the coastguard but they are unable to fly in these conditions.'

'The army, then!'

'The Territorial Army has been part of our search and we had the good fortune to have an Arctic-trained unit to call on. We really have tried everything.'

The call ended with tears, recriminations and a hail of abuse from Bill Saxby. Fenwick had volunteered to take over but Bernstein waved him away with a muttered: 'You're not even meant to be here!' and he backed off.

The hall was packed with stranded police officers and a few of the volunteers who seemed to be enjoying the experience.

Members of the local WI, without prompting, started a search for beds for them all. Juliette and John organised food to be delivered to the hall so that they could eat a hot meal. There was beer and wine to go with the meal, courtesy of the pubs, and spirits started to lift as they always do, even in dire times, when there is warmth, food, alcohol and convivial company, particularly after a shared risky endeavour. A flurry of carol singing broke out as they sat down only to die away before the end of the last verse as they remembered why they were there. Fenwick couldn't stand it and used the confusion to step outside.

As he huddled in the shelter of a wall, two volunteers left the hall. He pulled back into the shadows so as not to be seen.

'This is crazy, David. Gyp's a smart dog. She'll be home soon, you see.'

'I can't leave her out there, Fred, not in this. She's been in all sorts of winter weather on the hills with me before and she's never run off, not once.'

'But you're putting yourself at risk, man.'

'I'm dressed for it, so are you; and if you come along then I'll have my big TA-trained brother with me, won't I?'

'Mam will go nuts if she finds out. And we're due back for dinner at seven-thirty.'

'That gives us an hour, then. Come on.'

David switched on a torch and the two brothers strode away. Fenwick followed at a safe distance. The brothers headed back towards the footpath. It was still snowing but the wind was dropping. His breath misted in the air. Fenwick let them get ahead, switched on his torch and stepped into the snow to the north of the path, remembering what John had said about Issie possibly not being able to hear them above the storm. He could hear the two men calling, first '*Issie*' and then '*Gyp*', increasingly faintly.

'Issie!' Although the snow was deep the experience was

better than before as the wind had moderated and his boots maintained a grip on the freezing snow. 'Issie! Where are you? Come on, love, your mother's worried sick. You don't need to hide any more.'

'Issie!'

Behind him, the bells of St Andrews started to peal, as if urging him forward. Fenwick was sure that if he just kept on walking he would find her.

Issie slept, a deep comforting sleep that danced on the borders of oblivion. Beyond her eyelids the gentle glow of her dying fire played a game of shadows that fell into sweet dreams.

She was hiding but not out of fear; it was a game of hide-and-seek, in which her aim was to sink into the background, become invisible even to her family and friends. It was a familiar challenge. A short walk down this path, a quick turn of that corner, a slide along and down into the darkness of a concealing tunnel. She was so good at this.

They would never find her. She would burrow down deep into the cold earth; cold to them but welcoming to her; her natural element. A little cave of hibernation.

Her breathing slowed. It was comfortable here in this cosy den. She was snuggled up tight in a ball, curled like a full-term baby waiting to be born, one little fist under her chin the other hand a pillow for her cheek.

And it was peaceful. She felt a stillness like music all around her. The crack and rattle of her makeshift shelter had receded beyond her ears' hearing; the billowing pressure on the black plastic was a heartbeat. Her nose could no longer smell the acrid ash of her fading fire. She was beyond it all.

Floating. She had never slept on so comfortable a bed. The brittle branches were goose down; her toes were insensitive to the cramped, hard edges of her boots but twitched and stretched in her dream as she kept running farther and farther away. She was no longer shivering but yawned uncontrollably.

Someone was calling her name in a deep, masculine voice. They sounded anxious, scared even. Issie frowned in her sleep. She hoped they would go away soon. She was so tired. All she wanted was to rest, sleeping outside under the open sky.

It reminded her of Africa, when she had camped under the vast turning canopy of stars with her father. That had been the happiest period of her life. If she had died there and then, trampled by the poor, terrified elephant, she would have been content because nothing could ever again match the perfection of that time. Just the two of them and the tracker alone, camping rough but protected in the circle of light cast from their campfire. Like now.

Her breathing slowed infinitesimally on each breath, so gentle, so calm, no panic or fear.

That man was calling her again. Why was he so insistent? Couldn't he just leave her alone? She was at peace here under the stars, her father only feet away on the other side of the fire. Though her eyes were closed she could sense him there, a solid comforting presence in an otherwise uncertain world.

Was he awake and looking at her through the flames? Wondering whether she was dreaming or just faking sleep? The thought made her smile. Of course she was asleep but at the same time she was with him. Issie sighed and it was a long time before her chest rose again on a shallow intake of breath.

That wretched man. He was so loud now. Why wouldn't he just go away? Perhaps she should tell him, explain that she wanted to be left alone. Yes, that's what she would do. She would open her mouth; swallow, lick her dry lips and just tell him. Except that her jaw was so heavy and her tongue was like lead. It lay there as if held between her teeth by a thick elastic band. She strained but it just would not move. She tried focusing on the small muscles of her mouth and lips: open, shape, speak – she told them but they wouldn't obey.

Issie relaxed back into herself. There was no point worrying. She didn't really want to speak to him anyway and he would go away eventually. He'd never find her. She was so good at hiding when she wanted to.

Seconds passed and then minutes. His voice rose and fell on the wind, sometimes close, sometimes distant, as if he were on the far side of a valley that was impossible to cross. At some point she must have fallen into a deeper sleep because she could no longer hear him, though she sensed that he was still out there.

The sound of church bells almost roused her. They were insistent, demanding her attention, so that she half opened her eyes in wonder. How beautiful, she thought and held her breath in ecstasy. She was briefly aware of the cold, of the bitter chill rising from the ground; of the fire at her feet dwindling to ash. It needed more fuel. She should do that . . . put on another branch . . . now really, before it died down too far.

Yes, she should do that . . . in just a moment . . . but the cold receded again and faded with the sound of the bells to become a vague memory . . . Issie knew it was important that she did something . . . for a reason she couldn't remember . . . What was it she had to do? The action hovered at the edge of her mind as she sank back . . . It had been something . . . but what? Issie sighed.

Oh, that man was back; his insistence was almost sweet . . . the way he kept on looking for her. So kind . . . just like her father . . . and then she realised . . . of course . . . her father . . . Who else would be so determined to find her? . . . Why else would she feel no fear? . . . Just the opposite . . . she was cradled by a sense of security so absolute that she knew she was safe . . . Safe . . . in the right place . . .

It was her father's voice . . . there . . . again . . . his voice and behind it his music! Issie was suffused with a warm inner peace. Deep, deep in her dream Issie opened her eyes and with sight that could no longer see rested her gaze on the beloved face of the man sitting cross-legged on the other side of the fire, his head tilted to one side in that way he had; curious, alert, amused. Loving. Her father was smiling at her, waiting for her.

CHAPTER FIFTY-SEVEN

Fenwick could only just hear the brothers searching for Gyp now. In heading north away from the Way his path was diverging from theirs. He had to climb a hill and steeled himself for the blast of the gale at the top but it didn't come. The storm was passing. He looked around to gain his bearings and noticed that his tracks stood out black on the purity of the snow. There was light from somewhere. He looked up and noticed that the eastern clouds were slightly lighter than those overhead. As he walked on, the fallen snow slowly started to glow blue as the clouds thinned and moonlight filtered through.

'Issie!'

He knew the chances of her being alive were remote but perhaps she had found some shelter. And people could survive extremes of cold; he'd read about it. She had been outside at least five hours now in weather that could kill a healthy man in a fraction of that time but she would have found somewhere to wait out the worst of the storm: a barn with straw to keep her warm; or a stable among horses or cows whose animal heat could have saved her. Or she had made it to someone's house, and would be tucked up snug and warm right now, unable to let her parents know because the phone lines were down. There were plenty of reasons to hope and keep searching.

If he couldn't find her he would make a note of places to check, of ideas to follow, but for now he needed to keep focused. His mind was wandering and that wouldn't do anyone any good. He realised he was surprisingly hungry and that his legs were tiring quickly.

'Issie! Come on, love!'

He pushed forward and slipped on a patch of ice beneath a drift. He wobbled and almost fell. Pulling his leg free was hard but he managed it and then concentrated all his effort using his weight to crunch through to find a safer footing. He would have to watch every step this far away from the path, sometimes in snow above his knees, but he paced on and in that fashion made his way to the crest of the hill.

The countryside was silent. He could smell smoke from a chimney somewhere. Otherwise he could have been alone on the planet. His feet hurt, particularly one heel where the unfamiliar boot was rubbing but he welcomed the distraction to keep his mind from the cold.

There was a wooden bench on a viewing point twenty yards further on, thick with snow. By the time he reached it he needed to rest and paused, leaning on the back, breathing deeply, head down. He didn't know how long he stood like that but when he looked up again the moon was peeking from behind the clouds.

He forced himself to walk on, though it was more of a hobble now and his pace was slow. At least he could see a little better.

'Issie!' He realised that he hadn't been calling and was ashamed at his defeatism.

His voice was a croak but he kept crying her name as loudly as he could, turning three hundred and sixty degrees. There was an excited yelp from behind him and his heart leapt but it was only the missing Gyp, a black and white sheepdog with grey about the muzzle but a puppy at heart, judging by the way she ran towards Fenwick barking.

'Gyp, is that your name?' Fenwick called and the dog barked in reply, ran up to him and then backed away. 'I can't play now, Gyp.'

The dog was insistent, circling once around him barking insistently before bounding away. Fenwick followed her paw prints; it was a plan. The dog's barking had broken into the emptiness at the centre of his thoughts, leaving room for the pain of his imagining. If he could only find her, even dead, maybe he would be able to think straight again.

There was a slight dip ahead of him and beyond it a copse of trees, almost buried in the snow. The dog was running towards it, barking. Fenwick watched absently, noting the way it had found the biggest pile of snow to fight with, yapping fiercely. It ran in a circle around the copse, no doubt looking for a stick to play with.

Gyp's barking intensified as he walked closer. She must have found that stick she'd been looking for. Fenwick paid the dog no heed, not until he was almost level with a mound where she was standing rigid. It was no longer barking, it was howling. The hair stood up on the back of Fenwick's neck.

'Oh God, no; not so close all this time.'

He skidded down into the hollow and lumbered the remaining few yards to where the dog was staring at a scrap of black plastic beneath the hedge. As he approached the dog turned its head and whined, clearly scared.

'All right, Gyp, let me see, good dog.'

Fenwick patted her on the head as the dog carried on its high-pitched yelping. There was a mound of snow, almost like an igloo that had built up around the hedge. Poking out from it was the edge of a bin liner. *Please God, let her be alive*. He brushed some of the snow away to reveal more of the sack. It was pinned to the hedge, perhaps blown there? But that was string looped around one corner. He pushed the snow to either side and beneath was another mound, rigid, curled up tight beneath yet more black plastic.

Barely breathing Fenwick shuffled around until he found a hole on the far side with the remains of a fire extending from it that was still smouldering, melting the snow about it.

The dog's barking had reached a frenzy and he could hear in the distance the voice of its owner approaching.

'Over here!' he shouted. 'Quickly; I need help.'

He started to clear the snow from the entrance to the mound, keeping his torch pointed into the widening hole. He bent down to ground level and looked inside. The first thing he saw was the purple corner of a sleeping bag. Poking from the top was a tuft of auburn hair.

'Issie!'

There was so much snow above her he was worried it would collapse and smother her. He needed to be careful. Kneeling up, Fenwick scooped snow away to the sides as fast as he could, careful not to let if fall on top of her. His fingers were numb but he didn't notice as the snow covering the black liner was scraped away leaving only the sack between him and the silent girl. He managed to get a finger into the string holding one of the sacks in place and ripped it to make a hole. After several tugs the thing split and opened. He bent down and unzipped the sleeping bag a fraction . . . to reveal the pure, pale face of a child, resting as if asleep on the cushion of its hand.

Her eyes were closed, framed by the perfect arc of eyebrow, delineated by long eyelashes on which ice crystals were slowly melting. A snow angel.

'Issie, oh Issie.'

Fenwick bent his head and wept. The world faded around him, irrelevant, pointless.

'Gyp, what are you doing? Leave that alone. Come here. I said come here!'

David's voice returned Fenwick to the moment as the dog carried on whimpering behind him.

'What have you found then, girl? Oh my Lord! Fred, get over here; it's the girl. Is she alive?' He asked Fenwick.

'No, I don't think so. She's not breathing.'

'Let me look at her,' Fred pushed past his brother and Fenwick and bent down. He took in the fire, the remains of the little snow cave, the foil, her sleeping bag in one glance.

'She might still be alive even though she's not obviously breathing,' he said. 'In these conditions she could have cooled slowly and her body might have shut down enough to protect her vital organs from damage.'

Fenwick looked at him in disbelief.

'I've seen dead bodies before, she's icy to the touch, her lips are blue . . .'

'But in this cold that doesn't mean death. In the TA when we did our Arctic training the one thing they told us was: "not dead until warm". We can't give up on her.'

The rush of emotion Fenwick felt almost destabilised him. He made to start CPR.

'No! Don't do that. If she is alive giving her heart massage now could kill her. We need to be very careful.' Fred knelt down beside her and put his fingers gently against her neck. After what seemed to Fenwick an eternity he said, 'There's a carotid pulse. It's very faint but it's there, which means we are not dealing with cardiac arrest. But it's so weak she'll need to be stabilised before there's any attempt to move her.'

'Tell me what to do.' Fenwick recognised an expert.

'Breathe into her mouth hot, moist air, only a few breaths a minute – six to ten to start with, then increase up to twelve – but not with force. Just keep that going. But we need to get you kneeling on something dry or you'll be our next victim. Pull that sack down, Davey, and see about restarting the fire.'

While the brothers concentrated on the fire, Fenwick followed instructions. They managed to get a small blaze going and he shifted so that the heat could reach Issie. Gyp lay down gently on the girl's feet.

'Right, we need help on site. Give me your phone, Davey. Meanwhile, you stay close to her so that the air is warmer around her but *don't* touch her or try and rub her to get her warm. Treat her as if she is made of the most fragile glass you have ever known.'

Fenwick heard Fred giving instructions to someone on the phone and then he passed it to his brother to give a precise location.

For the next ten minutes they took it in turns to breathe into Issie's mouth. Kneeling for too long directly on the snow was too much for one person to do alone.

'Is there any way we can lift her further off the ground do you think?'

'It'll be very dangerous to try and move her at all. Her core body temperature is very low, maybe down as far as thirty or even twenty-nine degrees. So we should only move her once. I've asked for a tarpaulin, more sleeping bags or blankets and rope, plus some cushions of some sort to make a raised bed for her. As soon as they arrive we can wrap her up in a cocoon and put her on top of the cushions. Meanwhile, warm moist air is the best thing for her.'

Bernstein was at the front of the rescue team, followed by Nesbit and ten officers, each carrying something. They used spades to clear an area for a groundsheet, on top of which they arranged a bed of sunlounger cushions. Fred laid out the tarpaulin and blankets to make a nest ready for her. Then they needed to raise Issie.

Fenwick and David automatically bent down to do so.

'No, you two will be weakened by the cold. We need fresh strength for this.'

Fenwick wanted to protest but stepped back to make room, surprised at how wobbly his legs were.

Issie was lifted and placed with great care in the centre of the nest, then Fred wrapped towels around her feet, put two quilted hats on her head and layered the blankets over her before wrapping the tarpaulin firmly about her whole body from head to toe, leaving only a small hole for breathing. As he was working, others built up the fire with dry wood they had brought, lit two gaz stoves and deployed hurricane lamps around the copse.

'Put those two kettles on to boil,' Fred instructed.

'Are we going to give her a warm drink?' someone asked.

'No way, anything by mouth will kill her. No, I'm about to improvise something I saw our medic use on exercise. Did you bring that length of hosepipe I asked for?'

Bazza passed over a three-foot length of pipe. As soon as the kettle boiled Fred had it brought close to Issie's head and placed one end of the tubing over the spout and the other close Issie's mouth, with a dip in the middle so that the steam could reach her lips without the risk of water condensing and running into her mouth.

'Heat the other one and we can recycle them; they'll cool quickly.'

'For how long?' Fenwick asked, trying to mask his violent shivering.

'We'll need specialist advice on that.'

'Now that the wind has dropped, Sussex air ambulance is seeing if they can send a helicopter,' Bernstein advised, 'and there may be one coming from HMCG at Lee-on-Solent as well. They have the most experience of treating hypothermia victims in the south-east, apparently. If they've been able to fly, the first helicopter should be here shortly.'

Ten minutes later the air ambulance arrived but couldn't land at the scene because of the difficult terrain and deep snow. They found a suitable site a mile away and the doctor was with them at the same time the vicar arrived with thermoses for the rescuers but nobody touched them as they waited expectantly for the doctor's diagnosis.

'You've done well,' he said at last. 'What was her pulse when you first found her?'

'We didn't think to count, sorry, but it was very slow and weak.' Fred looked embarrassed at his oversight.

'Well, it's still a long way from normal but there is at least a little strength in it now. I need to consult an expert colleague on how long we should wait to avoid the risk of an after drop in temperature.'

The doctor made his call and was on the phone some time while the rescue party helped themselves to soup and warm drinks.

'We should give it another fifteen to thirty minutes. Hopefully the coastguard helicopter will be close by then. They will be better equipped and they have an expert flying with them. Who invented the respirator?'

'I did.' Fred looked sheepish.

'Well done. We shouldn't give her too much, not until we know she's warmer inside but my colleague says we can keep it up, a minute in every five say, but with the tube as you have it – well away from her lips so that we don't risk her gagging. It's going to help to stabilise her. Meanwhile, let's make sure none of the rest of you ends up in hospital. Fred, you've been out how long? An hour? Let me look at you.'

The doctor took the brothers off to one side and told them they had to get back at once or would risk being taken to hospital themselves. Fenwick stayed quiet at the edge of the group. He wasn't going anywhere until he had seen Issie safely into the helicopter. He noticed Bernstein looking around for him and crouched down next to a fire.

The wait was long and uneventful. Other than refilling the kettle with steaming water there was little to do. Bernstein sent all but three of the officers back to the village. With more space in the clearing she spotted Fenwick and walked over.

'You should go back.'

'I'm fine,' and indeed he did feel better. He was shivering less and the warm drink and fire actually made him feel hot, particularly his hands and feet.

'Don't be an idiot, Andrew. You've found her – against the odds and still just about alive – there's nothing more you can do for her now.'

'I know; and as soon as I see her into the air ambulance I'll leave. Are you going to call her parents?'

'I didn't want to until I had seen her alive with my own eyes. They've been through so much. If I tell them we've found her alive and then . . . then she dies on the way to hospital. It will be too little too late all over again, like everything else I've done on this sodding case.' Unexpectedly her eyes filled with tears.

'You've done a good job and you know it, come on.' He gave her a hug.

Bernstein sniffed and glanced over her shoulder to see if anyone had noticed but all eyes were on the wrapped bundle at their feet.

'Yeah, well. Why don't you do it? You found her, after all.'

He shook his head and waited patiently until she had dialled the Saxbys' number at which point he walked away, unsure how he would react. He needed to be closer to the fire anyway; he was starting to shiver again.

The three women were seated in an almost perfect triangle around the remains of the fire, which glowed and fluttered occasionally into flame as the logs crumbled to ash and dust. A choir service from a cathedral somewhere was playing on the television, largely disregarded.

Alice had nodded off and lolled back in her armchair, mouth agape, snoring softly. Nightingale watched her with envy.

'So he hasn't rung, then?'

Nightingale shook her head in response for perhaps the fifth time since the children had been forced to bed with threats that if they didn't Father Christmas wouldn't be stopping at the Fenwick household.

'You think he's out in this, don't you?'

Nightingale blinked and wondered how to answer. She hadn't shared her fears with anyone but somehow his mother seemed to know.

'It's the sort of crazy thing he might do, yes.' Brutal but honest; she thought his mother wouldn't appreciate anything else.

'That's what I feared, just like his father. He will push himself to the limit for a good cause.'

Nightingale looked up, trying to catch her eye and encourage the conversation but Gertrude Fenwick was staring fixedly at the dwindling fire.

The silence extended. On the television screen a solo chorister was singing the second verse of 'Away in a Manger'. They watched in silence until organ music announced the end of the recital.

'Shall we try and call him again?'

The spoke at the same time and grimaced a smile at each other. Nightingale dialled and schooled herself to listen to the electronic response with indifference. Instead a female voice answered.

'Yes?'

'Who is this? I was trying to reach Andrew Fenwick; is he there, please?'

'Who's calling?'

'Louise Nightingale.' For some reason she didn't give her rank.

'Wait a moment.'

There was a rustle and then . . . his voice.

'Andrew?' Her throat was tight.

'Nightingale? What are you doing calling me?' His tone was strange, almost as if he were drunk.

'I know; I . . . that is, we were worried for you. Are you all right?'

'We've found her, Nightingale. I looked and she was there. The

557

helicopter is going to take her away . . .' His voice slurred into silence and she heard someone take the phone from him to say, 'He's obviously not really in a fit state to speak right now.'

'What's the matter with him?'

She sensed Gertrude stand up and reach out for the phone but she gripped it tight.

'I repeat my question; who is calling?'

'I'm a friend . . .'

'Well, that's not good enough for me to be speaking to you.'

'Am I talking to Deidre Bernstein?'

'How would you know my name?'

'Andrew has mentioned you. Please tell me.'

There was a pause and before she knew it Fenwick's mother had lifted the handset nimbly from her fingers.

'This is Mrs Fenwick, Andrew's mother,' she said and Nightingale marvelled at the iron control of her voice. 'I insist that I speak with my son or, if he is not capable, you tell me at once, young woman, what the matter with him is.' She held the mobile at an angle so that Nightingale might listen.

'I think he's going to be all right,' Bernstein said obediently. 'He's reasonably safe and warm and the doctor is taking a look at him right now . . .'

'A doctor, what do you mean?'

'He went out looking for Isabelle Mattias and he found her, thank God. But he's probably been in the cold a bit longer than is good for him.'

'I see,' Nightingale noticed that Gertrude's jaw stiffened in the same way that her son's did. 'Well you make very sure that you keep him safe and send him home.'

'Yes, Mrs Fenwick.'

'And make sure he looks after himself. I'm relying on you to make certain he does.'

'Of course.'

'Well, I'd wish you a happy Christmas but somehow that doesn't seem right so I'll just say goodnight.'

'Goodnight, Mrs Fenwick.'

'I think we can go to bed, Louise. Oh dear, there's no point fussing yourself now that he's safe now, is there?'

'I know, it's just that . . . hearing his voice, knowing he's all right. I'm sorry . . .' Nightingale was deeply embarrassed.

'I think a nice cup of tea is in order. If you wake up Alice I'll go and put the kettle on.'

'Do you have a tissue by any chance?'

Fenwick's mother raised a surprised eyebrow.

'I have always found that tears dry best on their own, Louise.'

Nightingale stared after her; surely Mrs F wasn't an Amy Winehouse fan?

CHAPTER FIFTY-EIGHT

'Where are we going?' Bess asked for perhaps the tenth time.

'You'll find out soon enough. Now sit still, you're cramping Alice every time you wriggle.'

'But, Nightingale!'

'Enough, Bess; look at your brother and how he's behaving himself,' Gertrude Fenwick stepped in to support their driver who was managing with great skill some horrible road conditions as they drove towards Portsmouth.

Chris grinned but couldn't help asking, 'And we'll open our presents when we get back, Nanny?'

'Yes, Chrissy.'

'And will Daddy be coming home with us?'

There was an uncomfortable silence in the car before Nightingale and Mrs Fenwick said in unison, 'We'll have to see. Just be patient.'

They had left Harlden immediately after a hurried breakfast of porridge, bundled up in winter clothes and with boots, a shovel and blankets in the car in case the bad weather came back. Bess had sighed dramatically and pointed to the pale-blue, clear sky as evidence that they were being stupid but no one paid her any attention.

After nearly five hours of difficult driving they pulled into the visitors' car park of the Queen Alexandra Hospital in Portsmouth. Nightingale glanced in the rear-view mirror to see the children's reaction. She and Mrs Fenwick had decided not to tell them in advance where they were heading, only that their father would be waiting at the end of the journey.

Chris looked scared and even Bess's face went white. Gertrude Fenwick unclipped her seat belt and swivelled around in the front passenger seat.

'So, children, we're here to see your father. He is fine, don't worry, but he was involved in the rescue of that young lass, Issie Mattias . . .'

'Like on the radio this morning?' Chris asked excitedly.

'Yes; and the thing is that meant he had to be outside in the blizzard yesterday, so when he brought her here to this hospital, the doctors decided it would be sensible for him to stay in overnight.'

'Why, Nanny?'

'Because when you've been cold for a long time it's wise to be checked out by a doctor, and your father agreed.'

'Even though it's Christmas?' Bess asked sceptically.

'Yes, Bess. Now put on your coat and we'll go and see him.'

'I tell you what,' Nightingale suggested. 'Alice, if you could lock the car I'll go and find out where he is.'

'Good idea, Louise,' Gertrude Fenwick said, immediately understanding what Nightingale was thinking: she would be able to ask about her son's condition in private without little ears around.

'I'll come with you.' Bess was already opening her door.

'No, Bess, you will stay with us . . . Don't look like that, you heard me.'

Nightingale set off at once across the car park, glad yet again of her trusty rubber-soled boots. At reception she showed her warrant card and explained that Andrew Fenwick was a colleague.

'Oh, our resident hero!' the receptionist said. 'He's in Perry Ward, second floor.'

'And how is he, please?'

The cheerful woman in front of her, who must have been missing her family at Christmas but didn't show it, looked up over her half-moon glasses.

'Oh, I wouldn't know that, love. You need to ask the ward sister.'

Nightingale had a quick choice to make: run on ahead and find out or wait. She sprinted towards the lifts. On the second floor, she spotted the nurses' station and walked briskly to it. Again the warrant card was flashed.

'Please could you tell me where Superintendent Fenwick is and how he is . . . please?'

The senior nurse on duty was obviously less than pleased to be there, either that or something about Nightingale irritated her.

'Are you family?'

'No, I'm a colleague.'

'Then I can't tell you anything, with or without your warrant card.'

'Please, I . . .' Behind her she heard the lift doors open. It would be them. 'Can you at least tell me that he's all right?'

'Not unless you're family. Now if you'll excuse me, I have work to do.'

'That may be, miss, but I am family and I'm asking you the same question. I'm his mother.'

'Oh, ah . . .'

'Well, go on. How is my son?'

'He's being X-rayed in preparation for his surgery on Boxing Day, Mrs Fenwick.'

'Surgery?'

Gertrude Fenwick clutched Nightingale's hand.

'Yes, the consultant decided this morning when he did his early round that it will be necessary and your son agreed.'

'Agreed what?' Nightingale asked.

'The amputation.'

Mrs Fenwick was gripping her hand so tight she could no longer feel it.

'Go on.' There was steel in Nightingale's voice. 'Of what?'

The nurse paused and in the silence the lift doors opened. A bed was wheeled past by an orderly.

'Andrew!'

'Mum? What are you . . . ?'

'You go with him, Gertrude, while I get the details,' Nightingale said and turned back to the nurse, 'now.'

A few minutes later she was walking down the ward towards Fenwick's bed, a smile on her face.

'His little finger,' his mother said, 'on his left hand and probably the top of the ring finger. Apparently the consultant thinks he should remove them to avoid the risk of gangrene. But it will be a small operation, and on his left hand so no real harm done.'

She turned and smiled at him and her son's lips twitched but didn't manage to shape a response. Fenwick looked washed out. No, worse than that, Nightingale thought. It's as if he isn't really here. He saw her over his mother's shoulder and his eyes widened in surprise.

'Nightingale; you're here?'

'She drove us,' his mother said and before Fenwick could remark on the 'us', there was the sound of running feet and the bed was rushed by two children.

'We just saw Father Christmas, Daddy! He's here, at the hospital downstairs. He's going to visit everybody.' Chris made to jump on his father's bed in his excitement but Nightingale stopped him, afraid of the impact of his solid little body on his injured father.

'Father Christmas, hey? Well, that's good. He must have finished delivering presents everywhere else.' He tried a smile over Chris's head at Bess in adult complicity but she looked away, close to tears.

'He gave us both presents, Dad!'

Nightingale could see Fenwick struggling to concentrate and find an answer.

'That's nice, Chris, but Daddy needs to rest now.'

'Why?' Chris suddenly looked concerned. 'Are you poorly, Daddy?'

'No, not really Chris.' But Fenwick's eyes filled and he couldn't speak.

Behind her Nightingale heard Bess stifle a sob and turned to take her hand.

'Come on, Bess, we're a crowd here. Let's go for a little walk and leave the others to it. We'll have our turn later.'

Bess allowed herself to be dragged away, head down. Immediately they were outside the ward she burst into tears. Nightingale found a waiting area and sat down.

'Come here.' She patted the chair beside her and Bess obeyed, resting her head against Nightingale's shoulder.

She wept quietly for several minutes and Nightingale let her.

'He's very brave, you know, your daddy. He saved Issie's life. And, all right, you could say that maybe somebody else would have done if he hadn't but I don't think that is the case. He's in hospital because he was suffering from hypothermia yesterday. It's normal to keep people in if they get too cold.'

'And his hand?'

'Ah, you noticed that. Well he suffered frostbite and will lose his little finger, but he won't mind that.'

Bess's sobs had subsided but intensified at the idea of her father's hurt. After a moment she spoke again.

'But he could have died, couldn't he? I heard you last night with Nanny. You were worried.'

'Yes, we were, but I had a feeling your father would be OK and all's well that ends well.'

'What about Issie, the girl he found? Is she all right?'

'She's here in this hospital. It's the best centre for hypothermia and exposure treatment in the south of England. Your father's bound to ask the same question, so why don't we go and find out?'

Nightingale flashed her warrant card and was informed that Issie was in a specialist hypothermia recovery unit attached to intensive care. She was alive but unconscious and it would be a while before there could be a proper prognosis. The main thing was that she had withstood the transfer from Alfriston to the hospital with no deterioration of condition and that made the specialists treating her a little more optimistic.

Nightingale and Bess took the lift to the ICU floor but were stopped by a security guard as soon as they stepped out. Nightingale explained that she was a detective who worked with Fenwick and that Bess was his daughter. They just wanted to find out how Issie was doing so that they could tell him. The guard turned away and whispered into his radio. A couple of minutes later Lord Saxby appeared. He looked haggard, as if he hadn't slept in weeks, which Nightingale thought was probably the case.

'I'm Bill Saxby, and you are?'

Nightingale introduced them both. Saxby squatted down and looked into Bess's tear-stained face.

'So you're Andrew Fenwick's daughter. You must be very proud of him.'

'Yes, I am.'

'Well you tell him that Issie is making progress. She had a quiet night and her body temperature is almost back to normal. Her doctors are keeping her in an artificial coma to give her a chance to recover more fully. In the next couple of days we'll know what permanent damage has been done. Can you remember all of that?'

'Yes, sir.'

He stood up.

'Where is the superintendent?' he asked Nightingale.

'Perry Ward, sir. He'll be in for a few days. He has to have a small operation but then they'll let him home, all being well.'

'I see; well tell him I will pop down to see him later today. I want to thank him in person, as does Jane, though she won't leave Issie's side for the time being.'

'I'll let him know.'

Saxby shook both their hands and returned through the double doors to the ICU.

'Come on, Bess, let's go back. It's your turn to see Daddy now.'

They rode the lift back down in silence. When they arrived at Fenwick's bedside, Chris, Mrs Fenwick and Alice left to give them some room. As soon as they had gone, Bess threw herself on her father's bed and burst into fresh tears. He hugged her close and stroked her head with his good hand.

'It's all right, my love, don't cry. Everything will be fine. I'll be home soon and we can enjoy Christmas together.'

'But I'm so sorry, Daddy. I was mean and selfish and spiteful and all the time you were looking for that girl and if you hadn't she would be dead.'

Nightingale could barely hear the words muffled by Fenwick's hospital gown. She sat down in the chair on the other side and looked at his poor hand. Without meaning to, she touched his wrist above the bandages and he turned to look at her. He stared at her for a long time, saying nothing as Bess sobbed quietly to a standstill. He gestured with his head for Nightingale to come closer and she leant over until her ear was close to his lips.

'Thank you,' he whispered, 'for being there with them and for being here.' And then he kissed her cheek and let his lips rest there.

EPILOGUE

'Then let not winter's ragged hand deface
In thee thy summer, ere thou be distill'd:
Make sweet some vial; treasure thou some place
With beauty's treasure, ere it be self-kill'd.'

William Shakespeare,
'Sonnet 6'

CHAPTER FIFTY-NINE

May blossom festooned the hedgerows above verges dotted with the nodding heads of pink milkmaid flowers. It had rained solidly for a week but that morning had broken bright, with a clear high sky washed to blue perfection. Nightingale was singing as she drove, a hymn from schooldays that captured the moment.

As she swung onto the long drive to Saxby Hall she reflected that she had become almost a regular visitor, Fenwick's proxy while he struggled with his own recovery. The negative press coverage around the police investigation into Issie's prolonged abduction hadn't mentioned him at all. In fact, thanks to the *Enquirer* he had become something of a hero, credited with Mariner's arrest and saving the girl's life, but that meant nothing to him.

Her forehead creased briefly as she thought of her last conversation with him. He was still eaten with guilt for the delays in discovering Mariner's hiding places. If they had found her sooner Issie would have never embarked on her disastrous escape. She had told him not to be stupid, that his guilt was irrational, but inside she understood only too well.

Shortly after Christmas Jenni had disappeared from the shelter and, despite every effort short of a nationwide manhunt Nightingale had been unable to find her. Without their main witness the case against her cousin had been reduced fro attempted murder to assaulting a police officer. He might even escape without a custodial sentence. Nightingale told herself that Jenni had simply gone off somewhere she could be anonymous again, but even so she felt responsible and she could understand some of Andrew's deep-seated guilt.

She parked the car in shade and walked up a shallow flight of steps, to be greeted by Jane Saxby even before she could knock.

'Louise! It's so good to see you again. Come on in. How's Andrew?'

'A little better, thank you, Jane. Still not back at work but his psychiatrist is pleased with his recent progress.'

'Oh, good. Issie will be so relieved. She's desperate to meet her hero.'

Nightingale grimaced.

'She shouldn't call him that. Part of his problem is he just cannot accept it. People's praise makes him worse. He keeps thinking that if had found Issie at the pump station, or earlier at the farm, then—'

'None of that was his fault, as the inquiry proved. He was exonerated and deserved his commendation.'

'You know that; I know that; but Andrew . . .' Nightingale glanced away. 'He's still struggling.'

'Will the force accept him back?'

'With open arms! The assistant chief constable is working hard to keep him but Surrey has also indicated he'd be welcome there. The question is, will Andrew want to return? I've tried to talk to him about it but he's not in a fit state yet to make any decisions.'

'Well, at least he's starting to make progress at last. So is Issie, by the way. She's astonishing the physiotherapists and her special needs nurse has a joke that Issie's special and she's not needed!'

Nightingale watched Jane Saxby laugh, marvelling at her remarkable resilience. Like mother, like daughter, though Jane would never take any credit for her amazing child.

'Issie's in the garden. I know it's a bit chilly but she's wrapped up warm and was so insistent, and tomorrow,' a shadow crossed the sun of Jane's happiness, 'she's back to hospital again but Issie will probably want to tell you about that herself. She'll be pleased to see you. You're her only link to Andrew and she so looks forward to your visits.'

They walked across the tiled hall, past the stairs along a passage to french windows that looked over a flagged terrace towards a lawn that sloped down to a stream crossed by a Japanese-style bridge. Rhododendron and azalea flowers were bursting into life.

'She's on the other side next to the natural lawn. Issie's always liked that view.'

Jane led Nightingale down flagged steps onto a gravel path that curved away from the sculpted splendour towards a bucolic view of olde England. Ahead was a bank of hawthorn and new willow. Issie sat with her back to them, easel in front of her.

'You go on,' Jane said softly. 'I'll make us some coffee.' She turned back to the house as Nightingale continued.

'Hello, Louise!' Issie called without turning around. 'I recognise your footsteps.'

'Hi Issie, how are you?'

'Good today, thanks, which is why I'm out here. It's the way the hawthorn bows down under the weight of flower and the curve of the willow there . . .'

Nightingale had reached the side of her wheelchair and Issie turned to smile a welcome, radiant. The paintbrush was strapped to her left palm, gripped between her thumb and remaining fingers. The lower right sleeve of her jacket ended abruptly in bandages.

'What do you think? I'm having to learn a whole new technique but I've got a good teacher from St Anne's. She says this,' Issie nodded towards her right arm, 'could unlock a whol new creative side of me. I think she says it to be kind but, you know, she might be right. I do see things differently now.'

Nightingale had decided, even before looking at the canvas, that she would lie if necessary; but she didn't need to.

'Issie, that's amazing. So simple, just a few brushstrokes, but you've captured its essence.'

'Thank you.'

'And the colours; somehow you've stolen the soul of the trees.'

'Oh good! It's for Superintendent Fenwick. I was thinking of calling it *Spirit of Spring*. D'you think that's naff?'

'No; and Andrew will love it.'

A flicker of concern marred Issie's serenity.

'I thought he might be with you. Is he really OK?'

'Getting better all the time and when I bring him news of the progress you're making . . .'

Issie looked away.

'Don't tell him but tomorrow I have to go back. I was only allowed home because Bill has private nurses and a specially equipped room but I need another operation. No, that's not right. I *want* another one. This lower stump is useless.' She pointed to her right leg. 'And it hurts all the time. If I can just have it raised, then I'll be able to have a blade and I *want* a blade.'

Nightingale didn't know what to say but Issie didn't seem to notice.

'Bill's made a donation to a stable for the disabled over near Godalming. I think he's funding the whole thing, actually. He says it's because he was impressed by the Paralympics but I think otherwise.'

She gave Nightingale a knowing wink and turned back to the view as footsteps crunched down the path behind them.

'You know, Louise, I sometimes think that what happened – 'l of it, the horror as well as . . . well, that it somehow saved '. I was off the rails and heading for the abyss. If it hadn't happened I'd have ended up dead or dying of an overdose some day, locked in my own miserable, selfish world; doing nobody any good.

'Now I have all this and so much to be grateful for. You must make the superintendent realise that, please?'

Nightingale bent down and kissed the top of Issie's head, unable to speak for a moment; then she said, 'I promise to do my best.'

'Coffee!' Jane Saxby called out cheerily. 'And ginger biscuits.'

AUTHOR'S NOTE

The village of Alfriston is one of the most charming in the South of England. None of the characters in this book are based on anyone living or dead from the village, or elsewhere. However, the friendliness and warmth of the fictitious villagers is a true reflection of the hospitality and welcome visitors receive.

Those who know the South Downs Way will know that I have taken the liberty of moving the location of the copse in which Issie is found. Her grandmother's farm is not based on a real one so please don't search for it.

I would like to thank all the people who helped in my research for this book; and my husband Mike, who was a source of constant encouragement and who read early drafts with his customary critical – and invaluable – eye. Special thanks also go to Sara Magness for her important contribution to editing the draft; and to Sonia Land, my agent, and Allison & Busby for their patience in waiting for this fifth book in the series. The next one will not be so long in coming!

To discover more great books and to
place an order visit our website at
www.allisonandbusby.com

Don't forget to sign up to our free newsletter at
www. allisonandbusby.com/newsletter
for latest releases, events and exclusive offers

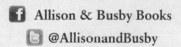 **Allison & Busby Books**
@AllisonandBusby

You can also call us on
020 7580 1080
for orders, queries
and reading recommendations